THE GLASS T

DISCLAIM.

Any names of people, companies ... in this work are completely fictive. If there are any similarities between the fictive entities described in this book and real ones operating in the world, the similarity is purely coincidental. If any attributes are associated with real places (as they are in the case of countries, cities, districts etc.) they are not meant to reflect any connection to the present situation in those places. They are simply meant again as devices to stimulate dialogue. The entire novel might as well be happening on Mars, but if it is set on Earth and references real places, readers might be able to relate to the happenings in it more intimately. Moreover, any descriptions of the workings of journalism are made with a very loose connection to present reality. The presence of different people in different situations is meant as a device to create dialogue rather than anything else. That holds true for all characters in the book, not just the members of the journalistic teams references in the text.

INTRODUCTION.

This story was written as a 'memory box' for my own thoughts and view of the world. It is a snapshot of how I see the world of the present and imagine the world of the future at this point in time. Not everything in there is meant to be a prediction, in fact most of it isn't. Instead most written 'units' penned -or rather keyed- in this text are meant to make a point, stimulate discussion and create questions rather than give answers. I don't necessarily believe all that is in there, but have expressed more opinions so that they could better contrast with each other.

The book can be read along 3 planes, either one at a time, or more together. The 1st plane is philosophical/political and deals with views I have come across in politics mostly, but also regarding what I think are really difficult questions of philosophy and more specifically concern human nature -although not exclusively-. The 2nd plane is a typical adventure novel where we follow the actions of a character placed into various situations. There is a storyline and it moves along, stopping at what I think are 'points of interest', which may be discussions or parts where the story intersects the other 2 'planes of reading'. The 3rd and final plane is the SciFi one. Here I describe futuristic technology. This plane contains elements that can be classed in a number of categories: 1)

Technology we know is possible and are actively researching. 2) Technology that is probably possible to achieve and eventually we will probably achieve as mankind. 3) Technology that most likely corresponds to wishful thinking -so not realisable- but looks and sounds quite realistic, and 4) Technology that's completely out of the question, but is in there just for the fun of it.

When I started writing this document I wasn't intending to show it to anyone except for very few people. If, however, it ever reaches more readers and you are one of them, read as much as you wish, take away as much as you decide and think about it and make your very own judgements about what is being written to your heart's content. In the end, it's all just a little bit of fun, no?

PART I: THE GLASS TOWERS.

CHAPTER 1: THE HIGH LIFE.

The view was breath-taking. Before Miles' eyes a vast expanse full of tiny little white lights was covering everything up to the line of the horizon; each of those little lights, an energy-saving Organic-LED array of residential or commercial, or even public lighting; each of them indicating its location in the dark background of the clear and warm summer night. In places, the white lights would climb above the line of the horizon, sometimes ascending and reaching out towards the stars, far above the horizon by a big margin, and the top of each such colossal pillar of little lights would invariably be crowned by a handful of powerful, slowly blinking red lights. Such red lights were often to be found above the horizon, denoting as they were, the tips of the various skyscrapers that populated the skyline of the capital of the United Kingdom of Great Britain and Northern Ireland. In fact, if Miles was to simply prop his head upwards to a sufficient degree, he would see the blinking red crown of the building he was situated in: the Kinroy bank tower. Yet, he felt little need to do so. The majestic view of the bustling metropolis was enough to keep him entertained. More so as the weather was being clement at that moment, gracing his presence with a gentle warm breeze and the few, solitary clouds in the sky far from the bright full moon, clouds which were exhibiting charming silvery linings at those edges that were facing the moon.

Miles had seen the very same view many times, yet still he could revel in its beauty every single time the occasion revealed herself and the night view of London was accompanied by such fine weather. As if to complement the feelings of primeval serenity that the view awoke in

Miles a handsome young waiter -about Miles' own age, he thought- graciously rested a glass of fine and very expensive champagne at the little table by which Miles sat. Miles nodded in recognition of the event and automatically uttered a barely audible 'Thank you' to the waiter, who in turn bowed and left. Subsequently, he proceeded to grab the glass with a gesture of utmost noblesse and bring the champagne gently to his lips taking the slightest sip of the silently bubbling drink. 'Ah, this is the life!' he thought with satisfaction.

And why should he not utter such phrase? After all he, Miles Fitzroy, was a handsome, young and upcoming investment banker. Having studied engineering at one of the most reputable universities in the UK, and the world for that matter, he made his way straight into investment banking after graduation never bequeathing so much as a second look again over those incomprehensible equations that plagued his 4 years in university. He never needed them in his new environment. As an investment banker he basically peddled money around, earning a living in the highly artificial world of finance. And boy was the retribution good. Within a few years he had managed to earn enough money to buy a flat in central London and an expensive German car. He was there, at the top of the world, or more precisely at the 95th floor of the Kinroy bank tower; one of the few who made it that far, that quickly. 'Most just end up like the cute guy serving me drinks by this age...' he thought with open self-satisfaction. To him, the present was paradise, the future, could only be better, the past, completely unimportant and therefore ignorable.

After another quarter of an hour or so of indulging in revelry under the charming view of nocturnal London he decided it was time to leave. The champagne glass stood empty to one side of the table, near the ash-tray. The only other object on the elegant, black metal/glass table was a little cubical device -also black- with a round, transparent disk on the top side, through which a dark red glow emanating from the inside of the small box could be observed. The edge of the disk was delimited by an ornate metallic ring. To this very top surface of this very little box Miles casually presented the back of his left hand, and in response the little box emitted a cheerful little beeping tune and as if out of nowhere and a thin, green LED array surrounding the base of the little box like a belt worn a bit too low, lit up. Miles then barely noticing the miniature ceremony unfolding as the Automatic Implant-Communication Payment box -informally just called AICOP- performed its task.

Miles would have probably found the idea of handling a fragile, plastic card that could be stolen at any time rather strange and clumsy. As for cash, that would be positively exotic, if not also disconcerting. He, however was born just as plastic money was replaced by bionic money.

As the last credit and debit cards were replaced by the Universal Use Implant and cash was just a memory a new era was heralded for mankind. Back in those days Miles would have had a 'wallet' used to store cash, plastic money, something the old folk called a 'driving licence' and other documents proving identity and linking to bank accounts, work accounts, medical insurance databases etc. etc. However now none of that was needed any longer. When we was just a toddler, his parents were getting their compulsory implant injections done -as was he for that matter- and ditching their wallets for good.

For Miles that was a mark of progress towards a life of more convenience. The deeper importance of the changeover from wallets to the Universal Use Implant (Uniusi for short) had eluded him. He never gave much thought to the possibility that this event is the beginning of the era where man and machine coexist, which could lead to what? Nobody yet knew for sure, but developments in medicine at the time indicated a continuous perfusion of machinery into the human body, advancing slowly, but steadily as scientists figured out how to either replace, or enhance or do both of these things on human parts by using electro-mechanical parts. Miles never gave much thought to such philosophical questions in general and this was no different. Instead, having reached the underground car park of the skyscraper he quite happily swiped the back of his hand in front of another dark red disk, much like the one on the AICOP system, situated roughly where the key slot of a car like the ones driven by his grandparents would normally be. The car responded by opening the door on the side of which Miles had swiped his hand, switching on the lights -it could detect automatically when headlights were necessary as well as figure out the optimal intensity for maximum useful visibility at minimum energy cost- and emitting a very gentle, muffled noise indicating that the electrical engine was testing itself for operational functionality.

Evidently content with itself the car powered up the TV pedestal embedded in the little table at the middle of the car and the hologram of a dignified lady of excessive sophistication appeared hovering over the said table. Without any delay the lady proceeded to greet Miles with impeccable courtesy: 'Good evening Mr. Fitzroy, sir. Where may I take you tonight?'. Miles lunged himself on two of the seats in the car, lying on his side, so that he could face the hologram. He propped his head against his arm, thought for the shortest of intervals and replied: 'Just take me home Hilda. I've partied too much these days. Now, I think, I deserve a rest...'. Hilda replied with a humble 'Yes sir. Calculating route sir.' and paused for a moment, her face assuming a pensive look. 'These Germans sure know how to pay attention to detail', Miles thought as he enjoyed for the umpteenth time the perceived ability of the on-board computer to mimic human emotions. This delightful thought didn't last long as Hilda soon resumed: 'Optimal route under current traffic conditions found, sir. Please be advised that it is illegal to start the car if even one passenger is not fastened with a suitable seat-belt, sir.'. Miles was galvanised into action by this announcement, at once sat properly and fastened himself with the seat-belt before uttering mockingly: 'Is this good enough, sir? May we pleeeease leave now, sir?', to which Hilda replied in a voice vibrant with resentment and just a hint of exasperation, the sort of which we expect to find in a person who has tried and tried to no avail to reform a delinquent youth: 'It is health and safety regulation I'm afraid, sir. I'm programmed to obey the law at all costs, sir.'. Indeed these Germans knew how to pay attention to detail...

    Soon enough Hilda aptly and most slenderly navigated the elegant vehicle through the pillared warrens of the underground car park and on to the roads of Britain, handling parking fees, congestion charging, street lighting tax, road tax, insurance, traffic light charge and in general all of the associated administration automatically for her lord and master. Following that she proceeded to integrate the vehicle into the traffic stream and navigate towards the final destination. This allowed Miles to enjoy the interior of the car. Unlike his grandparents' car, this one had four comfortable seats arranged so as to face each other in pairs, with a table in between. Thus at any given time two passengers would face the direction of travel, whilst the other two would face backwards. The table in between the pairs of seats also served another purpose: Hilda's elaborately groomed head apparently hovered at a low height above it. Underneath the table was the drinks cabinet and the phone system, as well as the docking station for the car's palm-top computers (often simply called 'terminals'). The engine was situated towards the front of the car, and the boot towards the back. There was obviously no driver. Drivers had been long since replaced by machines. First experimentally in the 2020's, then by 2040 by law, at least theoretically.

    As the car darted through central London's elevated highways heading from Canary Wharf, where the Kinroy tower was situated, towards Miles' apartment in Knightsbridge under the apt command of Hilda, Miles nearly dozed off. Despite the 100 mph the car's dashboard was showing the ride was smooth enough to allow for that. The complementary influence of the drink and the advanced hour of the night made sure that Miles had already showered and was sound asleep by the time Hilda had parked the car in the 'resident only' bay reserved for Miles in one of the back-streets of Knightsbridge. Hilda gently woke Miles up and advised that he went to sleep. Miles thanked her in a sleepy voice and complied with the advice, after which Hilda switched her holographic self off, leaving the less human parts of her to handle the recharging of the car's batteries. By the time she was done, Miles was in his comfortable bed, in the roomy Knightsbridge penthouse bedroom overlooking Hyde Park, already sound asleep.

The following morning Miles was woken up by his alarm clock. It was linked to the central computer of his residence as well as his main personal computer. In fact, all the electronics in the house were interlinked in a Virtual Private Network and could communicate with each other either using the Local Area Network wireless when inside the residence, or using internet infrastructure when some smaller consumer electronics -the palm-top, or the wrist watch for example- were outside the residence with their owner. As such, Miles could organise his agenda for the next week and at the same time set the alarm clock or the toaster if he so wished, but he didn't need to. The butler could handle that. That day, the clock had remembered it was an ordinary working day, Saturday, and he had to be in office by 09:00. Shortly after pressing the reset button on the alarm clock the robo-butler greeted him in his bedroom with a tray of breakfast. Caviar, the finest ham from Spain, cheese from France and British tea and toast. The robo-butler left the tray on Miles' lap, the disembodied holographic head of an amiable old gentleman with a rich moustache and a very retro-looking monocular paid his respects to the lord of the house and left. Miles always admired these high-quality holograms, this particular example coming from a large manufacturer in Japan. It hovered on top of the robo-butler's metallic body, crafted carefully to resemble what seemed to Miles like a headless penguin with wheels instead of the usual clumsy feet that he'd seen so often in history books, back in primary school. In any case, the robo-butler had left swiftly, barely giving enough time for Miles to idly read for the umpteenth time the engraved, golden letters on the back of his servant reading "Manufactured in China by Mizutomo corporation, Tokyo". Therefore Miles quickly turned his attention to the breakfast instead, forgetting all about penguins and product labelling.

Before too long the breakfast was all but gone. Miles placed the tray on the elegant table next to his plush bed and walked into the 'wardrobe chamber' in nothing but his most intimate undergarment. The collection of clothes in the actual wardrobe was small, and comprised of a set of very expensive clothes he owned for very special occasions: meeting highly regarded clients, meeting people far higher in the hierarchy of the bank etc. For daily usage none of that was needed. All the daily use clothing was made on the spot, by the 'wardrobe chamber' itself. The chamber was not a room inside a residence, but a large device situated in a corner of the bedroom. Miles stepped in it and the paper-thin flexible screen lit up, a set of weak, red laser beams swept his body from top to bottom and all the way around him from left to right and soon after

this welcoming ceremony of lights ended the screen displayed a menu and a 3D graphics-generated head of an elegant lady with an extravagant collie around her neck, a set of jet-black ear-rings and an elaborate coiffure. She spoke:
'Good morning Mr. Fitzroy. How may I dress you today?'.
To which Miles curtly replied: 'Smart and comfortable'.
'Gloves?'
'Not today, thank you.'
'Scarf?'
'No, thanks.'

After this short conversation, the lady in the screen nodded politely and without a further word the chamber was filled with a smooth buzzing noise. At the top of the chamber, the ceiling retreated to reveal a pair of long robotic arms, their individual sections folded neatly so as to take up as little space as possible. Along the arms ran a thin tube, ending at the small ampoules that signified the terminations of those robotic arms. The lady in the screen simply said what she said every time at this stage of the process: 'Please stand still with your arms up Mr. Fitzroy.' to which Miles complied without a word. Seconds later the robotic arms started spinning swiftly about the central axis of the cylindrical wardrobe chamber and slowly, with each revolution they made their way downwards. Reaching the top of Miles' hands, they started spinning around his limbs in smaller circles still going down with each revolution. Nothing else of significance happened until they reached his wrists. When that level was reached the ampoules, taking no break from their frenzied spinning, started squirting and spraying Miles with what appeared to be drops of a thick and viscous fluid. As they made their way downward it became clear that the substance stuck to Miles' skin where it solidified into a layer of elastic material. The clothing procedure continued down along Miles' arms, then his neck, then around his torso all the way down to the pelvis. At that level the robotic arms stopped in a smoothly decelerating motion and the lady in the screen spoke again: 'Please stand with your legs slightly farther apart Mr. Fitzroy if you please.'. Miles placed his feet rather apart giving the machine clearance to continue down his legs, where it was now busying itself with generating the trousers. Finally the machines reached the bottom of his legs and the lady in the screen issued her final command: she asked Miles to gracefully raise his left and then his right leg so that the wardrobe chamber could finish its task. Miles complied, his socks were completed, the lady in the screen bade a formal good-bye to Miles and he left the chamber fully clothed in a formal, black, nanomaterial full-body suit, decorated with tasteful, Chinese, red dragon outline motifs and a print-on tie decorated with Italian flower motifs. A curt command to the lady in the screen as he was exiting the chamber asking for his expensive French shoes and they appeared as if out of nowhere, right next to the bedroom door. Putting shoes and underwear on manually were the only annoyances consumer goods engineers had not yet managed to solve. The first one because it would make the wardrobe chamber much more expensive and bulky for a relatively small competitive advantage, and the second because of 'geometry issues' that nobody was willing to talk about openly...

The dressing procedure was followed by the traditional hygienic procedures people associated with the morning toilette since long before his grandparents. Fortunately, the nano-particle full-body suit was still designed with slits and flaps that allowed it to be taken off at will and put back on with relatively little difficulty. Thus, perfumed and freshened-up, as well as smartly dressed Miles set off towards his car. Hilda would take him to work while the robo-butler, with the supervision of his more human controller -the mainframe computer of the house- would take care of housework.

At 08:50 Hilda was pulling up by the main entrance of the Kinroy bank tower. Miles got off and set off toward his office. He passed through the metal detector and the full-body scanner and swiped the back of his hand against another 'reading eye' right before the lobby of the great tower. The light shone green underneath 'the eye' and Miles proceeded to the elevator. Before long he was in his office. A cup of tea was sitting on his desk and Miles sank into his comfortable swivelling chair and again swiped the back of his hand against the 'eye' that was conveniently placed just in sight underneath the surface of the desk. The paper-thin screen, supported by an elegant, slender arm came to life and displayed his work-software interface. It was a program designed specifically for Kinroy bank and displayed only what was necessary and useful for his tasks. At that moment, upon start-up, it was displaying his work dashboard, the shares and bonds and other financial products he was responsible for in a neat list and a live feed from the main financial-oriented news agencies of the world. A short-cut to useful applications was also there as well as a summary display of the calendar and clock.

Miles decided to start the day by having a look at the news. Scrolling quickly through the main titles and choosing to read the ones that looked interesting he gathered a few pieces of interesting information. The European Union was imposing new regulation on financial services and products, China and India were growing at a faster than expected rate, the debt burden on private households and businesses reached record highs all over the globe and so on. It seemed like a good day overall. Particularly in his sector, banking. So long as people were determined to continue borrowing to finance personal consumption or the growth of their businesses there was no way the bank could lose. Pay your dues with interest and the bank gets the interest. Fail to pay them and the bank gains your assets, which must exceed the value of the loan and include some sort of real estate. It's a win-win situation. Let others toil in factories, building machines and dealing with competition, struggling to survive in a hugely competitive world. The bank has money and so long as others desperately need it, it can impose terms on them that effectively eliminate risk for the bank. Of course there is competition amongst banks as well, but generally one would have to try really hard to make a bank go bankrupt.

Miles opened a news feed video. An economics professor was ranting on and on about something. Miles knew him. It was professor Aston Rodriguez of the 'Friedman' university of North Carolina. He was usually to be found on TV channels ranting on about extreme levels of debt everywhere in the world, warning people that a crisis was imminent just like in 2008, and shouting loudly about the lack of a social security network like what Europe used to enjoy until almost the entire continent went bankrupt in 2012. 'What is it now old fossil?' thought Miles. Professor Rodriguez was angrily arguing in favour of not just more regulation of the financial sector, but also a fundamental change in the way the system works. He was advocating such ridiculous concepts as the nationalisation of banks, the return of control over money supply into public hands and the formation of political unions EU-style all over the globe that would help regulate financial markets on a massive scale and if need be so, be able to isolate themselves from the rest of the world market to prevent capital flight to countries that rejected regulation. 'What a load of rubbish, nonsense.' thought Miles. The only thing keeping Britain great at the moment was applying the exact opposite. Nothing in the UK had been held by the public sector since the great wave of privatisation in the 2015-2040 era. Miles was too young and knew too little history to know about that. All he knew was that in modern Britain the government was nothing more than an assembly that collected a symbolic amount of tax -a few pounds per person per year on average- and did not even own an assembly hall of its own. Westminster was now a shopping centre and had been so since it was sold to a private developer. Parliament more often than not met in vast, luxurious hotels across the country, in a rented meeting theatre. The possibility that such pathetic group of people could take control of the gigantic financial industry that comprised 90% of the UK economy was truly comical.

As for the EU, it was nothing like it used to be. Anyone who had travelled to Germany, France, north Italy and elsewhere would simply see the remnants of once great countries. Vast arrays of collapsing infrastructure and abandoned factories, evident poverty everywhere in the streets and generally drab-looking people and antiquated cars on the streets of the main cities. All of this, set against a background of massive, empty, equally drab and unkempt tower blocks that signified that once the population of those states used to be much larger created a grim picture. The EU was a complete failure. Many British people were thankful that their country left it just before the collapse began really kicking in -the tumultuous year 2012-. To add insult to injury it was their own regulation of financial services and adherence to free market rules that ended up with the entire financial sector lifting its business off and moving across the channel or overseas. Environmental regulation too was more of a success than they anticipated by shutting down the entire, once proud, European industry and forcing it to move to China even faster than before. In general the world had settled into a comfortable reality. China and India would manufacture everything, Russia and the middle east would provide the fuel and energy, America would drive global consumption and generate technology, Britain would lend part of the money needed for all this bustling activity. There was no place in the new world for the EU any more. The same applied to bankrupt and forgotten Japan.

      Why would professor Rodriguez not quit defending a clearly failed model? Miles was thinking again and again. Also all this ranting about social injustice and dwindling social mobility was getting to his head. Why should he pay out of his pocket hard-earned money to help others? At the end of the day if professor Rodriguez was so concerned about the poor he might as well have donated his property to charities that still operated across the globe. Either way, Miles had been around London and the UK and all city centres were clean, organised and populated by very wealthy people. The UK was thriving.

      Annoyed, Miles shut down the video of the ranting professor and went on about his business. The stock market was on its upward spiral, massive gains were made by the bank and him personally throughout the day. Exhausted, but satisfied he finished the day at the regular leaving time, 21:00. This simply consisted of wrapping-up a few tasks still pending, taking a quick look at the news feed again, swiping the back of his hand by the desk 'eye' again and heading towards the elevator. Zombie-like he made his way to the elevator and headed downwards. The elevator was full of people, many of them working perhaps just the other side of one of his walls. Miles knew none of them. There was no need to know them. They never worked together, never met together, never dined together. All work-related activity as well as lunching occurred in their private offices. The only times they met was fleetingly and by chance when visiting the gent's room simultaneously. The same applied for everyone really. Thus, the elevator made its descent towards the parking lots quietly.

That night Hilda took Miles to a night club he enjoyed near Leicester Square. Leicester square and the surrounding areas were much like they would have been 100 years ago with the exception of few modern buildings as well as the elevated highways criss-crossing above the ancient, low buildings of London at a height that would correspond to the 10th floor. Miles walked the short distance between where Hilda left him and the club amongst the ancient buildings disinterestedly. That night he'd party because on Sunday he had no work to do! Kinroy bank was a brilliant employer! In other banks there would be no days off, but at Kinroy bank every employee got a day off every 2 weeks. These days (and their corresponding shifts) were staggered in such way that at every point in time about 47% of the company workforce was in office. That includes the night. But none of that mattered at the time. All that mattered was that the next day he could lie in bed all day if he wanted to. He thus went into the club, happy and excited.

The music inside was a deafening, boring rhythm with no melody or substance whatsoever. Yet him and the rest of the guests jumped up and down to it in near ecstasy. Every now and then, exhausted, he would head for the bar and have a drink. There was no sweat, for the nanomaterial suit would dissipate all the heat and expel the sweat that nonetheless was generated. Thus, he would happily rejoin the maddening dance after the short drinking break. Miles didn't know why, but he was enjoying himself and time flew past. Eventually, he decided to take one last break before heading home. 15 minutes later Hilda was picking him up from Leicester Square and shortly afterwards delivering him safely in front of his residence in Knightsbridge.

That Sunday the weather was nice and Miles woke up late, nearly noon must have been, under the rays of the sun. He pushed the red button situated on the bedside table and the robo-butler arrived ready to take orders. Miles, too languid to even talk, selected his breakfast from the robo-butler's touch screen. Then as the robo-butler left to fulfil its master's command he switched on the bedroom's TV. The news was on and Miles watched with satisfaction the story that the Chinese government allowed their national currency, the RMB to rise by another tenth of a percentage point. It might have seemed like little, but the bank's RMB assets, in the equivalent of tens of billions of pounds stood to gain massively from the move. China's policy of controlling the currency against a tide of upward pressure, and every now and then giving in to the pressure ever so slightly kept investors hopeful that their investments in RMB could only appreciate. It was a risk-free investment. At worst the government could halt the appreciation of the currency for a long time, they would never dare to push it back down or all that sweet,

sweet money that was resting in China would flee in panic.

The next story was all about whaling about the state of civil rights and living standards in China. Miles didn't care so long as the situation was stable and rife for business. Various guest speakers were commenting on the treatment of dissidents in China and how the government structures were not democratic enough. Others commented bitterly how the world's largest economy by a vast margin didn't manage to raise living standards for the masses to reflect even 1% of this incredible growth. Nevertheless out of China's billion and a half population about 100-200 million were living in luxury and enjoyed very high living standards, but that was just in the rich districts of the cities along the coast of the Pacific ocean. Miles didn't understand this argument either. Apparently the same situation reigned in Britain too. Supposedly there were only a few millions of very well-off people in an apparently invisible ocean of poverty. Wherever Miles travelled he saw people of various degrees of wealth, but nothing like the sad-looking people he'd met travelling across continental Europe. Next was again the familiar figure of professor Rodriguez. Miles had a faint suspicion that the venerable professor was being invited to speak his mind on TV more as an entertaining side-show attraction than as a serious guest. After all he was questioning a system that had worked brilliantly since the 2008 crisis according to the professor's own sayings.

With the news finished Miles switched channel to some reality show and kept himself entertained for a good number of hours. In the evening, he summoned the robo-butler with dinner on his mind, but the familiar, disembodied, dignified gentleman head didn't appear. Miles had only once ever experienced that before. It was when a circuit board inside the robo-butler burnt leaving the propulsion system disabled. Annoyed, Miles leapt from the sofa and started pacing about the bedroom impatiently, muttering incomprehensible words for a few minutes. Eventually his temper settled down and he went back in bed. There he reached for a transparent roll the size of the screen that was inside the drawer of his bedside table and unfolded it carefully. He then squeezed a little edge of the roll that was painted in red and the unrolled surface came to life indicating clearly that it was yet another flexible computer screen. This time, on the screen the dashboard of the residence was displayed, indicating the state of the electricity and gas meters, the state of the apartment's network, the heat loss/gain rate vs. the environment in W units and other important information regarding the operation of the residence. Next to the dashboard was the disembodied head of a very old gentleman, with a steady, lively gaze and a couple of small tufts of white hair protruding from behind his ears, leaving the rest of his head bald. His bushy, white eyebrows were another indication of the advanced age he was programmed to have and in the outer frontal reaches of his left eye-socket, just in front of his eye-ball, he wore an ancient-style monocular, a golden chain starting from the left-most end of the elegant, golden rim of the monocular and continuing downward out of sight. The already impressive ensemble was completed by an old-style snow-white collar adorned by a large, purple-red tie. This was Reginald, the residence computer. He issued orders to every other computer in the house much like a head-butler would issue orders to the entire personnel of a Victorian estate centuries ago. He possessed superior intelligence compared to his colleagues controlling the wardrobe chamber, the heating system, the home entertainment system, the plumbing etc. and unlike any of them he was manufactured with a name that he bore with electronic pride. The wealthy customers who could afford him were happy to have such a life-like electronic servant. He seemed more human and less of a yes-man with his amiable dignity and majestic composure. Moreover, he was capable of understanding a vast variety of commands and processing human speech far better than his colleagues. He was also capable, much like his electronic subordinates, of learning new commands.

'Yes sire.' Reginald spoke.

'I have a problem Reg.' replied Miles.

'Sire?'

'The robo-butler is not responding to my call. Can you do anything about that?'

'At once sire.' said Reginald and disappeared.

Reginald ran a diagnostic test on the robo-butler and sent a technical report to the 'human butler', in India. Sanjeev Sarmidjamal, technical support staff, was this 'butler'. A trained electronics and IT engineer he was responsible for ensuring that Reginald, as well as all his subservient computers in the house ran smoothly. He woke up by the beeping sound indicating that he had an incoming job and read the technical report. He then proceeded to switch on his work-computer, log on to his company's network and request permission to access the maintenance robot in Miles' apartment. Permission was quickly granted and Sanjeev diligently navigated the maintenance robot to the location of the broken robo-butler, taking extreme care not to damage any property of the customer by accident, for it could cost him his job and meagre salary. The maintenance robot's micro-cameras and robotic arms, each ending up in a useful tool worked together to unscrew the shell of the robo-butler and scan the insides of its electronic brain for any obvious signs of damage. Using information from Reginald's technical report, Sanjeev quickly spotted the loose wire connecting one of the propulsion-related integrated circuits to its corresponding PCB. It was a power transmitting pathway that had been broken for in modern electronics all signals were transmitted optically and only the power supply and ground terminals were still being implemented in metal. He guided the maintenance robot with precise movements and within minutes the problem was solved. He then proceeded to screw the robo-butler's shell back together and report to Reginald that another diagnostic was in order. Reginald performed the test and informed Sanjeev in turn that the problem was indeed fixed. 'Another satisfied customer' thought the meticulous and hard-working engineer and went back to bed.

Miles was unaware of all of this. He did now know how things worked and neither was he interested in knowing. He had no idea that in the few minutes that passed until Reginald rigidly informed him that his robo-butler was again up and running a miserably paid man from India who spent 5 years of his life studying engineering and IT had been summoned from his sleep to fix the problem. Even if he did know that he'd argue that it was his job after all and the market decided what that was worth and what working conditions he should be toiling in. Despite 5 decades of solid growth India was still lagging behind the west in development and remained largely a cheap-labour country, following closely behind China. After all the wages in the less stable and organised India would need to be below those tolerated in China by the government if India was to remain a competitive sweat-shop. These 5 decades were symbolic of the deep imbalances in the world system despite the liberalisation of global markets, as well as the tremendous rift in living standards and development between the West and India, which was evident at the start of the 20th century and to a significant extent still existed. However, life was sweet for Miles and that was all that mattered. The robo-butler was in service again and the dignified old gentleman took the order for dinner with a totally new hint of shame in his voice. The Japanese were also very good at creating emotions in computers!

Miles ate in his bed, rather than bothering to use the decorated dining room of his apartment and after dumping his tray on the bedside table for the robo-butler to handle, he unrolled the flexible screen again and started surfing the various social networking websites he was a member of, chatting to friends on webcam and e-socialising in general. If he so wished, he could link the system to the hologram generator in the sitting room and then friends of his with similar systems could 'scan themselves' into his own living room, as indeed he could do in theirs. Despite the mildly unnerving feeling created by the sight of the ghosts of his friends walking through furniture, or sometimes himself, the experience was very gratifying. It was as close as he cared to get to face-to-face relations between people. After a few hours of socialising and joining the idle gossip of his other high-class, young and dynamic friends from the world of finance he decided it was time for him to sleep for he had work the next day. 'Another 2 weeks of effort.' he sighed and headed to bed.

CHAPTER 2: CLOUDS ON THE HORIZON.

Life went on merrily for Miles. Before long it was new year. 2051 was coming with promises of more wealth. Kinroy bank had performed admirably, as usual, paid him his million-pound salary and bestowed upon him a generous million and a half-pound bonus and held a reception where everyone patted everyone else on the back in indication of congratulations and the president of the company himself shared his vision for even greater profits next year.

Despite the festive atmosphere and impressive numbers, something had changed that year. The president didn't seem as certain as usual about the future. Some senior members of the board were shaking their heads ever so slightly with evident scepticism when the president announced his projections for the coming year. In the past few months news feeds had been bristling with unnerving news that the housing market in many parts of the world was slowing down, growth was losing wind. Some countries were brought into difficulty by this situation. Vietnam in particular, in recent decades having been transformed into yet another Asian tiger, was experiencing difficulties paying back their national debt. Kinroy bank had lent tens of billions to Vietnam and as such the government of the south-east Asian country was a very important client to the bank. The coincidence of a housing market slowdown and financial difficulties in Vietnam hit Kinroy bank hard. On the one hand the properties acquired by the bank from borrowers who had been unfortunate enough to be unable repay their debts failed to gain in value and on the other a possible default from a major client was looming. However alarming the news, Miles had a deeply-rooted confidence in the system that soothed his soul. The system had worked fine for so long, why would it go wrong now? The market would eventually correct itself. It always did in the end. With that calming thought he headed back home. In any case he had a far more serious problem to contemplate. His throat was sore and he felt the fist hints of high temperature creeping upon him.

Once at home, he summoned the medical robot that he was fortunate enough to afford. It provided for efficient and relatively cheap home-care. Nothing like the vast, disorganised, inefficient and poorly stocked hospitals that were still to be seen in large metropolitan areas of continental Europe. Here technology brought right at his doorstep the very latest in medicine and he was only to go to a hospital if something very serious were to occur where self-treatment was not an option or practical. His dearly paid medical insurance to the high-end Medicorp corporation entitled him to consult a doctor online and if need be so, receive a visit in the event of a failed diagnosis. Thus Miles logged on to his Medicorp account and the automated doctor started asking questions about symptoms he was experiencing. As part of a massive international effort in the 2010's, a vast database linking symptoms to diseases had been created and was sufficiently advanced as to be able to identify the disease by receiving a small number of clear answers from the patient. The database was regularly updated at the expense of contributing research institutions, mostly funded by charities or governments of the EU and Japan. As a result, Miles could glide through his 10' diagnosis and receive the prescription indicated by the automated doctor. Miles then proceeded to receiving the medication that was indicated to him.

 Miles was grateful to have been provident enough to obtain for himself medical insurance again and thought that obtaining police and fire-protection insurance as well was also a good idea. After all, if your property was on fire and you had no suitable insurance, you were on your own or were forced to pay the exorbitant fire extinguishing fee. Similar conditions applied to the victims of crime at any level. If you had no police insurance you had to either pay the suitable -and expensive- crime investigation fee or let the case drop. Similarly judicial insurance would pay for setting up a court case and paying the trial costs -including lawyer or prosecutor and judge fees and court rental- in case of trouble with the law. The police force, the fire brigade and the entire judicial system had been privatised in the 2030's, a decade after the ancient organisation of the NHS and all the public education institutions were subject to the same fate. At about the same time local government was entirely privatised and governing councils were dissolved; a move that was greeted with cheers. More recently, in the early 2040's the last bastion of public power, the army had been privatised too and was formed into a corporation that handled military affairs at the request of clients and protected anyone's interests. Parliament still reserved the right to force the UK based companies to reject contracts against British national interests and deny them the right to migrate their business abroad. However, outside the borders of the UK what the companies did was no longer the concern of the government. Despite the fact that the UK government now consisted of exactly 1000 people, 646 MPs and 354 staff running the administration of parliament (responsible for renting a suitable room for house of commons and house of lords meetings as well as liaising with any company that was to provide services for the parliament), they still made the rules... Still Miles didn't vote. He didn't feel the need to. After all, the sole responsibility of parliament towards the people was to keep the country safe and rife for business, and possibly also declare wars when national businesses requested it and pay a suitable army company to wage those wars, but that hadn't happened in a very long time. Either way, voting was for important people who either had a say in such matters or 'just cared about such stuff' and indeed, the 1% of the population that turned up to the ballots were mostly such important people and lunatics that still professed political beliefs...

The following days Miles kept going to work as usual and everything seemed normal except a feeling of tension at the bank. The people he bumped into seemed more rushed and nervous than usual. Miles wondered what this dark cloud of negativity could mean. Perhaps his colleagues, just like himself were plagued by a tidal wave of bad luck. Suddenly it became much more difficult to make money on the financial market. Somehow the stock market returns were not quite so spectacular these days, businesses and even people were more reluctant to take out loans. Yet at the same time the figures coming out of the bank's central accounting office were healthy, and showed profits all across the board. 'Surely if I'm doing so much more badly but the bank overall is still looking good, others are doing better, no?' thought Miles and immediately started agonising about his job security. If he only had bothered to meet other people at work and get to know them... Maybe they could provide him with more insider information... Either way, Miles' routine kept going on, but was now constantly poisoned with this unnerving tension... Despite his enormous income, envied by anyone employed outside the investment banking and professional athletics professions he had never ever made any savings -besides his new residence in Knightsbridge had cost him 9 out of the 12 million pounds he'd earned at Kinroy bank over the few years he'd been there-. He always lived to the limit with cards over-drafted with amounts reflecting his huge income. Even so, he had to spend hundreds of thousands each year in his numerous insurance policies, motoring, police, fire-brigade, judicial, medical, etc. Either way, the experience of the past pacified him. Kinroy bank was a giant, one that would not fall easily. The bank had not cut jobs in decades, why would they do so now? After all, nothing could go wrong. The market would find its balance eventually; in the past every time it did and the bank got wealthier and stronger.

The following months passed and winter was about togive way to spring. Nothing dramatic had happened, but the string of 'bad days' persisted for Miles and judging by their nervous looks, his colleagues too. Still, the bank overall was reporting a healthy outlook. They had no reason to lie after all, no? Still, Miles thought that the EU regulations that once used to apply to the UK too might have actually forced them to tell the truth back in those days. He quickly dismissed the thought, however, reminding himself that the bank had no reason to lie. After all, in the City one trusted one's colleagues. There was nothing to be learned from the underachievers across the channel. Miles then proceeded to silently scold himself over showing so little faith in a system that had never betrayed him and went on with his life giving little more thought to the issue.

In reality, behind the scenes, Kinroy bank was hiding something from employees and partners alike. Kinroy had lent too much recklessly to people and businesses that had failed to pay back and whose real estate collaterals had failed to gain enough value to maintain Kinroy's profits. The meetings held in the round table on the top floor of the Kinroy tower were becoming more and more animated. If this situation continued at that rate, Kinroy would go bankrupt within one month, an old member of the board argued. Another shared his thoughts whilst yet another one expressed the view that Kinroy possessed the mass to sit out the crisis and use its money reserves to survive until the real-estate assets would appreciate to an acceptable level. This was occurring daily, rather than on occasion, but the underlings at the bank were none the wiser.

Then, on one day it happened. It was the first day when he did not make a profit for the bank. He finished that day disturbed, disappointed and ever so slightly frightened. It shook his world. In all the years he had been working happily for Kinroy bank, since his graduation in fact, he never once shamed himself by going in the red and that was the object of much pride for him. This shock made him realise that perhaps faith in the system will not be enough to avert a crisis if it ever arises. 'After all, I made a loss that day for the first time ever, that was just as unthinkable as the system collapsing, no? Well, perhaps not as unthinkable but still enough to make me stop and think.' Miles thought alarmedly. That really set him thinking. In the car on the way back home, and later that night in bed, unable to fall asleep. There was no partying that night for him. 'What happens if something serious fails in the system?' he asked himself. 'What happens if a bank goes bankrupt? Particularly a large one?' he continued. Following the logical steps he concluded that if many lenders had indeed provided loans for the failed bank and were in a similar financial situation as the one Kinroy bank might *really* be in, then the shock of such default may be enough to send them into bankruptcy too. In fact, the loss of confidence in the whole system after such disaster might pull everyone into bankruptcy. Miles shivered at the thought. 'Yet still, such thing hasn't happened since 2008, apparently.' he continued, the thought dampening his anxiety for the moment. 'Oh, I wish I knew more about 2008. Why didn't I learn anything about that all these years? I spent so much time ridiculing history as the science of that which can no longer be changed... If I had known...' his thoughts ran. Miles spent what seemed like hours trying to conciliate the truly frightening conclusions his logic was leading him towards against the clean record of the system for the past 40 years. Sure, there had been hiccups, such as local crises, but nothing that challenged the stability of the entire globe. 'Surely this one will be something local if it happens.' he consoled himself, satisfied with the conciliatory conclusion he reached.

As he was about to succumb to Orpheus' enticing song he suddenly had a flashback from when he was still a trainee engineer. He had a colleague of remarkable intelligence who every now and then would talk to him. He used to listen to him with bewilderment and pay generally little attention, particularly the times when he would mock him about his ambition to enter the world of finance after graduation. But on one day it was different. His colleague uttered a few things that really left a mark on him, despite the fact he didn't know it at the time.

They were in the departmental common room having cheap 'studenty' lunch that day, as usual during lunch break. Miles himself was ruffling through investment bank recruitment ads, looking for summer internships as his colleague marched in with his own equally 'studenty' lunch and sat next to him.

'Still trying to get a career in professional conning I see, eh?' he said in his usual humorously condescending fashion. He was well intended after all...

'Yes...'

'Well, we are young. We will live to see this unless something changes.'

Miles looked at his colleague inquisitively and puzzled.

'Now things are rosy and fine, and the City pays a lot, but we will see the day when hell breaks loose. A systemic failure. A catastrophe that will bring much of the financial system down.' the colleague continued. James his name probably was, Miles recollected vaguely.

'What do you mean James?'

'I mean like back in 2008, and before that in the 1930's'.

Miles recalled the vague knowledge he had about that event, over 35 years ago as it had been. After all he was a 2045 graduate.

'However, this time it will be different, and you know why?' he said.

'Why?' inquired Miles docilely.

'Because last time governments of the world bailed out the system at the expense of their taxpayers. Now that governments everywhere are outsourcing their power and privatising themselves what is our failure safety mechanism?'.

A silence followed. Miles thought about the problem and just as earlier that day, he had the clean record of the system for the past 35 years, now weighing against an opinion expressed by someone just as inexperienced as he was...

'Exactly', James declared.

'But why?' Miles asked genuinely interested.

'Well let me put it this way... Over the years and particularly as I learned more about engineering, I realised that behind everything in nature there exist some very general, extremely useful universal rules that seem to govern everything. For example trade-offs.' James uttered thoughtfully.

'And?'

'And these apply in science and in human relations and in economics and everywhere. Doesn't it seem strange that some concepts should apply to such diverse entities as the laws of the universe, i.e. physics, and something as contrived and artificial and human-generated as economics?' James replied, his tone indicating he had spent a lot of time thinking about that subject.

'I don't get you.' Miles replied. 'What universal concepts?'.

'Let me give you an example. You remember the trade-offs we have seen in the analogue electronics class in operational amplifiers? Our beloved OpAmps?'

'Vaguely... Please remind me'. Miles replied with a hint of shame. That was previous year material that he had memorised for the exam and promptly forgotten afterwards, something that brought him difficulties this year, by the way.

'Well, in the simplest case we have an OpAmp design and by applying different supporting feedback circuitry to it we can exchange amplification gain for bandwidth over which this amplification is reliable, no?'

The seemingly patronising reply was received with a silent thank you from Miles who suddenly felt his memory refreshed.

'Yes, and?'

'Well the concept of trade-offs is universal, no? It may seem obvious, but think of the implications of looking at the matter this way. It means that in most real-world problems there is nearly never a unique solution to a problem, but rather a multitude where different parameters are balanced against one another. If someone keeps that in mind the various political strifes and debates are explained. Everyone is right in a sense. Also, consider that if this concept of the universality of trade-offs is kept in mind, one's course of action in the face of trouble is set, no? One simply has to investigate the parameters involved and re-balance them to his advantage if possible, no?'

Miles tried to process the long string of data pouring into his mind. His countenance must have been exhibiting extreme intellectual effort since James asked him:

'Are you following me?'

'I'm trying...'

'Well, let's get down to a more concrete example'.

'Please let's'.

'Heh. All right. Remember the Boltzmann distribution and how it reflects on semiconductor physics?'

'Ugh, very vaguely' Miles cast his mind back 2 years when the memories of lectures were even more hazy.

'Well, the really meaty part is the one where there are a couple of reference energy levels, A and B and electrons in the low energy level can jump up to the high level. The probability that this happens is linked to the temperature, and therefore the available thermal energy that the electrons are privy to. Of course the same applies to holes.'

'Yeeeees...' replied Miles, his memory again receiving a boost.

'Well, if you replace the word 'temperature' with the phrase 'financial risk' and the energy levels now represent system stability as the low level and system failure as the high level you get something interesting. Can you see what?'

'Ugh... it means that the higher the risk, the higher the probability of system failure?' said Miles in exasperation.

'Exactly'. Replied James. 'We have a concept where a variable now influences the probability of another variable to take a certain value. This is another very universal concept, I find, and to me that is extraordinary. Again it seems obvious once all is said and done, but once again if you have this outlook on things your course is set out for you. Find the 'cause' variable and set it to an acceptable level. Also, most of the time it means that you cannot avert the possibility that your dependent variable reaches the undesired value, but you must satisfy yourself with a very, very low probability, and that will vary according to the situation.'

'Ugh...' replied Miles. 'Oh wait a minute, I get it now! It's so clear!' he exclaimed after a bit more thought in silence.

'Good man!' replied James.

'But how does that translate in economics for example? Does it mean that a financial entity must calculate risks so that it becomes very unlikely to succumb to failure?'

'Yes. It means exactly that. If we twist the probability problem and now assume that we have a single carrier and we want to see how often it will reach the high energy level, we should be able to calculate the mean time between transitions to the high energy level. In the example of financial system, this would be the mean time between a big systemic failure.'

'Wow. I'd never thought of it that way... But how about the

example where we design a beam or a table that is designed to sustain 10kg of weight and we know we'll never load it with more than 5kg. Isn't that a case where breakdown is impossible?'.

'Yes and no. It is still technically possible, but well, well, weeeeell into the realm of the unrealistic. Just like the possibility that your shattered pint on the floor where you just accidentally dropped it is going to spontaneously reconstruct, or the possibility that in a gas container all the molecules of air suddenly synchronise by pure accident and hit the edge of the container with enough force as to make it move, or that we ever get a prime minister who actually knows what he's doing, heh.'

'Heh.'

'In fact now that I think about it a bit more, in the case of risk and returns we have the general concept of a variable controlling another one in a stochastic manner and a trade-off at the same time. It's a stochastic trade-off! Heh. I must coin that term!' James concluded jokingly.

'Heh.'

'The difference with the OpAmp is that in our gain vs. bandwidth tradeoff we control a variable deterministically by exerting direct control over another one. In the stochastic control this dependence is probabilistic. As such, a trade-off may be stochastic or deterministic, like the cases of the OpAmp and the risk/return relationship.'

'Does this mean that we can design an economic system whereby failure is satisfactorily unlikely?'

'No! Definitely not! In economics, particularly globalised economics any single government holds far too little power to devise such fail-proof system. The best option is to devise a system that can respond to change easily and quickly and react to the economic situation as it unfolds. For example, provide stimulation to the economy it times of crisis, but be frugal, parsimonious even, and run surpluses in times of plenty; invest in public welfare when the population needs to be educated, but abandon it and simply outbid competitors to getting the best brains when the opportunity arises -like in the United States-; open labs when research can lead to a competitive advantage, and shut them down when following and copying is more profitable because you lack the means to be a leader. However, there may be a possibility to devise a fail-proof system...'

'What? How?'

'Create a vast economic and political union. Eliminate strife and competition on national grounds. Create a vast market space that acts in unison and is large enough to isolate itself from the rest of the world if this fail-proof model will be brought down otherwise.' James said assertively. 'But that would be just as unlikely as the spontaneously reconstructing pint, heh. We'd rather race each other to the bitter bottom in hope of out-racing competitors than unite and do what's best for all of us, heh.' he concluded humorously but with a distinct bitterness permeating his words.

'I suppose this explains why it has been so difficult to get people to start thinking about the environment in the old days.' Miles offered. It was one of the few things he remembered from history. In the late 2010's the leaders of the world finally agreed to adopt a global system of standards aimed to reduce pollution world-wide to acceptable levels, prevent the further loss of forests and preserve the biodiversity of the planet. It took a string of phenomenal natural catastrophes that hit every single country in the world to make everyone realise that the time for real action was there. He'd watched an educational movie about it at a school trip to some museum, as well as seen enormous piles of waste generated by previous generations, all of which would have been recycled had it been generated when he was watching the dreary piles as a visitor to the museum.

'Yeeeees...' James said slowly assenting.

'And I suppose this also explains why companies like to diversify their portfolios I guess'.

'Yes. Yet another example of trade-offs. In this case there are a multitude of parameters into play. Each financial product suits a set of specific needs and yet for that very specific set of needs there is always a multitude of competing options. Somehow every time there is not a single one ending up with 100% of the market share, which means that every competing product is somewhere on the trade-off limiting curve, plane, hyperplane even, i.e. every product is in some sense optimal. That is why trade-offs generate diversification as yet another universal rule. That explains why there are a hundred different mortgage deals out there, all still alive and well, as well as why the planet is populated by millions of species of animals, plants and insects, and not one single species...' James concluded pensively. 'Even though it could also be the case that the only reason we have not completely overtaken the planet as sole surviving species is because this multi-faceted 'optimality' needs to be of a multi-faceted nature in order to be sustainable, or to dampen down the statement, work optimally as a whole system... Complex eh?' he concluded with an almost cheeky smile.

'Quite.' Miles replied still a bit confused after the last torrent of information.

'Either way, I was expecting you to ask about things like imperfect markets and networking effects and imperfect information and brand reputation when I mentioned the mortgage example, you being a market person and all.' James said and chuckled -that cheeky smile again!-.

'Yes. Good point' said Miles interested.

'The answer is that parameters like brand reputation, information availability etc. are all taken into account when estimating this optimality. After all a bank loan may be the most suitable because the customer trusts that bank over any other, or because that's the only one he knows about, just like a backward and undeveloped alien civilisation can be there simply because it is too far away from anything that would overpower it. The optimality I'm talking about is something universal that transcends simple functional criteria, in the case of the bank loan, the interest rate and in the case of a civilisation, the level or military readiness. Everything out there exists because in some sense it was optimal under the rules of the universe, just like a stone is on the ground because it is optimal in terms of gravitational potential energy. However, mind that this optimality is something very different to purpose. Unfortunately, this also means that there is no meaning to life. It exists simply because it was in some way optimal.' pronounced James.

'So everything in the universe is basically rolling down some slope until it reaches some optimal point'. Added Miles.

'Yes, but possibly dotted with randomness, it's not necessary that everything is completely deterministic. In fact we may never know the answer to this. The only way to know whether the universe itself has a random nature or a deterministic one is to create perfect copies of it and set them off to see what happens. And of course hope that these universes are not perturbed by anything else from outside. But that's another story...' said James with yet another chuckle. 'Well, one thing is certain. There's much more out there to be taken into consideration. I don't profess to have the answer to everything... But the fact that there seem to exist such general universal principles to me is just amazing.' James continued. 'But I think it's now time for us to go to lectures.' he concluded pointing at the clock, indicating it was nearly 14:00. Miles nodded in agreement and they headed for the next class.

'So, could this be it? Could this be the moment when it is about time the system fails?' Miles thought. Then he remembered once again talking with James about acceptable safety criteria. James had memorably said: 'In the real world it is frightfully often that systems are designed with a mean time between failures that roughly matches the time the designers spend in the role of system administrator; not so much because after they're gone nobody knows how to run the system, but because after they're gone they don't care what happens to the system anyway...' and then added: 'Come to think about it in engineering we rarely get the chance to be that reckless and irresponsible, but go in politics and economics and god almighty the jig is on!' with his trademark cheeky smile. Miles remembered various news stories where

CEOs of large companies had left them with brilliant figures only to be later discovered that those stellar performances had been achieved while sowing the seeds of destruction long-term. James might have had a point there... Finally after all this exhausting thought process, Miles finally succumbed to sleep.

CHAPTER 3: DISASTER.

The day started normally, with the usual breakfast, dressing, and hygiene ceremonies. Miles, troubled by the thoughts that had robbed him of sleep and deprived him of the appetite for partying went to work under the safe guidance of Hilda. In the car he watched the news. He got used to it lately, watching the news in the car. The anxiety associated with the future was exhorting him to read the news earlier than usual. Search for anything indicative of victory or disaster. Searching through the headlines, one attracted his attention more than any others. Kinroy bank had filed for bankruptcy.

The news took a long while to sink in. He stood there dumbstruck, unable to move or speak. During the night Kinroy bank had defaulted against several creditors, admitting that 'they had lent the wrong amounts of money to the wrong sort of people'. All the talk about Vietnam defaulting proved to be bogus; a diversion at best. Kinroy bank had falsified information regarding their financial health. Despite them hiring external auditors to confirm the accounts to the world and boost confidence in the bank it seems that the ancient practice of 'cooking the books' was still alive and well. Kinroy bank was apparently in the deep, blood-red by sums in the tens, probably even hundreds of billions. That certainly explained why he was doing worse and worse, but the bank was apparently fine. What he blamed on personal failure was simply trickery on the part of the bank. Evidently that was the day when everyone was going to receive news about their futures at Kinroy bank. Perhaps the bank would continue in some form or another; a large chunk of the empire sinking while some small healthy bits being saved from the vultures. Nobody knew...

Certainly the atmosphere in the building was very different that day. People were nervously getting to their offices, not gaiting in their usual way, but rather pacing impatiently. Evidently they'd heard the news too. Miles entered the elevator and fidgeted nervously as shiny cabin was making its way to his office's floor. The elevator finally made it to the 20th floor and Miles', heart pounding with anxiety, left it continue transporting its equally unnerved passengers upwards towards their own offices. Reaching his office, he noticed that instead of the usual cup of tea, a red envelope was waiting for him on his desk. Miles raced to it, ripped apart the seal and violently pulled out the paper inside. It read:

'Dear employees of Kinroy bank,
as you may have heard in the news recently, the bank is now in severe financial difficulties. As a result, you have been given either a red, or a green envelope today. If this letter arrived in the red envelope, then your employment at Kinroy bank has regrettably been terminated. If you have received a green envelope, your employment at Kinroy bank shall continue until further notice.

To the recipients of the red envelope: please clear your desks within the hour. Your access to the non-public areas of the Kinroy tower, including the employee-only bar on level 95 will be revoked at 10:00 today.

Vice president Morency,
director of security.'

So that was it. He was fired, sacked, given the boot despite his track record at the company, despite the loyalty he had shown towards the bank. He cleared the desk of the handful of personal items he had brought along and called Hilda. Navigating his way past the crowd that was exiting the tower with their belongings in boxes and bags of various shapes and sizes he climbed into his car and told Hilda in a very run-down voice to just take him home. It was just 09:20. He had been really efficient at 'clearing his desk'. He then remembered that across the channel there was legislation that prevented such simple lay-offs without any warning or compensation, where even after the lay-off workers enjoyed a sort of benefit, what was it's name, unemployment benefit or something. The thought made his heart sting. He had laughed countless times at the continentals with their funny sense of social security but now he realised that perhaps there was a motive behind maintaining such systems in place. People in Germany might have been drab-looking, but they seemed healthy and were likely to be educated. Same in France and elsewhere. What was he to become now? His contributions to the private pension fund did not entitle him for any help from there and there was no way of receiving financial assistance from elsewhere given that his parents had long since passed on -tragic accident that was- and their family fortune had been all but spent trying to get him through the best education money could buy. His savings were near zero. He had been saving for far too little time, even for his enormous income. He was still too well-off to apply for charity too and even if he did he was not likely to be received well given the fact that a place for him would almost certainly mean no place for someone who had probably spent their entire life in misery.

Miles was lost in a torrent of thoughts swirling through his head. Much like a computer that is being given an impossible task and is forever trapped looking through countless alternatives that lead exactly nowhere, or more familiarly to Miles, when he loses some object and looks through his pockets again and again finding nothing, only to discover the desired object in an entirely different location, later on. Hilda was saying nothing, as if being too concentrated on her navigational tasks to strike conversation. Miles paid no attention. The old, low buildings of London swept past him way below as the car tackled the elevated highways. The few skyscrapers also swept past, hiding the car in their shadow for the briefest of moments. The impressive viaduct had been completed just before the privatisation of the ministry of transport. It was one of the last public projects and one that was still being used heavily by everyone in central London. Since the ministry was privatised, a company was formed to take care of the highway and charged toll fees for its maintenance. The same applied to regular streets for that matter. When it was time to build a new major infrastructure project, companies that stood to gain from it hired a private contractor, tried to gain the necessary land and then set the project in motion. At the end they created a company to manage it, in which all financing parties owned a stake and then typically sold it and made the said company independent.

Miles was darting on the highway with his mind totally away, panic filling his every vein and artery. Any solution he'd been able to scrap together in the few moments when he temporarily regained his composure was unsatisfactory. At that realisation he'd sink back into panic. Hilda left him, as usual, in front of his own home. He made his way to his apartment and then his bedroom and finally crashed into his bed. What was he to do? He looked around himself. The robo-butler, his wardrobe chamber, Reginald. Would he have to lose all of that? Cold sweat started running down his fore-head, the cold sweat of a desperate, most likely destitute man. 'Must concentrate! Must find a way out of this!' he kept saying to himself and for a second he'd regain his composure again and attempt to formulate a plan. But then sooner or later his gaze would fall upon a familiar object he would likely be forced to part with in the near future and a feeling of despair grabbed him and shook the deepest nooks of his insides with tremendous ferocity. Eventually he noticed the rolled-up terminal screen where he surfed the net. Perhaps some of his online friends would be able to assist him? Miles rushed to the terminal and unrolled it. He then hesitated and dropped the terminal. Quickly going through his 'friends' list he realised that none of them would be prepared to do that much for him.

A painful memory from the past came forcefully into his mind. A person named Alpman was his best friend long ago. They'd chat to each other for hours; they'd even spend hours together in virtual reality, either visiting places in a strange mix of vicarious and first-hand way of experiencing them or simply immersing themselves into some fantastic gaming world. They'd hold conversations about everything and nothing; they'd share their views and opinions. Eventually they'd share their most intimate secrets. Once Miles visited him and had great fun in Alpman's luxurious apartment in central Manchester. And then one day, they were discussing business. Miles shared some information that would have most certainly fallen into the 'strictly confidential' category with Alpman about certain investments Kinroy bank was preparing to make -it was the purchase of another bank, Miles remembered-. The next day, the bank that Alpman worked for purchased a large stake into the smaller bank in an attempt to block Kinroy bank from obtaining the deal. The directors at Kinroy were furious and tried desperately to find out who leaked the information. Ever since, employees with ranks similar to Miles' were put under surveillance. Their renewed working contracts demanded that surveillance cameras were placed in their offices, private cars and private residences. Otherwise they'd lose their jobs. Come to think of it, perhaps that's exactly why Kinroy decided to add holidays to the employee schedule: to balance out what would have been an outrageous invasion of privacy back when there still was some labour regulation... In any case, that day Alpman earned a huge bonus and a promotion and lost a person who had regarded him as a true friend. Miles had spoken to Alpman man-to-man, undressing his professional hat when he did so and putting aside any promises of profit, if gained on his friend's back. The trauma of betrayal had never truly healed. After all Alpman had been the only person to every invite him to his residence if one was to exclude childhood friends he visited on festive occasions, such as birthday parties.

Nevertheless, Miles' bitterness towards people after that fateful experience was not the only factor to blame for his lack of genuine friends. In truth, British society since the early 21st century had been changing from its deepest foundations. The culture of privatisation and suing for personal gain, the complete disengagement of government from its own citizens and its shunning of any responsibility apart from declaring wars and changing the rules when asked to, the knowledge that only the toughest would survive and those that used any means to get to the top; all of those prepared the scene for the advent of a new generation of people. Social Darwinism ensured that the people who survived the new order in society and done well enough to be boasting private quarters in London's so called "Zone 1" and have access to everything modern consumer technology could provide were self-centred, shallow fanfarons. Holding loyalties to nobody and nothing but themselves, their motives always selfish, image always more important than substance and possession of material wealth always reigned supreme. People able to navigate the perilous and reef-ridden waters of treachery and intrigue that permeated every important power structure in society and get ahead by manipulating a vast network of deceit and lawless competition. People in whom an insatiable lust for power, money and status had been instilled since they were competing with their peers to put up a vulgar and decadent show of wealth in primary school.

Miles, pondering all of this briefly, kneeling in his bed whilst looking at nothing, remembered James once again. "Society consists of rules and people. People can grow up to be anything within a vast range of possibilities, determined and in fact limited by our physical substance running from our most intricate molecular structures all the way up to the top-level design of the human brain. The rules, on the other hand, create a massive 'social potential field', much like a collection of charges creates an electric potential field in space." he said. He then continued to explain in response to the perplexed look Miles' countenance had assumed: "Imagine a 3-dimensional space where the x and the y axes represent various possibilities of behaviour. Let's say that the x-axis represents profession and the y-axis represents education. Now let's place a convenient variable called 'social success' on the z-axis. For the various combinations of x and y you will get different degrees of 'success', in other words success Z is a function of profession, P and education E." James said and paused to scan Miles' countenance for even the slightest hint of understanding. Finding a surprising amount of what he sought he continued: "Now imagine the system in its full complexity. We'll keep the convenient z-variable for the time being but have a multi-dimensional space where all the parameters play a role; parameters like the state of health, the social entourage at various stages of the human life cycle and the legal system. Society's system of rules shapes the function that links our z-variable to all the parameters mentioned above. It defines how being a lawyer from Zone 1 of London in a robust state of health and with rich parents one will wind up more successful than someone who is an assembly line supervisor from Zone 2 of London with a health ailment he can't afford to cure because his parents were also from Zone 2. Moreover it defines the nature of the z-variable, i.e. the nature of success itself. Of course all of this is stochastic rather than deterministic...". Miles was listening thinking that all of that made a lot of sense. Then James continued: "In our society, the market alone determines this function. Money is the sole indicator of success and the shape of the curve, pardon me, hyper-surface, is such that the tough, ruthless and strong survive to become stronger. Naturally, the set of rules applying to

Zones 2 or 3 may be different. That's why you are likely to find different sorts of people in different zones of London. Although if I am right in my assumptions you'll probably find that Zones 1 and 3 have a lot in common in this respect..." James said with a hint of that cheeky smile creeping on his face again. Miles never understood the meaning of that last statement. "Keeping this in mind may explain the behaviour many people exhibit in a multitude of situations, albeit that is not synonymous with agreement or even approval." he also stated emphatically. Miles could see the truth in that statement more easily.

"In conclusion we can say a couple of things in the way of useful conclusions: First, society is a system that works in feedback. In other words, change the rules and the people will change in time too, change the people and there will be pressure to change the rules in time too. That explains why propaganda works so frightfully well. It also lends credit to the argument that people here and now are truly different from people elsewhere and else-when. Unfortunately it also lends credit to the idea that national stereotypes and stereotypes about people in ancient times actually do have a basis in some form of truth, but at the same time also to the idea that any human could, can and will always be able to develop into any of these stereotypical forms if placed under those circumstances.". "And second?" demanded Miles. "Second, that our current system is frightfully likely to be the closest to THE human nature." replied James sombrely, even darkly, frowning menacingly. "THE human nature?" inquired Miles. "THE human nature." echoed James, then looking at the curious look exhibited by Miles he continued: "You see, I believe that humans have a true nature, one that is behind everything we do. We can seek to change it within strict limits and achieve doing so within even stricter limits. But always there will be a force pulling us down to that fundamental human nature, and the nature of that nature -excuse the pun- does not look good..." James uttered slowly now frowning even more intensely, his countenance even darker. "It doesn't look good and our system, the British system, the 'post-government' system as I like to call it, lets that true nature come out. Rules are made by the strong, for the strong, people adapt to those rules by becoming brutes, a situation not very much unlike what you would see in the jungle, or rather what's left of it." James concluded -was it possible- even more lugubriously. Miles nodded and memories of what happened later on were too hazy to recall.

Casting his mind on this conversation that occurred back in his undergraduate days helped him calm down. It was inexplicable but suddenly he felt composed, realised that there was no help to be found anywhere and that he would have to prepare himself for a set of very difficult decisions. It looked like Miles Fitzroy was moving job.

Otherwise, it looks like he was going to be moving a gear, and a zone down. So off he was, energised like a man who finally mastered his fear and turned it into action. Miles unrolled the terminal again, but instead of logging on to his networking sites in search for help that was unlikely to arrive he went straight for websites of major banks and corporations that might be in need of his skills. The City, after all, was full of banks of every sort. Even insurance companies might need his skills. London had been the centre of world finance since the government sounded its final retreat and was reduced to its contemporary form, so that fact alone should be an indication of the concentration of wealth in Zone 1. Surely he could squeeze himself in some sort of job and keep enjoying a sizeable chunk of the massive proverbial pie. At the end of the day the collapse of Kinroy bank hardly meant the collapse of the entire City. No?

The job hunt went badly. For some strange reason any company he called was informing him that there were no vacancies available. Some banks even notified prospective employees of that on their websites. 'Well, there is still time, no?' he thought to himself. For the rest of the day he felt excessively bored. Holidays were a necessary evil in the business world and for that reason they were kept short. As such, Miles only ever enjoyed very short one-day breaks at Kinroy bank which he normally spent recovering from the hangover, brought upon him by the drinking and partying throughout much of the night before. The amount of free time suddenly forced upon him was a recipe for boredom. In the end he decided to use the time-honoured approach of killing boredom by surfing the internet. He leapt back in bed and started surfing, alternating between the most random collection of websites about cats, national statistics, internet TV shows etc. and company websites of prospective employers. In the end, he somehow managed to go through his day and ended up in bed.

The next days passed in more or less the same tone. No luck at job-hunting, mostly boredom and the same on-off job-hunting on the net to end the day. It appeared like many banks and other finance-related companies were on a hire freeze, almost as if they were waiting for something. In fact, as the days turned into weeks and the fateful date when he'd have to 'shift down' approached, Miles began to grow suspicious that he couldn't obtain an audience for a job-interview, nay, a CV request, let alone a job. All the big players in the finance game were not hiring. Most suspicious indeed. Miles poured more and more intellectual resources to this as the fateful date approached. His thoughts started from the fact that Kinroy bank had ultimately declared bankruptcy and unleashed a massive scandal by falsifying accounts. How would that affect other players? Miles tried to put himself in the shoes of a different bank, one working with Kinroy, to see what conclusions he would reach.

"Let's say that I work for Barrington bank. Barrington lent a couple of billions to Kinroy just before I was made redundant. Money that they are not likely to receive back. Hmmm... This in effect means either less profit, or bigger deficit -or transition from profit to deficit-. It also means that all business linked with Kinroy bank, and therefore the man-hours dedicated to that will no longer be needed. This creates a labour vacuum already there." thought Miles. "But then, Kinroy bank is one of many financial giants. Surely if all other business partners do well this should be but a small hiccup for Barrington." he continued. "Think Miles, think!" he urged himself silently. "But Kinroy lied about their accounts, no? Who is to say that everyone else is not in the red and hiding it? After all, one wouldn't lend money to someone one wouldn't trust, would they? Interesting..." the thoughts rushed through Miles' head. "Well, in that case, it's very likely that business will not be brisk with anyone for quite a while. In fact, much of the economic-financial system will grind to a halt if many more banks go out of business... But will this happen? How long can a bank hide the fact that it's facing economic meltdown? Maybe this is what the big players are waiting to determine?" Miles' mind was frantically working. "Of course that's what it is! How could I have ever been so blind? And stupid!" Miles thought with bitterness. His blind faith in the system, the belief that the market would find its way, that a crisis could never happen again had clouded his thoughts. The possibility of a massive, systemic failure of this magnitude was simply unthinkable -ostensibly-. But the big cheeses knew about the risk. They were waiting to see whether this financial trouble would bust the entire system. They were either intelligent enough to figure it out despite the widespread belief in the system, or they knew because they were experiencing the same problems as Kinroy... In any case, the reluctance of banks to lend to one another would lead to the weakest links in the system collapsing. After all without a loan/life-line to extend their lifespans these weak links would surely collapse one after the other, like pieces of domino. In essence this loss of confidence amongst banks and their resulting reluctance to lend one to another was destabilising the system, in fact driving it to collapse.

  Miles kept figuring out parts of this scenario day after day until another shocking piece of news reached the press: Barrington bank declared bankruptcy amidst allegations of falsification of accounts, much like Kinroy had. Another army of unemployed people in London, and no chances that the employment market would rebound soon enough for Miles to maintain his present life-style until that time. It was time for action again, and it would be painful. Miles had to 'shift a gear down', but how? In Zone 1 estate agents in glittering skyscrapers would find and survey properties for the customer, and when the customer made up his mind to purchase one they'd take care of all legal matters. However, no estate agent operated in Zones 2 or 3. In fact Miles was barely half-aware of what lay in there. Come to think of it anything outside Zones 1 of each city that boasted one operated like different countries. In any case he would have to go out and see for himself. Hilda was summoned and Miles waited patiently for her call back, a call that would indicate that she was waiting for him at his front door.

In the meantime he pondered once more the other alternative that had occurred to him: to sell his residence and move somewhere cheaper. There were still a few snags with this plan, however. First, his property had lost tremendously in value. Worried about news of falling house prices he had the apartment surveyed. It was now worth less than ½ of its original value at 3 million. If he decided to sell now, he would lose an enormous amount and when things got better he'd have to work his way to such apartment all over again. Perhaps in the future, under these crisis circumstances, the work he did would be met with less emolument for a long, long time. How long would it take him to earn the millions that his beloved flat in Knightsbridge cost him all over again? The other snag was that he would have to rent a storage space to place all his possessions in, because it was more than certain that if he didn't pour at least a couple of million pounds into buying his new house he would never be able to find anything as spacious even in the outer rims of Zone 1, for example in Ealing Broadway, Richmond, Bromley etc. That was a significant loss again since such services were bound to become expensive as more and more people in banks, sharing Miles' predicament would no doubt seek such services for the very same reasons he did. Instead the best way out was to proceed with his current plan: don't sell the house, use the little savings he had left to obtain something, or even rent in Zone 2 and try to rent out his residence in Zone 1 along with all the furniture, robots and even many of the personal possessions he kept there. The rest of his possessions could go in the little storage locker at the basement of the building and the tenant would be forbidden from using it, i.e. its use would not be part of the rental contract. That way when things got better he'd end up with a valuable property again, perhaps some money if a tenant was found and thus a place back in high-class society, if only he could tolerate some time in the slums of Zone 2.

In any case Hilda was calling him. He interrupted his thoughts, satisfied with his plan, and left his apartment ready to receive a tour of Zone 2. Inside his car, Hilda asked politely where she could take her master, after greeting him in her usual, formal way. Miles made his intention of visiting Zone 2 known to Hilda and in response she warned him that in Zone 2 there are no known maps she can navigate by and that it was unlikely that there would be any charging tracks either. Miles heeded her advice but insisted that they travel in Zone 2.

    Charging tracks were much like rails in an ordinary railway; a pair of metal tracks whose gauge would perfectly match the distance between the wheels of any ordinary car. Each rail represented an electrical pole, left and right, negative and positive respectively, and cars with navigators like Hilda could run on the road exactly over these rails so that the car would recharge on the go. That is why the tyres of such cars were fitted with flexible metal rings that ran along the circumference of the wheels and made contact with the rails. Naturally, in contrast to railroad tracks these rails would not protrude from the surface of the road, but rather integrate into it. Thin channels each side of the actual track for draining rain-water would account for slight bumps felt when the car was aligning itself with the tracks, changing lanes or passing over a crossing. Moreover, the roads that were built and fitted with such tracks would boast a new kind of asphalt that possessed a spongy composure on the surface layer and absorbed rainwater easily, dumping it to yet more drainage channels underneath that superficial layer. The new asphalt in combination with the groves between the tracks and the asphalt ensured that rainwater wouldn't short-circuit the rails. The system was only susceptible to snow, as that could deposit itself upon the asphalt and then clog the groves as well. Nevertheless it hadn't snowed in London since the 2010's. The climate had been changing since then, always getting hotter and hotter. As such, countermeasures against snow, frost and other inconveniences caused by cold weather were, as a rule, not fitted to any public work constructed after 2020. Finally, only elevated highways were fitted with such system since it was too dangerous to fit such system on ordinary roads, crossed by pedestrians thousands of times every day. Not since the monumental lawsuit back in 2042 when the family of a man who slipped and fell over the rails of Cromwell road electrocuting himself horribly, successfully managed to obtain 300 million pounds from the company that owned that road, nearly driving it to the ruin. As a result the road charge in all the regions controlled by the Hammersmith road company (that owned the roads of London in the boroughs of Hammersmith and Fulham and Richmond, including Cromwell road but excluding the elevated highways) increased and never fell back again.

    In any case, Hilda was enjoying the benefit of such system despite her battery lifespan of roughly 60 hours of straight running. Back to the present, Hilda was darting skilfully over the elevated highways heading west, using the recharge tracks to the maximum. For possibly the first time Miles devoured everything that was passing by behind the window with his eyes. He wanted to see more, learn more so he could compare the world that he was used to with the one that he was about to be a part of. As he was taken westward by his trusted navigation computer he saw the old, low houses of London passing by his window and then being left behind. The people in the streets seemed so small, burrowing in and out of shops, or merely walking up and down the tight old streets of central London. Land was so expensive in London that all those old houses remained intact, their owners very reluctant to let go of them in anticipation of further increase in value. Some, were rich enough to knock down their old properties and replace them with skyscrapers which they then either sold or rented out for exorbitant profits. Others were lucky enough to entice the owners of the ancient establishments to sell them with contracts worth many, many millions. Their plan was as before, to replace the picturesque old residences with modern skyscrapers. Finally there were the few destitute people who could just about afford to still live in Zone 1. They were mostly people to whom fortune had once been kind but later abandoned. Elderly people who lost their younger brethren that earned the bread in the family by landing plush jobs in the City and thus had to survive on the tiny amount of pension they had earned from a lifetime's service in their low-paying jobs, the severely infirm who had spent their entire fortunes paying medical fees, the unemployed who were leading frugal lives with their little savings until they could hopefully land a job and many others who had been befallen by tragedy. These people often could not afford police insurance and judicial insurance and were thus the target of mafia-style strikes from property developers who wished to lay a hand on the precious London property. And developers knew exactly who was insured and who wasn't because all insurance companies were earning a sizeable income on the side by selling information about who they insure to special companies. They, in turn, would combine the data from the multitude of insurance companies that resided in the proud skyscrapers of the City and Canary Wharf, and create 'insurance maps' that showed exactly who had what kind of insurance. If someone could not afford judicial insurance, then contractors would know what to do. If, on the other hand, someone did have judicial insurance, but no police insurance, then development companies would organise anything from regular assaults by thugs, to hits and either force the residents out or outright kill them. Finally, if someone had judicial and police insurance, but no fire-brigade insurance, then developers would arrange arson. Very rarely different scenarios would make their appearance for generally people insured themselves in this order: judicial, police, fire-brigade according to their financial capabilities.

Despite this situation, in the decade or so since the complete dissolution of the state apparatus, people in Zone 1 generally possessed the means to insure themselves properly, but not enough to turn their properties into skyscrapers. After all, many still shared apartments in the same building, so even if one of the residents had the resources to turn it into something bigger, the others were likely to decline or demand a huge chunk of the profits in return. As a result, the rows and rows of Victorian housing, as well as some more modern, brutalist style tower-blocks from the 20th century still dominated Zone 1 of London by area. On the other hand, in height, the city was dominated by the skyscrapers that did manage to emerge. Land value was so high, and the desirability for office and residential space within London's high-end central zone so intense, that in the past couple of decades any skyscraper, no matter how massive and tall, would be sold out in record times. That explained the apparition of skyscrapers that appeared to touch heaven itself. Kinroy bank was one of them, and not a very large one at it. 125 floors, 450m tall, dwarfed by the Tokai corporation tower next to it at 200 floors and 800m height, or the J.D.K. Bank tower at 225 floors and 900m height to the top of the antenna. Many examples of such architecture were present in London and encompassed 100-floor residential buildings and much, much taller offices, the tallest of all being the gigantic 1050m-tall Royce&Boyce bank tower, right at the heart of Canary Wharf, where his grandparents would have remembered a meek little building called 'the One Canada' towering over even meeker towers that used to be in the area, the bright white beacon light on top of the tower helping identify it from afar and even from an aeroplane. Naturally these were dwarfed by the giant skyscrapers that reached up to 2,5km into the sky in China, or their slightly lower counterparts in Hong-Kong and India.

Nevertheless, London still boasted a fairly impressive skyline. Particularly at night, the sky would be littered with lights from the sparsely spaced skyscrapers of London; enough to make it a pretty sight, but not as many as to erase the darkness of the night sky and replace it with a wall of more or less solid light. Finally, at the top of each tower the red navigation beacons that warned air traffic of the tall structure would crown each tower and in a number of the skyscrapers, enormous, illuminated logos of financial giants would indicate beyond any doubt who was the master of the corresponding tower. Proud bastions of unfettered capitalism, evidence that the state is not needed to build a prosperous economy, Miles used to think. Now cold castles of heartlessness, they looked down at him condescendingly, if not with marked hostility and suddenly he felt unwanted, alienated, estranged and his heart sank a bit. Equally suddenly, something stirred within him and he felt a pulse of vengeance. He wished that those towers were destroyed with him. But then he calmed himself down. He realised that blind fury would lead him nowhere. Perhaps the vengeance that his innermost sense of justice was seeking would come with the collapse of the world financial system, perhaps it would never come and someone else would pay for the disaster... In any case the very thought of it was too painful to contemplate any further.

Before too long Miles was shocked awake from his tumultuous reverie by Hilda announcing their approach to the border of Zone 1. The road was descending as the elevated highway ended and turned into one of the even more ancient motorways. A dilapidated sign at the side of the road announced, in barely legible letters, that the motorway was once called the 'M4'. M4 linked London to the west of England and crossed through Zones 2 and 3 of London. As such, it was avoided by people since a company competing with the one that maintained the M4 built a by-pass that crossed the dreaded Zone 3 of London underground and re-emerged at a safe distance in the countryside. The maintenance costs of the tunnel were significantly lower than the costs incurred by the competitor in attempting to guard the M4. Guard from what, Miles didn't really know since the M4 had been left unmaintained for years. Hilda avoided the pot-holed motorway and turned away at an off-ramp. Signs indicated they were in Ealing Broadway, one of the border boroughs of Zone 1. As Hilda was navigating through the narrow streets near the border, Miles could see a very long and fairly tall structure that sometimes emerged from between the rows of low buildings, far behind. It was white and smooth with something messy running along the top like a garland and what looked like spheres interrupting the garland at even intervals. As the car moved closer to the structure Miles realised that that must have been 'the wall'. Back in 2044, following the chaos caused by the privatisation of the police force and the judicial system, and after the lines separating the haves from the have-nots, the wealthy people of Ealing Broadway, as well as a number of companies that supported the event put money together and hired a private contractor to build a secure wall separating them from the poverty in Zone 2.

The agreement had been done by a public mediation company. These companies gathered information on everyday issues from various people in the market and then, if promising enough they'd attempt to organise meetings for the public to discuss these issues and come down with a solution. There was a ticket to enter the events but representatives from companies and private citizens would attend if the topic proved to be of any interest to them. After that, it was likely that some solution would be found, probably requiring the involvement of some private contractor to build some form of infrastructure. The mediation company would most usually lead negotiations between the public and the contractor and then arrange the details of the contract. For example, in the Ealing Broadway wall project a local mediation company got wind of the fact that discontent about crime spilling over from Zone 2 into Zone 1 was on the rise. As such, they organised a meeting about security in

Ealing Broadway, which was a great success. Many members of the public and business leaders of the local area attended and put forward their views. The mediation company had been professional enough to create a table of possible solutions they had thought about. Then members of the audience proposed more possible solutions, there was a 4 hour debate session and at the end the voting results came in favour of erecting a wall at the borders of the borough. The wall was to be constructed on land in Zone 2 so that nobody in Zone 1 would be inconvenienced by the erection of the wall on their own properties. After all nobody in Zone 2 could afford judicial insurance, or police insurance for that matter. And thus it was done, the plans were laid out and the mediation company contacted a contractor to build it. Within months of the first hit of the shovel in Zone 2 territory, the wall was completed, full with barbed wire running along the top and spherical guard towers at even intervals, the mediation company got its commission and the gates to Zone 2 were closed.

    This action caused ripples in Zone 1. One after the other, all border boroughs decided to mimic the example of Ealing Broadway and integrate into the now growing wall system around Zone 1 of London. Pass-cards were instituted for everyone who worked in Zone 1 but lived in Zone 2. The unfortunate souls who had not been fortunate enough to be either employers or employees in finance, professional sport and a few other lucrative professions, but were essential to the daily function of Zone 1 were allowed to enter. Another private company, this one a security company, got a number of contracts via a mediation company to install implanted cameras in the foreheads of all those who worked in Zone 1 but lived in Zone 2. Anyone wishing a pass-card would have to be fitted with such device and maintain it in working order and on constantly. The slightest interruption in transmission to the private security company's servers and the pass-card would be deactivated. This often meant losing employment as well. It was a security measure many boroughs were happy to pay for. Not all boroughs had adopted that system though -in fact most hadn't because of the perceived low return on investment- and thus many Zone 2 residents continued to work in Zone 1 without such implant. Ealing Broadway was part of the boroughs that had declined to pay for such service, instead trusting their police force. Either way, people in Zone 2 were incredibly happy to be allowed the privilege to work in Zone 1 and would not dare lift a finger against a Zone 1 resident.

    On the other side of the wall, in Zone 2 there were equally consequential ripples. The population of Zone 2 found itself in need to obtain key cards, which to many was humiliating enough to begin with. Also it placed people beyond the wall in a different mind-set. They no longer though of people in Zone 1 as part of the same society, but a hated enemy that hired them only to carry out the most menial of tasks. Thus people in Zone 2 were forced to create their own society, their own set of rules. If beforehand many zones had already begun forming alternative governments (the communists and the royalists were amongst the first to form independent societies in Zone 2) now it became imperative that everybody does so. As such, the boroughs lying behind the wall found various alternative ways to organise themselves. For some, the name 'borough' was revitalised in substance. Borough was no longer a name for a geographic region, like it had been since the privatisation of local government. It once more became the name of a social entity. Miles was to find out a lot about these effects, largely unknown to the Zone 1 people, yet of that he knew not yet.

In any case, Hilda had stopped at one of the gates of Ealing Broadway and a screen at the side of the wall was activated. A uniformed guard appeared in the screen and inquired the identity of the passenger of the car. Miles identified himself and stated his intention to visit Zone 2.

'A Zone 1er? Going to Zone 2? Whatever possessed you. Either way, if you want to go that bad, I'm not going to stop you. Do you have a pass-card?' said the guard curtly.

'No.' replied Miles.

'You will need one if you ever want to return from there. We provide them here. £80 for a Zone 1 pass-card. Naturally yours will be a Zone 1er card. You will be able to return whenever you wish.' added the guard.

'Go ahead.' said Miles.

'Please scan your implant to the reader in your car.' asked the guard.

Miles swiped the back of his hand to the in-car reader, positioned there just for such occasions (including gaining authorisation for paying extra charges for tolls, road fees, parking fees etc. when the driver wasn't in the mood to confirm the commands verbally or transfer of identification information was required) without a comment.

'Identity confirmed, payment authorised, please wait a minute while your card prints sir.' concluded the guard.

Soon enough a card appeared from a slot in a machine not much unlike those used for paying for parking 50 years ago and Miles opened the window, reached out and grabbed it. The gate opened and Hilda set off into the unknown.

PART II: THE COUNTER-CLOCKWISE CIRCLE.

CHAPTER 4: NEW LAND.

As the gate opened slowly, it revealed a picture of extreme drabness. Dilapidated houses, still the original Victorian dwellings that for the first time transformed the timeless grassland that once stood there into bricks and mortar, were filling his field of view. The pot-holed street was giving Hilda a difficult time, however she managed to avoid the deepest and most vicious of them and maintain the car's structural integrity as well as part of Miles' comfort. People clad in dreary clothes that belonged to a different age were making their way on the cracked and grass-ridden pavements of Zone 2 to whatever destination they may have had; a very small number of vehicles was slowly making its way over the cracked and uneven roads, most of them service vehicles such as garbage trucks, all of them from at least 2 decades ago, all of them trying to tackle the rough and car-unfriendly road ahead of them. Overall it was a picture that arose feelings of sorrow in Miles' heart. Is this what people in Zone 2 lived like? What lay in Zone 3 then? He shuddered to think and for that reason he abandoned any attempts to do so.

He always suspected that Zone 2 was not a very nice place to live, however as the heavy gates closed behind him with the sound of a heavy metallic object being dragged on dirt the picture that was greeting his sight seemed surreal. Sure, Miles had travelled around the globe, but it was always in the richest parts of the richest cities in various countries. China, India and America, the greatest superpowers in the world -in that order- were full of brilliant cities with grandiose city centres. Whenever he visited a customer anywhere in the world he would typically land in a private jet -property of Kinroy bank-, be escorted by neatly dressed servants into the most lavish of executive lounges and after spending some time in luxury waiting for his luggage he'd be taken by a limousine with tinted windows over elevated highways straight to the heart of the city, where all the money was. He had never seen any scene matching the one that filled his field of view on any level, except on television. Only when he travelled to continental Europe he'd see scenes of unfamiliar poverty, but not to the extent he was witnessing at the moment. At least the roads were clean and fairly free of cracks and potholes in Europe. In Europe, there were trees along the streets, just like in Zone 2, but they always seemed to be cared for and trimmed, unlike the unkempt monsters that were looming before his eyes. In Europe there were a number vehicles running on the streets, both private and public and even though they were fairly old and of cheap brand, they were present and looked well maintained. At least the paint wasn't falling off like on the garbage truck he'd just seen and the small bus that was moving perpendicularly to his own direction along a side-street just farther down the street.

In any case, the locals were also shooting curious stares at his car and himself. It seemed, he was just as unfamiliar a sight for the people of Zone 2 as Zone 2 herself was for him. Many people were positively following him with his gaze. Had they never seen a modern car? Miles thought. In that case they can't be workers in Zone 1. How did they earn a living? Miles wondered. Hilda brought him back to business.

'We are in the Osterley/Hounslow area now sir. Where should I take you next?'

Miles scratched his chin in sign of thinking.

'I don't know. Let's just drive around London, along the wall.' he finally said.

'Clockwise, or anti-clockwise sir?' inquired Hilda.

'Anti.' Miles replied. 'How are you on battery Hilda?'

'59 hours remaining. It will not be a problem for quite while sir.' she replied to Miles' query respectfully.

'Let's go then Hilda, shall we?' he added with slightly more politeness than usual in his voice. After all he could not take Hilda for granted any more now, could he?

'Of course, sir.' she replied as formally as ever.

Following the brief exchange of words Hilda took a corner left and started heading south-south-east, towards Whitton. The scenery remained mostly unchanged as the car made its way towards Whitton. Maybe other boroughs would be different? Miles was absorbing everything he saw and Hilda interrupted once more.

'We are approaching Whitton, sir.' she said in her usual soft and always formal voice.

'How do you know? I thought you didn't have any maps of the region and the navigator doesn't work here, does it?' Miles inquired with observation that positively surprised him.

'That is correct sir, but I took the liberty of consulting the internet and found some old maps from the last surveys commissioned by the last local authorities, back in 2031.' she explained.

'Good, it looks like it is unlikely that anything has changed since then.' Miles exclaimed more to himself.

'May I inquire why sir?' said Hilda. For all her sophistication, she was still a man-made machine and as such her judgement still lagged behind that of a human.

'Well, it doesn't look like the area has received any major infrastructure investment in quite some time, no?' he explained slowly.

'As you say sir.' replied Hilda showing no signs of understanding. She simply obeyed her master's orders and continued approaching Whitton.

Less than a minute after the conclusion of that small conversation a man in a blue police uniform like he'd seen in history books was asking him to stop. Hilda stopped the car even though she was not programmed to stop at the sign of anyone but automatic traffic control signals. Perhaps she did possess more judgement than Miles had originally thought. The officer sported a tall, black hat with an old badge bearing the barely legible letters CR and a small III symbol between them. The badge was dirty and decayed, but clearly there had been effort put into making it look as decent as possible and clearly that had had some success since it was at parts shiny. Miles did not know that the $C_{III}R$ stood for Carolus III Rex, Charles the 3rd, king (of England) and therefore dated from the time of king Charles the 3rd, son of Elizabeth the 2nd. The rest of the uniform was dark blue with buttons in the same state as the badge on the hat. Finally, the officer wore old, black shoes that had at one point clearly been shiny and was armed with a pistol. Behind him a shallow fence made out of barbed wire and what appeared to be sacks of sand blocked the road with the exception of one lane, just wide enough to allow a bus or truck to go through. The buildings nearby had their windows barred although a dirty little corner shop was open for business on his side of the barricade. There were no trees at the side of the road and the pavements were narrow. Farther ahead, beyond the barricade, the scenery was more or less unchanged, although the roads did seem to be in a slightly better state. The majority of potholes was filled with gravel which indicated that some effort was being put into road maintenance by someone who, albeit, lacked the proper means to carry it out to its full extent. A very small number of what looked like private vehicles from the 2040's was crossing the road he was looking into, certainly more in density than he'd seen that far. All in all, it looked like whatever administrative region lay behind the barricade was better off than the one he was still present in.

    In this setting Miles stepped out of the car, to engage the police officer in conversation. He wasn't used to having to get out of the car to communicate with anybody in any official capacity, let alone an officer of the law. In Zone 1 all of that was done through computer screens. It was more secure and convenient for everyone. Nevertheless, Miles figured out that as a stranger, and one considerably better off than most in those regions, it would only be respectful to step out of the car. The officer greeted him first:

    "noon sir.'

    'Good after noon to you too officer. What can I do for you?'

    'Well, showing me the Whitton community passport might help, sir.' the officer said grinning friendly.

    'Sorry, the what?'

    The officer grinned again and continued the dialogue with the following words:

'Not from around are we, sir? I figured that much. Are you by any chance from Zone 1?'

'Errr... yes actually. Did my car give it away?'

'The car, the cologne, the elaborate, modern haircut -or wig, no offence,sir-, the expensive-looking shirt with the shiny buttons. The list could go on forever, sir.' the officer continued cheerfully.

'Ow...'

'Nothing to worry about, sir. In this community we have long since taught ourselves not to hate people from Zone 1. Here you should be safe, although I still do not recommend passage if you are going to be condescending towards our community or look down on it. It might cause trouble...'

'Ow...' Miles had not thought that Zone 2 would be actually unsafe for him.

'Now, about the passport, sir.'

'The passport.'

A short silence followed. Then Miles realised what was going on and said:

'Oh, the passport. Yes, I don't have one. May I still visit your community, please?'

'Hmmm... I suppose so. But you will have to go through the formalities first. Applying for a passport, providing some paperwork and then obtaining the right to travel here. Should be quite fast, won't take longer than a couple of days.'

'Paperwork?'

'Yes, sir.'

'What's that?'

'Well, documents providing information of your identity and basic background.'

'I have none. All I have is this.' Miles flashed the back of his left hand to the police officer, pointed to it with his right hand and said: 'Implant'.

'Ah, I see...' replied the officer. 'We have none of that here. Too expensive.'

'Any other way I can convince you of my identity?'

'I'm afraid we are not exactly fitted with systems to deal with guests from Zone 1, sir.'

'So I am denied access to your community? Now I'm really intrigued to see what's ahead.'

'Heh. Isn't that so, sir? Let me see what I can do. I'll talk to my authorities and see whether we can do anything about you, sir.'

'Truly thank you.' said Miles bowing slightly with his left hand on his chest in sign of respect. The police officer then bowed in turn and retreated a few meters away where he had a conversation on an old-style walkie-talkie with someone on the other line. Miles kept looking about idly for what must have been at least 20'. In the end, the officer returned after the prolonged conversation and spoke again, unsurprisingly addressing Miles:

'I think we have just made an arrangement, sir. One of our elders wishes to speak to you in person.'

'Elder?'

'It's part of our system of government, sir.'

'And how...? Will I meet him, may I inquire?'

'You certainly can, sir. He will arrive soon enough. Then you shall head to the council building together.'

'On foot?'

'Yes, sir. Unless, of course, you wish to lend them a ride in your vehicle.'

'Them?'

'The elder is coming accompanied by another officer of the law. We respect him too much to leave him unguarded with a newcomer, no offence sir. I hope you understand.' said the police officer thinning his lips in sign of concern. The gesture made his rich moustache look even bushier.

'Totally! Please do not worry. Now we wait?'

'Yes, sir.' concluded the police officer with a cheerful smile, emanating politeness.

For a significant amount of time neither of the two men said anything, courteous comments on the weather aside. Finally, after a 20' wait Miles spotted an old man with a snow-white goatee and rich snow-white hair approaching in the company of yet another uniformed officer of the law. The old man wore what looked like an old-fashioned and warm green cape, carefully thrown over his shoulders, a big triangular flap hanging in front of him and what looked like a square flap hanging behind. It was after all, February and even though the sub-tropical zone only ended as close as southern France, Mediterranean London still enjoyed some cool days during winter; some perhaps a bit too cool. Behind the green cape was presumably a jacket of sorts, one that belonged to a brown suit. The white sleeves of a white shirt could be seen protruding from underneath the larger sleeves of the jacket. The old man wore brown trousers, presumably from the same suit and black shoes. He walked with the aid of a walking stick, just a piece of wood with a bent end for a handle and a rubber end at the bottom. The ensemble was completed by a pair of thick, black glasses that looked like a century old. Overall everything about the old man's attire gave the impression of amiability in poverty. The wrinkled face, the bushy white eyebrows and the benevolent smile all contributed to this image.

In time, the old man approached in his slow gait. He stopped barely 2 meters away from the newcomer and spoke in a slow, tired voice but maintaining a benevolent grin:

'So, you must be the Zone 1 newcomer I presume. Yes. No mistaking it. You radiate wealth young man. Good afternoon. I am Stephenson, Irving Stephenson. Political philosopher by profession and one of the elders of the Whitton micro-community. And who may you be young fellow, and most importantly what brings you to our humble commune?' inquired the old gentleman.

'Greetings Mr. Stephenson...' Miles started saying but was interrupted by the old man's escort.

'That would be Dr. Stephenson, thank you.'

'That's enough Amit. I appreciate your zeal, but please make allowances for the fact that the young man here is a newcomer.' said Dr. Stephenson and then addressing Miles: 'Please continue young man.'

'Emmm... Good afternoon Dr. Stephenson. My name is Miles Fitzroy and as you correctly guessed I'm from Zone 1...'

'Please continue.' said Dr. Stephenson as benevolently as ever.

'And the reason I'm here is...'

'Yes?'

'The reason is...'

'In your own time.'

'The reason is...'

'Hmmm...' exhaled Dr. Stephenson after the pause that succeeded Miles' last, faltered, half-finished statement. He continued:

'Well, young man, if you are so hesitant to answer such question, it means you came for a reason that is difficult for you to admit to. I'm certain that if it was anything malicious you would have turned away already. So it must have to do something with... shame? Tell me young man, are you here because you have no alternative?' remarked Dr. Stephenson.

'Well... yes. You see, when the financial crisis hit...' offered Miles in the way of explanation.

'I think I understand. Please do not continue if you do not feel comfortable with disclosing such information at the present time.' politely interrupted Dr. Stephenson.

'Thank you sir.' Muttered Miles respectfully and went quiet.

The conversation was picked up by Dr. Stephenson after a short pause:

'I must not forget my manners. Please accept my invitation to a meek meal at the council building. If you wish so, of course.' he offered politely.

'Would that be all right?' asked Miles blushing slightly. For the first time in a very long time he was the recipient of an honest invitation. He felt the old vaguely familiar feeling of not wishing to impinge upon the comfort of his host. A feeling he never felt at the parties of his upper-class colleagues since 'the Alpman incident'.

'You are being most kind, young man. And displaying manners I didn't come to expect from a citizen of Zone 1.'

'Citizen? That's what we used to be called before the national-ID system was privatised, no? You still use this concept here?' asked Miles suddenly curious of politics.

'Heh, heh. You have a lot to learn, young man. I take it this means my invitation is accepted then?' uttered Dr. Stephenson grinning.

'It would be my honour!' exclaimed Miles and pointed towards his ride adding: 'May I offer you the ride Dr. Stephenson?'

'You certainly may young man.' concluded the Dr. and both men headed for the car with the accompaniment of Amit, the officer.

They all sat down in the luxurious vehicle and Hilda moved the car in the direction indicated by Amit. They passed the border guard who first greeted Miles and he paid his respects to the passengers of the car with a brief salute.

'Impressive vehicle, young man.' remarked the Dr.

'It is a nice model, isn't it Dr?' agreed Miles.

'It certainly is.' mechanically replied the Dr, then he switched topic:

'Tell me young man, what do you think about this whole crisis situation?'

Miles was startled by the question, emitted a slight, short, high-pitched noise, the beginning of an answer, and then said nothing. He needed more time to formulate an answer, so he tried to buy some time:

'Any particular aspect of the situation?' he asked.

'All I wanted to know was whether it made you think about politics. For example, did you ponder at all why the system was driven to this? Whether there may be a better alternative? Or even whether this current system could be fixed somehow?' replied the old philosopher.

'Ugh.. Well... In the month or so I spent unemployed, I had a lot more time to think than usual. The matter did cross my mind. I mean why the system failed. I didn't think about alternatives or solutions.' admitted Miles half-embarrassed, half-pensive.

'That's understandable. A destitute man only has time to ponder ways out of his predicament and ask why did this all have to happen.' Stephenson uttered with sympathy. Then he proceeded to ask: 'So what are your answers? Why did all this happen?'

'Well, Kinroy bank started the crisis by going bankrupt. Turns out the accounting department was hiding data from investors and partners. It looks like transparency in transactions could have mitigated the problem, no?' offered Miles in the way of an explanation.

'Quite correct. However, perhaps the problem is more general. The problem really started when a vast number of people took advantage of the freely available loans, then were unable to repay them. Many of those people were buying houses with the loan money, in fact. Houses that at the rates of appreciation seen before would quickly become valuable anyway, so why should Kinroy bank not lend recklessly? People who can, pay back the loan bring interest back to the bank. Those who can't, bring a house that stands a good chance of gaining value, in fact the bank may stand to gain more from exactly those bad loans. Unregulated banks in this country had enough free hand to set this perilous situation up, no?' inquired Stephenson.

'Y... Yes.' replied Miles, thinking back to the times when colleagues of his had been promoted for providing such 'bad loans', resulting into a quick growth of the collection of estates owned by the bank.

'This has nothing to do with transparency, does it?' the old Dr. stated.

'N... No. It doesn't.' came the reply.

'If Kinroy bank had not been lying, then their partners would be able to disengage from Kinroy and diminishing their exposure to the risk. The whole collapse of Kinroy would be cushioned, yet at the base the system is still unstable. The saturation of the housing market, the resulting stall in the housing prices, the reckless lending are creating this precarious situation, no?'

Miles nodded in agreement silently.

'But how can you regulate such that banks don't over-lend? It's difficult, but perhaps not impossible. I'm no economist after all...' Stephenson concluded just before the car stopped.

Hilda parked the car outside what looked like one of those medieval churches that often litter English towns and cities. The passengers descended from the vehicle and headed inside the old church while Hilda switched off all systems and ran on minimal power supply. Miles was shown inside the church. He then walked slowly with Stephenson along the main aisle of the church, flanked by benches and pews, Amit following closely behind. Once in front of the altar they all turned left and headed down the stairs into the church crypt.

'Where are we going?' Miles inquired simply.

'The crypt of the old church. That's where our community is being ran from. This here church is where we hold our community meetings as well; in the area we just crossed in fact. For that reason we call the old church 'the council building'.' clarified Stephenson as the two were making their way down the stairs, each step resounding strangely in the narrow, stone staircase.

'Wait a minute, how did you get furniture down here?' suddenly exclaimed Miles, examining the staircase they'd just used as well as the crypt's old and voluminous furniture. Having reached the bottom of the staircase he could partially see both.

'Observant young man. We have opened a service entrance a while ago from the side of the old church. One that's wide enough to fit everything you see in here through.' patiently explained Stephenson.

The two men then continued walking through what appeared to be the main corridor in the layout of the crypt, eventually reaching the end. At that end, there was a large wooden door that might have dated from the time when the church was first built. That made it differ from the other doors in the corridor, which were modern and connected the rooms and the corridor, which were otherwise completely separated from each other by what looked like thin, possibly cardboard walls that had been added later to the architectural ensemble of the old church. In fact, the entire corridor was defined by such 'new type' walls with the sole exception of that little section that featured the old, wooden door. Lighting in the corridor was provided by a set of OLED panels.

'Here we are young man.' said Stephenson opening the old wooden door. Miles read the inscription on the door, a neat paper sitting inside a thin glass case added to the door fairly recently. It read: 'EXECUTIVE COMMITTEE CHAMBER.'. Miles curiously asked:

'What is the executive committee?'

'Well, it's all part of our system of government. I am guessing I will have to explain soon, so don't worry. All will be explained if you really wish to know. Please have a seat.' Stephenson beckoned while politely indicating with his hand towards a chair, one of 12 sitting around a round table. The room, like everything else, looked like a relic from the recent past, but at the same time was maintained clean and tidy. Miles sat down at the indicated place, Dr. Stephenson next to him. The latter then nodded to Amit and pronounced 'Thank you Amit.', at which the taciturn and always zealous officer saluted respectfully and left, leaving just the Miles-Irving duo in the chamber. The Dr. spoke first:

'Young man, were you an employee of Kinroy bank, by any chance?'

Miles blinked and stared blankly for a moment. Then he composed himself and asked:

'How... How did you know that?'

'I didn't, I just figured it out.' Stephenson answered calmly. Then he continued: 'A young man, obviously wealthy with no reason to visit

Zone 2 suddenly appears at our community borders. He wishes to see our community but something holds him back from revealing the reason. He says that it is connected to the crisis. I think the conclusion is fairly obvious no? That is why I interrupted you back there in front of the officers. I wanted you to speak your mind freely, and I figured you'd do so if we talked in private first. So tell me: did you lose your job back when Kinroy bank went bankrupt, lived on savings hoping for a job elsewhere and then when Barrington bank failed decided that it might be time to shift down a Zone?'

Miles was flabbergasted.

'To the very last word.' he uttered lowering his head, an expression of pain dominating his countenance.

'We don't normally get curious travellers or visitors from Zone 1 for any reason, you see. They would send servants. That helped with the conclusion. Either way, you actually entered our community from the north, from the Osterley area, no? That's still Zone 2. So if you're not coming straight from Zone 1, it means that you might have been touring Zone 2. Are you testing the waters for where to shift down and settle into a new home?' asked the old Dr. politely.

'Once again, to the last word.' replied Miles.

'So, tell me, young man, what have you seen so far? Where have you travelled? What have you seen? What have you learned about the places you visited?' asked Stephenson eagerly. 'I can help you by sharing the information I have about the politics, societies, and generally the situation in Zone 2. It's my job to know, after all.' he concluded placidly.

'Well, all I've seen is Osterley, and all I can say about it is that it is not in such good shape as your community.' Miles declared honestly.

'I think the same. That is because they use a different political system than we do.' explained Stephenson.

'I didn't know there were more political systems out here. In fact, there is a lot I don't know about the outer Zones.' admitted Miles.

'Outer Zones... So that's what the people of the Core call us. Well, I do inform you that there are a number of political systems out here, in Zone 2.' said Stephenson beaming ever happy.

'So what keeps your societies moving? How do you organise your economies? Who runs things, if anyone?' emitted Miles in an eruption of curiosity.

'Let me explain. First of all, a little geography.' started Stephenson. 'London, as you know, has been divided into 3 Zones for quite a long time. Zone 1 concentrating all the wealth and high-end jobs upon itself, Zone 2 containing all the people that are essential to Zone 1, but who earn too little to stay in it, and Zone 3 where chaos rules.' said Dr. Stephenson while at the same time he stood up, made his way to a dusty cabinet, picked-up an equally dusty map that was carefully rolled and stood upright, leaning against the said cabinet, and returned to the table. Then the Dr. proceeded to unfold the map on the table as one would unroll a mini-carpet, causing plumes of dust to stir as he did so. It was a map of London, one of the last maps ever to be printed for a public comprehensive school before their disappearance or conversion to private institutions.

'Map of London, 2028 edition, last one we got in our local public school, with additions we made ourselves to keep it up to date. Of course schools operating in this region after 2028 had access to maps that were specifically made for them, however when they left because Zone 2 citizens couldn't afford them they took everything they owned with them.'

The map was rather large, must have been 2x3m and showed the entire region of greater London, as well as much of the surroundings. This provision that had been designed into the original map came to service well when the members of the Whitton community completed the map with later additions to the enormous city complex of London. The map was drawn painstakingly and with craft, Miles could clearly see, and what obviously were the 3 Zones of London were covered in light shades of colour: blue for the Core, yellow for Zone 2 and red for Zone 3. Various lines of different colorations criss-crossed across the map. What those may have meant, Miles had no idea. Presumably they were borders of some sort, or maybe they indicated transport links. Dr. Stephenson grabbed a pointing stick that lay on the table, next to the map and pointed to a small area, surrounded by a blue line and said:

'On this political map of London, this little area here is our community. You can see it is surrounded by a thin blue line except the North and East borders, which are represented by a thick blue line. The thin blue line thus delimits what is officially called 'The Whitton Anarcho-Syndicalist Commune', the Whitton commune in short. The thick blue line encompasses our commune and many others, each little commune delimited by similar thin blue lines. The thick blue line represents the Commune Confederation. It is a political structure based on mutual assistance in times of need. We have isolated members farther North and East as you can see...'. Stephenson pointed to a number of places on the map, all surrounded by a thick blue line. 'But the main body of the confederation is here.' he concluded.

'But this only covers, what, 10% of Zone 2. What lies in the other places?' inquired Miles.

'9% to be accurate.' corrected Dr. Stephenson. 'As for what lies elsewhere, the lines say it all. This is a political map after all. Apart from the dotted lines denoting transport links, everything else on the map is there to indicate who rules what. The red lines indicate regions that have been operating a communist system. They represent about as much area as the Commune does, but a lot more population. The yellow lines indicate feudal districts, where governors that have been self-ennobled pledge an allegiance to the King of England and then rule pretty much as monarchs in their own districts. These are rather surprisingly large and occupy about 17% of Zone 2. Green lines denote areas under the old system, where the local governments have been revived and act as the sole government of those areas, in fact taking upon it even authorities that used to belong to the central government. This is what 52% of Zone 2 London decided to revert to after the central government abandoned them. The remaining 13% is shown in purple and consists of dictatorships of various sorts. In essence, the 2nd Zone of London is a collection of micro-nations sharing the same culture, language etc. but using completely different power structures.' lectured sagely Dr. Stephenson.

'Fascinating!' exclaimed Miles. His expensive education did mention various political systems, but he had never paid particular attention to them at the time. In any case his freshly kindled interest in how societies work made Dr. Stephenson's lecture most interesting to him.

'You might ask why there are no republics on the map. Actually, a single district left white does operate this system. Less than 0,5% of the area. We have good relations with them.' notified Stephenson.

'May I ask a question?' Miles interrupted the silence that followed the old Sage's last statement.

'Please do.'

'How do all these systems work? How do these societies fare in terms of living standards and economy? How safe and easy is it to travel to all these places?' blurted out Miles.

'Well that's a lot of questions young man. Let me begin from the simplest, as the more complex ones may take a while to answer.' started the venerable Dr. Then he continued: 'As a general rule you will be safe and welcome within the anarchist zone, the zone we are in. You need a pass-card to travel from outside the zone, to within, but other than that there is no need for such formality. In the communist zone you will be subject to various controls upon arrival and will need again a document proving your identity. Within it, you will always be escorted by an officer of the law so you will be safe there, perhaps more than here. In the monarchist boroughs you will find things pretty much work similarly to the communist zone in terms of identification, but there will be no police escort. Again, fairly safe. In the old-style democratic zones with the old system of local government you will need no passport, movement is free, but also crime is fairly high. As an outsider you will be asked to pay if the police needs to rescue you or provide any other service. Generally, they are the 'un-safest' areas, if I'm permitted the use of the term. In the dictatorial zones it all depends on the dictator. Anyone between 'enlightened despots' and 'blood-thirsty tyrants' can be running any of those areas. As a result some areas are doing fairly well and are quite safe, but in others you may end up murdered. In the republic, you will need identification, but once inside you are free to move about.' concluded Dr. Stephenson.

'So the fact that I entered Zone 2 without being subject to any controls this side of the wall was mere chance?' Miles inquired pensively.

'Serendipity, yes, but don't forget that more than ½ of London Zone 2 has chosen this model to operate in. In terms of external policy, this zone keeps a balance between the other zones, acts as a buffer.' said the Dr. slowly.

'Balance? What balance?' Miles expressed his confusion.

'The delicate balance that keeps the different regions from descending into perpetual war with one another. Our different political systems are creating tension amongst us. The precarious conditions we live in do not help either. After all, our societies live off the scraps that fall off from Zone 1. The more of us scrape a living here, the more competition for work in Zone 1, the less the retribution for our work in Zone 1. All the leaders of the various independent regions of Zone 2 understand that. On the other side, the outer border, the border with Zone 3 is part of another dangerous balance.' calmly explained the Dr.

'Why?'

'Exactly because out of Zone 2, there is Zone 3. A Zone of constant chaos and proxy wars. A Zone where the tensions of Zone 2 are let loose. A Zone where all there is left is a primitive agricultural economy that provides us with cheap food, war for control, and ruin. The protracted war in Zone 3 serves to keep that area poor and therefore forced to provide us with cheap food to earn the right to some luxuries. Much like in backward African states. Meanwhile, the master of whichever militia controls various parts of Zone 3 gets to project power in that region and usurp the resources it contains. Put briefly, Zone 3 is a collection of anarchic areas and colonies of Zone 2 and lives off the scraps we, here in Zone 2, leave. To make things worse, bands of armed goons roam Zone 3 and sometimes even venture into Zone 2 and plunder everything they see, thus earning their living. Zone 3 is fuelled by a war economy, in short.' the Dr. said resentfully.

'But where do they get the military supplies from? How come there is farming in Zone 3? Why is there none here, in Zone 2?' Miles asked scratching his head in sign of curiosity.

'Well, the supplies come from private companies that sell armaments to anyone, anywhere. Zone 3 bandits obtain money by selling products and items they loot, often metal that goes to scrapyards. As for farming, Zone 3 is the only one that has access to the country-side. The outer rims of Zone 3 reach into the plains of the north-west, as well as the coasts of the east and south-east. Moreover, the people farm every open area available, such as parks and yards. Zone 2 also does some farming with people growing food in their yards and some of our parks. However, with what we earn from our labour in Zone 1 we can afford to buy our food. This, in turn, frees labour forces for our militia that keeps us safe from the incursions we suffer from Zone 3. Other than that, it frees labour forces for other tasks. We have officers of the law, our own fire brigade as well as local shop-keepers. All of these people don't actually work in Zone 1, but their businesses are largely sustained from money brought in by labour in Zone 1.' explained the Dr. frowning darkly.

'So in effect the economy of Zone 2 has degenerated, but not as much as that of Zone 3 and is thus floating somewhere between the skyscrapers of Zone 1 and the empty husks of the ruined tower blocks of Zone 3.' completed Miles.

'Exactly.' confirmed Stephenson.

'So if I wanted to settle anywhere in Zone 2, is there any advice you could give me?' Miles veered the conversation more towards his own business.

'Ah, yes. There is of course the matter of your resettlement.' agreed Dr. Stephenson. 'Well, in Zone 1 it may depend on what property you can get for what you wish to spend, but here things work a little differently. The major deciding factor will be what system of government you wish to live in. This time, I'm guessing for the first time in your life, politics will play a genuinely huge role in your predicament. Don't start by looking at the kind of cars people drive in various areas of Zone 2, but who runs things and how. That's my best advice.'

'But I know very little about politics. Sure, you mentioned the names of the political systems in use over the 2nd Zone, but that in itself is not enough information for a decision is it?' retorted Miles with concern.

'Not for an informed decision it isn't.' agreed the Dr. once again. 'All right, let me offer more in the way of explanation then. In every community you go there will be rules you have to obey, naturally. These will affect the way you live, your rights and your duties, as well as your station in each particular society and many more. In our community, the rules you need to concern yourself with are the following: You have to share any income with the community, but what is your property stays your property. However, we feel that in the spirit of collegiality the decent thing is to share everything we own. We do this purely voluntarily and we never abuse what we are bequeathed by others. This is the mind-set that governs our collective. Everyone has to contribute to society in a certain profession, if able to do so. Otherwise that member of our society will receive the utmost care we can provide. You are free to choose your profession and we'll try to accommodate you. If personnel of your profession is not needed you may choose another one and then another one and so on until you find such profession that you may carry out and enjoy doing. The collective is run by a council of 10 members, 3 of whom are elders. You may stand for the office of council-man, in which case you wait for your turn and then sit on the council. The council is replaced every 2 weeks. Justice is dispensed by officers of the law who obey a code of laws we have all agreed upon. You will be given the chance to read it and agree upon it before you join our community if you wish to do so. Any bodily harm committed by anyone against anyone is forbidden so unless you attack first, nobody, not even an officer of the law will attack you in any way. If one is able but unwilling to work, then they are expunged from our society. It may seem harsh, but it is the only way our poor community can stay strong. Ideally, everybody will work voluntarily and nobody will be forced to work, but we simply cannot afford laziness. Does that cover everything?' ended the Dr. muttering to himself.

'I think so. What will happen to my flat in London? Do I have to give it up?' asked Miles.

'You have a flat in London? Then you are simply here until the crisis is over, no? Keeping the flat in anticipation of better times, maybe rent it out. Eh?' remarked the Dr.

'Er... Yes.' admitted Miles.

'Don't worry. Your property stays yours, however if you rent it out and your income is more than 5 times our benchmark, then you'll have to share the rest with the community. That's the only downside I can think of for you. In return you get to be a member of a society that will fight for you and stand up for you when you are in need. A society that will place trust in you. A society I suspect you haven't been part of in a long time, if ever. A more or less self-less society.' emphasised Dr. Stephenson.

'A self-less society...' repeated Miles with an empty stare. It was difficult to him to grasp the concept that there could be a situation where others had a chance to harm him for personal gain but wouldn't do so out of affection, or friendship, or honour.

'Must be quite a foreign concept for a young City-boy, no?' offered the Dr.

'Yes...'

'Well, it may take time for you to trust us, young man, but we will give you time to fit in our society. In time you will get to know us all and trust us.' soothingly pronounced the old sage.

'All of you?' inquired Miles.

'Ah, of course. I forgot to mention. There's only 258 of us, living in this community. The commune system does not scale upwards very well, you see. That's why we are a confederation of communes rather than a large anarchist state, unlike the communist zone, which is the largest, genuinely united entity in Zone 2. If any of our communities exceeds 300 members, it splits into 2 halves, which always maintain cordial mutual relationships thereafter. I believe you will find the solidarity our communes show to one another in the confederation assembly to be quite moving.' clarified the Dr.

'That explains why the Confederation is made up of this enormous variety of small communes as I can see on the map.' concluded Miles.

'Yes. And it gets more complicated in the vast tower-blocks of the outer regions of Zone 2. There, some of the tower-blocks contain even 3 or 4 full communities, one on top of the other. In any case, we all pool our resources and expertise freely. So a mechanic from Hounslow may journey all over the Confederation offering his assistance wherever needed. We have a centralised system where every man of every profession is listed. Then, requests for assistance are made on that system by various citizens of the commune. The specialists then attempt to service the requests in rough first-come first-served basis with some consideration to geographical location. Despite our poverty, we do have computers, you see. Modern technology allows us to procure computers at no more than a couple of hundred pounds from abroad and thus everyone in our Confederation has access to one. In fact, this is the case for the vast majority of the 2nd Zone.' filled-in Dr. Stephenson. 'I forgot to mention that earlier. For you it implies that if you have expertise that is needed everywhere but found only in very few people, you might have to travel a bit. Fortunately we have public transport here too. Old buses from 20 years ago, but still functional.'

'I see. One more question.' indicated his wish, Miles.

'Of course.'

'What prevents Zone 1 from invading Zone 2 and extending its territory?' said Miles puzzled.

'You are from Zone 1, you should know better than me. Tell me, young man, what is the main concern of Zone 1? The main thing to fight for?' retorted the Dr.

'Money.' single-wordedly replied Miles without the slightest sign of hesitation.

'Exactly. Now, you already know that there is a wall that separates Zone 1 and 2. This wall immediately creates an atmosphere of security within and insecurity outside. As such, land in Zone 2 is worth nothing compared to land in Zone 1. Therefore...' said the Dr. with a tone of voice that made it evident that Miles was meant to complete the sentence.

'...any reasonable company would rather build upwards than expand side-ways!' exclaimed Miles.

'Exactly.' confirmed the Dr. 'However, the only danger is that at some point a very large developer will decide to take out an entire region of Zone 2 and develop it from nothing, spending billions in the process. However, we have armed ourselves and such operation would require hiring a private military company, for the developer's side. At the moment the pressure for space in London is not high enough to warrant such intervention, but if it ever does... As I said again and again, the balance is very delicate, very unstable. It may topple any time.' said the Dr. worriedly. 'The communists also realise that, which is probably why they are making a huge effort to arm themselves.' concluded the Dr.

'Ow...' exclaimed Miles.

'But to business, young man. Do you wish to become a member of our community, or do you need more time to consider?' the Dr. once again brought the conversation to the meat of the business.

'Ow. I still don't know what the rules are in other regions. I may travel around Zone 2 a bit more before I make a decision.' replied Miles.

'A wise decision. After all, before you make a decision it is most certainly best to see for yourself what is going on in other parts of the metropolis. I have already given you a taster of what lies outside our community. In any case, will you accept a humble invitation to spend a night here?' said the Dr. pointing to an old 7-segment display digital clock on the wall, just behind and above Miles. It indicated that the time was 23:00. 'The gates of the wall are shut from the inside. Traffic may only flow one way from 22:30 onwards.' explained Stephenson.

'I believe I should stay then, if you are certain I'm not impinging upon your hospitality.' stated Miles at the height of politeness to the elder that had been so kind to him.

'Your manners surprise me more and more, young man. Are you sure you are from Zone 1?' said the Dr. smiling pleasantly and then he continued: 'Of course you are not impinging on anything. Please, enjoy our hospitality for the night. I think we happen to have some free space in one of the houses around here.'

'Nice. Where can I buy some toilette supplies?'

'There will likely be a local corner shop at the bottom of the building you'll be lodged in. Please follow me when you're ready.'

Miles stood up in indication of his readiness and soon the two men were making their way first back outside the crypt and then outside the old church. At the exit they found Amit, enjoying a tobacco-filled cigarette.

'Where did you find that?' inquired Stephenson. 'I thought we were not importing any cigarettes in the Confederation.'

Amit muttered that he got them from Osterley when he last travelled there and blushed. The Dr. let the matter drop and continued: 'These things will harm you. Please try to quit. Anyway, to business. Will you be so kind as to escort Mr. Fitzroy here to one of the rooms in the cylinder?'

'Certainly Dr.' replied Amit.

'The cylinder?' inquired Miles.

'It is the closest we have to a hotel.' replied the Dr. 'Mostly intended for people who travel from other communes to help us with something or other. For example electricians maintaining the electricity grid, coming here from the other end of the Confederation to do a 2-day job will use the cylinder for temporary lodging.'

'Ah. I see.' replied Miles.

'Now, if you'll excuse me young man, I would see you to your room, however my old age imposes upon me the need for some rest...' said the Dr.

'It's all right, I understand.' said Miles. 'Where can I find you again when the need arises?'

'Well, Amit here will issue a special pass for you allowing to enter the commune. It will also act as a form of identification allowing you to travel through Zone 2 as an official guest of our commune. I will write a special recommendation for you. Then you can always make your way back to the commune and ask for Irving Stephenson from the Whitton council. People will then help you find me.' said the old man.

Miles and Dr. Stephenson bade each other good-bye and each left to his own way, any thoughts about dining having been completely forgotten in the heat of the discussion.

CHAPTER 5: THE RED KINGDOM.

The following morning, Miles woke up in his Spartan room. His back hurt from the uncomfortable sleep he had endured in the old, metal bed that screeched at every move of his. The brown blanket he used was of a rough fabric and featured some holes, but was otherwise clean. Still his skin was irritated from the constant turning and twisting in the uncomfortable bed. The small necessaire containing all the bits and bobs he'd picked up from the corner shop for the purpose of servicing his personal hygiene both that morning and the previous night lay on a small and worn-out wooden bed-side table, just beside the equally old and worn-out lamp that provided guests with a reading light during the night.

He put all his clothes back on, this time plain clothes rather than the nano-fabric suits he was used to. He had procured those from the boot of his car. He always carried at least one change of plain clothes just in case the nanomaterial suits he usually wore failed for any reason, or he was unable to replace his nano-fabric suit after 24 hours. His providence served him well on that occasion. The plain clothes felt ill-fitting and disturbing to wear, but the feeling was not completely unfamiliar to him.

Having worn his spare clothes he went to the communal bathroom that the entire floor was sharing. He walked along the circular corridor that connected the series of rooms, regularly aligned along the outer side of the corridor-ring, to the elevator, the bathroom and the pantry, all of which featured doors on the inner side of the afore-mentioned ring corridor. The bathroom was relatively modern, with sinks made of glass and tasteful mirrors with lights embedded in their structure. Even though the little chips in the glass of the sinks and the mirrors were difficult to miss, they were all clean. The same could be said about the floor- and wall-tiles: clean although old and full of chips.

Finally, having properly concluded his morning ablutions he left to meet Hilda. He did not have to pay anything at the administration of the cylinder. Everything was provided for free. It was an early hour of the morning, as Miles' body clock had gotten used to waking up just in time for his morning commute. Miles felt a cold breeze going through his entire body as he exited the establishment of the cylinder, the ill-fitting plain clothes clearly shielding his body only inadequately against the draught. He entered his vehicle and bade Hilda to take him to the old church again. Hilda complied with her usual formality. Once at his destination he asked the officer on duty whether he could possibly see Dr. Stephenson and, in a stroke of luck, spotted him making his way slowly towards the old church before finishing his own sentence. From afar he greeted the respected old man and he, in reply, nodded with a wide smile. Before long they were standing opposite each other at a distance comfortable for conversation.

'Dr. Stephenson.' said Miles.

'Young man.' replied the Dr.

'Since I'm setting off to travel the 2nd Zone, I was wondering whether there is one more thing I might ask you for.' Miles said timidly.

'Ask away.' the Dr. replied warmly, almost paternally.

'Along with my special pass-card, may I also have another look at the large map of London?' Miles asked respectfully.

'Certainly. You pass-card is ready, by the way. Please follow me, young man.' said Stephenson gesturing with his hand in beckoning. Miles took the hint and entered the old church.

The duo made their way to the crypt again where from one of the offices an officer of the law emerged with Miles' document at the request of the Dr. Having received the document with all the proper expressions of thanks Miles followed Stephenson to the council chamber. The old man took the map, but before he could unroll it, Miles stopped him.

'Actually, I think I have a better idea. If we scan this map into the memory of my vehicle's computer, then it will always be available to me, no?' said Miles.

'Can you really do that in your car?' replied Stephenson excited.

'Oh yes. Hilda, my on-board computer can read maps I lay on the table, even if piece-by-piece and store them in memory.' explained Miles.

'Most wonderful vehicle you own young man.' exclaimed in awe Dr. Stephenson.

And so they put the new plan into action. The map was shown to Hilda piece-by-piece and she would memorise the section of the map she was shown and then combine it with previous segments of the large map until she reconstructed the full area of the political map of London. At the end of that not particularly lengthy procedure, Dr. Stephenson rolled the map back up, bade Miles good bye and good luck and with the advice of keeping away from the purple/pink areas denoting dictatorial regimes they parted. Keeping those words in mind, Miles made his way to his car and then to the unknown.

The car was heading south-east now, towards Kingston-upon-Thames. Once a wealthy suburb of London, now it was part of Zone 2. During the large shake-ups of the last few decades -from about 2020 onwards- the wealthy residents moved towards the centre, pushing those of meeker social status away. On the other hand the out-flux of poorer people from the centre outwards accelerated the flux of richer people towards the interior of London. It was a feedback loop maintained by the natural property of immiscibility that social classes exhibit. Naturally only a very, very small number of extremely wealthy residents moved all the way to the centre of London, in places like Knightsbridge, Kensington, Edgeware Road, Canary Wharf etc. Most just settled in areas like Wimbledon, Clapham, Brixton etc., which were cheaper to begin with, but later on gained in value as the poor moved out to be replaced by the rich. In stark contrast, areas that lay more peripherally and were rich to begin with, soon lost their inhabitants to more central regions, house prices fell and poorer people, often from areas exactly like Clapham, Brixton etc. moved in.

The reason for this shake-up was the collapse of the social state, the exacerbation of the gap between rich and poor. This meant that as time progressed, the central regions became way too expensive for common folk to afford. Rents and house prices went through the roof. In turn local shops, mostly operating in rented space, became too expensive.

The fully privatised transport system became even more expensive, especially since roads were privatised, the congestion charge was turned into a road-use charge and tripled in price, and similar charges were instituted to all the roads in London. The richer residents of the centre could afford the charge, so it remained in place and the roads kept being maintained. To top that up, train and underground and bus companies increased their fares to roughly match road charges so that they make the most out of their market. This combination of rocketing prices of everything in the centre was the driving force behind both the mass outflow of the poor towards the outside (for obvious reasons) as well as the influx of the rich (who worked in the plushy jobs of the centre, could afford a house in the centre -though nothing like the comfortable manors they enjoyed farther out-, but did not enjoy paying the sky-rocketing, money and time, commute costs 'New and privatised' London involved). It was this initial driving impulse that was reinforced by the feedback loop discussed not long ago.

London of 2051 boasted a population of 32 million souls, or rather that was the best estimate the UN could provide. 6 million lived in Zone 1 and enjoyed the high-life. 11 million lived in Zone 2 and kept Zone 1 alive earning a meagre existence in the meantime. The remaining 15 million barely scraped a living in Zone 3. Miles tried to visualise all the information he had, as if trying to mentally populate the image of the map of London, now projected by the holographic display instead of Hilda's familiar figure, with a multitude of tiny human beings, each group living under a completely different political, economic and social regime. However, not much came into mind. He had no idea what attributes to equip those human beings with anywhere outside Zone 1, the regions controlled by the commune Confederation and what he'd seen in Osterley. His meditations were often interrupted by long sessions of gazing hungrily through the window, absorbing everything he saw with his eyes.

The Confederation looked pretty much the same wherever he went. It seems it was true that the people in the commune Confederation did share everything amongst themselves in a spirit of true solidarity. Suddenly, something changed. The concentration of officers of the law increased and before long he reached the border of the Confederation. Miles saw, far ahead, a barrier of barbed wire and sacks of sand, much like the one connecting the Confederation to Osterley. An officer of the law stood in front of it and he raised his hand towards the car in indication of his request that the car stops. Hilda stopped the car a few meters away from the barrier and the police officer approached. Miles stepped out of his car in sign of respect. The officer spoke first:

'Good morning, sir.' he said with a polite smile.

'Good morning officer. Would you kindly guide me through the procedure?' replied Miles.

'I most certainly will, sir. To begin with, I would like to see some identity proof.' said the policeman placidly.

'Here we go.' uttered Miles, showing his special pass.

'Ah, a special pass-card for an official guest. Recommended by one of the elders of Whitton. In fact I see it was old Dr. Stephenson himself. You are very lucky to have made his acquaintance young man.' said the officer with a hint of envy in his voice. 'Always wanted to meet the man.'

'You know Dr. Stephenson?' exclaimed Miles with no little degree of genuine surprise. 'I thought each community had 3 elders and there were thousands such communities!' he completed his thought. The officer keyed the number on Miles' pass on his palm-top. An old version and apparently a very cheap one. Procured from India that particular model. Either way, it worked.

'Yes, but Dr. Stephenson is the one who placed the foundations of the entire confederation. Perhaps not the original ideological founder, but the one who worked tirelessly to make it happen in practice. Created the commune in the dark times we live in, he did. Here's your pass, sir.' said the officer and returned the evidently valid pass that belonged to Miles.

A short silence followed and Miles was the one to break it.

'Well?'

'Well what, sir?'

'What do I do now?'

'You continue your journey I would expect, no? You've cleared our border control.' said the officer smiling.

'But when I said I need help with the procedure I was also hoping I'd get some advice on what to do at the other side of the border.' explained Miles.

'Oh, I see... Well, to my knowledge once you are in the communist sector you will be asked for identity, for which your current document should be sufficient. Then you will be searched for weapons, propaganda material or forbidden substances. If you clear those you will be permitted into the zone after an officer has been allocated to be your escort for the duration of your stay in that zone.' said the officer.

'Forbidden substances?' said Miles ever confused. Nothing was forbidden in Zone 1. If it could be sold or bought it was all right. However, anything that could be used to hurt people was seized by the security companies that intercepted them. The law allowed them to confiscate any of a list of 'harmful materials' and then sell them outside the borders of the UK. That law was promulgated to replace the pre-existing law on illegal substances, at the request of the security company lobby.

'Well, things like drugs, ammunition, explosives. People are just not allowed to possess those. Not in the communist zone, and not here either.' explained the officer. 'Don't you forbid people carrying such stuff in Zone 1?' he then inquired puzzled. Miles explained the situation in Zone 1.

'Strange fellows you are in Zone 1. So your companies will sell crack to children abroad if it makes them money and that has the silent endorsement of the government? Really strange fellows you are...' the officer concluded. He then courteously nodded and in his previous cheerful disposition he asked: 'Is there anything else I can do for you, sir?'

'I think not. I'm ready to go... Will I be safe there, you reckon?' Miles uttered.

'Beyond the slightest shadow of doubt, sir. You will be escorted by an officer of the law and the entire country is more or less a massive complex of barracks and factories.' replied the officer.

'Factories? Oh well, I guess I'll see when I'm there.' Miles finally said before bidding good-bye to the commune officer.

Miles, therefore, returned to his vehicle and instructed Hilda to move it forward slowly, at about 5km/h, the speed of an average walker. The car passed by the officer from the commune, then left the barricades of the commune behind. A short ride through a neutral zone followed and he spotted ahead another set of barricades, these fitted with guard outposts, more barbed wire and sand sacks than the commune's barricades and vicious structures littering the ground ahead of the barbed wire. They looked like a physical manifestation of the three principle axes, x, y and z, only made out of old-style railroad tracks, possibly looted from the ancient, disused underground railway system that London used to boast before it became too expensive to be of any use and subsequently technology left it behind the times. Public transport after all never paid for its own expenses and in Zone 1 all the important people had cars, running smoothly on autopilot on the elevated highways of London. Any plans for a modern, yet low-cost public transportation system was always sabotaged by the car companies that had set-up headquarters in London to avoid taxes elsewhere and the car lobby was always stronger than the train lobby. At any rate, it seemed that the rails of the the 'district line' that once ran all the way from central London to Kingston were now employed as a defensive installation, although, of course, the rails may have easily come from any other source. Left and right of the barricades there was a defensive wall, not quite as tall as the Zone 1 peripheral wall, but equally fitted with sentry towers.

Between the barricades there were two guards. At the nearby

sentry towers two more guards, one in each tower within the field of view Miles enjoyed, were looking without any particular interest towards the confederate zone of Kingston. The car approached the barricades and stopped at the command of one of the heavily armed guards. It seems the communists were indeed arming themselves, evidently preparing for the worst. The guard approached:

'Good evening comrade. Your identification documents please.' the guard half-said, half-barked, in an official, formal, yet slightly terrifying way, as if announcing somebody's arrest.

'Ugh, good evening.' said Miles ruffling his pockets for the pass the commune had issued him. Finally finding it, he handed it to the guard.

'Special guest of the Confederation? Is that not where you are originally from then?' barked the guard again.

'Ugh... I'm from Zone 1, but my only identification from there is my implant.' said Miles showing the back of his left hand to the guard.

'Scan it here please.' the guard barked as officiously as ever showing a portable scanning eye to Miles. He let out a brief, sharp noise and complied.

'You sound surprised comrade.' said the guard slightly less terrifyingly this time.

'Well, I... I mean, they had no such scanners in the commune.' said Miles.

'Commune? You mean the Confederation? Our good western socialist neighbours in the Confederation are not as advanced as we are.' said the guard with formality and evident pride. She then looked at her palm-top and stated firmly:

'You are a first time visitor to our sector. We need information on you. I will ask you the questions. You reply as we go.'

'Can't you find all that from the Confederation pass-card? It must contain all the information you need.' proposed Miles.

'You speak correctly comrade. I forgot you have a 2nd form of ID. I will pursue that path of action.' barked the guard and inserted Miles' pass-card into a slot of her palm-top. Few seconds passed, information about the dates of his entry and exit to the Confederation was extracted and the guard spoke again:

'Done comrade. Please proceed to baggage control.' she barked again handing him back his pass-card and saluting militarily.

Miles entered his vehicle and moved it about 10-15m into a part of the road that was covered by a roof, large enough to cover both lanes and fit 4-5 cars underneath it. A set of tables, specifically designed for the purpose, were laid along the road on the pavement, just under the covered section; they were metallic and fairly modern-looking. A large sign hanging from the roof of the road indicated that it was the luggage control area. Beside the benches along the road were customs control buildings either side. Behind those, the wall continued, detouring from it's normal course, so as to create a little pocket in which the customs to the communist zone were situated. A couple of uniformed officers were chattering about some topic in one of the customs control buildings. One of them spotted Miles and walked to the car that had now stopped under the roof. The officer greeted Miles, who'd just descended from his vehicle, with the same formal bark and demanded to see his luggage.

'I have none apart from a toilette kit.' Miles replied.

'Reveal it please.' the customs official curtly replied.

Miles opened the boot, showed the little neccessaire to the officer who opened it and checked every single item for god knows what. He then announced:

'Body scan next. Please step inside the customs building and head to the scanner unit.'

Miles complied and entered the indicated customs building. Inside there was a scanner that could perform an MRI on the human body in a matter of a minute. It was not quite of the resolution that one would find in the advanced hospitals in Zone 1, but an old, yet functional and fit-for-purpose model. Miles went through the procedure and when the customs officials were satisfied with the result of the search, they released the next order: Vehicle control. Miles asked Hilda to move the car ahead, beyond the roof and inside a cylinder whose structure had been integrated into the road. In other words, the lane of tarmac run uninterrupted, however all around the road ran a cylindrical structure that resembled a gigantic ring that was partially buried. The ring was white on the outside and black on the inside, long and tall enough to contain a bus. Hilda stopped the car inside the ring and the black part started spinning slowly. After about 2' it had completed a revolution. There was a moment of waiting while the customs officials consulted their monitors and soon enough Miles was told that he could re-enter his vehicle and prepare for departure into the communist sector.

Miles did as he was told and Hilda drove the car for another 5m to the gate of the customs zone. That was the innermost part of the border control post. Behind it, lay the communist zone, none of which he had seen until that moment. The heavy gate, which was integrated to the perimetric wall of the communist sector opened outwards slowly and noisily. Behind the gate stood another 3 guards who saluted and said: 'Welcome to the people's republic of Anglia.'. Then, the 3rd one added: 'I am your assigned police escort for the duration of your stay in our zone. That billboard contains a map to help you with orientation' pointing somewhere to her left. There, a large bill-board map (digital of course) indicated to him that he was in segment 7 of the zone under the name of East-Kingston. Miles made an overture to the dame in uniform by indicating he was done consulting the map and attempting to introduce himself:

'Thank you very much dear lady. I had a look at the map now. I think I want to visit the centre of the city first. I am Miles Fitzroy by the way.' he said bowing politely and smiling pleasantly.

'Martha Dominique. Internal security officer.' replied the lady in uniform officiously, although clearly not as much as usual.

'Pleasure to meet you Mrs. Martha. How do we proceed now? I have a vehicle, so will you ride alongside me?' Miles inquired.

'Pleasure to meet you too comrade.' indirectly corrected Martha and continued: 'Yes. That is correct. Say the word when you are ready to go.'

Miles nodded and the two of them entered the car. Hilda got the order to proceed by just following the road ahead for the time being, and Miles dedicated himself to absorbing as much of the scenery as he could with his eyes.

The sight that greeted him in the communist sector was very different from the ones he'd seen in the Confederation. The buildings were well-maintained, even though mostly old. Some fairly tall buildings had been obviously recently built. Far behind in the horizon were 25-floor tower-blocks for residential use from what Miles could tell and looked a lot like what he'd seen in his journeys across continental Europe. Of course Miles didn't know the buildings were rising for that many floors, but 25 was the number he was (correctly) guessing. In any case, they were tall enough to be seen creeping up from behind the old houses that lay near the border to the Confederation. Taking his eyes away from the communist sector's skyline and lowering them he had a closer look at the objects nearer to him. More rows of Victorian housing left an right along the road and a little roundabout ahead. The roundabout was small and denoted by a little green knoll surrounded by the kerb. Some 40-50 years old buildings rising up to 5-6 floors were also littered in the area, beyond the roundabout, and their windowless walls were adorned with massive paintings glorifying the working man and woman. Naturally, the sides of the buildings with windows on them showcased no such decorations. The streets were clean, litter-bins were neatly positioned at every street corner he could see, along with 4 recycling bins around the one for general refuse. A small, but substantial number of vehicles were moving along farther ahead, none turning to the piece of road he was situated on, which only led to the border gate and the driveways of the few residences that lay on it. The overall impression was uncannily like what he would get when travelling in, say, Germany and could be summarised thus: Cleanliness, order, fairly old, drab-looking buildings. At that moment Miles realised that what he thought were drab-looking buildings in Germany and now in the communist sector of Zone 2, were actually a matter of perspective. The buildings might have been old, might have been made out of concrete with thermal insulation layers and automatic ventilation shafts, all of which was trivial and boring compared to the glittering glass giants in Zone 1, but they were always clean and freshly painted, which is more than what he'd seen in the Confederation, or even worse, the old-fashioned city-council governed Osterley zone.

Much more appreciative of what he was seeing, and with the boon of perspective and experience he asked Hilda to give him a battery check and then proceed towards the centre of the sector. Hilda replied that she had 55 hours of running left. Of course they had not been travelling for 5 hours on the roads of Zone 2, however Hilda's static power dissipation, small as it might have been was not entirely zero. In any case, because Hilda consumed little power when the car was not moving the 55-hour statistic was encouraging. Perhaps Miles could complete the tour of London Zone 2 in one charge.

Whatever concern they had about was going to happen during their journey aside, for the time being, Miles and his police escort were heading to the heart of the communist zone. Miles saw street after street and building after building slide past the window of his car as Hilda navigated her way to the centre. Fairly neatly dressed gentry, some even in nano-fabric suits was everywhere to be seen, however, the shops they were passing by looked fairly poorly stocked. Finally, having seen a great deal and feeling that perhaps it was impolite to seemingly ignore his travelling companion for too long, Miles spoke to Martha:

'Umm...'

'Yes comrade?'

'I... I just wanted to talk.' Miles uttered uncertainly.

'Certainly.' said Martha in reply with a smile on her face. Her smile was something quite magic. Her brightened-up countenance suddenly made Miles feel he could talk much more easily than he ever would to any of the officious robots back at the border station.

'I have been travelling Zone 2 for a couple of days now, and I think out of Zone 2 this sector is the most neat and tidy.' Miles attempted a compliment. Martha smiled.

'I hear that is the case too. I believe we can be proud of our system that made all this possible and our general secretary of the party.' she said still sounding somewhat officious.

'However, permit me to ask one question.' Miles inquired timidly.

'Shoot.' Martha said simply.

'Why do shops here seem to be so poorly stocked?' Miles said and without the slightest pause Martha replied, suddenly frowning:

'Because they are poorly stocked.'. A long pause followed. Miles didn't dare ask why, and Martha was intensely concentrating on something in her mind. Finally, it was she who broke the silence:

'Our general secretary explained it to us, that our system suffers and always will suffer to a certain degree from shortages of various goods. I know you wanted to ask me that, so I'm telling you.' she uttered leaning her head back on the comfortable headrest of one of the seats in Miles' car. Miles, on the other hand, replied with a confused look on his face. Martha felt the need to clarify more.

'You are from Zone 1, yes?'

'Yes.'

'Can everybody there buy everything they want, need or think they need?'

'Yes, more or less. All inhabitants of Zone 1 are very wealthy.'

'So everybody can have whatever car they want, whatever food they want, whatever clothes they want, whatever service they want?' Martha said staring at Miles searchingly.

'Yes.' Miles said but after the briefest of pauses he corrected himself: 'Wait a minute... No!'

'Please clarify comrade.'

'Well, there are always cars too expensive for many, food sorts that are too expensive for many and particularly houses that are too expensive for many. In fact, prices are set so that supply just about meets demand, although it is a bit more complicated than that. That nearly always leaves some people out. This is particularly true in goods that are in shortage, i.e. many would like to have one, but there is simply not enough of it produced...' said Miles confusedly, then he proceeded to exclaim: 'Hang on a minute, let me think about this a bit more.' After a long pause he resumed:

'An industrial sector tries to sell to a market of given size. They want to sell as much as possible, as expensive as possible. However, as price increases, the market shrinks because fewer and fewer of the interested customers can afford the product. At the end there is always a sweet spot where the industry makes optimal, or rather maximum profits. The market balances at that point in ideal conditions and that always leaves the poor chunk of the market out of that product. However, there are non-idealities. Often the optimum point is where a large number of people still buy the product because it is necessary to them, even though too expensive, however, competition shifts this point downwards so that the final price better reflects the effort and money put into making it. That grants access to that product, to many more people, but always the poorest layers get left out. The rest depends on the product and where its own 'natural' balance point lies. If enough bread is produced, then everyone can afford it because of the inherent productivity associated with the process of making bread, but you never have enough luxury cars made for every single inhabitant of Zone 1 because if that many were made, the price of one would have to be below production costs in order to sell.' Miles asserted confidently.

'Eloquently put.' said Martha. 'Here, on the other hand, we don't like the idea that the richest only get all that's best. For that reason we lower the prices on many products artificially. That causes our factories to be overloaded with work and almost invariably fail to meet demand. Nevertheless, the artificial lowering is not too steep. Certainly not as steep as our predecessors in the ancient Soviet Union had implemented. For that reason, you will not see too intense shortages. Moreover, we have good estimates as to what the needs of the population are in food and clothing, so we adjusted our production and import of such articles to the point where there is enough for everybody. So, yes, our supermarkets have half the shelves empty, but nobody suffers from starvation or lacks the means to clothe himself. Moreover, because there is still a difference in living standards between those who earn more and those who earn less, people have a motivation to earn more and strive to occupy those positions in the labour market that do so. In our society these are factory directors, professors of all ranks, engineers and scientists etc. In your society it is people in the financial sector. No?'

Miles nodded in agreement at Martha's statement.

'That's why our society creates shortages, and your society creates haves and have nots. The competition now, within our society, lies in who can provide more wealth, be it material or not, to more people. Productivity will determine that as well as the strength of the industry and generation of money in our society, on the other hand only the creation of money will determine it in your society.' said Martha. Miles shot her another look of confusion.

'We actually produce a lot of what we use here, comrade. The rest we import from abroad. That's why the size of our industry and its productivity matter. With the money we make, we can import goods we lack, just like Zone 1 does.' Martha explained sternly. Miles understood and that galvanised him into asking the next question:

'There are factories here? I thought no industry was left here whatsoever!'

'Well, our government committed resources to re-creating an industrial base here. We produce armaments, industrial machinery and process most of the food we import as well as most of the textile raw material we import -cotton, wool, that sort of stuff- into clothing. After all, our sector does contain 2,2 million people. That's the size of a small country. Also the other communist zones in Britain are also part of our new communist country. We can support this small industrial base, a large university and an equally large research institute.' clarified Martha.

'You have a university and do research here?' asked Miles, his countenance revealing even more curiosity than ever before.

'Why, of course.' said Martha simply.

'Why don't your engineers then leave to go to America to do research? Surely you don't pay better than the Americans do, do you?' asked Miles. Martha sighed and answered:

'This is the price we pay for our little country. We are forbidden from emigrating and travelling abroad is extremely difficult, particularly for scientists and engineers. That's why our scientific community only participates in tele-conferences and we use holographic displays very often to demonstrate new products, rather than actually going to where the products are and touching them with our bare hands. Imagine this in the context of heavy machinery.' Martha said suddenly looking very sullen.

'As such, your sector conserves its scientific potential and general intellectual potential.' Miles concluded.

'It is unpleasant, but it is a sacrifice we have to make...' Martha said and soon after she added: 'Oh, how I'd like to travel like you are!'. Another pause followed. Martha broke the silence again:

'Tell me, comrade Fitzroy...' she started.

'Ow... please just call me Miles.' cheerfully interrupted Miles.

'All right, comrade Miles then, tell me: why do you think a person with such interest in politics as myself decided to join the security services, foreigner escort team?' she asked inquisitively.

'What else could you have done?' asked Miles in return.

'I could have attempted to join the political division of our university as a lecturer, no?' she replied.

Miles looked at her in disbelief, she frowned indicating she felt slightly offended by Miles' tendency to believe that all of Zone 2 was a desolate, underdeveloped wasteland, he took the hint and then uttered: 'Ugh... Yes... Well... Yes... I think... I think you joined this profession so you could talk to foreigners. Although your job is to watch them closely, no doubt.'

Martha nodded in agreement and added: 'This job gives me an opportunity to see people from 'outside'. People who can either be talkative and teach me more about the world outside, like you do, or people who are less talkative, in which case I enjoy scrutinising their character.'

'But why can't you do that socialising over the internet?' inquired

Miles.

'Oh, I can and I do. But there is still something different when talking to someone face-to-face. I can't explain it. It just feels much more real. It is the difference between listening to Tchaikovsky on the internet and actually being there when the orchestra is playing, or enjoying a scenery in person and listening to a description, no matter how poetic and accurate it may be...' Martha replied quite more sentimentally than Miles had thought her capable of.

'Which explains your desire to travel despite the internet bringing it all to your own home.' added Miles.

'Precisely. Until our scientists manage to connect electrodes directly to our brains and artificially create the sensation of being there, vicarious and first-hand experiences will always be different.' Martha said.

It was true enough. Scientists had been developing ever finer, ever less invasive, ever more accurate neural stimulators and micro-electrode array readers, but the brain still refused to give up its secrets. The best neuroscience had to offer at the time was the electronic scalp; a vast array of micro-electrodes that could read neural activity over the majority of the cortex. It could read information like a recalled memory or a motor command and even some feelings, and upon command it could link those to some action. For example, a person could see a robotic arm, think of it moving in a certain way and the thought of that would be configured to cause the robotic arm to move in exactly that way. Typically, in experiments, the subject would define motion along a degree of freedom by thinking of the arm moving only in that degree of freedom, then another, and then another until all the degrees of freedom were configured; typically in a double joint (elbow-wrist) arm the configuration would touch upon first rotation, then elevation, then extension, then wrist rotation about its own axis, then wrist angle with respect to the forearm, then wrist rotation with respect to the forearm and finally grasping at an arbitrary (yet constrained) force. After practice the subject could move the robotic arm as if it was one of their own limbs. Studies showed that after practice, those areas of the memory that when excited, elicited a move in the robotic arm started behaving like a motor cortex area and certain regions of the brain became dedicated to the task of controlling the robotic arm exclusively. The same principle could be applied to other Human Peripheral Devices (HPDs) such as keyboards, cursors, domestic appliances etc. More recently the device had managed to recreate images and sounds from a human memory and store them, although if the memory had to be recalled, it would still be recalled from the cortical area where it was stored amongst countless other human memories cramming the gyri and the sulci of the cortical surface. At the same time in beta version there was technology for aiding humans not recall memories from an external hard disk (that was still too difficult), but replacing some of the neural circuitry in the cerebellum or adding extra control circuits in various areas of the brain in order to stop epileptic incidents by cutting off looping signals that became too strong, or replacing lost dopaminergic neurons in the brain to cure Parkinson's disease, or even replacing whole chunks of demyelinated neurons with electronic circuits after diagnosis of multiple sclerosis. It was hoped that eventually, if the replacement was done slowly enough, people could gradually 'migrate' themselves, their personalities, their thoughts and their memories from their old biological circuits into fully electronic ones and end up with a fully electronic brain. That way people would be able not only to have effectively brains with replaceable parts and brains that are impossible to destroy by something as clumsy as a cerebrovascular failure, but also obtain ports that would be able to link them directly to machines in a way that was much more intimate than ever expected. On the other hand, the newly acquired handicap would be vulnerability to EM pulses of high magnitude and software viruses. At any rate, all of that, including the ethical debate that would inevitably be born under the circumstances was still a thing of the future.

The car was still heading towards the centre of the communist sector. Realising that he didn't exactly know where that was, but that his travelling companion probably did, Miles asked:

'By the way, where are we going?'

'Well, I thought you asked the car to navigate you to the centre of our sector, no?' Martha said with a slight hint of incredulity.

'Yes, I did, but the car knows where that is whereas I've never been there before and don't even know what it's called.' explained Miles.

'Ah. I see. Well, I can tell you we call it Epsom and is mostly built over the last 3-4 decades. It is where our government sits as well as all the important institutions of the state.' Martha gave the sought answer.

'And how about private institutions?' Miles inquired idly.

'There are none.' Martha replied simply. Then noticing the confused stare appearing again uninvited all over Miles' countenance she proceeded to clarify even more: 'Yes, you heard well. We have no private institutions. All economic, scientific, social activity is done by the state. Our factories are all government-owned, the universities too, schools and hospitals, transport and utilities as well.'

'But, but...'

'You wonder how they can possibly work, no? You were taught that nothing owned by the state can ever work because nobody needs to work to get paid, no? You have read about the failure of the Soviet Union, no?' Martha said anticipating what was probably going on through Miles' head. Except the last one, which Miles never read about, she was right.

'A... Yes.' he said feigning reassurance.

'Well, here we employ a rather different system of management. Here we reward results.' said Martha with a triumphant smile.

'How exactly?' inquired Miles fascinated at the prospect that people have finally found a way to make a state-run enterprise actually run.

'Well, let's take an example of an industrial machinery factory.' said Martha. 'The factory needs to somehow ensure quality, productivity and customer satisfaction in non-free market conditions. So, somehow our system had to create pressure to satisfy those conditions without placing too much power in the hands of too few individuals. The best solution we came up with is the so called '3 director system'.' she said and paused for a second. Miles said nothing, so Martha resumed in her own time:

'The basis is that every factory employs 3 'big-cheese' directors. One of them is the technical director, another is the personnel director and finally, it is the quality control manager. Each of the 3 has a base salary that is not very high and bonuses depending on different variables of production. The technical director is rewarded for increases in productivity, i.e. value generated per employee. So he pushes for fewer staff, better quality, newer machines. The personnel director is rewarded on quantity. So he pushes for more staff and more production in absolute numbers. The quality control manager is responsible for quality, but is also rewarded for un-rooting corruption. When he sees corruption he alerts the authorities. The authorities then place the factory 'under inspection' and send monitoring teams and inspectors to see how things run. For the duration of that activity all bonuses are cut from everyone from the top to the bottom of the hierarchy, so having the factory put 'under inspection' benefits nobody including the quality control manager. If after 1 year of the factory being run effectively by the police things improve dramatically and the quality control manager is found correct in his allegations of corruption, he gets richly rewarded and the corrupt members of the management are penalised. Otherwise, if it was a scam, he'll have to deal with the workers' wrath... So it only benefits him that the factory is 'under inspection' if it is genuinely corrupt, but not otherwise.

This now creates a natural balance. The technical manager now blocks the personnel manager from flooding the market with an enormous quantity of cheap junk, the personnel manager prevents the technical manager from creating shortages by obsessing with quality and artificially increasing prices, the quality control manager prevents the two from cooperating somehow against the factory and none of them has enough power to impose himself too much. Above these 3 sits the general director who is holistically responsible about the factory and earns bonuses dependent on doing well in quantity, productivity and keeping corruption down. He has the final word in the factory and is personally responsible for every time the factory does badly. If any of the 3 parameters of productivity, quantity and low corruption is indicating a critical situation, the director responsible for it is bound to take action, protest or even report the factory to the higher-ups complaining that for example all the achievements of the factory are based on quantity and not quality (the technical manager would usually also file such complaint). For that reason, the general director can and will rain fire upon anybody who doesn't work to the maximum. We are effectively creating a race to the top of productivity and production.' concluded Martha. Miles had another question brewing:

'You mentioned higher-ups to the general director. Who are they?'

'They are the people responsible for the organisation of production in the entire sector of industrial activity. For example if our machine-building factory was one out of 20, the higher-ups of each general director would be the board that runs the entire sector and we call it the 'machine building central command'. They, in turn, have their own higher-ups, who now work for the ministry of heavy industry, who, in turn, have their higher-ups in the higher echelons of the ministry that coordinate between the various branches of industry. Finally, at the top of the economic pyramid sit the ministers who constitute the Government Planning Committee (GPC) and decide how much investment goes where. Then, depending on demand, national need and other factors the ministers in the GPC decide which sectors of the industry to 'water so that they grow' and by how much. Then, their underlings at the ministries try to distribute the funds between branches of the industry, again depending on demand for those branches under the GPC's strategic development plan for the economy. Farther below, the ministries distribute these targets to the central commands, who then split it between factories.' Martha said hardly taking a breath. Miles had yet another question:

'How do they know how much demand there is or will be?' he requested to know.

'How much demand there will be is just an estimate. As for how much demand there already is, consumers, factories and every single group of people that needs to procure items has 'supply officers' of 'consumer ombudsmen' whose sole task is to seek shortages and inform higher-ups; in specific the ministry directly. The ministry, in turn, has a whole department that handles this shortage data from across the country and feeds back this information to the planners in the 'upstream' phase of planning. Generally speaking, these shortage inspectors as we normally call them have pressure placed upon them to reveal shortages to the higher-ups because shortages hurt production and productivity, no? The technical director will therefore make sure the higher-ups hear about shortages.' Martha explained calmly, yet Miles had more questions:

'What is the 'upstream' phase of planning?'

'It is when lower ranks of management starting from individual factory provide information upstream until it reaches the GPC. This includes information on shortages, but we have a specialised department to deal with just that because we consider it too important to leave to just one mechanism of gathering and processing information. The downstream flow is when targets are disaggregated and passed down to individual industry sectors, then central commands and then factories.' she tirelessly explained, but Miles had yet another question:

'And how does price integrate into all this?'

'Factories have a certain freedom to set prices, and so do shops. Profitability is rewarded all over the economy by returning part of the profits back to everybody working in the factory as a direct bonus. Prices can change every 3 months, but not more frequently. That's how we alleviate our shortage problem, by making sure that not so many people can afford to buy the items in shortage. It might seem harsh, but if we didn't act so all we'd achieve is gigantic queues forming before the morning delivery in shops and that would just be a waste of time for our citizens. At the current level of pricing we also have no queues anywhere for the additional reason that all that is essential for life is either produced or imported at a sufficient rate. If we get over-production, we cut from the imports or if it's not something we import, we keep making the industry more productive but allocate less workforce to it and use the extra manpower elsewhere. In these essential goods, we keep prices such as to reflect the actual effort put into making them. So food costs as much to buy as it does to produce and we import and process just the right amount to top domestic production up, each year more and more productively and cheaply. By wielding productivity and technology as weapons we try to push products of all categories, from essential to luxury, to the point where everybody can afford them. To answer your question in a very short sentence: we use prices to eliminate queues. As an extra boon, we also don't have the problem where profit-mongers inflate prices way above production cost when a product is in urgent need. The best example to illustrate this point is thinking back to the oil crises where cartels were keeping prices artificially high, although the way justice is dispensed in your Zone would probably be another good example of that.' Martha kept explaining. Miles nodded in sign of understanding. Justice was indeed extremely expensive in Zone 1. It didn't cost that much to set-up and run a trial, yet law firms charged exorbitant amounts of money and justice insurance was one of the most expensive types of insurance around. He contemplated all this for a minute and then, he fired his next query.

'I understand that a factory can't then plunder its own goods because then their customers would be after their heads and other directors would report them, plus in their triplet of directors and the general director there would be some protest from somebody for sure. Presumably if all 4 of them decide to plunder their own factory for personal gain and even the quality control manager gains more out of this than reporting the corruption, and their customers report them, the quartet is in for some hard time, no?' said Miles.

'Yes, in forced labour.' came the brief reply.

'And what happens if the two factories get engaged in warfare because for some reason some goods were produced all right but destroyed by accident and everybody is looking for someone to take the blame?' Miles inquired again.

'Well, every time an institution receives resources or sends away processed goods they record the event with a ministry agency that monitors such transactions. Every time a factory loads goods on a train, a representative of the factory signs, and a representative of the railway signs and a ministry transactions department representative oversees and signs as well. The ministry official has the responsibility for this. This is a situation where if the cargo is not there, intact and transferred properly somebody of the 3 is going to get into trouble for it. For that reason the 3 signatures are required; all of them. The ministry oversees such transactions so at any point in time they know who was responsible for what.' Martha clarified placing her index finger on the side of her head, just in front of the ear, and winking in the international sign that we all associate with the phrase: 'clever, eh?'.

'So that's how accountability is guaranteed. Although to me it still seems like a bulky and bureaucratic system...' Miles said. Martha wasted no time in replying:

'Perhaps, but in return you get a centralised, coordinated control mechanism that can steer the economy in places the market never would.'

'Finally, what happens at the end of the chain? At the shop? How do you make sure that the shop doesn't plunder the wares before they reach the customer?' exclaimed Miles.

'Every time an item is sold, it is scanned on the bar-code. That scanner is connected to the ministry servers which count products and compare with the stocks of the shop. Accidents do happen, and goods are declared 'deceased' as if I were to say, but if those overshoot logical limits the shop goes under investigation, which is just as pleasant as being 'under inspection'. Moreover evidence of the destroyed goods is asked, and if there is none because, say for example, a fire burnt all the candles, then the threshold for investigation lowers. Finally, for every such incident a series of counter-measures to prevent such incident from reoccurring is demanded from the central command of the shop. If the event reoccurs for the same reason and it is found out that the counter-measures had not been taken when the time was due, then somebody is in for a lot of trouble.' once again patiently clarified Martha.

'You still use candles?' incredulously asked Miles.

'Definitely not. It was just the best example I could think where an accident would totally and utterly destroy the product and every trace of it.' replied Martha, a pleasant smile painted on her face.

Following that conversation Miles fell silent and returned to looking outside the windows of the car. His head hurt from the overflow of information. Getting the enormous bureaucratic system of the communists round his head was a gargantuan task. So many rules, so many extreme possibilities where the system might malfunction. Just like a computer program with an endless chain of 'if / else if' statements, where every possibility had to be dealt with by the program or terrible consequences would ensue. If he were to discuss every single possibility with Martha, they'd probably grow old together in that car... Martha also fell silent and occupied herself with looking outside the window as well. The car proceeded for a little while in silence until Miles broke it with yet another, albeit simpler, question:

'What is that?' he said pointing with his finger at a tall structure ahead of them.

'Ah that...' said Martha. 'That is our government's central command HQ tower. 250 floors of bureaucracy. It might seem much, but remember that large corporations yielding turnovers close to our national economy have administrations of similar size, just not all concentrated in the same building. At the base of the tower is a concert hall, a congress hall, a museum, a shopping centre and a vast public sports hall. Believe it or not it was completed last year. We may be in Zone 2, but we are united and led by a monolithic government and thus still capable of completing major projects. As for running them, that's a different story, but I'm being unfair. Doesn't work perfectly, but it is actually not too bad.' she concluded pensively, talking more to herself than to Miles.

Miles sensed that and kept to himself. Hilda navigated quickly over the well-maintained avenues of the communist zone towards the centre. Before too long they were at the base of the 250-floor, 1009m tower with the sharp antenna at the top. The skyscraper's base was surrounded by a large wing of the building that rose between 12 and 30 floors at different angles around the building creating the impression of a steep staircase as one moved right-to-left around the building and then dropping back down to the base in the outline of a more steep staircase. This surrounding wing featured a cylindrical projection on to the ground plane. The tower of the skyscraper itself on the other hand left a triangular projection and its top was at that moment hidden behind the low clouds so often flying over London. Miles was looking at the edifice with interest when Martha interrupted his thoughts:

'This is where this whole sector is ran from. And back there you will see the new London academy towers under construction.' she said pointing towards the west where the outline of some large building with a large central tower and at least another 7, lower spires surrounding it at various distances could be distinguished against the grey background of the cloudy sky. Evidently the communists had managed to get their economy moving again despite the problems their bulky bureaucracy was causing. Could it be that the secretary general's modifications to the system had done it?

Miles looked at the government tower, then he looked at the academy tower, then he had another look all around him and noticed the gardens in front of the main entrance of the government building. Beautiful gardens with colourful flowerbeds, surrounded by the asphalt of the boulevards that ran in the vicinity of the tower as well as the 'double roundabout', two concentric ring-roads, one running exactly around the pavement surrounding the base of the government skyscraper and another one running in a circle with its centre also at the government tower, but about 75m away from it. Five boulevards left in five different directions from the inner ring and went on, seemingly forever, straight as rulers. In the five plots of earth that were delimited by the double roundabout and the 5 straight boulevards flowers grew in ordered arrays in a multitude of colours. The one in front of the main entrance to the tower also boasted a large fountain with decorations in the form of statues of burly working men and women as well as scientists and artists surrounding a central urn-like sculpture, the top of which was spurting water vertically up. At the periphery of the admittedly large, circular fountain stood yet more water pumps, at even intervals, harmoniously squirting water towards the central sculpture at an angle of about 60 degrees, calculated so that the falling water would land just short of hitting the urn and the stone figures surrounding it. All around the fountain stood 6 pillars of shiny black marble, which got thinner and thinner as one moved upwards, until near the top the material changed to brass and at the very top of each pillar stood a large, nearly human-sized 5-spike ruby-red star that glowed, evidently with the power of OLEDs. The side-wall of the fountain, as well as the urn were made out of red granite and the statues glorifying different segments of communist society from white marble. Finally, although Miles couldn't see that from the car, passers-by casually walking through the park on a good day could enjoy the mosaic that was laid carefully on the floor and depicted snapshots from the lives of Marx, Engels and Lenin, mixed with yet more images glorifying the working man and woman.

After taking all that in, he addressed his new travelling companion:

'Say, Martha. Can we perhaps pull in somewhere for the night? A hotel or something.'

'Certainly. There is a small number of fairly good hotels that could accommodate you for a modest price. I recommend the hotel Kalinin near the Kalinin square underground railway station.' she replied.

'You have an operating underground railway system?' Miles said with surprise, but having caught sight of Martha's rather disturbed countenance slightly faster than the previous time he inadvertently offended her, he swiftly apologised and steered the conversation back to business.

'And what about you? Where will you stay for the night? I mean, you are my escort guard, but at night how does it work?' he inquired curiously.

'All our hotels have an extra bed and small room for the police escort. It's been thought of, don't worry.' she clarified.

'Ah, I see!' Miles exclaimed and without any further delay asked Hilda to take them to the Kalinin hotel. The minor difficulty that arose when Hilda made it known that such hotel was not on her maps was resolved quickly when Martha declared she would show her the way.

The car went around the external roundabout that was surrounding the government tower and then took one of the large boulevards leaving north-east. Before long, the boulevard started sloping upwards until it became clear that it was part of the old elevated highway system. Hilda had a chance to recharge her batteries on the go. Miles enjoyed the view from above, still not entirely free from the headache that was precipitated by the complex explanations of Martha's. Either way, for the moment he was happy enough to simply enjoy the views; the endless rows of Victorian houses, the outlines of the newly-built tower-blocks, the outline of the imposing new academy building, the various parks, most of which were converted to farmland. Far ahead, the skyscrapers of Zone 1 were towering over the landscape like a wall of glass and light. The cloudy day was making the imposing Zone 1 skyscrapers look like faint ghosts, emitting white light from various parts of their bodies and some emitting those eerie, blinking red strobe lights at various heights from the ground, always at least 2 visible at each level in each building that exhibited them. The miserable weather, the bad memories that came to be associated with the skyscrapers of Zone 1 and the whole general attire of the clinically clean communist zone were making him melancholic, even depressed. He must have looked really miserable because Martha patted him on the shoulder to attract his attention and spoke:

'Are you all right?'

'What? Oh yes. Yes. I'm fine, thank you.' he lied.

'I've been thinking.' Martha said after a little pause. 'What we just talked about, how our system works, might be a little overwhelming for a first-time visitor.'

'You don't tell me!' Miles replied with evident sullenness.

'Yes, but there is a basic principle behind everything we did to create this bureaucracy.' she insisted. Miles suddenly got interested, raised his head that was previously reclining against his fist and made it apparent that he was all ears. Thus Martha, encouraged, continued:

'The entire system hinges on this pattern: You have managers who need to get tasks done. Then you reward these people if they achieve them. If they don't, however they can often lie and pretend they achieved their targets. For that reason, when they fail for whatever reason, our system makes sure that somebody else profits by reporting them. For that reason you must make sure that you have people fighting for everything that needs to be done, in the case of factories, quality, quantity, productivity and low corruption. To keep these interests in balance you then add a general manager over them who needs to keep the conflicting interests in harmony and advance the factory by taking all key performance parameters into consideration. If the general manager doesn't maintain balance, somebody's 'interests' will get hurt too much and the factory will be reported for failing miserably in productivity for example while over-stressing quantity. So the general manager keeps the individual managers in balance, while the individual managers don't let the general manager ignore key metrics of good factory-running for too long. The ministry-controlled mode of good transactions also ensures that all factories have to face up to their responsibilities. Finally, barriers and difficulties that arise if a factory is put 'under inspection' make sure that reports for bad quality, slobbing around at work etc. do not arise unless there is a serious reason for them to appear. This is our basic blueprint that we replicate and apply with appropriate modifications to each and every aspect of our society.

For example, in services, where you can't have such rigid ministry-controlled goods transaction system and the final customer is people, rather than an institution which can defend its own interests, we have a customer satisfaction manager whose sole task is to make sure that the 'consumer ombudsmen' are happy. The ombudsmen themselves are elected every 3 months and enjoy good bonuses, so they have a motivation to do well in their jobs and be incorruptible. They then produce and publish lists that indicate shortages, quality complaints etc. Finally they rate companies on the quality of their services. If their companies provide poor services, the customer satisfaction manager reports it to the directors, who then either take appropriate action, or the matter goes to the higher-ups.

In even more general terms the pattern can be described as 'if you screw up, I pay for the disaster too so you'd better do your job well or I'll rain fire on you' and its twin 'if you screw up and I report it, I get rewarded'. This is how the managers keep the general manager in control, how the customers keep the mangers in control etc. I don't know how to describe it more simply.' she finished her attempt to explain once again to Miles how the communist society achieved production. Miles thought in silence for a while and the replied:

'I see. It is effectively the same as creating a 3D map where you bend the function in such way that the 'valleys' of the function sit exactly where you want the ball to roll into. Then you place a ball on the map and let it roll down to its natural equilibrium, as James would say.' exclaimed Miles suddenly understanding.

'Who?' said Martha, evidently confused.

'Oh, just an old friend of mine. It is exactly how he would explain it, I mean the way I just put it. Or even better, he'd say you have to construct a function where the local minima lie at the values you wish them to, which is easier said than done.' Miles said.

'Hmmm. Clever fellow your friend. That does make a lot of sense. We are still tuning the system, but the idea is this: That each person is put in a position where he must do what he is supposed to in order to gain the maximum benefit out of his station in life and society. And I suppose that's exactly how you could put these words into mathematical terms.' she said pensively. Then went on to utter: 'But I think this enough politics for one day.' just as the car was parking in front of the Kalinin hotel. Miles nodded in agreement and very soon they were entering the hotel's impressive reception area.

Martha handled the administration for Miles' 1-night stay, Miles handled the payment using his implant and the companions made their way to the room. It was a very clean and tidy room of decent size. Modern furniture, a nice TV-mirror that was obviously used as a TV when on and as a mirror when it was off, a place to put the various suitcases on and a desk with a nice, leather swivelling chair before it adorned the room. Colourful OLED lighting was providing illumination to the room and could be customised to change colour and intensity according to the lodger's mood. Miles quickly crashed into the lodger's bed while Martha was preparing to install herself into the special guard escort bed (in a separate, small chamber) when he thought: 'I'm going to regret this' and then uttered: 'Oh Martha...'.

'Yes?'

'How do you keep your hotels so clean and tidy?' he inquired.

'Oh, haha. Hotel inspection in this country has been elevated to the level of a science. We have inspection districts and inspector groups. Each group corresponds to an inspection district. Within 3 months all the hotels within that district must be inspected, then the groups get reassigned to different districts. Each hotel gets inspected twice. That way, if the 1st hotel inspector reveals himself to the management and requires money to cover up a disaster or to grant a merited positive review, in short blackmail, the hotel management has either the option of reporting him, or taking the risk of playing along. However, if the 2nd inspector comes down with a different verdict, then both inspectors come under suspicion of corruption and everybody including the hotel is in trouble. For that reason, any behaviour apart from two options for both hotel and inspectors is a risky gamble with potentially very serious penalties. Either the hotel is consistently bad and both inspectors tell the truth, or the hotel is consistently impeccable and the inspectors both tell the truth. Any inconsistency from the hotel or foul play from the inspectors has a potentially very serious aftermath. The only way corruption can go through is if they all orchestrate something together. For that reason inspectors don't know which hotel they are inspecting until they are being taken there in their office cars. Even if that evil concert succeeds, any report from customers indicating that there is any foul play going on would cause the secret police to send an inspector of their own. As you can see, the secret police has a very important secondary function here that is to provide information on corruption to the higher-ups...' said Martha with an unspecified expression that seemed to contain a peculiar mixture of worry and satisfaction.

Miles said nothing in reply, choosing to nod in sign of understanding instead. Clearly a communist society required an enormous amount of bureaucracy to keep the wheels of the entire society running in one, grand mechanism. With this thought he lay in his bed looking at the ceiling, contemplating. Yes, the communist society was based on a very strict bureaucracy that was supposed to keep the entire society in tune like a strict orchestra director waving his baton to keep a giant, million-people orchestra playing the correct tune in perfect synchrony. Whether it worked or not was a different story. After all, Martha told him that shortages were natural in her society, just like poverty was in his. Moreover there seemed to be a serious issue with personal liberty. Not that he wasn't enjoying Martha's companionship, on the contrary, however being escorted by an officer of the law wherever he went was not something that made him feel comfortable. It made him feel under suspicion. Giving up travelling also didn't sound good to him. Perhaps in this society, despite its impressive infrastructure, cleanliness and even economic development -for Zone 2 anyway-, the price to pay to be one of its members was too high for him. Either way, he decided to ask:

'Say, Martha.'

'Yes?'

'What would it take to become a citizen of your zone?'

'Ah. It's quite simple really. We need your identity and background, which are all on your implant. Then any real estate property or means of production you own should be transferred to the state. Here the state owns all land, including real estate and all means of production from shops to factories.' she declared. Miles said nothing in reply. He was thinking of his multi-million-pound flat in Zone 1.

'Still own significant property in Zone 1, eh?' said Martha most perceptively.

Miles nodded in agreement, but said nothing.

'May I see it?' inquired Martha with expectation. Miles was perplexed.

'How?' he simply asked.

'Surely you must have some pictures of your house or flat, no? I always wanted to see what a house in Zone 1 looks like!' she replied exhibiting the expectation of a child that's about to receive presents for Christmas.

'Yes, but they are on my computer mainframe. If I could log on to my console I could even have the robo-butler give us some live feed from the apartment.' Miles replied.

'Please do so then!' said Martha with the same excitement.

'But, how?'

'Just scan your implant at the reader on your desk. How else?' said Martha pointing towards the implant reader. Miles turned his head, looked at the desk and sure enough there was an implant reader on it; a most elegant one too.

'What are you waiting for? Swipe!' Martha encouraged him excitedly. Miles complied and after completing the manoeuvre the TV/mirror screen came to life. The locally written software initialised and a red star appeared on the screen. Soon afterwards text appeared:

'Welcome to the People's Republic of Anglia, citizen of Zone 1. This software has recognised you as Miles Fitzroy from Zone 1. With your authorisation the hotel may provide you with any service you would normally have access to in your homeland. When you finish reading this message press any key to see the main menu.'

Miles complied and the main menu appeared. Much like in regular Zone 1 terminals the left side was taken up by a menu indicating various usual options and the right side was taken up by a floating head, this one an old gentleman with balding head, tiny spectacles and a very small, curvy moustache. He announced himself as being Monsieur Deuxville.

'French?' he asked Martha with disbelief.

'Yes, we found that people tend to think of mainframes with French personalities as more, how do you say, chique, than plain old English ones.' she said giggling with amusement.

'Oh well, then. Deuxville, can you connect me to my own mainframe?' he asked.

'Certainly Monsieur.' answered the mainframe with a French accent that greatly amused Miles. Soon Reginald's head replaced that of Mon. Deuxville.

'Sir?' he declared as sternly as ever.

'Reginald, my companion here would like to have a virtual tour of my residence. Would you kindly oblige?' said Miles politely.

'Certainly sir. Please lead the way.' said Reginald and disappeared. Miles understood and simply said to Martha pointing towards the screen at the same time:

'This is my bedroom'.

An image of the bedroom appeared. Miles explained to Martha all the wonders of technology that adorned his most private chamber, paying particular attention to the wardrobe chamber. Apparently, in the communist zone these chambers were only something the political elite had access to, but they were getting more and more popular slowly, as the economy of the communist zone improved. Along similar lines Miles proceeded to show all the machinery that made his life so comfortable, machinery he now realised he had taken for granted for too long. Martha looked at the images before her with the most peculiar mix of awe and envy. How could people who in her mind -as well as many others'- did nothing productive, earn such a plush and luxurious living? At long last Martha familiarised herself with the latest in appliance, consumer and home comfort technology, Miles thanked Reginald and bade him good bye. The connection was closed and the terminal shut down. Miles then asked:

'How secure is the connection, by the way?'

'Very secure, why?' Martha answered.

'Is it being monitored by the authorities?' Miles inquired.

'Good question. I don't know. There certainly seems to be a great deal of secrecy around here though.' she replied lowering her voice.

'Worrying indeed.' said Miles in an equally low tone of voice and then started more boisterously and cheerfully: 'But what the hell, let's go dine and then retire for the night. Any nice places you know where we can dine?'

'I certainly do. There are a few good restaurants in the area, let's walk there.' Martha replied with her usual, radiant smile. Then the companions left to dine and in an office, deep underground, in the warrens of the national security building that ran below even the deepest underground tunnels, an employee finished his work for the day.

CHAPTER 6: BANGERS AND MASH.

The following morning Miles woke up in his comfortable bed and went to the little, but well laid-out bathroom of his room in order to carry out his morning ablutions. His travelling companion had already concluded hers and was patiently waiting for him. After a short interval of time spent packing, the two of them went to the hotel reception and checked out. Martha then asked:

'Where do you intend to go now then?' all the formality from their 1st encounter having completely washed away.

'I will continue my journey west. Do you know what lies beyond?' he asked Martha, also more informally than he would have upon their first meeting.

'Why, the old-style boroughs where the local government has been revived and now controls affairs. There is a border control post at West Wickham in fact. Shall I indicate the way?' replied Martha.

'Please.' said Miles bowing respectfully and showed her to his vehicle once again.

The time between their departure from the hotel and the arrival at the West Wickham border post flew by as the two companions were engrossed into conversation. But it was not the heavy, political conversation they were indulging in throughout much of the previous day; it was more personal and casual. Miles talked about what it was like to live care-free in Zone 1 as a City-boy and always return to the luxury of a very expensive residence and Martha was telling him about the daily life in a state where everything was ran from the government tower, how she led an interesting life with rich access to culture and information, but lacking travelling freedom and sometimes goods that she could really make use of. Meanwhile, the scenery flew past them and consisted of the usual mix of old Victorian houses with new tower-blocks growing amidst them, clean roads and alleys, the occasional park that hasn't been turned into a farm and here and there various impressive public use buildings.

Naturally, all large windowless walls were adorned with propagandistic works of art which the locals called 'agitki'.

At some point, the car passed under a fairly large and impressive glass building in which enormous chandeliers with intricate patterns could be seen. This building was so strange that it deserves a proper description. Its curious structure appeared to be sitting on a bridge, and its exterior consisted of what appeared to be a metal skeleton and glass. The metal skeleton was in the approximate shape of a ribcage taken from a vast ocean mammal, with the spinal vertebrae running along the top of the building (at least 25m from the ground) and the individual ribs descending down, embracing the interior of the building, getting thinner and thinner as they descended until they touched the base of the building. This left spaces in between in the shape of very elongated and curved windows like the ones one would expect to find in a medieval cathedral, with a basal edge of roughly 5m at the base of the structure, getting gradually thinner and thinner running upwards, until it disappeared at an apex. Every 4th such window was a mural, depicting yet another scene glorifying the working man in bright, but tasteful colours. The other windows were clear and the interior of the building could be seen. At the top, hanging from the 'vertebrae', large chandeliers with intricate floral patterns descended for what must have been about 4 meters and illuminated the interior of the building with the OLED lights that were arranged in 3 circular tiers, the lower tiers being of a larger diameter. In front of these circular tiers of OLEDs stood rings of crystals that refracted the light creating an effect that was very pleasant to the eye. These rings were made out of crystals of the triangular prismatic sort, aligned in such way that if seen from above their exterior outline resembled that of a saw-tooth and the interior a regular polygon with at least 120 sides. Below them a crowd of people was shuffling about and what appeared to be trains were coming and going. Miles did not hesitate to inquire about the precise nature of the building. Martha was only too happy to explain:

'This is Croydon underground railway station. I know it's actually overground technically speaking, but we call it the underground anyway. This one has 4 platforms and serves 2 underground railway lines. It's part of our public transport. The newspapers called it a gift to the working people when it was completed.'

'It is... It is... simply impressive. Are all stops like this?' inquired Miles, still in awe.

'No, this is a newer one. In the last 3 years we have been expanding our public railways and revamping our stations. You should have seen some of the old stations. They were a disgrace.' Martha said rather nonchalantly.

'It certainly beats our public transport system in Zone 1. Our mostly disused stations are disgraceful compared to these. These are works of art. Ours are just concrete. Apparently there's no money to be made in maintaining museum galleries as railway stations...' said Miles with what he recognised to be the first signs of genuine envy towards something that was related to Zone 2. Martha picked that up and felt a tingle of pride.

The rest of the journey towards the West Wickham border post was uneventful and the car soon reached the heavy gates that indicated that beyond lay a different land. Martha explained the situation to the guards manning the interior of the gates and they ceremoniously opened the gates for the visitor to enter the control area. Miles and Martha took their goodbyes in the most emotional way possible. With a hug and a fleeting kiss on the cheek. Then they parted as Martha returned to her administration building ready for her next assignment and Miles crossed the gate, a tiny tear at the corner of the eyes of each of them.

'Oh well... We'll talk again, I'm sure, even if over the internet.' Miles thought to himself as the arduous procedure of scanning every nook and cranny of his car, then his person and then going through the 'passport control' phase were carried out. The exit procedure was much like the entry procedure, but the order of all activities had been reversed. In the end, after his implant was scanned, the equivalent of showing his pass-card, the guards at the barbed-wire and sand sacks saluted him officiously and he was free to move on. About 10m far from the barricade the road quality suddenly worsened significantly, the pavements suddenly were full of cracks and grass growing between those cracks, the amount of vehicles reduced substantially and the people looked again dressed in drab clothing and wandering around like vagrant souls. He knew he had entered the 'green zone on the political map of London'.

The images he was seeing were familiar. He'd seen it all again back in Osterley. Hilda was navigating slowly past the pot-holes and the cracks in the road and slowly made her way deeper and deeper into the 'green boroughs'. Eventually she asked her master:

'Where exactly are we going, sir? For the time being I'm following our north-east bearing with no particular destination in mind.'

'Ah, well...' said Miles 'Let's go to Bexley...'. A groan from his stomach reminding him that he had skipped breakfast interrupted him. '...and I think we can find a nice pub there to eat a thing or two.' he concluded taking the hint from his bowels.

Hilda nodded with her usual, formal 'Yes, sir.' and went on to preoccupy herself with the treacherous navigation issues the ramshackle roads of the area were constantly presenting her with. Miles looked out of the window at the roads, the people, the houses, the shops and one question tortured his mind with persistence. Why did these boroughs that chose to return back to the old system of government did so much worse than either the communists or the anarchists? To this, however he found no answer. As such, he continued to absorb everything he saw flying past him with his eyes, sullen as it may have been to watch. Every now and then the monotony of street after street of boring Victorian housing would be broken by a dirty and miserable high-street with shops that were very well stocked, but rather empty of customers or some public building, for example old and poorly maintained hospitals or a disused and weedy railway track. Less often he'd pass by a school, where the little children's floral-themed drawings on the sides of the school building, drawn in chalk, would create an island of youthful warmth and optimism in what appeared to be an endless ocean of misery. In one case Miles' heart beat boisterously with excitement and melancholy at the same time when he passed by a school during a break. The little kids were practically in rags, but playing joyfully in the sand pit of the school court, or playing football in the school's overgrown football pitch. Memories of his own childhood in one of the poshest schools Zone 1 could offer overwhelmed him and suddenly he realised how well he'd had it. After all, his parents spent their entire fortune trying to educate him, and that was no trifling amount of money. Before tears could swell up to his eyes the car had passed the school and Miles' attention was turned to other scenes.

For mile after mile nothing exciting was to be seen. Rusty, old signs were informing him of his whereabouts as the car tackled the ruined roads of the area, but the scenery was mostly unchanged. Then, he entered an area dominated by semi-finished tower-blocks, each between 5 and 12 floors tall, many of them with old, rusting cranes still standing right next to them and metal rods protruding from their tops, indicating that they were abandoned in the middle of building. 'Abandoned project' Miles thought and he knew what he was talking about. A few construction companies had undertaken projects in Zone 2 trying to get a share of the less important, but still sizeable market for cheap, mass accommodation for Zone 2. However, as the various areas of Zone 2 dropped in value with increasing poverty after the complete dissolution of the social state, the expected return from the completion of various housing projects that were in progress in these areas at the time (late 2030's and 2040's) gradually dropped until it was below what the companies carrying them our deemed worthy of the effort. Yet it seemed that in the empty husks of the unfinished buildings people had taken settlement. Somehow they had managed to connect themselves to the electricity grid as evidenced by the lights that were still on in some rooms despite it being closer to lunchtime than dinner (not that the murky, cloudy sky would make that obvious). These areas must have been particularly underdeveloped; the evidence was everywhere. At the base of the buildings, what plots of land once were most likely planned to be parking lots and gardens, were just a wasteland, littered with wilted, red-brown flora and mostly metal junk spread all over the place. There were very few vehicles to be seen in the area and most of them were in a pitiful state: utterly destroyed and rusting with any possibly valuable parts they may have once had, missing. The state of the roads was even worse than elsewhere in the borough and the cracked and dirty pavements had to suffer the presence of lamp-posts with broken glass and benches that consisted of mostly broken, graffiti-ridden planks of wood. Miles started to panic at the sight and he urged Hilda to get out of the area as swiftly as possible, however she could not execute her master's order without putting the structural integrity of the car in peril. To complete the picture, the streets of that area were completely deserted, which should have calmed Miles down by convincing him there was no immediate threat, but somehow achieved the opposite effect. When a few more hundreds of meters into this desolate zone, he spotted what once had been a playground, but now was a depressing collection of completely unusable, rusting children's playthings, presently oscillating morbidly in response to the winter wind, Miles got so scared and depressed that he sunk into his seat and curled in a ball, though still the right way up, until all he could see were the eerie, almost ghostly metal-ridden tops of the unfinished buildings around him and decided not to re-emerge until all of those terrifying buildings had vanished from his field of view.

Luckily, the housing project was not all that extensive, and Miles felt safe enough to re-emerge from his rather un-heroic position about a quarter of an hour after assuming it in the first place. He was back to the usual, boring rows of Victorian housing once again, and this time he felt relief, nay, almost joy about it. The only thing that struck him in the rest of the rather long and monotonous journey towards Bexley was that the parks of these boroughs were not being farmed, like in the confederate or the communist zones. Instead they were overgrown and unkempt and felt like nobody had taken care of them in ages. Curious as to why that might be the case, Miles searched in vain for an answer. Finding none, however he returned to his meditations. His most serious problem at the time was how he would be able to learn more about these areas that had reverted to the old system of government. In the commune he was lucky to find himself in the gracious company of an elder who took interest in his visit. In the communist sector he was escorted, as the rules required, by a charming officer. Here? Oh well, he'd figure something out, he thought after no obvious answers came to mind.

The difficult and slow journey continued for a while, until finally around noon, and to the great delight of Miles' stomach, Hilda announced that she was on the final leg of the journey and they were effectively in the centre of Bexley. Miles expressed his wish to descend, the car stopped and he leapt out bidding Hilda to park. He then started walking along the local high-street, checking his pocket for the remote beacon that connected him to his car at all times; particularly useful in situations like this, where he asked Hilda to park in an unfamiliar area and pick him up at a later time in equally unfamiliar surroundings. Miles cheerfully trotted along the high-street of Bexley looking for an establishment that could provide him with some sustenance.

Not much time had passed when his keen eye spotted an old pub, called 'The fox and the crane'. Miles, succumbing to the rumblings of his protesting stomach entered to see a fairly large room, littered with old and rather worn-out sofas and wooden tables, a long bar counter extending for about 15m just about a dozen meters from him. In the far ends of the room, small compartments were formed by wooden separator walls, 6 seats arranged in triplets facing each other across an ancient oak table, much like Miles imagined the compartments of 1st class carriages would have looked like in the historic steam trains that ran across the country back in the 19th century. The walls were decorated with various paintings that seemed to actually date from the Boer war and mostly depicted either English countryside scenes or uniformed officers that once might have fought against the Zulus. The ceiling of the pub was criss-crossed by thick, heavy wooden beams, on some of which rows upon rows of little decorative plates with Victorian scenes were giving the pub a rather homely appearance. Miles, satisfied with the look of the establishment proceeded to explore with the intention of occupying a table and lunching there.

Off he shot towards the left and started observing the architectural layout of the pub. Upon taking a number of steps in his chosen direction he noticed a little staircase, no more than 5 steps tall leading to another room with yet more worn-out sofas and sturdy, wooden tables. It quickly became evident to Miles that the back-room was far roomier than the front room, and also that the seating area of the pub was shaped like a picture frame, wrapping around a central area that was apparently used as a kitchen, a liquor cabinet and the counter at the same time. The back-room possessed a rather different atmosphere than the front room. It was darker, the walls were dressed in heavy wooden wall-panels with simple decorations that Prime Minister Gladstone would have found familiar, the lights were OLEDs shaped so as to emulate the flame of a candle and most importantly there was a fireplace in the centre of the room, on the outer wall rather than the one that presumably separated the seating area from the pub's kitchen. The fireplace was rather large, and much to the delight of Miles, housed a strong and warm fire, consuming a bunch of large, thick logs on top of a sturdy metal grid. In front of the fire, a thin filament-grid surrounded by an elegant old brass frame (itself decorated with floral-themed bas-relief just at the top part) was protecting the guests of the pub, as well as the rich and dusty carpet, from smouldering fragments of charred wood that the fire would emit at times. Around the fire, a pair of white marble columns rose either side to support a thick mantelpiece, on top of which two, double-barrelled shotguns were lying proudly in special holders, facing each other. Farther up a large painting of dubious artistic quality depicted a crane with his beak halfway inside a deep amphora with a long, thin neck while a fox was trying to bite upon the lips of a similar amphora, evidently in a futile attempt to reach its contents. These surroundings pleased Miles who took a seat in the close proximity of the fire and engrossed himself in the detailed examination of the menu.

After a short time spent fantasising about steaks, meatballs, fish&chips and the like, he set his mind upon a dish called 'Bangers & mash, truly traditional' and headed for the counter to order it. He did so, paid with the antiquated chip&pin method they were still using in this sector -using his pass-card- and then promptly returned to his table, only to find that in the other sofa that corresponded to his table a stocky old man that Miles clearly recalled being right in front of him when ordering, was sitting idly. Miles approached his seat, pointed at it looking confusedly in the very same direction and opened his mouth, as if to utter something, but only a vague 'Agh...' sort of noise exited through his lips. The old man noticed this peculiar behaviour and spoke:

"allo there. Can I 'elp you?'

'Agh... I... I...' said Miles not knowing what to say. If he indicated it was his table the old man was sitting in, he might be perceived as rude. If not, he had nothing of substance to say. Either way, lately he seemed to be much more preoccupied with what those around him had to say in reaction to his actions. All these thoughts passed through Miles' brain while he was stuttering in confusion.

'Was you sittin' on this 'ere table before I got 'ere?' he asked simply.

'Well, yes, but I don't want to impinge on...' Miles started saying politely, but the old man interrupted him.

'If ye don' mind, ye can sit right 'ere and we can talk an' everything. No?' said the old man invitingly. He then continued: 'Ye're a strange fellow ye are. Not from around 'ere are ye?'

'Well, indeed.' said Miles sitting.

'So where'ya from then young geezer? What's yer name? Tompkins is mine, Jack Tompkins.' said the old man.

'Well, I am Miles, Miles Fitzroy from Zone 1. Investment banker, at least until I recently got fired, and you sir?' asked Miles in return.

'I'm just a retired builder.' replied Tompkins. A pause followed. Old Tompkins broke it again:

'Great place 'at Zone 1 'at is I 'ear.' he said.

'Sorry what?' said Miles and after barely half a second: 'Oh yes, sorry. Please continue.'

'Great place 'at is. Ye can see all o' them skyscrapers from 'ere. I bet it's a right old plush-cushion place to live, 'at it.' the old man continued while Miles struggled to follow. When the man concluded his last statement Miles added philosophically:

'Yes, it is, isn't it? If you have money. A lot of it. Otherwise it gets quite, quite different...'

'Heh. All 'ose geezers up t'ere 'ave it all. Tons o' money, plushy jobs, all o' it.' replied Tompkins without the slightest hesitation.

'Yes, I suppose you are right... That's changing though now. The crisis and everything you see.' Miles said fully understanding the old fellow's yearning for the rich Zone 1 and its glittering skyscrapers, yet at the same time fully aware of his inability to comprehend just how bad life got in Zone 1 if you lacked the money to afford it.

'Meh, nonsens' young lad. Life up t'ere is great. Ye said ye lost yer job, ye came from t'ere and look at ye. Nice clothes, all polished up and perfumed...' said Tompkins carelessly pointing in the general direction of Miles. Miles, in turn, realised that the old geezer was right. There he was, unemployed, yet his few savings had granted him an extension to his plush life in Zone 1 and enough to get by while travelling Zone 2 like a tourist, or even worse like a visitor to a zoo flashing past thousands upon thousands of people who were condemned to live there possibly for their entire lives, gazing at the skyscrapers of Zone 1 that were tantalisingly and mockingly towering over everything in their areas.

'You're right.' Miles finally admitted.

'And what did ye think of our 'here boro' then?' asked Tompkins as if he'd never heard Miles' admission.

'Well, I've been travelling, and I've seen a lot here in Zone 2...' started Miles. Tompkins interrupted again:

'Aye, aye lad. But what d' ye think of this 'ere boro'?' he said excitedly, almost in expectation.

Miles had not been impressed by the general outlook of the borough, but he didn't wish to appear impolite in front of his companion:

'Well... well... I was impressed by... I mean I liked...' clumsily stuttered Miles, desperately trying to think of something that left a positive mark upon him. Finally, he thought of something and added with reassurance: 'I liked this pub a lot!'

'Meh, 's a ****hole.' replied Tompkins disarmingly in what seemed to be a very British answer.

'I beg your pardon?' said Miles rather surprised to see such expression fly past him like a tossed grenade, ejected from a figure of such age.

'It is, ain' it? Must've seen it all. Weedy roads, cracks in 'em pavements, trash in 'em streets.' replied the old man once again with disarming honesty.

'Well, to be honest I wasn't very impressed with this place either...' admitted Miles encouraged by the aforesaid.

'Oh well, te hell with it.' said Tompkins again and the changed the topic of conversation: 'Tell me lad. Ye said ye'd been travelling 'round Zone 2. What've ye seen?' he asked.

'I've been in the commune and the communist sector so far and seen how things are there. They both seem to enjoy better material welfare than people here. The commune amazed me by how they made their simple society work, something I would have never thought possible.' said Miles pensively.

"Em communards stick to'ether they do. Shifty fellas if ye ask me.' said Tompkins disapprovingly.

Miles realised that despite his old interlocutor's rather misguided conception of the communards he was right in one respect: The communards did have solidarity going for them. Their society might have been simple, organised on the basis of micro-cells of no more than 300, however their solidarity made them strong. In the commune, if a road was presenting problems with potholes, they'd have a meeting, the residents, and people would volunteer to fetch gravel and fill them in what was a temporary, yet rather effective solution. Here, who knows? Miles contemplated all this in silence and finally spoke again:

'Do you know any people from the commune by any chance?' he inquired of his old table-mate.

'Nay, but I've read all aboot it in it electronic noospaper, the Daily Email.' he replied and Miles left it to that. He then changed the subject by asking the old man yet another question:

'Say, if the road here shows a pothole, who is responsible for fixing it?'

'Is the ol' council, ain' it? Well, in theory at least.' Tompkins replied. He then continued disinterestedly: 'In reality nobody ain' responsible fer all this 'ere lot.'. A small pause followed, swiftly broken by Miles going:

'Lot... Ah, road repairs and presumably street cleanliness and everything.'

'Got it in one young lad.' Tompkins confirmed and that marked the start of yet another long pause, during which the food arrived: two dishes of bangers & mash. The strange duo started eating, interrupting every now and then to continue the conversation.

'So, what do you think of the communists then? I can tell you that they boast impressive infrastructure...' Miles said choosing to leave the whole civic liberty issue out of the conversation, however his old table-mate brought it in anyway:

'Don' trust 'em old reddies. Can't even pop open a bleedin' bottle 'o liquor without the whole bleeding police knowin' all aboot it. I'll tell ye what it is, is a big barracks is what it is, that place.' blurted Tompkins.

Once again a gentle smile quivered on Miles' lips at the contemplation of his interlocutor's misguided ideas -no doubt from the Daily Email-, yet again, he realised that he was right about something: the communist sector did have the army look. He realised that there was an unnaturally large number of uniformed people in the streets of the clinically clean 'red' zone. Also, the entire communist zone seemed to move at the beat of the numerous retro-looking 7-segment display digital clocks that were ubiquitously encountered on the clean streets of the various 'red' neighbourhoods. In fact he just realised that after 18:00 – 18:15 on the evening he spent in the 'red' sector, traffic on the streets, both pedestrian and vehicular, suddenly increased, probably indicative of a large number of enterprises changing shift at the same time.

'So I take it you would never move across to the neighbours form the West then.' said Miles.

"em reds? Nay. Never. I'm prood of me liberty young lad, I am!' exclaimed old Tompkins making his feelings of pride very clearly known to Miles.

Miles contemplated the full implications of that statement. On the one hand Tompkins was right. He could travel around, he didn't have to look over his shoulder wondering whether we was followed whenever he was about to do something which though legal, might have been socially unacceptable, he didn't have to adhere to strict schedules and a million rules and regulations like his fellow men from the communist zone no doubt had to. On the other hand, the abject poverty -by British standards- that his borough was living in was anything but empowering. The public libraries, concert halls, museums and other public amenities Miles had fleetingly seen in the communist zone had either badly run-down or conspicuously absent counterparts in what he came to call the 'green' boroughs. So, in terms of personal freedom of action, Tompkins was far better off where he lived, but in terms of potential and real empowerment, perhaps the case was different.

Meh. At the end of the day it all comes down to preference. Some people would gladly give up personal freedoms, a lot of them, just to be part of a society that offered them a high enough standard of material welfare. And come to think of it wasn't that the trade-off we all had to be subject to, regardless of the sort of society we live in? After all, in terms of direct personal freedom of action, arguably a hermit is the freest man of all. Nobody there to limit him in any way. But add even a single other person into the mix and suddenly rules come up. Suddenly you have to create rules for sharing, distributing labour and duties. In return you get the benefit of having someone to do the laundry while you are out picking nuts, someone to keep the fire going while you gather firewood, someone to sew newer or better clothes while you fetch freshwater. Naturally, it isn't always the case that societies with many rules generate more benefits in return. The quality of life in each and every society will intimately be linked with not just the quantity, but also the nature of the rules that are in play. And these rules will in turn determine the natural equilibrium that society will reach, in other words the very nature of the society that will emerge from them. And that's where unfortunately it gets a bit too complicated.

Miles was contemplating the trade-off between simple liberty of action and the more profound meanings that could be attributed to the notion and their balance in various societies while munching on his fatty sausage. Tompkins was equally silent.

'Say Tompkins.' exclaimed Miles after attacking a spoonful of mashed potatoes.

'Wot is it young lad?' replied Tompkins.

'You said you are retired. Do you get a pension from... I don't know. Some sort of pension fund you operate here?' he inquired and then hastily added: 'If you don't find the question excessively personal.'

'It's all right young lad. I get a bleeding hundred quid from t'at ol' council pension fund. Barely 'nough te buy me vegetables for the month.' he complained.

'That's terrible! How do you survive?' exclaimed Miles with surprise and concern.

'Got kids an't I? Son's a police officer in it Zone 1. Daughter's a secretary in Zone 1 too.' explained Tompkins with a smile on his face. Evidently the thought of his children gave him a warm feeling inside.

It was very clear to Miles that old Tompkins had loving children who paid his bills and that was a nice thought in those dark times.

'Just to clarify, we are talking state pension here. Who pays for that?' asked Miles.

'Ol' council tax, ain't it?' replied old Tompkins, then continued finally perceiving the insatiable curiosity of his table-mate: 'Listen up sonny. Ye're new to this 'ere boro'. Let me explain just how things work 'ere.' Tompkins said. He then went on to explain the essence of government in Bexley and the other 'green' zones. For the benefit of our readers we render the rest of the discussion with funny old Tompkins in 'corrected' and 'refined' English. Thus, so went old Tompkins' lecture:

'You see, in this borough we we have reverted to the old system of government, reviving the old borough city council. We vote in elections every 4 years and the party that wins those elections takes control of the council. The parties here are the same as in the central government, up in your world. However, ever since local governments were privatised and faded into insignificance, the connection between our parties and the central parties also waned and eventually dissolved. Be that as it may, people who do well in government here still hope that one day they will be noticed by the main parties and taken in. A life in the benches of parliament -or rather the hotel seats, heh heh-.' Tompkins sniggered, then resumed: 'They figure the only way to do it is by making money, so they tax us and then give us nothing in return. We pay tax in and all they provide back is a measly state pension, a worthless road service, dysfunctional state education, carried out in what looks more like prisons than schools, a healthcare system tottering on the verge of collapse and a variety of other services we get in name, but not in deed.'

Miles was listening closely to all this, making superhuman efforts to decipher the old fellow's English. Thankfully Tompkins had taken a pause after his long, but evidently fully justified rant-storm. Miles had just digested all the incoming information when old Tompkins started again:

'You see, the thing is that the communards have their solidarity going for them, the communists have their steel, military discipline going for them. Here, we sank into the apathy, lower voter turnout and general disengagement from politics that brought about the collapse of state power in the first place and its placement in the hands of the private sector.' Another pause ensued.

Miles was contemplating the gravity of the statements just made. Indeed. All this explained why everything in the green zone was abandoned and left to its fate. Apathy and a general simmer of helpless ranting seemed to sweep across the green boroughs, if Tompkins was a representative enough sample -which he was-. Put it simply, if there was a pothole in the commune, volunteers would go and fix it, in the communist zone a specialised brigade of road workers would be scheduled to do it at a certain time with a certain amount of resources and then do it, but in the unkempt boroughs of the green zone, everybody would stay home and rant about how the council isn't fixing it. And after all why shouldn't they? It was a democracy, every man for himself. If someone wanted to waste his time foolishly doing something in the service of others, in effect be used, they were welcome to it, but such idiots never survived for too long. This seemed to be the prevalent mindset of the populace in this part of London. A micrography of Zone 1, equally mean and selfish, but far less successful in terms of wealth. To be fair there was some form of state education, funded from the council tax, and state healthcare operating, however its quality would elicit tears of sympathy and pity even from continental Europe, as evidenced by the ramshackle buildings he'd witnessed bearing the red cross or the illuminated white letters that were aligned to form the word 'school'.

For the inhabitants of the boroughs that chose to revive the old system, the new and improved councils handled the usual local affairs they were traditionally associated with, as well as duties imposed upon them by the pressing needs created as a result of the central government washing its hands clean off them and saying to the people of the United Kingdom: 'it's your problem, not mine'. The people felt betrayed by the central government as Tompkins continued repeating over and over again, yet the councils that were attempting to cover for it were also part of 'them', part of 'the enemy', part of that remote and distant class of people that make their fortunes in politics. The whole society anguished under the tensions created by powerless protest. 'No matter who you vote for, it's all the same ****.' as the saying was amongst the locals. Councils were elected for 4 unaccountable years and for 3,5 years of that period they loathed the people they were meant to serve, as fervently and totally as the people loathed the council. Then, for the last 6 months, campaigning was on and suddenly every candidate was everybody's best pal. Councils realised very quickly that they had pretty much free hand to set the rules in their little kingdoms and demand arbitrary amounts of taxes. Then they could simply carry out the one task every council was always able to execute with impeccable efficiency: collect money, let the quality of public services slide even more and blame it all on inflation. And taxes were not the only points of friction. Speed limits on the roads of these boroughs had been steadily declining in magnitude, ostensibly in response to a health & safety drive, but in reality so that the police could collect more fines (god help you if you don't own a car with a navigator mainframe to do the driving for you). Roads were left weedy and unkempt routinely, but traffic wardens were always plentiful to look out for people who parked in areas that were designated illegal for parking for no conceivable reason. Naturally, all these tasks laid upon the shoulders of an already battered police force, struggling for money, did little good to the image of the once respected law enforcement that was Britain's pride.

On the other hand trade unions, or rather the faded ghosts that are what was left of those unions were the recipients of equal amount of scorn and resentment. Their weak and feeble efforts to create resistance to the councils were first of all centred mostly around their members rather than society at large, which meant they often claimed boons that even the most willing and generous council would find impossible to grant. Secondly, every time they attempted to organise resistance to something or protest, even for the most legitimate of reasons (for example teachers demanding that less money is spent in the set-up of speed-cameras, already present in most roads, and more on education), people not directly associated with the industrial action would simply find it a nuisance and impart scorn upon the activists. 'Why should I not be able to use the A2 if some pathetic teachers insist that more money is spent on education?' Was the prevalent mentality.

Thus, in this environment of social self-sabotage and mutual hatred, the green boroughs of Zone 2 London could only elevate their living standards to their market value: i.e. live off the scraps that fell off from Zone 1 and drop their living standards until some of the economic activity going on in their areas was cheap enough to compete with tough rivals from China, India and other cheap-labour providers. Upon reflection on this torrent of thoughts Miles realised that Zone 1 was simply the partner in a gruesome game of poker that had been dealt the best hand, and Zone 2 was one that had been dealt an awful one, and that Zone 1 for so long sat comfortably behind a wall of bricks and mortar, but also behind a wall of ignorance and decided to do nothing about it. How could such injustice be allowed? Why did he not so much as contemplate the goings-on beyond his tiny, super-luxurious bubble-world before? He thus realised in the flesh that injustice stung really badly for the recipient, even though it must have felt pretty good for its dealer. A wave of bitterness overcame him. Never before did he care so much about the plight and lives of the people that were cast out of Zone 1, and now that he was joining their ranks he knew that those left behind, in the comfort of London's core would do the same to him. Finally, as he finished his meal, he asked Tompkins a simple question:

'Say Tompkins, are you happy here?'

"appy young lad? Aye. I 'ave me wife, bless 'er doin' some shoppin' right about now I'd expect, two wonderful kids, a place to put me old 'ead on when I go to sleep and 'nough food and medicines to live. Cheers.' said Tompkins with a smile under his small, white moustache and downed the pint of ale that had arrived with the food. He then leant back in his worn-out sofa, placed his hands on his belly and his entire outlook irradiated satisfaction with the meal he'd just consumed. Miles smiled benevolently and started thinking again. That man, sitting across him was a citizen of what Miles had determined to be one of the most desolate boroughs of Zone 2, yet there he stood, perfectly happy. Martha was filled with concerns and worries far more than Tompkins. Was it because Tompkins was genuinely happier? Or was it because Martha was living in better living standards that allowed her the luxury of worry? It was like a circle, wasn't it? The larger the radius, the greater the area, but also the greater the perimeter. If we replace in this analogy the circle's area with our level of development, both material and spiritual, and the perimeter with worry, the point of it all becomes clear. Once the brain snatches the luxury of engaging in fervent activity, you can't stop it. It is in the human nature after all: plenty creates anxiety about how to retain this plenty, as well as yearning for more.

This applies to material wealth, but also to spiritual wealth. A wise man will seek more and more knowledge just as a wealthy person will yearn for more money and a powerful ruler more power. However, because the pursuit of wisdom and knowledge is far less likely to harm people and usually leads the people who follow its path to be more understanding and diplomatic, rather than narrow-minded and violent, an aura of sanctity and purity has been bestowed upon it. In complete opposite the sweet, sweet pursuits of wealth and power have been many times vilified, perhaps for good reason. For that reason alone, he who has attained vast wealth is more often than not, a greedy tycoon, he who has attained vast power is similarly a bloody tyrant and he who has attained vast wisdom is a revered sage.

At that point Miles consulted his amusing holographic watch that projected a 3D image indicating it was nearly 14:00 and realised that it would be better if he found some accommodation sooner rather than later. What better solution that to ask Tompkins if he knew of any decent hotel he could retreat in for the night. Thus, he spoke:

'Say Tompkins.'

'Yes lad?'

'Know you of any decent and clean hotels one may retire to for the night?' inquired Miles more gracefully than he thought possible.

'Sure I know lad. But it's far. All the 'otels round this 'ere area are ****.' explained Tompkins colourfully.

'Where is that? What's the name of the place?' inquired Miles.

'Is an old 'otel called Upminster towers. Is in Upminster t'at is. Grand 'otel. No idea how they survive. None o' their customers have the money to afford it, ye see?' said Tompkins with a non-descript expression that could either be disapproval or pity.

'Thank you old Tompkins. I have truly enjoyed your company today a lot. But I guess I need to get going if I am to reach the hotel before sundown.' Miles excused himself.

'Right ye are son. It'll take you ages to get 'ere by bus. Shoddy buses we have 'ere son. Even if you 'ave a car, can't drive too fast in these 'ere roads. Still take you a bleedin' long time to get t'ere. Good luck son, enjoy yer journey.' said Tompkins with a big smile and waved his hand in indication of good-bye to Miles who returned the gesture.

Miles made his way out of the pub, then pressed the button on his portable, remote beacon that summoned Hilda and went outside to wait for her. He stood at the side of the pavement waiting while a chilly winter afternoon wind prompted him to start shivering and curse his lack of providence for having left his thick coat in the car. His agony was not to last long, however, as Miles' car soon appeared, slowly making its way towards him. Miles, noticing the car approaching walked briskly towards it, thus shortening the time that elapsed between optical and physical contact between the car and its lord and master. Wasting no time with pointless moves Miles darted straight inside his comfortably air-conditioned car and made his wish of going to the Upminster Towers hotel known to Hilda. She calculated the route and set off. Few minutes into the journey Miles realised something and asked Hilda with great curiosity:

'Listen, Hilda. I've just realised something funny.'

'What would that be, sir?'

'I remember you telling me you have no maps available for Zone 2. How come you know where to find Upminster towers?'

'Upminster towers is a 5-star hotel that offers a small selection of very luxurious rooms. As such, it is also included in my tourist information guides along with sat-nav latitude and longitude data. I can navigate based on such data.' said Hilda simply.

'Interesting.' said Miles more to himself and less to Hilda and the journey continued in silence. How come in all this misery such luxurious hotel, what's more connected to the sat-nav system, makes its appearance? In Africa you can find luxurious hotels in places where one would think no sane tourist would ever go, however business still flourishes. Despite its troubles the 2nd zone was still a large market and Miles was guessing that important, wealthy people still had reasons to visit Zone 2 in sufficient numbers as to warrant the operation of a top-notch hotel in the region. At any rate, Miles was going there so he would see for himself what that place was like. For the time being he was enjoying the ride. Outside his window, the same sort of sceneries that have been already described only too often. Miles himself had seen such scenes way too often, so he slowly dozed off in the slow-moving car.

About an hour had passed and Miles woke up when one of those bumps that Hilda just couldn't avoid shook Miles and forced him back into reality. As it quickly became apparent the car was crossing through a novel sight for Miles, an industrial zone. Or to be more precise the car was crossing an old and battered bridge over the river Thames, at the other side of which large structures with tall smoke-stacks could be seen. Miles enjoyed the view of London's river and then started consuming with his eyes the factory buildings.

They were all abandoned. Enormous factories that had done business in manufacturing, mostly of military equipment -as was well known- on the soil of the once burgeoning Averley industrial zone, now stood as empty husks with broken windows, their business long since moved to China and other places where labour came at a lower cost. As the car finally crossed the bridge and entered the former industrial zone, Miles realised the size of the edifices and saw all the broken windows that helped create a sullen atmosphere around the empty buildings. Suddenly, being amongst terribly maintained roads, dark and ramshackle buildings and empty pavements gave him the chills again so once again he sunk into his car. Every now and then he could see, from his sheltered position, people coming in and out of the empty shells of what had once been large factories. All those people were dressed in rags and paid very little attention to him as they went about their business. But why were they walking in and out of the factories? Despite improvements in recycling technology that meant that almost 99% of all waste in the industry could be recycled given enough energy, a small, but conspicuous trail of (harmless) white smoke was always present over each smoke-stack to indicate that a factory was alive. Miles could see no such smoke anywhere, which begged the question of what all these people were doing in the factory buildings.

With this issue in mind Miles kept observing from his fortified position; on his knees with just 4 fingers from each hand and everything on his head above the eye-line visible form the outside of the car. The car went on and on, tackling the usual poor quality roads in that zone and Miles saw factory after factory sweeping past his eyes. The large industrial doors that many of these buildings featured were a bit of an amazement for Miles. He had never seen gates of such size. Most of them were simply heavy, steel gates that lay there bent by some force, probably the labour of many men with rudimentary tools, so as to create an opening large enough for maybe a couple of normal-sized people to go through side-by-side. But then he spotted one where the industrial doors were different. Not heavy steel ones, but a couple of long strips of thick rubber, running in parallel from the top of the massive frames all the way to the dirty floor, and overlapping both with the side walls and with each other so that they don't leave an open gap when left hanging undisturbed. Miles was coming to terms with this sort of strange gate as the car was approaching, making the details of the rubber strips more clear, when he saw a man pushing one of the strips aside. The entire strip of rubber opened outwards, making it clear that the rubber strips were actually hanging from metal rods (clearly visible from the inside only) that were hinged on the door-frame. The purpose for such 'flexible' door mechanism was unknown to Miles, and very likely to the man who exited from the factory too. Miles followed his actions as the car slowly advanced. The man wasn't simply exiting, he was holding the door open as if in anticipation of someone's arrival or departure, and sure enough shortly after the man opened the door more of less fully, a woman with a very old pram exited the factory, probably to take her little toddler out for a walk in the sunny, but chilly afternoon. The woman turned right and was on her way walking the toddler and the man was preoccupied with closing the large rubber door when Miles' car passed right in front of the still open door.

    For the brief second that Miles caught a glimpse of what was inside the factory the image swept before his eyes and shocked him. He couldn't be certain his eyes weren't deceiving him, but it looked like the interior of the old factory was a vast industrial hall with large metal girders supporting the ceiling and rows upon rows upon rows of bunk-beds, neatly arranged at even intervals with an old metal school-style cabinet corresponding to each single bed. What looked like hundreds of people were either lying in bed, or moving about their business, mostly women and children. It was a scene that made a profound impression on Miles. Did those people live there? Hundreds of people sleeping and storing all their belongings into a single, massive room. Miles jumped from his position and stuck his nose and palms on the windows of the car trying to see more, but the door was already merely ajar, nearly completely shut and nothing of the interior could be discerned any more. Miles looked carefully at the entire factory building trying to commit it to his memory with the intent of inquiring as to its nature and function at the hotel reception, when he spotted a characteristic that was to greatly aid his attempts to describe the structure to the people at the hotel reception: high up, on the factory's front side, large, white letters that might have once been illuminated, read: 'Averley automobile parts factory.'. Cementing that into his mind he preoccupied himself with studying his surroundings further.

    The rest of the journey to Upminster was more or less uneventful and slow as ever. Hilda's competent navigation meant the despite the quality of the road, the car made its way out of the Averley industrial zone with relatively few bumps disturbing Miles' delicate balance, as he was precariously attempting to prevent himself from falling back from his fortified position. Thankfully, the time came when the industrial zone was left behind and the surrounding scenery was replaced with much more agreeable scenes. Parks, shops, endless rows of Victorian housing and the occasional tower-block, all so familiar to Miles already, once again filled his entire field of view. However, something was different here. All of a sudden, the roads seemed less shabby, the trees somewhat cared for, the people slightly better-looking. In fact, some of the streets he saw could easily have been in the Commune, although probably not in the communist zone. From behind the rows of Victorian housing some tall buildings were showing their outline, roughly 10-12 floors high (Miles thought) and presumably one of those was the hotel where he was about to spend his evening. Curious as to the causes of such sudden change in scenery, Miles was all the most determined to ask about the characteristics of the borough he was traversing, particularly details pertaining to the way society was organised as well as the differences between it and its neighbouring boroughs. Of course, he didn't forget the large old factory, back in Averley; he was sure to ask about that too...

Not 10' had passed, and the car stopped in front of a most peculiar building. It was rather large in area and built in an imitation of the celebrated Tudor style, 6 floors of large scenic window arrays with the traditional protective metal grids, all capped by a complicated array of slanted roofs. The ground floor walls were lined with bricks on the outside, whilst higher up the walls were a delightful clean, creamy colour that blended very elegantly with the tar-black wooden poles of what in a genuine Tudor house would be the skeleton of the building. In fact that building was reminding Miles of a genuinely old Tudor-style house on Carnaby street in Zone 1. As he was continuing the examination of the scenic building, Miles finally saw an old-style wooden sign hanging from a couple of delicate chains. It simply read: "Upminster Towers Hotel" and right underneath the name 5 golden stars were glowing a very discrete, dim yellow. Miles smiled; 'not exactly towers, but nice', he thought. He then proceeded to instruct Hilda to park the car in the hotel's garage and proceeded towards the reception desk.

He crossed the threshold of the hotel under the watchful eye of a security guard and the polite simile of the usher, then stood for a minute to admire the homely look of the interior of the hotel. The interior walls were all lined with wood, arranged in large rectangular panels that were delimited by the large wooden beams of what ostensibly was the interior skeleton of the building. Every single panel had a modern addition to it though, which clearly indicated that the building was not quite as old as its architecture would have customers believe: a thin line of pleasant, pale fiery orange strip of OLEDs lining the top of the panel, providing a gentle, uniform light in the hallway that led to the reception area, farther inside the building. The portraits of Henry the 8th, Queen Elizabeth the 1st and other illustrious members of house Tudor adorned the hallways at regular intervals, interposed by various potted plants the size of a child.

Miles expected nothing less of such hotel, and indeed nothing short of such image of Tudorian grandeur was provided. Miles walked with gratification through the homely, yet grand corridor and made his way to the reception area where a very beautiful lady had intercepted him and smiled placidly in anticipation of his arrival. Funny thing this, in good hotels the reception desk was always manned by humans, not androids or disembodied heads of people. Customers being human beings themselves found it more natural.

Be that as it may, Miles approached the reception desk where he was greeted by the attractive young lady:

'Good evening sir.' she said with a formal and officious tone, as well as a smile that seemed to have been honed over the years as to achieve absolutely optimal attractiveness. Somehow, that supernaturally perfect smile put Miles off.

'Good evening. I was wondering whether you have a room for me to spend just a night. I have no reservation, however, so I understand if that would be slightly difficult. I simply didn't anticipate I would be spending my night in this here establishment.' Miles answered excusing himself.

'Certainly sir. I shall attempt to assign a room for you, for one night. Are there any special requests you may have of the room?' the lady replied. Miles noticed she was wearing a name-badge with the inscription: 'Ophelia O'Brien'.

'Well, I'd be more than happy if it was en-suite. I need nothing more for such short stay.' he replied, attempting to think what else he might wish to request of the room.

'All our rooms are en-suite, sir, so that should be no problem at all.' Ophelia replied with her unnatural smile.

'I also have a car...' Miles added.

'If it has a navigator computer, sir, please swipe your implant by this here machine and the rest will all be taken care of.' Ophelia said indicating with the palm of her hand -most courteously- towards an all-familiar implant scanner. Miles followed her advice and seconds later Hilda was past the barrier and handling the parking manoeuvre of the car in the basement of the building. Miles was oblivious to all these happenings although he trusted they were in progress. Ophelia broke the silence again:

'It would seem we have a large multitude of rooms available, sir. What floor would you like to be on? Or shall I assign you a random room? They are all exactly identical and so are their nightly rates.' she explained.

Miles made his intention of being somewhere as high as possible known, so he was allocated room 606 and promptly left towards it after dispensing with the ceremonial goodbyes. He needed no key. The implant was going to be his key. After all, every room had an implant reader for that specific purpose. Miles, thus, went straight to the elevator and pressed the top button, leading to the 6th floor. After a handful of seconds of enjoying the gentle classical music at the speakers of the elevator (a part from Beethoven's 7th symphony at that moment) the elevator doors slid open and Miles stepped on to the carpeted floor of the 6th floor heading for his room. He navigated around the corridors of the building until he found his room and just as he was about to open the door he realised that he had forgotten to ask about Upminster at the reception. Face-palming himself he returned to the down-bound elevator, but this time made his way to the reception area. Ophelia greeted him with her unsettling, perfect smile and bade him a very formal good evening. He replied:

'And good evening again. I was just wondering... I have some questions actually.'

'Certainly, sir. What about?' she said, and then without a pause added: 'If it is tourist information you seek, the terminal in your room might help. We offer a tourist information service at no extra charge. Moreover, if you so wish, you may speak to a human employee whilst using the service at no extra charge.'

Miles simply uttered: 'Good; and so I shall, thank you.' and after Ophelia's polite reply he left for his room again. After listening to a few more seconds of Beethoven he eventually found his way to room 606 and entered.

The room was rather similar to what he'd seen at the Kalinin hotel. Large, clean, well laid-out room with a comfortable bed and a large terminal whose screen dubbed as a mirror when not in use. The only difference was that here a lot of the items, furniture and equipment were of renowned brands and certainly very, very expensive. It struck Miles as very odd that such place in Zone 2 would operate this kind of extremely high-end hotel. Yet another question to ask, he thought and idly switched the terminal on. A familiar interface menu with a disembodied head of a French waiter appeared on his screen and Miles went straight to the 'tourist information' option, choosing to speak to a human, and also choosing bidirectional image transfer. A dignified gentleman in an old-fashioned suit with a white bow-tie appeared on his screen, greeted with the utmost politeness and introduced himself as Mr. Doyle Parker, the tourist concierge of the Upminster Towers hotel. Miles greeted in reply and then went straight to business:

'I actually arrived here by car, and I saw a number of interesting scenes on my way here. Perhaps you could clarify a few things for me, if that's all right with you?' he said equally politely.

'Certainly sir, anything. I trust you enjoyed our luxury limousines?' replied Mr. Parker.

'Limousines?' inquired Miles slightly puzzled.

'Umm... yes. We offer a luxury limousine service at this hotel, connecting you directly to any point in Zone 1 or any airport in London. Presumably you arrived thus?' inquired Mr. Parker slightly confused.

'No. I didn't know there was such service. I arrived in my own, private vehicle.' clarified Miles.

'Ow... I was about to say that you would be the first customer not to use our limousines' window screens. I apologise for my hasty arrival at such erroneous conclusion.' apologised Mr. Parker.

'Window screen?' inquired Miles.

'Certainly sir.' replied Mr. Parker. 'Our limousines' passenger windows are covered in a thin film of that same nature as ordinary TV screens. Moreover, each limousine's mainframe is provided with special software that allows the passenger to name a place of his liking, real or fictive and based on that location the limousine's window screens create the illusion that the car is travelling in that very vicinity. Here at Upminster towers we host hundreds of businessmen and many ask for tourist information, however you would be the first one to inquire about something you've seen from your car, on your way here.' he clarified.

'First one, eh? So, my interest in the conditions that seem to prevail in this part of London has so far been rather unique.' Miles said, thinking aloud.

'Precisely so, sir.' replied Mr. Parker and went silent in anticipation of receiving a question. Indeed such question did make its appearance.

'I have to say, that travelling through the 2nd Zone of London I get the impression that this is one of the cleanest, more developed and generally well-off parts of it, and I was wondering why that might be.' he said.

'A good question indeed, sir.' said Mr. Parker, suddenly refreshed. 'Well, the mayor of this borough is a man of business. He quickly realised that in a globalised world, where capital can more or less move freely but people can't, the important thing is that a country occupies a good spot in the global economy. Some people farm, others mine, others manufacture and the luckiest have money and lend it to everybody else demanding great returns for that. Zone 1 does that, so it's found its way to the top of the global economic pyramid. Here, we instituted a similar system to Zone 1, but focused on something different. We successfully strove to become the heart of the business activity in all of Zone 2 that has decided to continue the old system of government. As such, public services here have been privatised, with the exception of some that support the function of our business centre. You must have seen the 10-floor buildings near the hotel. These are offices where the companies that do business in our parts of Zone 2 operate from. Energy providers, supermarket chains, public works companies all have their regional Zone 2 headquarters here. Thus we have floated up in the globalised economy and took up a comfortable place here.' concluded Mr. Parker.

'So in effect, the way you've achieved this, is that you privatised everything except those services that serve the companies around here, which are now financed by tax from the population presumably; a form of subsidising corporations.' astutely observed Miles, who found a lot of familiar phrases in Mr. Parker's little speech. Phrases often said to him before by James, phrases about the globalised economy where nations are now irrelevant. People and regions must attempt to float up and occupy the highest echelons of the world economy, i.e. banking and insurance...

'Astutely observed, sir.' Said Mr. Parker positively delighted to have such brilliant interlocutor. 'We have done exactly that. Moreover, corporate tax here is zero.' he added.

'I guessed so much.' muttered Miles and then asked another question: 'Don't you find this rather sad?'

Mr. Parker looked at him with slight disbelief, hesitated for a while and finally uttered just:

'Sir?'

'You heard well, Mr. Doyle.' said Miles reassuringly.

'I... well... Forgive me Mr. Fitzroy. I have simply never met a man from Zone 1 who is quite like you before.' apologised Mr. Parker.

'How do you know I'm from Zone 1?' asked Miles genuinely surprised, but then he realised that Mr. Parker was looking at him with the sort of countenance that unmistakeably indicated its bearer thought the matter obvious and thus fell silent. Mr. Parker eventually answered:

'You see, Mr Fitzroy...' he started.

'Just call me Miles.' interjected Miles.

'A... well... Thank you. You see Mr. Miles, I've always realised that what we are trying to do here in the Upmnister borough, is a pathetic attempt to mimic Zone 1. In fact, it has succeeded to some point. We even got a mini Zone-3 all around us. You might have seen it on the way here...' Miles remembered the industrial zone in Averley and shivered, but Mr. Parker didn't seem to notice and continued: 'Yet at the same time I realise that I owe my own and my family's relative well-being to this exactly sort of policies. Something inside me tells me we're inherently doing the wrong thing, yet my stomach is never empty, my children never lack clothing...'.

It took Miles quite some pondering before he could address Mr. Doyle again:

'True...' he simply uttered, not quite sure what to say next. He could obviously not start criticising the system the mayor of Upminster was employing to keep his borough afloat. The man, despite his motives, had managed to bring relative prosperity to his area, Mr. Doyle's family seemed to enjoy a fairly decent living standard -well, he was happy with it at least- and Miles himself came from 'the mother' of the system after all. He could hardly lecture the people of Upminster on the invalidity of their points of view when he came from where it was championed more vehemently than anywhere. As such, he opted for changing the subject instead:

'Say, Mr. Doyle.' he started.

'Yes, sir.' replied Mr. Doyle, suddenly formal again, as if woken up from some reverie.

'Have you by any chance heard of some place called the "Averley Automobile Factory" by any chance?' Miles asked gently.

'The Averley Automoblie parts factory?' corrected Mr. Doyle.

'Oh yes. That one.' replied Miles suddenly realising that he indeed forgot a word.

'Well, sir, what can I say about it...' said Mr. Doyle pensively, trying to recollect any pieces of information relating to that particular place that might be of interest to his guest. 'Oh yes, it has been recently occupied by the international red cross organisation for a start.'

'Occupied?' said Miles, curious as to why his tourist guide would use such term.

'Yes. Averley industrial zone has been abandoned years ago. In fact decades. You will find nothing there, no human life, I believe. I don't know what the red cross might be using the old car parts factory for, probably a medical supply deposit I suppose...' said Mr. Doyle, not quite certain.

'International Red Cross.' repeated Miles slowly, stressing each word quite heavily.

'The very same, sir.' added Mr. Doyle.

'As you might be gathering already, I passed by that old factory...' started Miles ending the sentence and then pausing.

'And presumably it made an impression on you, sir.' chimed in Mr. Doyle.

'Well observed.' confirmed Miles. 'But it wasn't the size of the building, or its shape that imprinted themselves into my memory.'

'Oh?' exclaimed Mr. Doyle.

'What would you say if I told you that Averley is not as abandoned as it looks? That people live there?' said Miles.

'Oh?' replied Mr. Doyle with more surprise than before.

'What would you say if I told you that the red cross uses the old factory to house what seems like hundreds maybe even a whole thousand people in refugee camp conditions?'

'Ooh?' exclaimed Mr. Doyle with even more surprise.

'What if I said that my Zone 1 and your Upminster have both had it very wrong for very long? That we created societies that need a ring of misery around them to function?' said Miles dramatically.

'But... but, how? Why don't the people of Averley go seek employment in Zone 1 as so many Zone 2 inhabitants do? Even if we do underpay our staff in the name of outsourcing, they can always cross the wall and seek better employment in Zone 1, no?' said Mr. Doyle in shock, leaving all formality aside. Miles had an answer that came from the news, a few years ago.

'Actually I think I know the answer to this...' Miles started. Mr. Doyle was not even breathing, in a mix of exasperation and outrage. Miles continued offering an explanation. 'I heard, long ago in the news that Upminster and Zone 1 businesses just across the wall came to an agreement. Have you ever travelled to Zone 1 Mr. Doyle?'

'Why, no. Never.' Mr. Doyle admitted.

'Truth is that as a result of that agreement, back in 2046, you would not be able to unless you travelled quite far. Far enough, in fact for it to be impractical for people living in Upminster and the neighbouring regions to commute there daily. As such, the effective commute distance between these neighbourhoods of Upminster and Zone 1 is comparable to what we see in Zone 3. Which means...' Miles said, leaving his sentence unfinished, for his interlocutor to complete at his own leisure. Mr. Doyle caught the hint and did continue the semi-finished sentence:

'...that effectively everything in those zones affected by the Zone 1 wall restrictions has turned into Zone 3, except for the very centre, which has for some reason turned into a mini -Zone 1.' Mr. Doyle aptly completed.

'Precisely. This, in combination with Upminster's pro-business policies and effective subsidies to the companies that operate in Zone 2 pulled the region out of the pit the other boroughs have fallen into, and as a result it is now hovering at a higher level of economic development, mirroring the practices of Zone 1 at a lower level.' concluded Miles.

'I can't believe it.' said Mr. Doyle at a loss for words.

'The micro-community of office workers, hotel workers and other people that are lucky and good enough to work for these top-tier companies indeed created such mini-Zone 1. Once again, the people necessary for the function of the core have to scrape off a living from whatever crumbs fall from above. I know, I come from Zone 1 and I only recently realised what my well-being was built upon.' said Miles genuinely self-critically.

Mr. Doyle said nothing. He evinced pain and guilt. He was a tourist guide, yet had never looked beyond the comfort of his own little successful islet. His only experiences of life beyond came from the TV and the internet and were as such merely vicarious experiences. At the realisation of the fact that the success he, as well as his fellow citizens, were so proud of was built on an unholy agreement he felt uneasy. At least people in this Zone were not dehumanised, thought Miles. They had a sense of dignity and feelings of understanding towards fellow human beings, they could not simply observe idly as they made gains out of other peoples' pain, like in Zone 1. Zone 1 did create that sort of characters. It was after all social Darwinism.

With all these thoughts swirling in Miles' head and similar, equally tumultuous meditations occupying Mr. Doyle's intellectual equipment it was no wonder that a protracted silence ensued. Miles was the first one to realise this and figured out that it might be politer to end the conversation there and leave Mr. Doyle to his own thoughts.

'If you wish to retire now Mr. Doyle, please don't hesitate to do so. I understand if you need some time alone.' said Miles respectfully. In response, Mr. Doyle nodded his head slightly in sign of agreement, his gaze directed at nothing in particular, his countenance indicating his need to contemplate a matter of urgency. Perhaps his reaction seemed rather extreme, but on the other hand Miles understood that it would be rather difficult to realise all of a sudden that such poverty and misery existed so close to one's home and that one could have been so blind of it for so long. Eventually, the grim reality would become knowledge and experience and incorporate itself into everyday life, accepted as a full-fledged part of it. Thus, Mr Doyle Parker departed and the connection was closed. Miles headed downstairs to enjoy a simple, but filling dinner and shortly after its completion he carried out his usual evening ablutions and went to bed.

CHAPTER 7: OATH OF FEALTY.

The morning following his stay at the Upminster Towers luxury hotel Miles woke up, enjoyed a delicious breakfast, checked out of his room and entered his car, that was waiting just outside the red-carpeted front door for him at his request. It was a cloudy day, typical for February and Miles had no intention of spending more time in the insufferable company of the morning chill. He entered his car, that had been conveniently fully recharged during the night, with brisk movements, sat on one of the comfortable seats, clapped his hands together, finishing the gesture by rubbing his palms to one another -a clear indication of eagerness both for the impending journey and to get his frozen fingers warm-, and addressed Hilda. Their next destination was determined to be Epping. Apparently there was a border crossing there that led into the zone where the royalists had gathered and created a strange feudal system. The so-called 'royal zone' was by no means politically consistent, or indeed stable. It was merely a fragile confederation of various duchies and counties, ridden by intrigue and kept together only through fear of their western neighbours: a fearsome dictatorship. That was Miles' intelligence on the royal zone and he was keen to see for himself how much of it was valid.

Thankfully, Hilda navigated to Epping fairly swiftly, using one of the old motorways. Old, rusted signs indicated that it was once called the M25 and historical archives show that it once encircled all that was then called London. Now it was just another old road left in Zone 2. In any case, traffic along it did not seem to be particularly brisk, and its rather more solid construction meant it was not as badly ridden with potholes as its less significant counterparts that didn't bear the capital letter 'M' before their names. As a result the journey to Epping lasted surprisingly little although the scenery of endless rows of modern, as well as modest dwellings of 4-5 floors height somehow managed to render even this short journey impossibly boring. In the end Miles was most gratified to hear from Hilda that they were approaching the Epping border post. In response to the announcement he beamed ahead and sure enough, he saw a familiar sight: sacks of sand and barbed wire. However, this time something was different.

The guards that seemed to man the border guard-posts were clad in a rather odd fashion. The two guards wore red uniforms with white belts and grey trousers, but more unusually, also shiny black shoes and the vast black, fur hats that the Royal Guard was equipped with. They carried long, antiquated weapons that the Royal Guard normally would and Miles suspected that they could either only fire blanks or nothing at all; that's how ceremonial they looked. In fact, they might as well have been issued with muskrats, thought Miles merrily. The car finally slowed down and Miles could descend in order to encounter the guards that were greeting him officiously.

'Good morning.' Miles started with a respectful bow.

'And good morning to you too sir, and dare I say so, welcome to the Duchy of Epping & Waltham.' said one of the guards with impeccable politeness, whilst the other one maintained a respectful position of 'attention' and smiled warmly.

'Excuse my clumsiness for I am merely a traveller, and as such unfamiliar with your procedures. Is this the part where I show my identification credentials?' Miles inquired exceedingly politely.

'Absolutely correct, sir.' replied the guard. Miles showed his pass-card from the commune.

'Ow...' said the guard.

'Anything the matter?' inquired Miles.

'You are from the commune, sir?' the guard asked confusedly. He was a faithful royalist, ardent in fact, and the anarchists and communists were not too much to his liking, yet at the same time he knew better than to insult foreigners who might be visiting the zone for perfectly legitimate reasons, particularly if those reasons involved business.

'No actually. I am a guest of honour to one of their elders. A traveller who has had the fortune to fall in the grace of an illustrious philosopher.' replied Miles and then added: 'I'm actually from Zone 1.'

The guards seemed amazed by the discovery and scrambled to a position of 'attention' again, hastening to add that he was most welcome into the Duchy. Miles thanked them and turned towards his car when he was stopped by one of the guards.

'May I inquire just one thing of you, sire?' he said with even more respect than usual.

'Certainly, kind sir.' replied Miles.

'Why don't you use a Zone 1 pass-card as identification instead?' was the inquiry.

'Because in Zone 1 identification is provided by means of scanning an implant.' Miles explained cheerfully, pointing at the location on his skin, underneath which the implant was to be found. A gesture he was very used to doing. He then added: 'In my travels through Zone 2 I have often found that border guards lack the means to check for identification directly from the implant.'

'A... you... are quite right sire.' said that guard. He then thanked Miles very respectfully, bowed with his right hand on his chest and wished him a very pleasant stay in the Duchy. Miles responded by wishing both guards a happy and long life (each) and went back to his car. Hilda was promptly instructed to head towards Enfield, where according to the political map of London, the capital of the royalist confederation was to be found, at the palace of the Archduke of Enfield. Miles was keen to see the infrastructure and inquire of the living standards of the people in this strange zone so the capital region would be of interest to him. Then he planned to go through the Barony of Barnet and finallt stay the night at some inn at small fief of Edgeware. It was a plan, and seemingly a good one. Hilda servilely agreed and started fulfilling her tasks as the car's navigator once again.

The first impression he got of the Duchy of Epping & Waltham was rather mixed. Business didn't seem to be particularly brisk anywhere, the people were dressed simply and conservatively, vehicles seemed to be few, but those that were to be seen seemed to be of superior quality, the roads were in rather good condition, but the pavements were dreadful. As the car started making its way deeper into the Duchy, Miles noticed that side-streets tended to be rather miserable and unkempt, with cracked asphalt as bad as anywhere in the previous zone. Moreover, the drabness of the buildings he could see, seemed to be a function of the distance between their façade and the main road. Strange, he thought. As the car continued he noticed that to a large extent the people's clothing was also a function of their distance from the main road. Generally speaking those who could be seen frequenting the numerous shops by the main street seemed to be simply and conservatively, but rather well-dressed, whilst those who could be seen wandering about farther away looked far, far less presentable. The same with the cleanliness of the roads and everything. With the experience that Miles had gathered from all the travelling he concluded that the system here must be such that the rich get all the perks, but through a government rather than simply through their own forces. Which is why infrastructure was built to the pleasure of the gentry in this society, as opposed to Upminster and Zone 1 where it was built for profit and nothing else. This impression only consolidated itself as the car approached the centre of the Duchy. During this interval of approach, the road Hilda was following got progressively wider, then the pavements alongside it also got wider and better maintained. Next, trees appeared on the pavement, carefully grown for the delight of passers-by and finally fancy lamp-posts and benches took their places on the pavement making the street look rather picturesque. Naturally, during this progression the attires of the people showed similar improvement and the density of vehicles increased, despite still being rather low.

In the end he saw it: the old church at the centre of the Duchy, standing in front of a large square where the local gentry was committing itself to long walks with their pets, enjoying the delightful play of water at the various fountains, particularly the large one at the centre of the square. To the left of the church a small palace stood proud, flying a most peculiar flag that seemed to feature some sort of coat of arms, right next to a Union Jack. On the other side a much more modern edifice of similar size and bearing the exact same flag pair completed a picture of royal serenity. Miles instructed Hilda to drive around the square once before moving on east-south-east towards Enfield. Hilda nodded politely and complied. The car drove around the square giving Miles ample opportunity to examine the church, the modern edifice with the flag pair, the ancient edifice with the similar flag pair and the gentry.

The little tour was of little educational value. The church was simply a modern copy of a rather old church from Zone 1, apparently built for no other reason, but to gratify the gentry with a piece of architecture that was pleasant to the eye and elicited thoughts about medieval history. It bore a simple inscription indicating that it was attributed to St. John and possessed very little else that would interest anyone. As for the modern building, it was apparently the central government building for the Duchy. The inscription 'Duchy of Epping & Waltham central administration' made that much clear. The exterior of the building consisted of a rather large number of elegant glass panels and a lightweight metal skeleton, creating an ensemble that was rather pleasant to the eye. Inside it was all concrete, lined with very long, light-coloured planks of wood, lit at night by rather sumptuous chandeliers modelled on floral themes (and the occasional nondescript fish). There seemed to be little pedestrian traffic within the building and that was pretty much all that can be said about the administration building of the Duchy. Moving on Miles had a look at the older-looking building; another copy from an old building. This one was a copy of Blenheim palace, in Oxfordshire. Miles found it rather pleasant to the eye despite its somewhat too obvious perfection. Too many block edges were suspiciously straight for a century-old building, the columns that supported the roof were too smooth and unadulterated, the statues that adorned various parts of the palace too shiny and untouched by time. A new and shiny inscription in brass indicated that the edifice was the official residence of the Duke of Epping & Waltham. Finally, the local gentry seemed very well-dressed and was clearly rich. Most members were preceded by a dog, cat or other pet (as described before) and followed by a servant who would tend to all their needs and step in whenever the pets (particularly the dogs) were not behaving themselves, more specifically placing 'little mines' for other unfortunate pedestrians to 'step into'. Finally, as the car completed the circle around the central square, Miles gazed upon the 3 buildings, the fountain and the gentry that was blissfully strolling up and down the park, snorted half-disapprovingly and half-amused and quickly turned his attention elsewhere.

 Hilda turned the car more towards the south and followed what looked like the main road linking the Duchy of Epping & Waltham to the Grand Duchy of Enfield. In the beginning, nothing changed in the scenery. Modern, low housing with shops along the main street and a gradual decay as a function of distance from the main street dominated the scenery that was zooming past Miles' eyes. Every now and then the monotony would be interrupted by a little park, perhaps a statue of king Harry, or king Charles the 3rd, or every now and then a little public fountain; certainly nothing to indicate important economic activity. Then, a road sign indicated that he was entering the Grand Duchy of Enfield and slowly the scenery changed in so much as one kind of monotony was replaced by another one, which, as one might guess, revolved around the legacy of queen Victoria. What did not change, however, was the general phenomenon of wealth and well-being being a function of distance not only from the main road, but also from the centre. Miles could feel it when he approached the centre of Enfield. Similar to the approach to the central square in Epping & Waltham the approach to the central square of Enfield was marked by the gradual appearance of well-trimmed trees, elaborate lamp-posts and benches, only everything at a grander scale. It felt like the difference between a small provincial town and a large capital city. Even the buildings were getting taller.

In the end he saw it in front of him: the central square of Enfield. It was all completely modern. There was none of the fake Renaissance style grandeur he'd seen in Epping & Waltham; simply modern design and art at the maximum. Apparently the Archduke of Enfield was a fan of modern architecture and probably had quite an attraction to the work of Escher. Miles remembered a lot of optical illusions that he had seen in school mathematics books, when teachers desperately tried to make their unruly students gain an interest in the science/art of mathematics. He remembered because he could see them in front of him, on a grand scale, 'in bricks and mortar' so to speak. Right in front of him, in fact, was a building where each floor seemed to consist of a row of alternate black and white squares. Generally speaking, 'the floor underneath' was similar, but not perfectly aligned with the squares of 'the floor above' and each floor was separated by the ones above and below it by a thick, silver line. The silver lines were parallel, but did not seem so. In front of the strange illusion building, a positively gratifying garden was the attraction of the local gentry. The garden was rather large, at least 200x200m as it became apparent when the car reached the street that was surrounding it, and possessed a medium-size lake along the shores of which various pets ran playfully.

Reaching the threshold of the garden also meant that Miles' field of view now included the buildings at either side of the garden. Unsurprisingly, perhaps, they were both illusions. The one on the left had a façade made out of dark glass squares. The squares were divided by thick silver lines and at the intersections between these lines stood large, white dots. As for the building on the other side, its façade was made out of dark brown glass, as dark as the polished wood of an oak. This time the glass was separated by thick vertical lines only. The lines themselves, however, were coloured in a strange way. On a white background, thick black lines were positioned at an angle such as to create the illusion that the separator lines between the slabs of glass were bendy. Overall, the impression was rather pleasant. Moreover, the rich trees that were growing rather densely over the entire surface of the park (the lake and the vicinity of its shores notwithstanding) were creating a very serene atmosphere, engrossed in which the gentry of Enfield was most justified in enjoying long walks in the park.

Once again, Miles required of Hilda that she drives the car around the square once before moving on to the next way-point, in Barnet, and so she did. The car turned left and started heading towards the building with the white dots. Along the street 4-5 floor modern buildings adorned the left side of the street, creating a rather nice visual effect, while on the right side of the street trees and other delightful flora maintained balance with the bricks and mortar. Other than that, the approach to the optical illusion buildings was not marked by anything else of significance. The car reached the base of the building with the white dots and turned right, going right past it. Eventually, the entrance of the building made its appearance. Miles noticed and looked around for any inscription, road sign or other clue that would indicate the purpose of that building. He was not disappointed: a large, brass inscription evinced that the building with the white dots was the central administration of the Grand Duchy of Enfield. A large number of people were entering and exiting the building, everybody dressed fairly formally, some dressed in rather sumptuous clothing; a fact that indicated that amongst the crowd that was making use of the main door of the central administration were some individuals that probably ranked fairly high within the bureaucratic structure of the Grand Duchy of Enfield. Miles looked at the car's clock. It was nearly lunch-time. It made sense that there would be significant traffic by all public buildings. More importantly, Miles was longing for something to eat for lunch.

He took his mind off grub for the moment by directing his attention towards his surroundings once more. With the gate of the administration of the Grand Duchy left behind, Miles was now looking at the building ahead and slightly to the right of him, the one with the alternating black and white squares. It was funny how the lines separating each floor seemed slanted although he knew they were perfectly parallel. Either way, he was wondering more what sort of function the building served at that moment. His curiosity was soon to be satisfied as the car turned right again and started running along the side of the strange edifice. As usual, the main gate made its appearance and a very shiny brass plate announced to all that cared to gaze upon it and read, that the building was the official residence of the Archduke, but also that it housed the headquarters of the military of the Grand Duchy.

Miles thought that this made sense that a building of such function should be situated next to the central administration and was beginning to turn his attention to the last optical illusion in the square when he noticed a group of people moving together in a tight formation. At least 6 people were moving towards the entrance of the palace in a very tight group, as if 5 people surrounded the 6th. In front of them another pair was moving at the same pace, both looking around rather tensely, whilst behind the large group a trio was checking that everything behind was in order. All members of this peculiar party were dressed in impeccably clean and ironed military uniforms, with perfectly shiny golden-coloured buttons. Their uniforms were navy blue and every single one of them was wearing at least one full row of decorations on his chest and at least a couple of large medals underneath the row (or rows). Their hats were apparently metallic and featured a small white feather on top, that was lazily hanging downwards towards the back of the wearer's head. Everybody was armed and in white gloves. Amidst this performance, much akin to a parade, Miles noticed that the person in the very centre of this procession looked completely different. Between the ebbs and flows of the guards who were oscillating around the dignified gentleman in the centre, Miles could catch glimpses of the clearly illustrious person; glimpses that were summed together over time to create the full impression of the person for whom the entire procession had been formed. To begin with, the 'man in the centre' was wearing an exceedingly sumptuous green uniform. From bottom to top we could describe him as such: His shoes were black and shinier than any Miles had ever seen. They were like mirrors and if Miles was closer he was certain he would be able to examine those shoes and see the reflection of his face on them clearly enough to shave with its aid. Above those shiny shoes, the trousers extended from the tops of the shoes all the way up until they were hidden by the bottom part of the gentleman's coat (the coat's skirting). Miles could see that the outer side of the trouser-legs of the gentleman were featuring a thick, red line. Naturally, Miles could only see one such line, on the trouser-leg nearer to him, but it was a fair assumption to make that the other trouser-leg would be adorned with the same little textile band. Thus far, nothing out of the ordinary; well not by much anyway. Farther up, things became much more sumptuous. The green coat was held together by a white belt, with a very intricate belt-button made of white metal with a bas-relief possibly depicting some old battle, Miles lacked the necessary ocular resolution to be able to tell at that distance. Above the belt, there was a very wide, blue band running from his left shoulder to his right hip and presumably wrapped around his back to form a loop. On the blue belt there was a couple of very large badges. Both of them consisted of a large frame of golden-coloured metal (might have even been actual gold) in the shape of a star that consisted of many, many little beams of light and a core. One of the cores (the one belonging to the large badge) was made out of a shiny, crimson red material with a very delicate and smooth, white cross at the centre. To Miles it elicited memories of the flag of Switzerland. As for the other badge, the smaller one, its core had a background that consisted of a shiny, dark green material, on top of which a figure that was made out of a variety of precious and semi-precious stones could be seen. The figure was too small to discern clearly, but judging from the position of the body, and combining the incoming information with memories he had from school he made an educated guess that the figure was, in fact, St. George; a most correct guess. On the left side of the man's chest stood 3 rows of medals in the largest variety of colours and shapes, and his shoulders were crowned by a pair of very old-fashioned epaulettes. The green jacket was fully buttoned up, all the way up to the collar, which was lined with golden strips along the edges. On top of that collar stood the man's head. He was a rather old gentleman, with snow-white hair that covered the entire top of his head, or at least as much as could be seen under his hat, as well as a fair part of his face. A combination of large side-burns merging with a bushy moustache and a little goatee beard made him look like the sort of person that would have been around when his colleague, Archduke Ferdinand was still ruling the Austro-Hungarian empire. The man looked rather cheerful but other than that his countenance revealed not much more. Finally, above the gentleman's head stood a very tall, dark green hat, matching the colour of his jacket, with crimson red lining along the edges and a vast white feather. Miles took all of that information in during the interval of time in which he could maintain optical contact with the gentleman. Little did he know that that day he caught a glimpse of Archduke Archibald the 1st himself.

With the Archduke out of his field of view, Miles turned his attention to the last illusory building. Once again the car travelled along the entire façade of the building and unsurprisingly at the main gate a large brass plate was announcing that the building's function was to serve as the headquarters of the confederate government of the 'royal' or 'feudal' zone. Satisfied with this little tour of Enfield's heart, Miles politely asked Hilda to direct the car towards the Barony of Barnet. She complied and the car headed dead West. Once again, the same views zoomed past Miles' eyes, revealing nothing extra about the nature of the royal zone. The only sight of any significance was a bridge crossing over a couple of grassy and abandoned railroad tracks that once belonged to the underground railway system of London. A train lay at a distance on one of the tracks, abandoned, worn-out, a victim of the times. The tubular shape of the carriage reminded Miles why people used to call London underground 'the tube' and that memory created a quiver of a smile on his lips, ridden with melancholy. The front of the train was painted red, the cabin visible behind the large driver's window was empty, the two round headlights, dead. It looked as if the train was lying there, dead, its wheels worn out and unused. Before too long that sad picture vanished as well as the car proceeded westwards towards Barnet.

Miles reached Barnet when the clock showed 13:15, saw the central square, which was to say the least unimpressive and instructed Hilda to move the car south-west towards Edgeware, a borderline fief of the royal zone. He intended to occupy a room at a local Edgeware inn, spend the night there and continue his journey the next day. Said and done, Miles was reaching Edgeware just a bit late for lunch. After a little exploration around the streets in the vicinity of Edgeware's miniature central square Miles' gaze fell upon a very little inn, a single floor above ground level with the inscription 'The knight and the lark' on a small wooden sign just above the door. Miles descended and asked Hilda to wait for him for no more than 5'. If he wasn't returning after the lapse of 5 minutes, she was to park the car somewhere nearby. Hilda nodded in understanding and greeted her master as he descended. Miles returned the greeting and then proceeded to explore the interior of the inn. The inside was homely, even more so than the Upminster Towers hotel. Contrary to the towers, though, this building was genuinely old and Miles could tell. Everything from the wooden beams that supported the structure to the furniture looked like they came from an ancient time and had been painstakingly maintained and renovated to look presentable in the modern era. The carpeted floor was an exception as it looked like a fairly recent job. Behind the wooden reception desk stood an old lady with silver-grey hair, clad in a blue 'sari' dress with white roses painted on it. She beamed and greeted the young customer with a smile; a very natural smile. Miles returned the smile politely and bade the lady good evening. She then spoke:

'And good afternoon to you too young man. My name is Amina, how can I help you?'

'Oh yes, it is not yet evening, is it?' said Miles touching his nose lightly, in admittance of his error to refer to the evening previously. He quickly recovered though and continued: 'I was wondering whether there is a room available for me. I just intend to spend a single night here.'

'Certainly, we have 3 or 4 rooms available, all en-suite all with a terminal.' replied Amina.

'Any of them should do, I'd say.' stated Miles with satisfaction.

'Room 28, upstairs?' Amina asked.

'Certainly, why not?' replied Miles and then inquired: 'How do I pay?'

'Either by card, or by implant I'd think. You are bound to have one or the other, no?' Amina replied naturally.

'You can process implants? I didn't think it would be something particularly popular around here.' said Miles with evident surprise. Amina confirmed his conclusion and explained:

'You are right. Implants are not something most people will have around here. However, those belonging to the nobility, or many of those belonging to the middle class for that matter, do have them, mostly because it is a convenience they can afford.'

'And are there many such people around, in general, as a percentage of the population?' Miles inquired very interested.

'Good question.' said Amina. 'Not really. The nobility measures only a few thousands of people. As for the middle class, they are probably in the few hundreds of thousands. For that matter, our region has a population of about 2,2 million.' she explained using the few statistics she had bothered to memorise. 'So not very many, but on the other hand, they are the ones that tend to be able to afford to travel around. As such as a percentage of our clientèle they constitute a far more important percentage. For that reason we are equipped with the necessary infrastructure to accept payment from implants as well.' she concluded, answering fully to Miles' query. After that he had not much more to ask. Thus, he simply swiped the implant to the reader, bade the old lady good afternoon again and retired to his chamber.

Room 28 was a small, old-fashioned room with plush curtains, a comfortable-looking bed adorned with nice embroidery, a very old, varnished wooden desk, a large mirror and a separate TV screen. A small chandelier with OLED candles (OLEDs made to resemble candles) provided illumination to the room whenever summoned by the press of the suitable switch. The room was fully carpeted in a thick, dark green carpet that made moving on the swivelling chair by the desk a rather difficult task. An old-fashioned oaken wardrobe was there to accommodate any clothes he might wish to hang during his stay and a little wooden table was carefully positioned out of the way so he could place any heavy luggage on top of it. The bathroom was clean and permeated by a distinct, yet discrete smell of roses. Other than that, the sink, the toilet and the shower facilities were all white and presented nothing worthy of particular description. Just the handles of the 2 different faucets of the sink were made of brass and boasted a small disk of smooth, white plastic with the letter 'H' for hot water on one, and 'C' for cold water on the other. Miles turned the cold water faucet and suddenly the white disk started glowing a gentle, dark blue. Experimentation revealed that the hot water faucet's little disk would glow an equally gentle, dark red when switched on. It turns out he was lucky. He somehow ended up in yet another high-end hotel. Very satisfied with his chamber he left for a quick lunch at the inn's restaurant and after gorging himself on Cornish pastries baked by Amina herself he thanked the brilliant old lady and returned to his room where he promptly napped until dinner time.

Time goes on relentlessly -except in special relativistic

circumstances- and eventually it was time for Miles to wake up and attempt to find himself dinner. Having taken a liking to the inn's restaurant, as well as not wishing to walk about too much that evening, Miles decided to dine one floor below his room, in the very restaurant of the inn. He dressed himself appropriately for dinner and made his way downstairs where the serving girl seated him at a table for 2, right next to a large table for 6 where 4 gentlemen were absorbed in a fervent game of cards, apparently Whist. Miles paid little attention to them and preoccupied himself with examining his surroundings instead. The dining-room was small and as homely as the rest of the inn. Wooden poles supported the roof, beautiful, slender lights provided illumination to the entire area and at rare intervals some of the walls were lined with old books that nobody bothered to read. One such bookshelf lay next to Miles, on the right side. He extended his arm and grabbed a book at random. It was a 20th century treatise on electronics using bipolar transistors for analogue filters. The book quickly found its way back to the shelf. Another book was drawn, this one an even older 20th century treatise on the comparison of convective heat transfer between laminar and turbulent flow. Needless to say, this book also found its way back to the shelf where it was exchanged for another one. The 3rd book was entitled: 'From Albion, to England, to Empire to United Kingdom: a journey through time.' and underneath the sub-title indicated that it was the 7th volume dealing with the interval of time between Elizabeth the 1^{st}s reign to the rise and fall of house Stuart with the English revolution. Miles thought that that topic might be something he could take interest in, but certainly not in the relatively short interval of time between then and the moment at which his food was bound to arrive. As such, Miles started skimming through the book, paying attention at the titles of the various chapters and the pictures that adorned its pages, mostly ancient sketches depicting historical events, portraits of royalty and nobility and pictures of old estates where the aforementioned persons of high standing lived, or where some important historical event took place. After killing about 5-10' with that book Miles replaced it in its original position and drew a final book, determined that it was either going to be interesting or he was going to spend the rest of the waiting time looking at the gentlemen to his right playing Whist. Upon being informed by the title that the book he'd just drawn contained a treatise on the various birds of south-west England and south Wales he replaced it hastily back on its shelf, sighed in exasperation and propped his head against his arm so that it rested in a position from which he could look at the Whist-playing quartet.

    All of the Whist players looked to be of a high station. Overhearing their conversation for the remaining few minutes until the arrival of his meal, he gathered that the old gentleman with the dark hair and the military uniform was a colonel in charge of the Barnet border guard, the slightly younger man in the suit with the white bow-tie was an illustrious knight, adorned for his artistic talent for he was the Archduke's chief musician back in the court of Enfield, the stocky and plump man with the bushy beard and the empty pipe was a Baronet, the chief councillor of the Baron of Barnet and the relatively young man in the rather more modern cladding was the son of the Seigneur of Edgeware, although he called himself a Knight of the Manor. So all of them were nobility. Their conversation revolved mostly around tedious matters such as who invited whom at some or other ball party, who was having an affair with whom or less gossipy, but even more boringly who won the last horse-race at the local match at the recently built Newgate track etc. Miles felt like he was sinking in a lethargy, or even a coma when the waitress brought forth his dish of grilled salmon and mushrooms with white wine sauce and filled his glass with a bottle of champagne. Finally he had something to occupy himself with. Thus, without any further delay he preoccupied himself with doing justice to his dish copiously.

It was a most enjoyable meal and Miles thanked the waitress when she cleaned up the table and bade her to convey his most sincere compliments to the chef. He was then left in peace with only a bottle of champagne on his table and his already half-empty glass. Minutes later and as boredom began to once again rob the life out of Miles the chief musician at the next table excused himself and left. But Whist is a game of four and the company was deeply disappointed to lose a vital link in the chain of players. Following the departure of the musician, the colonel declared that it couldn't be helped and his eye caught Miles looking in the general direction of the trio that was left with their cards in their hands. The colonel waved his hand with grace and addressing Miles he said:

'Sir, sir! Hallo sir!'. Miles suddenly looked at the colonel as if just woken up from a reverie.

'Hmm? Oh hallo. May I help you, sir?' he said as benevolently as he did respectfully.

'Pardon my impudence, but I couldn't help but notice that you are alone at your table, just in the company of a drink. Perhaps you would like to join us for a game of Whist?' the colonel proposed with a benevolent smile.

'Oh. Certainly. It would be my pleasure to engage in a game of Whist. Thank you for your most kind offer.' Miles replied smiling and swiftly transferred the bottle and his glass to the table of the company of three.

'Mathilda, another champagne if you please!' bade the colonel to the waitress whom he was was clearly familiar with. She nodded in understanding and left to bring another bottle for the group.

'Please accept it as a token of my gratitude, sir.' Said the colonel, then added: 'But I must not forget my manners, I am colonel Sir Lionel Champs, Edgeware border brigade. This here is Baronet Aldous Wilfred, councillor to the Baron of Barnet on matters of defence and the military, very good friend of mine, and this here is Mr. Brent Dreyfus, esquire, son of the Seigneur of Edgeware, capital young chap, very intelligent.' he concluded as Miles shook hands with the people he was being kindly introduced to. Once these sundry introductions were completed, Miles introduced himself as Mr. Miles Fitzroy, adventurer from Zone 1 travelling in Zone 2 and collecting impressions of the people and the government systems he saw. The group of three were gratified to be in the company of such exciting person and soon the game of Whist was all but forgotten. But let's follow the dialogue in detail. Immediately following the introduction of Miles, young Mr. Dreyfus chuckled rebelliously and spoke:

'Collecting impressions of the people and systems of government here, are you, sir? Heh heh. I guess we should be blushing right now then.' he said facetiously and chuckled again at the hilarity of his statement.

'Come, come Mr. Dreyfus!' said Baronet Wilfred. 'Why should we be blushing? What is wrong with us? We are perfectly respectable gentlemen!'

'I don't deny that for a moment Baronet Wilfred.' replied the young Mr. Dreyfus. 'What I'm less convinced about is our system of government.' he explained.

'Always the rebel, Mr. Dreyfus, eh?' interjected colonel Champs. 'What, I pray is wrong with our system? There is order in the kingdom, everybody has a strictly determined station in life and we all fight in the name of King Harry the 1st. Surely that's all a man can ask for, no?' he argued.

Mr. Dreyfus sighed loudly. 'That is exactly the problem Sir Champs.' he finally uttered. 'That is exactly, exactly the problem. There is no real social mobility here. People are selected for office based on their social rank and bloodline rather than merit. How is that fair? We are condemning very capable people to poverty in this society.' he continued with a hurt tone.

'Yes, but tradition my dear fellow! Tradition!' exclaimed with gravity the Baronet.

'What tradition?' interjected Mr. Dreyfus. 'What tradition are we talking about? The entire sector was instituted formally only about 9-10 years ago, a few years before the erection of the wall! Before that there was no meaning in the concept of lineage!' he protested.

'That's true.' colonel Champs added pensively.

'Yes, but before all this madness we've been trough for the last hundred years or so, we were a great nation. We were an empire that spanned a quarter of the globe, and we did that under the sage leadership of illustrious kings and queens with a society like what we are attempting to revive here, sir!' the Baronet argued heatedly.

'That's not fair to say!' protested the young Dreyfus again. 'What lost us the empire was our inability to accept others as part of our group. The people of India suffered to make the empire strong, the people of Africa were treated as slaves even long after their emancipation! During the entire imperial era we, the wealthy English, were masters in other peoples' homes. We refused to make amends by apologising, accepting them as our equals and striving to build an empire all together for a brighter future in unity rather than discord. In other words what lost us the empire was our own very noble arrogance!' he eloquently discoursed.

'This is outrageous!' started the Baronet, but was swiftly interrupted by colonel Champs.

'Enough, both of you! Please! We are all gentlemen here!' he insisted, then turned to Miles and explained: 'I apologise for the improper behaviour of my colleagues Mr. Fitzroy. It seems we can never hold a decent political conversation together without resorting to shouting...' he said looking at his two companions with that countenance that says very clearly 'Look what mess you've gotten into now.'.

'Oh no, no! It is most interesting for me to listen to this conversation. Heated as it may be, it certainly brims with educational quality.' Miles replied. 'Please continue at your leisure.' he then beckoned.

'Perhaps an introduction to our system would be in order?' offered young Dreyfus.

'Certainly, if you wish, sir.' replied Miles. Dreyfus was only too happy to oblige.

'Back in 2042, as you are no doubt aware, the political situation in Zone 2 changed a lot when the Royalist zones were instituted. These zones here, sir, were the second ones to declare effective independence from the central government, just like the communists had already done a few years before. The people rallied under different factions, a referendum was organised and the people came in favour of the royalist faction's proposals of instituting a traditional monarchic state, loyal to the king. Thus, a number of illustrious leaders from within the royalist faction left for Buckingham where they met the king and asked for his blessing. The deal was that the royalist boroughs would swear an oath of fealty to the king and provide him with tax money that would help sustain the royal palaces and the expenditures of the royal family. The king accepted the deal and anointed 8 people as nobility of different ranks to lead the now royal boroughs. The highest ranking of these nobles is the Archduke of Enfield, the leader of the royal borough confederation. He holds council with the Duke of Epping & Waltham, the Duke of Newgate, the Baron of Potter's Barn, the Baron of Barnet, the Seigneur of Edgeware, the Marquis of Shenleybury and the Marquis of Hatfield and together they run the confederation. They are the crème de la crème. Just below them sit the other nobles that hold various positions in ministries of each Duchy, County, Barony etc. as well as the high-ranking officers of the army and the civil administration. These people together with their families and a small number of business people are the upper class. Beneath them sit the lower ranked officers and administrators, as well as those who own businesses within our region and are as a result relatively well-off. They are the middle class. Below them sit those who work for them, the bulk of the army, and those who make a living in Zone 1 and bring in money from Zone 1. They are the lower class, or working class.' aptly explained the young man. Nods coming from the Baronet and colonel Champs confirmed the young man's statements.

'I see.' said Miles. 'That explains the politics. The upper class exercises power. The middle class holds wealth and the lower class sustains the entire structure.' More nods followed his conclusion. Miles continued: 'So economically what can you tell me about the classes?'

'Ah.' Said Dreyfus. 'That's where we begin to have problems. The upper class survives on the taxes of the middle and lower classes. The middle class is what keeps the economy moving and the lower class is the engine of the entire society that gets just the short end of the stick. Have you noticed, in your journeys, how the distance your are at from any major political centre can be judged by the quality of the infrastructure and the cleanliness of your surroundings?' he inquired.

'Yes, actually. I found it most peculiar.' said Miles.

'This is because that's exactly what our society creates. Wealth flows from below, to above and then to the centre, and from there it gets redistributed to the higher echelons of society and what is left for the lower ones is just scraps. For that reason we have massive public works like the central square in Enfield and the avenues that lead to it, or for that matter, the buildings around the central square in Enfield. On the other hand we have back-streets that I wouldn't dare walk through during the day, let alone during the night!' continued explaining with passion Mr. Dreyfus.

'Outrageous!' exclaimed the Baronet, but the colonel held him down.

'I think our young friend's analysis is rather accurate, actually.' he said. 'Now whether we believe that this is the correct order for a healthy society or not is another matter.' he stated solemnly and calmly.

'The are huge barriers to social mobility!' kept protesting Mr. Dreyfus. 'The jump from lower class to middle class must involve either a lottery ticket or the formation of a new business out of a meagre salary. As for the jump from middle to upper class... that one entails marriage.'

The Baronet and the colonel kept quiet. Miles simply said 'interesting' and then fell silent again, but before he could contemplate for too long, Mr. Dreyfus asked:

'What is interesting, sir? Please do share.'

'I was just thinking what you said about the distribution of wealth and comparing it to what I've seen so far.' Miles replied.

'Oh, do share, please!' exclaimed young Dreyfus with excitement.

'Well, you see, it's this way: In the anarcho-syndicalist confederation, wealth is shared voluntarily and they have a culture of solidarity. That is why wherever I travelled in that zone, I saw the same, equally distributed drabness, however, at the same time the attempts to make things better were equally ubiquitous and equally distributed. For example the roads with potholes were filled with gravel, everywhere, the streets were all reasonably clean. I saw no inequality, but witnessed a great deal of solidarity.' Miles said. The Baronet sighed condescendingly but the colonel urged him to listen further.

'Then?' inquired young Dreyfus with undamped excitement.

'Then I went to the communist zone. There, wealth flows from everywhere to the centre, and then gets redistributed everywhere through a very complex bureaucratic system. What I saw there was mechanical order, cleanliness and uniformity; in fact frighteningly much.' Miles said again and paused for a little to gather his thoughts, but Mr. Dreyfus was anxious to learn more.

'And? And?' he uttered excitedly.

'Then I went to the democratic zone, where each borough is on its own, there is no state-like organisation and things are much like they used to be before the last, say, couple of decades. There, wealth flows from the bottom to the centre and then gets distributed to the top, just like here. However, because the rulers of those zones have a limited tenure, unlike here, they tend to give back even less to the population. I couldn't believe my eyes when I was crossing some of those regions. At the same time though, I realise that those zones have greater potential for change. Who knows? Maybe at some point in the future, a charismatic leader will be elected and he will bring genuine change. I saw a single borough in the democratic zone that had managed to lift itself off poverty, although at a terrible cost to its neighbours.' said Miles. 'Then I travelled here to see what things are like here.' he concluded.

'To be fair though, this only applies because the people of Zone 2 can't even be bothered to go and vote. If a democratic system can only achieve turnouts of a few percentage points, and all the parties end up equally irrelevant, then the system reduces to a monarchy like ours, only with less long-term visions. Am I not right Mr. Miles?' said Mr. Dreyfus.

'Yes, although there is always the possibility that somebody has enough and forms a radical new party that rekindles local interest in politics and sweeps the next elections.' clarified Miles.

'But something of that sort has not yet appeared so far. From what I know the various politically separate regions of Zone 2 have been formed years ago and only cemented themselves ever since. In the meantime, those regions that chose to revive the old system simply stagnated. The councils of their governments are more corrupt and less professional than our aristocratic government.' argued colonel Champs.

'Besides, look at what happened to this country's central government. It lost all real power since the globalisation of markets created a race to the bottom. The only alternatives were to reach the bottom first or perish. Thus, with no political party ever achieving any good results people lost interest in politics. It is not the people themselves alone to blame for the apathy that fills the democratic electorates. Whoever gets into government in those zones stands little chance to change anything. The success of Upminster was an exception and only worked by passing on the misery to the neighbours. Instead in all the other zones we've seen departures from the full free market system, I suspect including here.' said Miles.

'Indeed. We have raised trade barriers and attempted to create our own economic base locally, and it seems to be paying off, at least for the moment. I mean of course trade is generally beneficial for everybody, but sometimes the imbalance is just too great, or you have countries that play foul and spoil it for everyone. It's the old convict's dilemma: if everybody plays right, everybody gets out. If everybody plays foul, everybody loses a bit. If everybody plays right, but one plays foul, the one who played foul wins the jackpot and everybody else loses terribly. It's the race to the bottom as you just mentioned, sir. ' agreed Mr. Dreyfus.

'I don't disagree. After leaving Zone 1 and seeing the reality of Zone 2 my faith in unfettered free market rules and trade has been shaken. I think you are being much more careful here. Certainly this royalist zone seems to have more ample opportunities to escape the 'poverty trap' than the democratic zones have.' said Miles pensively.

'Ha! You see? We are doing better than the old system! I knew it! It is a step forward!' exclaimed the Baronet with excitement.

'Not quite.' replied Mr. Dreyfus. 'A society that has lost its ability to change dynamically, in response to its environment, is doomed to fail, and fail miserably. The ultimate survivor is not a castle that is built to stand to centuries and then is left to its fortune. It is a castle that is built solidly and is subsequently religiously maintained.' contradicted the young man bringing the attention back to the matter of social flexibility.

'That makes sense to me. Perhaps we now have illustrious leaders. After all, the Archduke of Enfield was a most charismatic, pragmatic and wise leader of the royalist faction. He rose to the top as a result of his political shrewdness. Who is to say that his son in 20 years, or his great-grandchildren in generations from now will be the lucky possessors of such capabilities?' interjected the colonel.

'Well spoken dear colonel.' said Mr. Dreyfus gently clapping his hands. 'Couldn't have put it better myself. We have stumbled across the most perilous point of any hereditary system.' he asserted.

'But... but king William the conqueror! Queen Victoria!' protested the Baronet.

'In your place I'd be more concerned about the last Russian Czar and king Louis the 16th of France...' calmly uttered the colonel and the Baronet fell silent.

'We must take care of our people, provide them access to healthcare and education, give them a chance to shine if they possess talent, regardless of their origins.' said Mr. Dreyfus slowly. The colonel nodded in agreement.

'Some of my best officers come from the lowest ranks. Very often they are better and more competent than any of the officers I'm being sent directly from wealthy noble families... but don't tell them I told you that.' said the colonel sipping champagne serenely, with the air of a man who's fully accepted reality and can thence pass judgement without any emotional passion.

'Equally, if not more importantly, this climate doesn't favour the development of a strong consumer base and a large market.' said Miles.

'Consumerism! Pah!' exclaimed Mr. Dreyfus with contempt, disgust even.

'Well, we do operate a market economy. So long as we continue to do so consumerism will be what drives it ahead. And indeed not letting the people gain wealth and prosperity is like refusing to feed a steam locomotive with coal and water.' said the colonel shaking his champagne glass. Miles nodded in agreement and the Baronet stood silent, evidently slightly calmer than before.

'Either way, it can't be that bad yet.' philosophised Miles. 'The monarchy here is young. The people that reached the ranks of the nobility were those who could pull themselves up there. They clearly must have some special character traits like a talent in leadership. However, as time will go on, the monarchy will gather rust, corruption will settle in and eventually it will either stabilise in a stagnant society or end up in disaster.'

'Disrupted from time to time by the appearance of a truly talented leader.' completed the colonel. Miles nodded in agreement. The Baronet stood silent.

'Well, at least the law here is applied equally.' the Baronet finally said drily, avoiding to look at Miles.

'Oh yes. The application of law in Zone 1 is a disaster.' said Miles. The Baronet was expecting resistance from Miles at his last statement, but receiving none he shook with surprise.

'I beg your pardon?' the Baronet asked.

'The law only protects people in exchange for a fee. Surely, you know that.' Miles said. Judging by the expressions of shock on the countenances of Mr. Dreyfus and the Baronet and the expression of disturbed surprise showcased by the colonel, Miles realised that his interlocutors were not aware of the workings of justice in Zone 1.

'Surely you are referring to fees for lawyers and solicitors of various sorts, barristers...' said Mr. Dreyfus.

'No. I mean everything. You pay for the trial, you pay for the judge, you pay for the guards in the court-room and so on. Miles said and then proceeded to explain more details of the judicial system in Zone 1.

'I fail to see how our monarchy is worse that what lies in Zone 1! After all, the rule of law in any sort of society, from the most oppressive to the most liberal is the cornerstone, the foundation of good governance!' exclaimed the Baronet.

'Agreed!' said Mr. Dreyfus.

'Same here.' said Miles. 'Material welfare aside, I now came to realise how brutal and dehumanising society in Zone 1 is...' he concluded with pain. The other 3 stood silent and simply looked down.

'Oh well, at least this means your society has its redeeming features. After all, look at mine!' said Miles jokingly and chuckled weakly. The others followed equally weakly.

'Still, coming from me, it must sound rather rich, but I do believe that the upper classes are exploiting the lower ones. We are a weight to society.' started Mr. Dreyfus again.

'And how do you propose we fix this inequality then?' malevolently asked the Baronet.

'Open society to the idea of mobility. Let people rise to their ranks rather than inherit them. Get a government that distributes wealth more equally over society; in other words, open government to the voice of the poor.' said Mr. Dreyfus beginning to steam again.

'Letting the ignorant plebs govern? Outrageous!' said the Baronet starting to steam himself.

'They'll surprise you.' said the colonel. 'At least if what I've seen in the army also applies in politics.'

'So what does your army do then?' inquired Miles desperately trying to veer conversation off dangerous ground.

'Ah!' to colonel exclaimed with great satisfaction as the conversation was entering his domain of expertise. 'You see, the army here is constituted to protect us from incursions from the north, where Zone 3 lies. Moreover, it is there to protect us in the frightening event of an invasion from the West.'

'What invasion from the west? I don't remember what lies there.' admitted Miles.

'In the west lies an odious dictatorship.' said Mr. Dreyfus.

'More terrifying that anything you've ever seen, I guarantee.' said the Baronet.

'The things they do to their people there you wouldn't believe.' completed the colonel.

'How do you know what happens in there though?' asked Miles curiously.

'Simple.' said the colonel. 'We have a military surveillance facility. We can see what's going on in their streets by using simple auto-focus telescopes. In fact, I can take you to our military facility tomorrow for a tour if you would like to enrich your travels with more impressions.' he offered.

'Certainly! It would be my honour!' exclaimed Miles with great interest.

'There you will find that all that is being said about the odious dictatorship covering Harrow and Watford is no mere rumour.' the colonel said with great gravity, his countenance darkening with a very serious frown. Miles was intrigued, but said nothing.

'There are a few dictatorships out there young man.' said the Baronet. 'There are some religious lunatics in the south-east, some regions in the far west where a group of generals has taken over control, even some small regions in the north-west where powerful crime lords decide the politics, but no other dictatorship can rival the one to the immediate west of us in brutality.'

'I concur.' said Mr. Dreyfus.

'But let's not spoil the surprise for the young gentleman here, nor riddle his night's sleep with tales that could keep an experienced soldier awake at night.' said the colonel.

Miles shook in horror. What manner of beastly regime could possibly elicit such reactions from his interlocutors? Miles was guessing he'd find out in the morning. He preferred not to think too much about it at that moment. A discomforting quiet ensued after the colonel finished his sentence.

'Well, perhaps we should retreat for the evening now.' said the Baronet breaking the uneasiness.

'It is rather late isn't it?' confirmed Mr. Dreyfus.

'Agreed.' said the colonel as the other two were taking their leave and Miles politely waved at them, and then addressing Miles: 'Young man, if you wish to take a tour of the Edgeware monitoring tower military facility you have a couple of options. You may meet me at 07:30 sharp here and join me for breakfast, or you meet me at 08:15 when I'm ready to depart. Is that a suitable arrangement?'

'I believe it is, kind sir. I shall see you tomorrow at daybreak then!' said Miles excitedly.

'Let it be so then, Mr. Miles.' said the colonel and continued: 'Now if' you'll excuse me, I'm getting rather old and I really believe I should retire to my own quarters.'

'You are not staying here, at this inn then, sir?' asked Miles realising that suddenly all the formality had returned as the spirits of the conversation dampened.

'Oh no, no, young man. I have come here merely so that I may indulge myself in a game of Whist with 3 of my most illustrious and respected friends who happen to be visiting our little fief; capital chaps they are, capital.' the colonel said waving his arms in the direction his fellow had chosen to retreat in just a minute ago. Another short pause ensued as Miles nodded in understanding and then the colonel broke the silence for the last time that night: 'And now if you'll excuse me...' and bowed respectfully. Miles said 'Of course! Of course!' bowing in turn and the two gentlemen parted.

Miles headed to his room where he went, as usual, through his evening toilette routine and then promptly fell asleep in the comfortable bed of his hotel room, setting the alarm clock for 07:10 the next morning.

CHAPTER 8: DARKNESS AND LIGHT.

The next morning, Miles woke up very refreshed. He had enjoyed a good night's sleep on the comfortable bed of the inn and thus felt comfortable waking up even at that early hour of the day. He promptly proceeded to dispense with his morning ablutions and then swiftly made his way to the reception desk. Amina greeted him politely and inquired of his nocturnal experience of his room and the hotel in general. Miles smiled and immediately replied that his night stay was most comfortable. He complimented Amina for the well-kept and nicely ran establishment she owned at which point Amina irradiated genuine happiness and Miles felt really happy for her. Miles let her rejoice the feeling for a second and then announced his intention to take breakfast in the dining room of the inn. Amina said simply: 'Be my guest young sire.' pointed with her hand in the direction of the dining-room and flashed Miles a happy smile. In turn, Miles bowed respectfully and left for the dining room.

At a table by one of the large windows of the inn, bathed in sunlight -it seemed to be a good day-, sat colonel Champs. Taking notice of Miles' approach, roughly a couple of minutes before the nominal meeting time he waved his hands and nodded approvingly finally beckoning him to occupy the seat opposite him. Miles complied and upon seating himself comfortably and pulling the chair so the distance between his torso and the table was satisfactorily small he greeted the colonel with a cheerful 'Good morning'. The colonel answered:

'And good morning to you too, sir. I trust your night's sleep was comfortable?'

'Most certainly so, sir. Thank you. And yours?' Courteously replied Miles.

'So was mine although I do remember the beds in this here establishment are of a superior quality and comfort. Ah. There is Mathilda, presumably ready to take our orders.' said the colonel as he noticed that the waitress of the inn was making her way towards them. The two of them ordered breakfast; sausages, beans and bacon with mushrooms and an omelette. The future was there, but some things never change. So long as there will be English people, there will be English breakfast. Naturally, everything was topped up by the obligatory cup of tea. Mathilda placed the serving tray carefully on the table and unloaded the dishes, distributing them to their proper consumers. She then uttered a jolly 'Enjoy your breakfast sirs.' and gracefully departed taking with her the actual tray.

'Lovely girl she is, sir, I dare say. Most polite, most proper.' exclaimed with pride the colonel.

'Indeed so, sir.' agreed Miles.

'But let's not trifle over matters of little significance. Here, have a look at this.' the colonel said unravelling his flexible terminal. He then manipulated the images displayed on it via the touch-screen device until he found the main page of the 'Royal Courier' newspaper. He opened an article with quick and precise moves and then passed the terminal to Miles. Miles received it curiously and looked at the article. It was rather long article about the situation with lending. Apparently, the newspaper had done a survey and commissioned the Statistics Office inc. in Zone 1 in order to get information on the historical daily rates of lending first between banks, then between banks and states, then between banks and businesses and finally between banks and private consumers. Most of the information was in the graph that indicated a sharp drop in all daily loan volume indicators. Miles examined the figure closely and noticed that a visible dent in all indices was to be seen the day Kinroy bank collapsed. The dent persevered and got gradually deeper at a slow rate until a few days ago when Barrington bank also collapsed. A more severe dent followed into the present. Upon finishing the examination of this article Miles looked at the colonel pensively, still holding the flexible terminal (some people called these devices Flexinals) in his hands. The colonel was eating calmly. He noticed that Miles was looking at him and simply uttered:

'I am no man of finance, but you young man, must be. You are from Zone 1 after all. Tell me, what do you make of all this?'

'Worrying. Most worrying. For us, and for you. We are at the eye of the storm, you are largely dependent on the labour force that brings in money from Zone 1.' Miles said worriedly.

'Yes, yes. But is it just business slowing down, or something...' the colonel let his spoon down and looked at Miles with concern '...more serious?' he said stressing each word.

'Difficult to tell. We don't know how far and deep the rot goes, no? Maybe in a few years when everything becomes clear we'll be sitting somewhere and talk saying it's all obvious, completely oblivious to the feelings of confusion that dominate our spirits in these uncertain days. I can at best surmise that the rot will not stop here. I'm expecting more collapses, but whether there will be enough living part to sustain the weight of the crumbling rotten part of the financial tree -if I'm allowed this simile-, nobody yet knows. After all who are we, mere mortals, to speculate upon the deeds of the almighty up in their glass towers?' Miles offered in the way of an answer, trying to mix some humour to lighten the atmosphere.

'Hmmm...' mumbled the colonel 'I feared so much. Problem is that if the wave of collapses continues, eventually the unemployment will spread to affect people living in our Zone. The collapse of Zone 1 will take us down too.' he completed.

'Is that a concern that is already sweeping the population here?' Miles inquired. The colonel nodded in the affirmative.

'The Baronet might think so, but the people are not idiots. They read the news, they worry about the future. They seethe with anger when they see how the people of Zone 1 live in comparison. Make no mistake about it, the happenings in Zone 1 will send shock waves here too. I simply wanted to know your assessment of the situation there.' colonel Champs muttered sombrely.

'I must apologise most sincerely for my inability to be of more assistance.' apologised Miles.

'Don't worry young man. I believe you didn't know as a result of your station in Zone 1. The ones higher above you, in fact a lot higher above you hold the answer, and even they only hold pieces of it.' said the colonel most politely.

Miles now realised better than ever before that everyone in Zone 2 was tied up to Zone 1 and depended upon it for a vast chunk of its wealth. Even for the communists, the people who worked in Zone 1 were bringing a vast amount of Zone 1 pounds into the economy, pounds that could be exchanged for tradable goods from abroad. After all, even those zones that had decided to rebuild their industries would have a hard time facing up to competition unless they were willing to reduce wages and living standards to the low level imposed by China and a few other sweatshops that provided the wealthy bankers of Zone 1 with cheap goods. Even if those industries did a good job at providing goods for the local population with little regard for exports, still trade was paramount in so much as these industries needed resources and fuel from abroad to work. Indeed, everyone in Zone 2 was in mortal danger if Zone 1 collapsed. Miles then naturally wondered whether the people governing the various parts of Zone 2 had done anything to counteract this perilous dependency. Dr. Stephenson back in the commune would know for sure. He had to remember to ask him, Miles' thoughts raced.

At any rate, as the conversation above was unfolding with an abundance of interruptions so that the two gentlemen could do justice to their dishes and take sips of tea, by the time it was over, it was already time to go. The colonel proposed they depart:

'Right. Shall we?'

'Certainly.' replied Miles cheerfully.

'I do believe you will enjoy the walk Mr. Miles. It goes through a nice little park and the weather is most clement today.' said the colonel as they were making their way outside.

'One minute, why don't we use my car? It must be parked somewhere in the vicinity.' proposed Miles.

'You have a car, sir? Oh, of course you do. You are from Zone 1, no?' replied the colonel.

'Indeed so. A very good vehicle as well. Please allow me to offer you a ride to your workplace, dear colonel.' said Miles with utmost politeness.

'You are most kind, young gentleman. I shall seize the opportunity to examine what sort of vehicles people from Zone 1 are used to as well, on this occasion.' said the colonel with a slight bow of the head and a warm smile.

Said and done, Miles summoned the car via his beacon and soon enough Hilda brought the vehicle to a stop right in front of the passengers. The colonel nodded approvingly and soon the two gentlemen were inside. Miles presented Hilda to the colonel, who took the opportunity to ask her to navigate them to their destination, and then started explaining the various functionalities that the car offered. TV, terminal, navigational aids, GPS, the housing of the mainframe that generated Hilda, an implant reader and a very small, hidden drinks cabinet that was full of tiny bottles of liquor. At the offer of a drink made by Miles towards the esteemed colonel, the latter refused citing the early hour of the day as the sole reason for such perceived breach of protocol. Next, the colonel, impressed by the quality of the car, declared that such vehicle would usually be found in the service of a high-ranking officer of the army, or a minister. The heads of the governments of the royalist confederation usually possessed larger cars which, however, offered little extra in the way of comfort. He then expressed the view that it was indeed interesting that in Zone 1 people of even a relatively junior rank could afford to live like ministers of the crown in Zone 2. Miles felt a little tingle of guilt but did not otherwise react to that statement. Silence ensued.

     Fortunately, the destination was already marked on Hilda's maps as a landmark. For what reason, Miles could only guess as such landmarks were not usually on Hilda's maps unless within Zone 1. In any case, even if it wasn't they could see it from afar, as it was a rather tall building.

     'Quite a structure isn't it?' said the colonel pointing towards the structure with his hand. 'Used to be an office block but then as all real business migrated to Zone 1 during the rearrangements of wealth that brought about the present situation, it was left empty. For years it was an empty husk until the royal confederation was formed and soon turned it into a defence facility. The colonel imparted the short, but interesting history of the building with Miles and then started talking about the building, its staff and the facilities inside it, taking all due care not to disclose any confidential information.

     'You see, that tower spans 35 floors and possesses a large antenna, giving it a total height of 135m. From there we can monitor our fearsome neighbours to the west with the latest technology in surveillance we could procure from the best labs in the United States. We constantly sweep the region beyond our barricades with everything from radars to Gamma ray detectors, thus covering the entire electromagnetic spectrum. Our automatic systems sweep the entire field of view every few seconds, auto-focus by use of invisible lasers well into the UV-range and generate a 3D image with all the information they collect. Naturally, we use powerful computers to aggregate data from all bands of the EM spectrum and at the end we create a large, almost real-time 3D image on hologram and our expert gene-drones search through it for suspicious activity. That is the bulk of what we do, in principle. You will understand me if I don't go to specifics, I hope.' said curtly and concisely colonel Champs to a very attentive Miles.

'Of course, of course. The defence of the realm is a sensitive issue and all too often secrecy is paramount.' Miles said. The colonel nodded in agreement and Miles continued: 'However, I hope I'm not impinging upon state secrets if I ask you what those gene-drones are.' asking very politely and even more indirectly. The colonel nodded again, now in sign of assent.

'Most certainly not. I can tell you what they are and what they do in principle. You see, about 30 years ago, in the 2020's, there was a revolution in genetics. Many people will tell you that the revolution started in the 50's with the discovery of the DNA, and then in the 70's and 80's with the first, primitive genetic engineering, and finally in the 90's with the development of the first genetic therapies to diseases. However, I believe that the revolution in the 20's was the truly important one: when we learned how to create humans with specific characteristics on demand.' said the colonel. Miles knew all this already, but listened on trying to guess where the colonel was leading. The latter continued:

'In the 2020's, long before genetic screening and reparation of all embryos was instituted as standard practice in all hospitals, researchers attempted to create test humans for the military. They were engineered primarily so that their senses were sharper than those of normal humans and with the prospect of using them in various positions of the military when they grow up. All this you probably know.' said the colonel and paused in anticipation of some nod or other signal of understanding. Miles did nod in understanding.

'What you probably don't know is the result of this grand experiment. As you are no doubt well aware, gene-drones are not exactly something you will encounter anywhere in your daily life, and there are good reasons for it. First of all, any gene-drone must grow to a useful age. Second of all, all gene-drones need sustenance and suffer from the same weaknesses and high maintenance cost as regular people. Third, as technology progressed, more and more of the tasks originally denoted as ideal for gene-drones gradually came within the territory of machines. For all these reasons gene-drones have not taken off as an idea; instead, the genetic screening and reparation before birth has. Nevertheless we still use gene-drones in a very narrow band of applications.' said the colonel, giving a mysterious aura to his last sentence.

Miles understood now how the system of births employed for a brief period before the government absolved itself of any responsibility for demographic change, was founded. Every citizen that wished a child, had to register with the national demographics bureau, take a written exam in parenting and then if they passed, get issued with a breeding licence. Subsequently, the man in discussion would provide sperm, the woman in discussion would provide an ovum and the two would be combined under laboratory conditions. During the first few crucial cell divisions, specialist doctors would take a sample of the embryo and test it in large PCR (polymerase chain reaction) vats with specialised PCR accelerating enzymes for a vast variety of genetic diseases and deformities. At the same time the embryo would be frozen. The doctors would then compile a list of all the genetic faults found in the embryo and the computerised database would then generate an 'antidote virus'. Despite the scientifically rather improper name, an antidote virus was nothing more than a genetically engineered virus that would attack only cells derived from ova a few divisions before and then it would shuttle inside those cells genetic material that had the capability of destroying dysfunctional DNA and replacing it with healthy one. The virus attacked all cells, changed all the faulty DNA with healthy one and subsequently having no other cells to attack simply died having completed its mission. The proper procedure for using it was to unfreeze the embryo, place it in a vat with plenty of suitable antidote viruses and then wait for a specific amount of time during which the embryo continued dividing. The rate of cell division in the embryo was taken into consideration and enough viruses were added to the vat to ensure that absolutely every single cell of the embryo would get repaired before the embryonic cell conglomerate reached critical mass and started differentiating into cells of various specialisations. Finally, the 'corrected' embryo was implanted into the mother's womb, or often into another woman's womb and the rest of child birth went on more or less as nature had always intended -still cheaper than growing babies in hospital vats-.

    This entire system started with experiments that ran along the same lines, but with viruses that instead of repairing damaged DNA, they attempted to alter healthy DNA in order to obtain specific properties from those embryos. As such, the gene-drones were created. Naturally, the concept was not only applicable to humans but also various animals and plants as well as -with suitable modifications- to bacteria, protozoans and fungi. This gave rise to genimals, geniplants, geniteria, genizoa and gengi. The names were not particularly poetic, but had managed to burrow their way deep into the English dictionary. Thus, the new way of having children, involving simply bureaucracy and gamete donation, the genimal husbandry and the geniplant farming industry had all originated from that military project; a pattern often to be found in the course of human technological progress. Finally, it is rather interesting to mention that in Miles' world sex and reproduction had become to entirely different things. Sex was merely a fun past-time. Reproduction was a scientifically regulated and industrialised procedure where the contribution of the parents was limited to donation of gametes and the use of the woman's womb.

In any case, despite hugely beneficial applications in civilian healthcare and the primary industry sector of the economy, the military branch of the project was not stopped entirely. True, new human gene-drones stopped being produced a few years into the project, however research on the properties that the individuals born as gene-drones possessed went on with time. According to the colonel, they had managed to find areas of human activity where gene-drones were actually better suited than machines. Miles was curious to hear more and the colonel happily provided him with the information he sought.

'Now, you may be wondering what those applications where gene-drones proved better than machines are. I won't disappoint you, I'll tell you. They are applications where human judgement is still more valuable than the ability of machines to crunch numbers. No matter what we say, machines still don't possess the reasoning abilities of humans.' said the colonel.

'More specifically?' inquired Miles fearful he might be sailing into the waters of secrecy.

'More specifically those 3D maps we are generating from our surveillance cameras are searched for suspicious activity by gene-drones.' said the colonel with signs of a gentle smile quivering on his lips.

'Oh yes, that one. You already told me and I forgot.' said Miles face-palming himself.

'Heh.' chuckled colonel Champs and continued: 'Our gene-drones have eyes that could best those of a good hound, competing with the likes of eagles. Brilliant resolution they have those eyes. Where a regular human would need a lot of zooming in and a lot of time to uncover details in a large 3D image, our gene-drones can look at them 'from above' as if we were to say and spot suspicious details at a fraction of the time necessitated for a regular human, in fact almost immediately. Naturally our computers are also 'trained' with neural algorithms to look for bomb-shaped objects and other clearly suspicious material, but when it comes to judging people's actions or objects of ambiguous uses, our gene-drones have the upper hand. So thus they sit, perched up in high seats in the holographic projection chamber and watch. Whenever they spot something suspicious they send the coordinates of the suspicious spot to regular human controllers who scrutinise them more carefully.' he explained. Miles was astonished.

'And these people, these gene-drones. Are they otherwise normal people?' he inquired.

'Oh well. That's a sad story. For the most part, yes. However, having tampered with their eyes and other body organs in such invasive ways has to this day almost always created horrifying side-effects. For the most part their faces are malformed as a result of eyes that are bulkier than usual, and their brains are not as fast in areas where humans normally are as a result of too much processing power being bound for the processing of optical information. For example, ask a gene-drone to spot the villain with the bomb in a crowd and he'll do it in seconds, but ask him to join you in a game of chess and suddenly the level of mental faculty decreases to a painfully low level.' said the colonel. 'To be honest with you, it pains me to see them sometimes. I can't help but get a feeling that they are like innocent children that we exploit to our own ends... but then again, they are invaluable to our surveillance system and ultimately the defence of our realm.' he added speaking emotionally and leaning closer to his interlocutor as people will often do when they want to impart deeply emotional or personal information. Miles could understand the old colonel's moral concerns about using gene-drones. He too found it rather cruel to have people manufactured as tools, people who were condemned to live with the effects of that manufacturing process for their entire lifetimes. For all he knew the gene-drones were happy in their blissful ignorance, perching on their high seats and looking at things, yet still something deep in his soul was telling him there was something fundamentally wrong with this situation.

    Miles stood silent in contemplation after the colonel's statement on his personal views on gene-drones and so did the colonel himself. In the meantime the towering figure of the military surveillance tower from Edgeware drew closer and closer. Before long the car was at the base of the tower and the colonel descended, followed by Miles. Miles asked Hilda to park somewhere in the vicinity and the colonel recommended a spot just around the block. Hilda thanked the colonel after Miles' assent to the recommendation, and promptly left to park the car. At the same time colonel Champs and Miles headed for the entrance of the building. A guard recognised his commanding officer, who for the sake of formality was displaying his identity credentials anyway, and saluted cheerfully. The colonel returned the salutation and explained that Miles was a traveller whom he had invited at a reconnaissance of the dictatorial country of Harrow and Watford so that he would be convinced not to travel there. The guard saluted again and nodded in understanding with a terrified look on his face. He addressed Miles:

    'I really think you should not go there. It's hell out there. Please listen to me. I know. I've seen what goes on in there.' he said worriedly.

    'I appreciate your concern for my safety. I think I will avoid that region after witnessing first hand the terrifying stares everybody shoots at me when I say I intend to travel there. Still, I would like to see here, at this facility, exactly what is wrong in the west. I want to see with my own eyes.' Miles said. The guard simply replied: 'Certainly, but I warn you it will turn your stomach.' and greeted as the colonel and Miles both headed towards the interior of the building. The two gentlemen reached the elevator and entered, then the colonel pushed the button to the top floor. Miles broke the silence:

'Is it really that bad in there?' he inquired.

'Well, I want you to be the judge of that. We're going to the top floor so that you can take a look at the region with your bare eyes first. Then I'm going to take you to the viewing arena we built around the holographic projection chamber. There you can observe our gene-drones at work and see our holographic projection being generated real-time. In the same room we have terminals where our regular human military personnel analyse spots where suspicious activity is scrutinised. I'm sure it will do no harm to take over one of those terminals and zoom into, say, a small square inside the dictatorial zone. There you will be able to see more details, as if looking through a very high-quality spyglass.' said the colonel smiling cheerfully.

'I... I... I can't express my gratitude for your kindness, sir. I truly, honestly thank you so much. This is a real experience for me!' said Miles excitedly. 'At the same time though I would like your assurances that I impinge upon nothing secret during this tour. I by no means wish to compromise the job of someone who has been so kind to me.' he continued.

'Don't worry young man. This is simply a surveillance station. They know we are monitoring them and they are probably guessing we are monitoring them closely. There is nothing secret here. The secrets are in the buildings where we keep information on our own defences and troops.' said the colonel after a brief, but wholehearted laugh, patting Miles on the back. Miles smiled in response and the elevator continued ascending. It was a rather slow one.

At the end, the doors opened and as the two sliding elements of the elevator door were pulling apart from one another Miles' sight was greeted by a vast, open-plan office space that seemed to take over the entire floor. The most prominent feature of the floor was the array of windows that Miles could see covering what would be the left, right and front external walls of the floor; in other words instead of having walls with the exterior, the entire floor had glass spanning its entire height and perimeter. Miles could not confirm that this was the case since one of the four walls of the floor was behind him, hidden by the elevator, but he later found it was indeed the case. On the floor, a number of supporting pylons, sparsely spaced, held up the roof with the antenna structure and a thick, blue carpet covered the entire surface. In the interior side of the building, rows of desks sat arranged in regular patterns and uniformed employees were toiling over paperwork with their backs acutely bent over whatever it was they were reading at the time. In general, the entire level was bustling with activity. Meanwhile arranged around the sides of the level were a number of spyglasses, particularly many in the side that was facing the Harrow & Watford area. Even there. a number of uniformed people were peeping through the various spyglasses, thus adding to the activity on that floor, however, since most of them held sandwiches or coffee in their hands Miles presumed that they were simply taking a short break and he was correct in his presumption. Large OLED panels provided dim lighting to the level and some employees at the desks even lit up their desk lamps since in the interval between breakfast and Miles' arrival at the military surveillance tower, the weather had changed from sunny and bright to murky and ready for a cracking thunderstorm. It was in this surreal atmosphere of 360-view all around him, dark clouds in the sky and a dimly lit floor that Miles stepped out of the elevator, behind the colonel. Hardly had he taken a couple of steps out of it when the colonel stopped, turned left, raised his arm and pointing with the palm of his hand right ahead of him and said:

'Here, young man, you can see what the so called 'Harrow & Watford Empire' looks like with your very own eyes.'

Miles turned left as well and gazed upon the sight that was unveiling before him. He could see very little since he was shorter than the colonel (the colonel being a giant of a man who could sit eye-to-eye with the legendary general De Gaulle) took a number of steps until he reached the glass wall of the building. Once there he gazed again upon a much larger area and his heart immediately sunk. Below him he could see the buildings of the Edgeware district in the Royal zone extending normally until a point about 500m away from the tower. At that point, the colour of the buildings changed. The various Victorian houses, old factories, new buildings, old rail-deposits and other structures turned a sick, soot-grey colour. Miles could literally see a line of soot-grey defining the border between the fief of Edgeware and the land beyond. Even farther behind Miles spotted a dark silhouette of a building that appeared to be completely black and plain, like a vast, blank piece of domino, or equally well described as a large, featureless black parallelpiped. The darkness of the sky, the extremely fast moving clouds and the general grey sullenness that the Harrow & Watford Empire seemed to emit, combined with each other to create a sinister impression that the thunderstorm was actually being generated over there. Of course that was utter nonsense. Despite many attempts to control the climate at will, people had found many technologies that could achieve that but all at a prohibitive energy cost. The best bet were those technologies that sought to manipulate the climate when it was on a so-called 'knife edge' i.e.

balancing between two possible states that would lead to very different future outcomes; not just different within the normal borders of chaotic systems, but so different as to switch to a different chaotic attractor altogether. However, the inherently chaotic nature of the climate and the difficulty intrinsic to determining the so called 'chaotic attractors' -we can't really reasonably speak of equilibria in such chaotic systems- and the borders between their basins of attraction made this technique at best unreliable. Of course, if the ITER (the international fusion research project commenced at the start of the millennium) project, long delayed by the collapse of state power in the participating UK as well as engineering delays, was ever going operational and opened the doors for fusion power on a mass scale, perhaps climate control would come within grasp practically, rather than just technically. Until then, no chance. Back to the story, Miles reacted with terror at the sight. He raised his hand pointing with the finger towards the Harrow & Watford area and uttered:

'That line... what is it? Why is everything grey? What is that massive, black building?'

'That's a lot of questions young man.' said the colonel. 'Which one shall I answer first?' he concluded with a smile that showed benevolence and worry at the same time. Benevolence towards his guest, worry that the answer was unpleasant.

'Well. Let's start with the greyness that seems to start abruptly at what I presume is the border with your country.' said Miles, composing himself.

'Correct, that line is the border. As for why everything is grey behind the border, it is because none of those buildings ever got painted since the institution of the dictatorship there. They spent all their money elsewhere.' said the colonel.

'Where?' inquired Miles curiously.

'You will see later. Don't worry. You won't leave this place without the answers that you seek.' reassured the colonel.

'And that building far behind?' Miles inquired again.

'Oh that one. That's one of the very few new buildings that have been built by the dictatorship. It is the central administration of the region. That's where the dictator rules from.' said the colonel.

'Very few?' asked Miles with curiosity.

'Oh yes. Very few. Here, look through the spyglass... Wait. Let me go first so I can lock the sights on to the new buildings. One minute... here we go.' said the colonel and after affixing the line of sight of the spyglass towards some, still unknown to Miles, objective he beckoned his guest to take a look through the eyepieces. Miles complied with eagerness.

What he could see was a large, dark building that looked like a stepped pyramid. On each level of that grotesque, ash-grey pyramid were endless rows of windows with heavy metal bars through their concrete frames. On the ceiling of each of the pyramid's levels there was barbed wire; enough to to cover the entire surface. Overall, the size of the building was enormous, about 20 pyramid levels equivalent to 20 floors in a normal building, but because it was situated even farther than the central administration of the region he didn't notice it with the naked eye the first time. Miles guessed what the building was for, but asked anyway. The colonel was ready to answer.

'That is the central prison of the so called Empire. We have virtually no idea what goes on in there. Our imaging from the surveillance equipment we have can penetrate that far at decent resolution but all we can see is tiny cells. In the lower levels we suspect they keep a forced labour factory and at the top couple of levels we think they keep torture chambers.' he said with a dark frown. 'Those bastards. They come into power years ago and all they manage to build is a tower for their oppressive government, a prison and a few other things along similar lines. Here, let me show you.' concluded the colonel and assumed control of the spyglass again. Barely a minute later he had locked onto yet something else he wanted Miles to look upon. He beckoned and Miles looked through the eyepieces again.

This time he could see the vast court inside a large building. The court was full of police cars. There were hundreds of them and parking space for probably ½ a thousand, or maybe even more. Riot vans, ordinary cars, armoured vehicles and rows upon rows of motorbikes, all belonging to the police were stationed inside. That was presumably the force that kept the government into power.

'Is that the force that keeps the government into power?' inquired Miles.

'Correct.' answered the colonel curtly. Then he assumed the control position at the spyglass again and while he was setting up the thing he uttered: 'There's just one more thing I want you to see.'. He finally found his objective and let Miles peek through the eyepieces one more time. Miles took the opportunity.

This time Miles saw a building that was presumably at the other end of the Empire, near Watford. It was a tall and slender, cylindrical tower with a top that split into what looked like a dozen tentacles, which in turn left outwards in various directions. The tower itself was pitch-black except for thin, iridescent blue/blue-green lines that criss-crossed the structure in angles that were always either parallel to the ground, or perpendicular. The appearance of the building was truly grotesque and terrifying. Miles felt chills run through his spine and after a few seconds of gazing at the monstrosity he abandoned the spyglass agitated.

'What... what the hell was that?' he said with profound agitation. 'I've never seen anything so disturbing in my whole life.'

'I saved the best for the last.' said colonel Champs with a bitter smile. 'That, young man, is the headquarters of the secret police of the Empire. It is a dark and evil place no matter how you take it. 60 floors of pure evil. Those tentacles at the top are meant to symbolise the all-reaching power of the service within. Why do they need so much space for their secret services when there are barely ½ a million souls living in that desolate place? You will find out...' concluded the colonel mysteriously.

Following that eerie statement, Miles requested permission to go once around the floor, following the glass wall so that he could admire the view all around. The colonel politely accepted and Miles took the opportunity to see what the rest of London looked like from that particular spot. He first walked to the northern wall. Here he could see parts of the Royal sector as far as the eye could see. Nothing significant. Once he had looked enough, he moved to the Eastern wall. Here he could discern the bulk of the Royal sector. He could not see the optical illusion buildings in Enfield with sufficient clarity though because he was too far. Once again, nothing significant. Finally, he moved to the Southern wall. From there he could see the glass towers of Zone 1, protruding through the cloud bank to their dizzying heights. The familiar flashing red beacons, the lights at the various bank and insurance offices that they contained were all visible. Miles knew some of the structures he was seeing could be as much as 20km away, but their enormous heights as well as the height of the tower he was in at that moment made them still visible. These towers were so big, they dwarfed the secret services HQ in the Harrow & Watford zone. 'Oh well, perhaps it's better that our towers are banks and not secret police HQs.' thought Miles not realising the profoundness of the statement that had just passed through his mind and the implications it had in philosophical terms. That statement alone could open vast discussions about the nature of happiness, fairness, the innate human craving for freedom, the nature of freedom in various societies etc. all things Miles had had a chance to think and discuss about a lot more in the recent past. Finally, Miles sighed and turned back to encounter the colonel once again. After doing so he communicated his readiness to move on to the next part of the tour and the colonel pressed the elevator button in response. While the two of them were waiting for an elevator to arrive (there were 4 in the building) the colonel asked:

'Now do you see why I think you should avoid that area?'

'Definitely yes.' responded Miles with terror. Neither of them spoke again until they were exiting the elevator again a few floors below the top.

'Here is the holographic projection chamber control room.' said the colonel simply.

Miles saw a small room in front of him, which itself had windows looking into yet another room. The room behind the windows was clearly spanning more floors as Miles could see its ceiling, but no sign of its floor. In that large chamber, roughly 100 square meters in area, a number of egg-shaped capsules were hanging from the ceiling with a tunnel, much like the ones they use at airports to guide passengers from the aeroplane to the terminal, connecting the back of the capsule with the walls of the said chamber. Presumably behind those walls stood either more rooms, or corridors. Judging by the size of the top floor and given that the military surveillance tower possessed the same top-view trace from the top floor to the ground floor, Miles judged that this must be indeed the case. Each capsule had a large window that covered almost 1/3 of its surface and allowed the beings inside it to gaze down unto something Miles could not yet see. The beings inside the capsule were humans with severely deformed faces, huge eyes and a look of intense concentration on their task, dominating their malformed countenances. They were gene-drones. In front of them they had a terminal, but none of the drones was using it at the moment. Meanwhile, inside the room that Miles had just stepped in, the control room, it was dark. The only light inside the room was coming from the chamber where the drones were sitting in, and even that was coming from below and dispersing on the walls and ceiling of the drones' room before entering the control room. This dim and dispersed, pale yellow-white light that was illuminating the control room was creating a very eerie and almost alien atmosphere. Miles shivered at the feel of it. Around the chamber, against its walls there were 4-5 workstations where people with large, military headphones covering their ears entirely were sitting and... playing games? At the arrival of the colonel the games immediately disappeared from the screens and images of various city scenes appeared in their place. The colonel was not happy.

After shouting for about 2 minutes to his heart's content about discipline and readiness the colonel let out enough steam and remembered his guest. He addressed Miles:

'Excuse me, young man, but I had to restore order. Here is the control room of the holographic projection chamber. Back there...' the colonel said pointing towards the room with the drones '...is the actual projection chamber. Here, let's go and have a look at what's in there, then we'll go at this here terminal...' the colonel indicated by pointing again '...and see an example of surveillance in action.'

The two gentlemen approached the window and Miles saw that at what would be a couple of levels below them, a 3D holographic image was covering the entire floor of the drone/projection chamber and what's more, the image was constantly moving from left to right at a rate that was just about enough for Miles to follow without finding it excessively annoying. Miles examined the image briefly and then looked at the drones again; fearful mutants they were.

'Don't worry, they can't see you. These windows are half-mirrors.' said the colonel reassuringly. 'Down there is the image we are getting from the surveillance equipment. We render all the information we get in visible light, yellow-white to be more precise. We found that our drones can detect edges more easily if the dominant colour is this white-yellow. The image is moving because it updates in real-time. If you wait for about 10" or so you should be able to recognise the periodicity of the image.' explained the colonel.

'Fascinating! And from these images the drones can spot suspicious activity? I can barely see the people.' said Miles genuinely excited.

'I told you the drones have their uses...' replied the colonel. 'Now let us see an example of surveillance in action.' he continued and beckoned Miles to go to the terminal towards which he had previously pointed. Colonel Champs then asked the uniformed soldier who was manning the terminal to move aside a bit so they could see as well and soon the three of them were bent over the image that was being displayed at the holographic projector of the terminal. This one was clearly a zoom in from one very specific part of the image, some street inside the dictatorial zone. The image refreshed every 10" or so making it hard to see the continuity of motion, but colonel Champs pushed some buttons and soon enough the image became continuous and flowing.

'Our system has the capability of activating auxiliary surveillance cameras for focus on specific areas we wish to survey. That way we can keep track of up to 5 small regions constantly without having to overexert our computers.' the colonel said correctly anticipating Miles' question.

Colonel Champs then pushed yet another few buttons and the image changed colour, suddenly becoming solid and naturally coloured.

'I've just switched off any other EM wavelength apart from optical ones.' the colonel explained patiently. 'Now we can't see details from, say, inside the cars and so on.'

Miles was astonished. That was some serious surveillance going on. He was standing there, in a dark control room in the fief of Edgeware, looking at a piece of road with its associated pavement in the dictatorial zone about 1km away from him as if he were watching television with the sound off. He could see the people walking about and vehicles going about their business.

'I chose to monitor this part because there are no buildings in the way to hide it from us. It's a good example to see clearly.' explained the colonel and then zoomed in until the people became large enough for Miles to see their countenances. The image now included only a very small piece of road and pavement.

'Hang on a minute. What do those people have on their foreheads?' inquired Miles after a handful of seconds he spent scrutinising the pedestrians.

'Ah. That is one of the things the dictatorship has spent all of its available funds on. It is an implanted camera. Wherever the people of Harrow & Watford go, whatever they see, the cameras record everything and send it to the secret services HQ. I believe this answers two of the questions you asked me when we were on the top floor.' said the colonel.

It was indeed so. It explained why the dictatorship did not have money to maintain the buildings within its jurisdiction painted, as well as why the HQ of the secret services needed to be so large. Because a vast part of the population was monitoring the other part!

'And those gruesome earrings everybody seems to be wearing?' inquired Miles upon noticing black spots on everybody's ears.

'Microphones.' said the colonel. 'Whatever the people hear, so does the service. Naturally all of these implants are powered by scavenging body heat energy, so as long as the person is alive, the devices work. Also, if anybody fails to transmit information for even the briefest of intervals, they are likely to be interrogated, tortured, or even killed.' he concluded frowning darkly. 'This takes the meaning of 'odious' to a whole new level.' added the colonel frowning even more intensely, now with disgust. Miles shivered again as chills ran through his spine once again. What manner of beastly regime was that?

During his contemplations Miles kept monitoring the people on the street going about their businesses, some looking deeply unhappy, the vast majority looking completely neutral and very few people looking cheerful. It seemed that people who were condemned to live in the dictatorship of Harrow and Watford had adapted to the situation and had learned how to keep a perfectly expressionless, straight face at all times as well as, presumably, keep their thoughts securely to themselves. Meanwhile, the few vehicles on the street that passed by were mostly police cars on patrol. After a few minutes of watching, a large, black bus with metal grids on the windows passed by. Miles was intrigued:

'Was that a bus?' he inquired of the colonel.

'Yes.' colonel Champs replied.

'They have public transport at least.' commented Miles.

'Yes and no...' said the colonel mysteriously.

'What? Why yes and no?' asked Miles.

'Well, you see, young man. These are buses, but they don't serve urban transport purposes, they serve something different. They shuttle workers in and out of Zone 1. Now it is late so only few of them are running, you should see them in long chains like ancient merchant caravans during rush hour. They are secured with metal grids on the windows and a lot of police inside so the people don't escape in the democratic region of Zone 2 that they need to traverse when going from their own home region to Zone 1.' explained the colonel patiently.

'But if the people are free to go anywhere in Zone 1, why bother with all this police? I mean they can always escape in Zone 1.' argued Miles.

'Oh yes? And go where? You are from Zone 1 young man and know better than anyone that without money you are a non-person there. They would not be able to survive or even get out of the Zone 1 walls. You have to pay a charge to open the gates of the Zone 1 walls, no?' said the colonel and Miles nodded in agreement. 'Exactly. It is the perfect trap.' concluded the colonel.

Miles thought about that for a minute. Society in Zone 1 was so perfectly market-oriented that for somebody without money it was not even by an inch better than the most hostile frozen wasteland or desert on the entire planet. That really put things into perspective. Suddenly Miles' insides were filled with intense hatred. Hatred and contempt for Zone 1 and for the evil dictatorship of Harrow & Watford and for everything they stood for.

'Can't we do anything about it?' inquired Miles, seething with anger.

'Not much at the moment. They are armed too. What's more, the only reason they aren't invading the weak, democratic zones they share a border with is that they are afraid we'll seize the opportunity to hit them, which we most likely would.' answered the colonel.

'Colonel, I have to confess something.' said Miles sombrely.

'What is it young man?' asked the colonel patting Miles on the back.

'Up until now I always thought that intervening with another country's internal affairs was... was effectively blasphemy. I thought, let the people decide for themselves whether they want to be part of a country or not, what government they want to have and so on. It was quite convenient for me, in Zone 1, where this idea was absolving us of any responsibility towards the outer Zones of London.' said Miles, red with tension. 'Yet at the same time, what is there to prevent us from using the excuse of responsibility to attempt to turn everybody who is weaker than us into a copy of our own image?' he continued, torn apart by the moral dilemma.

'Interesting thoughts.' replied the colonel. 'Believe it or not there is a conceivable state where the people living in such world are actually used to it and have no moral qualms with it. I mean a world like the Empire. There is a conceivable state where people live in a society we would find odious and oppressive, but would even give their lives to defend the very sort of odious society they live in. Do we still have the moral responsibility of liberating them?' he argued evidently himself trying to put his own thoughts in order.

'I suppose we don't, do we? If the people are used to that and are happy with it...' said Miles with great difficulty.

'Oh my, oh my. You give up so easily young man. All right, let's add something to the mix. Suppose that a couple of radically different societies live close by, just as we do. What if each of these societies is dangerous to its neighbour? Then do you invade?' asked the colonel. Miles was taken aback but could produce no satisfactory answer.

'Fine, suppose that they are poised to strike, do you pre-empt it?' asked the colonel again.

'I... I... Agh...' was all Miles could utter. The colonel was smiling radiantly.

'Well, how do you know they are poised to strike? How do you know there is no room for negotiation?' Miles finally exploded.

'You don't. You're sitting in the chair of the Archduke of Enfield and have to make a decision. A practical decision, not a philosophical one. One that might condemn thousands or save thousands.' the colonel said simply.

'In that case... argh... Well... I suppose it is a risk you have to take. You have to use your judgement and accept the consequences. Like Neville Chamberlain. He is the perfect example of a man who sought peace to the very bitter end until war was imposed upon him in the most unfavourable terms. Or... Or on the other side of the table Hitler who started a war when it could have easily been avoided. On the other hand, Nikita Khrushchev and president Kennedy managed to stop a nuclear meltdown by keeping their cool. All these are decisions that were taken based on judgement more than simply principle.' said Miles arguing most eloquently. The examples of world war II and the Cuban missile crisis were all well studied in history classes at school, or at least used to be before education was privatised and started becoming more and more 'labour market-oriented' with time. Miles was lucky enough to have had a solid comprehensive education that taught him all these subjects that were considered irrelevant in modern society and dismissed as not useful to land their possessor a good job. The colonel was older than Miles and was privy to such education as well so he caught the references.

'Bravo, sir. Bravo.' he exclaimed. 'Now you see how philosophy and practice sometimes don't correspond to each other perfectly. How people in power have to make decisions on judgements and how the lines separating right and wrong are often very wide and ill-defined. Oh well. Follow your heart to discern between good and evil. I do. For that reason I believe we must be on guard and if we get the opportunity, destroy the evil Empire of Harrow and liberate its inhabitants from the outside.' said the colonel. Under any other circumstance Miles would have protested, but having seen the evils of Harrow and Watford it was difficult to do so.

'It feels wrong, I know. But think of it this way. We wouldn't do anything extreme unless we felt cornered and left without choices. And we feel pretty close to that... Does that make you feel a bit better?' asked the colonel benevolently.

'A little.' said Miles still feeling uncomfortable. For the time being he decided to trust the colonel's judgement. If he said that there was no room for negotiation and that the royal zone was under threat, perhaps he should trust him. Even if things did end up in a balance between the two zones, what sort of terrifying balance would that be? Living in constant fear that the other side would one day attack. It was for the best that one of the two collapsed. But then again, if the balance was there, perhaps eventually the two sides would come to a conciliation. 'Argh!' thought Miles. 'So many thoughts! So many possibilities. What do I choose? Everything is statistics, chances and risks. Nothing is clearly defined! No clear right or wrong!' he kept thinking angrily. 'It figures. All important questions in life are not clear black-and-white issues.' Miles concluded bitterly.

The colonel was probably able to literally see Miles thinking by the look on his countenance so he stood silent and let his guest contemplate in peace. When Miles looked back at the colonel again the latter spoke again: 'Oh well. Think about it. For now, take away the main message, that is: people in power have to use their judgement and make decisions on a case-by-case basis. It helps if they are guided by strong principles, but sometimes that will simply not be enough and they must be ready to act against their hearts if need be so. The rest is for you to think.' he said calmly, almost paternally. 'Think about all of this.' he recommended. Miles stood silent for a little while, then thanked the colonel:

'Colonel, I truly thank you for this opportunity to talk to you and see your wonderful facility, as well as have a peek into life in the dictatorship of Harrow and Watford.'

'Oh, not at all my dear chap. It was extremely interesting talking to you too.' replied the colonel with a cheerful smile.

'And thank you, sir, too for lending us your monitor for the duration of this conversation.' Miles said addressing the soldier who normally manned that terminal.

'Oh not at all. Not at all! It was my pleasure. Besides your conversation was very interesting for me to listen in on as well.' replied the soldier saluting casually.

'Colonel, I believe I am now ready to continue my journey through Zone 2.' declared Miles assertively but politely. The colonel nodded in agreement.

'I have shown you everything I could as well. Young man, I shall escort you to the entrance. Courtesy forbids any other course of action.' he said and the two of them took their leave.

At the base of the military surveillance tower the honourable colonel Lionel Champs grabbed Miles' arm with both his hands, shook it with vigour and said: 'Good luck, traveller. May your experiences on the journey give you what you seek.'.

Miles bowed courteously and thanked the colonel from the bottom of his heart. He then entered his car (he had summoned Hilda by using the beacon while he was still in the elevator and descending), waved at the colonel goodbye and left for his next destination as the colonel was waving back to him.

Hilda knew that their rough direction was counter-clockwise around Zone 2 so she headed West towards the borders with the dictatorial zone. Miles, however instructed her to change course and head South. They would cross the border at South Queensbury, a region where Zone 1, the Royal boroughs of Zone 2 and the democratic borough of Brent met together. That way they'd avoid Harrow & Watford. The plan was to then head West towards Uxbridge, where in a small zone with barely 10.000 people an Athenian-style republic was in operation. Hilda comprehended the plan and set course for the borders with the borough of Brent. The journey to the borders was uneventful as Miles passed the ubiquitous rows of Victorian housing, mixed with more modern council flats arranged in messy and poorly laid-out council estates that even Hilda had trouble navigating through, small clusters of light industrial buildings -all abandoned- and the occasional rail deposit or station, ridden with weeds and long since left to its fate. The rather depressing surroundings did little to impress Miles since he was still rather shaken by the images he'd seen through the spyglass and then in the holographic projection control room. Thus, he sat on the comfortable seat of his car, propping his head in his hand and looking at intervals either at the surroundings or at the dark and murky sky.

Eventually, Hilda announced the approach to the border of the Royal Zone. The border crossing procedure was short and involved the display of the pass-card Miles had acquired at the anarchist

Confederation. Happily it was carried out with the utmost formality and politeness. After Miles waved cheerfully at the border guards, and they returned the hand wave, he was free to go and thus headed West, at full speed towards Uxbridge; or at least the maximum speed the roads would allow as he was once again in old-system democratic territory again. The car proceeded West-south-west towards Brent park area with little of significance to attract Miles' attention and then proceeded dead West towards central Brent. At about this point Miles noticed something peculiar. One of the people walking merrily on the street was armed with a pistol that showed clumsily from within his trouser holster. The man was not a police officer and that's what attracted Miles' attention. He was wondering whether the possessor of the gun owned it legally when just a few tens of meters farther down the street he saw yet another man with a gun. Miles got suspicious and from that point onward he actively looked at all passers-by in search of hidden weapons. To his incredible surprise, Miles found out that a rather sizeable number of civilians bore arms in this borough. He wondered why that might be the case and then a thought passed flashing through his mind: This borough shares a vast border with the dictatorial zone of Harrow and Watford. Perhaps all citizens here were allowed or indeed required to bear at least small arms in case of an invasion. To take it even further, perhaps they were also trained to use them by the council itself.

His suspicions were confirmed when his car was waiting at the traffic lights, at an intersection with a large street. The area was full of people perhaps as it was nearly lunch-time by then, and sure enough, most were armed. Then, as the traffic lights facing Miles still persisted in maintaining a deep red hue, a large, black bus with metal grids on the windows passed by. The people inside it featured grotesque 'third eyes' on their foreheads and had pierced ears. They all looked down at their laps with blank, zombified stares. There was no doubt about it. These were workers from the dictatorship crossing over to Zone 1 for labour. Miles was diligent enough not to waste all his stares on the bus itself. He perceptively looked at the people on the streets to gauge their reactions to the crossing bus and it would be fair to assert that an absolute majority of the passers-by gently brought their right (or left if left-handed) hands to their holsters and discretely caressed the butts of their issued handguns. At the same time they avoided looking at the bus directly, electing to instead direct their gazes towards other targets and act disinterested. 'So it is for defence against the dictatorship.' thought Miles. 'How can these people live under such permanent fear? It really puts things into perspective I suppose. I never had such fears in my entire life and yet everywhere I go here it seems that people have at least one big fear. Fear of being arrested in the communist sector, fear of endless, inescapable poverty in the democratic zones, fear of collapse in Zone 1 for the royal sector, fear of their own government in Harrow & Watford, fear of their safety, in Brent and fear of war in the generally ill-defined Commune.' thought Miles with small stings of guilt.

Miles sat back in his seat, looking at the sky through the glass ceiling of his car. He preferred not to think about anything at that moment, but just enjoy sitting back comfortably and let Hilda take him up and down the hills of Brent borough. Eventually he dozed off in an afternoon nap and Hilda's careful driving meant that he was not woken up until the approach to the border with the republic of Uxbridge. It was just as well, he didn't miss anything; nothing passed by the windows of his car that he had not already seen plenty of: Victorian houses, abandoned industries etc. etc. etc.

The borders with the republic were of the traditional sack of sand & barbed wire sort with a couple of guards on duty, however, the difference was that the guards wore bright white uniforms instead of more traditional blue or green hues. Miles was rather surprised to see uniformed personnel in such choice of garments but that did not impede him to greet them politely and announce his intention to visit their little republic as a tourist. In turn, the guards themselves were hindered by nothing in their intention to greet the newcomer equally politely and ask for identification documents. Upon the guard seeing the special guest pass from none other than the legendary Dr. Stephenson himself that Miles carried upon his person, there were excited exclamations from both border guards.

'Wow! You know Dr. Stephenson? He is a hero around here. An ideological father of our friends in the commune and uncle of our own republic over here, in Uxbridge. He visited us very often to see our proceedings in the Agora and gave us a lot of advice on how to trim the system and make it work better!' one of them exclaimed with vigorous excitement.

'The what?' inquired Miles with confusion. 'I apologise, I am not yet fully familiar with all the political systems currently in existence around Zone 2.' he then said apologising humbly.

'The Agora. The Forum. It is our open, public assembly. Anyone may attend, listen or speak on it on a first-come first-served basis.' explained the guard. 'It is how our system works. With nearly full participation in politics of the entire active population.' he concluded.

'How do you listen on a first-come first-served basis? Ah, I see. You only talk on that basis, the listening and attending part is just open to anyone. Right, I see.' said Miles blushing a little at his blunder. The guards unsuccessfully repressed a chuckle in response and beckoned him to enter their beloved republic.

'Please come in, come in friend.' they said and showed him into their small region. Miles crossed the border on foot and Hilda followed.

'Brilliant vehicle you have Mr. Miles!' exclaimed the guards with cheerful, almost childish smiles. They had, after all, just crossed the threshold of adulthood.

'Thank you gentlemen.' replied Miles. 'To me she is more than my car, she is my companion.' he said warmly. The guards looked at him with a look that indicated a mixture of confusion, curiosity and the slightest hint of disturbance.

'I... I mean the navigator inside the car. She is named Hilda and is a holographic projection of a German woman. It might seem stupid, her being an android and all, but after being on the road in her companionship for so long I am beginning to regard her as human.' said Miles blushing at his 2nd blunder in a record time.

'Aaah!' said the guards understandingly and smiled without adding a word.

'And now, if you'll excuse me, I must take my leave...' said Miles still rather reddish on the face. The young guards chuckled and said goodbye at the traveller before attending to their own business once again.

Miles re-entered his car and asked Hilda to take him to the dead centre of the area. Perhaps he could partake into lunch at some nice restaurant and quell his hunger and thirst. Also, maybe there he would find someone interested in talking politics with him, like Tompkins in Bexley or the noble trio in Edgeware. Hilda complied and the car headed towards the centre of Uxbridge. The distance was evidently rather short since Hilda crossed it in a very short interval of time. The good quality of the road also helped. During this short trip, Miles realised that people here looked well-dressed, the streets clean and taken care of and the buildings presentable and well-maintained. There were few vehicles on the streets and some of them were little buses, 20-seaters, all of them with either the number 1 or 2 on them. Evidently the Uxbridge area was too small to warrant the constitution of more bus lines or the use of larger buses.

In this region Miles also noticed a few interesting details: benches were made out of metal, but boasted a coating of plastic and little holes all over their surface. The coating, however was not simply plastic. It had been manufactured to resemble the surface of a lotus leaf, so that water and dirt would tend to be repelled by the surface of the seats. The slanted nature of the seats would then ensure that all dirt and water fell through the little holes and the seats stayed dry and clean even in the most intense weather conditions. What a brilliant idea! Just a bit farther down, a public clock was displaying the time, weather conditions and predictions for the weather in the next 6 hours. The weather and clock displays of the public clock-tower were separate so at any given moment the time and either the weather at that very moment or the weather over the next 6 hours could be seen simultaneously. Another great idea. Meanwhile at every crossroads there were little roofs supported on slender metallic bars, roofs that would shield pedestrian from precipitation while they were waiting for the green light to appear. Yet the attention to detail Miles was noticing all around him did not end there. He noticed that for those who did not yet own a car with an automatic, almost sentient navigator, there were speed limit signs. On smaller streets, older signs, dissected in 4 quadrants, indicated the speed limits for conditions of clear weather during the day, rain, night and heavy fog. The day speed limit was black against white, the rain one was black against grey, the night one was white against black and the fog one was a black outline of the numbers against white. At the same time on large streets, modern signs, all effectively computer screens, displayed the speed limit for the current weather conditions in a rather artistic way. For example as the clouds loomed above, the speed limits on the main road were shown as black numbers against a background of dark clouds. Clearly this system of government was ripe for the propagation of fresh ideas, thought Miles.

 Amused by what he was seeing all around him he reached the central square of the Uxbridge republic. The square was quite impressive. Over the entire square, large enough to fit 5000 people at least, was an enormous glass dome that shielded all the people underneath from the elements of nature, surprisingly including wind. Trees were growing here and there and a road circled all around the square, which if seen from above would look like a huge disk. Miles asked Hilda to get to that ring road, allow him to descend and then seek parking, for he had noticed that the area to the interior of the ring-road was delimited by the glass walls and gates that shielded all those inside from wind, and at that very time a vast crowd was making use of that comfort. Miles wished to see what all the clutter was about, so after Hilda dropped him at a convenient location, he walked straight towards a gate, opened the outside door of the gate, entered the little antechamber in between the doors, then opened the interior door and found himself at one with the crowd. Apart from a low pitched and incessant murmuring noise the vast enclosure was silent. Miles looked around at the people and quickly realised that everyone was looking towards a point at the edge of the circle that was elevated by the equivalent of one floor from the pavement. That point was the top of a peculiar structure that looked like a miniature stepped pyramid with an orthogonal block on top of it sitting in such way that its long side was vertical. Miles was rather far from that peculiar structure, but could already tell that it was made of very good quality, polished, white marble.

Miles was idly examining the interior of the dome for quite a while, in fact at that very moment he was gazing straight up towards the pinnacle of the dome, where above the glass roof stood a statue in the shape of an ancient Greek goddess -it was Athena, the goddess of democracy and reason in ancient Greece-. His idle examination was interrupted when the crows burst into an explosion of exhilaration; a man was taking his position on the podium. Miles asked a random person standing next to him what the fuss was all about. The man replied that the great orator Jones Ember was taking the podium. He also managed to fleetingly add that Miles came just in time to miss the president's introductory speech for the general assembly, before the speaker addressed the crowd with immeasurable eloquence.

'My dear, fellow citizens of our glorious republic. I am immensely honoured, as I am indeed gratified, to be given the opportunity to step on this very pedestal of freedom and democracy and speak my humble mind to the assembled citizenry of our beloved homeland.

In today's general assembly I would be most inclined to touch upon a very serious issue that affects all of us, an issue that pertains to events that are currently unfolding very near us, an issue that can gravely affect the future of our beloved republic, even its very existence. Therefore I beg your leave to touch upon the subject of the recent collapse of a couple of very large banking giants in Zone 1.

A small number of our fellow citizens, who were working for Kinroy bank and Barrington bank have as a result lost their jobs. Small as their number might be, first of all we may not for one minute abandon them to their fate, and second of all we must be prepared to face the same fate if the wave of collapses in Zone 1 gathers momentum rather than diffusing and vanishing in the near future. Let us face reality, fellow citizens. Our economy is heavily dependent upon those of us who commute every day to Zone 1, toil in labour for a meagre income of Zone 1 pounds and return home every evening tired, but happy in their knowledge that the hard-earned money they bring back will constitute a blow of fresh air and invigorate our economy. That money is what allows us, as a community and a republic, to procure the items and services we here may not ourselves produce, from abroad. That money is what is vital to our continued existence and without it we shall all for sure either perish, or be reduced to living from charities that arrive from abroad, or join another political formation in Zone 2 of London and lose the supreme privilege of living in a republic.

However, fellow citizens, the crisis threatens our Zone 2 workers and by extension the very existence of our dearly beloved republic. And please allow me to assert that even if this crisis does vanish and we avoid the worst, it is not necessarily true that the next crisis will not be the big one. For that reason I maintain with all my heart and spirit that we as united people with an independent economy must break out from the shackles of dependence on Zone 1. We must find a place in the globalised market, a place in the world economy, a place high up at the most productive echelons of the enormous machine that is the world economy, a place from where we may exercise our greatest competence and hold our head high amongst the nations of the world.

And what, I ask, dear citizens, is a better place than that which entails holding to our very bosom one of the world's leading humanity academies and pulling our sovereign wealth together to create one of the world's largest conglomerates? By maintaining a humanity academy of such illustrious standard we shall gain respect abroad and capitalise on our core competence of freedom of expression. We shall exert vast cultural influence by preaching the inherent purity and righteousness of our political system. Meanwhile by pooling our wealth as a sibling would do for another sibling, or even more dramatically a son towards an ailing father, we can create a sovereign fund of biblical proportions, income from which shall be enough to sustain an elevated standard of living for all of us; eliminate poverty from our entire nation, something no other nation has ever achieved in true essence!

Thus brothers and sisters, let us join forces. Let us pull together in the harsh times so that we can enjoy the good times together. Let us break free of the shackles of dependence on the decadent and arrogant Zone 1 and soar like freed eagles up to heights we can now only aspire to! Let us create a vast sovereign fund and propel our little educational college into an academy of international standing. Please vote for the Ember plan for the future of our republic!' concluded the illustrious orator and stepped off the podium amidst a torrent of popular applause, coming from a public charmed by his eloquence and ease and elegance of expression.

Miles, in the meantime, had listened to the entire speech and upon clearing the rhetoric artefacts and exposing the essence of the speech, realised that the proposals of Mr. Ember were actually quite sound even though his plans for an academy of world standing in a community of barely 10.000 people may have been a bit on the optimistic side.

As he was still contemplating these ideas, Miles saw that a second orator was taking the podium. Miles' neighbour, clocking the fact that Miles was a newcomer, bent slightly in the direction of our character and whispered:

'This is Arthur Segner. The main opponent of Jones Ember. These two are the main politicians in our community.'

Miles thanked with a nod and a whisper of 'thank you' and the two men fell silent as the 2nd orator began his speech:

'Dear fellow citizens. We are here today to decide upon a matter of the utmost importance, as my honourable contestant just mentioned. What is the future of our republic going to look like? Let us talk about reality; plain feet-on-the-ground reality. Fancy words and ornate expressions can not mask the fact that we face a tough future. We have been dependent on Zone 1 too much and for too long. This has got to change. We have all read the news, I was sitting with my wife the other day in the living room reading our own Uxbridge Gazette and saw reports that there was something amiss in Zone 1. The article was saying that in Zone 1 there is a hire-freeze and lending has decreased sharply. I know what you are thinking ladies and gentlemen. I know what you are thinking because I had exactly the same suspicions as you, fellow citizens. Namely: what are they waiting for? Hire freeze? Stop lending to each other? Why this sudden suspension of activity? What are the big cheeses in the City hiding and won't tell us?

One thing is for certain. Whatever this crisis is about, it is something big, something that will not blow over quickly. Mark my words brothers and sisters, it will not blow over quickly. I am worried about the future, just as I suspect we all are. My illustrious opponent is right in saying that we need to break off from the shackles of dependence, as he likes to call it. I simply say we must not put all our eggs in the Zone 1 basket. Our fellow citizens who labour in often humiliating conditions for the pleasure and benefit of a number of over-wealthy elite have so far done a brilliant job in providing for their brethren back here, in our beloved republic. For too long have their efforts been inadequately rewarded by the fat-cats of Zone 1. For too long have they wasted their talents for our sakes, sacrificing dignity and talent for the disproportional benefit of the Zone 1ers.

But I say enough is enough, dear citizens. It is high time that our people's talents were recognised, their efforts properly rewarded, the fruit of their labours remaining in our homeland for themselves, their families and all of us to enjoy together. Now more than ever it is time for decisive action. Decisive, united, strong and unrelenting action. The time for words is over.

For that reason let me propose the Segner plan for the future of our republic. We all know that in the real world you need to produce real stuff in order to secure your being. Money will not feed you, stocks and bonds will not either. We need industry of some sort in our community. We are few, but if we pool our wealth together we can create a medium-sized industry and become the very best in the world at producing something very specific that everybody needs. I am thinking of our republic as becoming a great producer of software. We can thus capitalise on all our technical expertise, currently wasted on 3rd rate jobs in Zone 1. To support this we must create a technical university of international reputation. History and philosophy are great objects of academic interest, but technical skills are what will pull us out of the crisis pit.

Dear, fellow citizens, please, remember: in the real world we need real solutions. Vote for engineering, vote for a solid industry, vote for the Segner plan and secure the future of our little, homely republic.' said the illustrious Mr. Segner and stepped down amidst yet another torrent of applause, even more tumultuous than the one offered to Mr. Ember. It seems Mr. Segner's populist, 'man of the people' style was more effective at swaying large parts of the crowd to his side.

As for Miles, he could see the benefits of both plans. Generally speaking, whichever way the republic was going to take, it involved extreme specialisation either in industry, or business. Either way would succeed in breaking the heavy dependence of the republic on labour in Zone 1 equally well. The industrial approach though was slightly more risky. The republic would face stiff competition, although on second thought that was also true if they decided to create a large sovereign business. The industrial approach, however, would be slightly less flexible. It is easier to abandon a business you own that is sinking and use the remaining money to invest elsewhere than abandon a business you own and operate that is sinking. Miles was thinking quickly and in disorder until he stumbled upon the best argument there was in favour of the flamboyant Mr. Ember: If Mr. Segner's plan succeeded, the end result would be a large software company employing a very large part of the republic, earning software developer wages. However, if Mr. Ember's plan succeeded, the end result would be a nation of wealthy industrialists. The risks involved in Mr. Ember's plans were much larger and the time needed for the plan to reach fruition would be longer, but the promise of a very high position in the global economy as an end result was much more appealing.

Miles was satisfied with the quick and apparently correct conclusion he reached and started making his way towards the exit when he stopped all of a sudden. What if they started off with Mr. Segner's plan and then using it as a stepping stone they moved on to Mr. Ember's plan at a later date? Yes. That was definitely the best way to move forward. Either way, the people of Uxbridge already possessed great technical skills in the software department and it would be a pity to abandon them rather than hone them to world-class level. The more Miles thought about this specific contemplation, the more he liked the idea. With that satisfying thought he left and headed out of the Agora, looking for a place to eat at.

Very soon he noticed a very welcoming little tavern at the side of the road and decided to attempt to eat there. The tavern was called 'O Vaggelis' and specialised in Greek food. After all, where else, but in front of the Agora would people pay homage to Greek culture, especially culinary culture? Miles smiled upon seeing the small statuette of Athena just by the entrance and the meandering shapes adorning the door frame and went inside the tavern. Unlike any other restaurant he'd been to, there were only about 3 tables in the entire establishment. They were not, however, ordinary tables, but extremely long ones where maybe 30 people could sit at the same time. Miles assumed a place and started consulting the menu for ideas. He decided to go for traditional Greek 'gyros' and 'tzatziki' and placed his menu on the table upon finalising his decision. Soon afterwards a waiter arrived and took his order. Miles paid at his own request before eating so that he wouldn't have to wait for the bill at the end of his meal, and then sat comfortably and started examining his surroundings at his own leisure.

The restaurant was modern and clean, and its decorations were brimming with references to the Greek antiquity. At the wall that defined the bottom of the restaurant was -what else?- a giant painting of the Acropolis of Athens, framed by a couple of simple, Doric columns either side, a small marble step as the bottom and an ornate slate of marble with various scenes of daily life at the top. The whole ensemble was illuminated by a triplet of lights that shone upwards from inside the floor and were slanted at an angle that gave the Acropolis a very majestic illumination. All around the large dining area there were large, seemingly heavy, stone columns with vases on top of them, some melanomorphous, most erythromorphous and in between the vases stood various paintings of ancient monuments of Greece or pictures of natural jewels of the Greek mainland and islands. All in all, it was a clean and rather cosy restaurant with a relaxed atmosphere. The only rather unsettling thing about the restaurant was that he was the only customer at what must have by all means been lunch-time.

'Are you all right? You seem a bit lost, sir.' asked the waiter noticing that Miles was looking around with ample curiosity.

'Who, me? Ow... well... I was just wondering why there are no other people here at the moment.' asked Miles.

'Oh, I see. Well, we do have a general assembly at the moment. It will be over in...' the waiter checked his watch '...about 10' now, I think.'

'Oh that! I saw part of it. What is it exactly? People were talking about the economic future of the republic from what I could discern.' inquired Miles with interest.

'The assembly? It is the act of gathering our citizens together -as many as possible- to the central square so we can decide upon matters of utmost gravity and vote on them. These last 10' will be dedicated to the voting procedure.' said the waiter. 'In fact, I have just cast my vote myself.' he concluded smiling.

'But, how? When?' asked Miles not quite seeing how that was physically possible.

'Through my personal terminal.' said the waiter showing Miles a terminal neatly rolled into a rather tight cylinder. 'I watched the proceedings through my terminal too.' he said.

'And did that not interfere with your work in any way?' asked Miles with concern.

'Not at all. Pretty much the entire population that has come of age was doing the same as me. So there were no customers around to serve. That is why during general assemblies we only maintain a skeleton workforce and resume work in full swing after it. In that way you're lucky. You got to order first.' said the waiter and smiled.

'Heh. True.' said Miles and fell quiet again.

This idea of full participation in democratic procedures rather appealed to him. He had already seen that this system was ideal for the propagation of ideas, judging by the number of brilliant ideas he spotted on his way to the centre from his very car. Now he was also seeing that people here were genuinely asked for their vote and held general assemblies to make their views heard.

'Say, waiter.' said Miles.

'Yes, sir?' answered the waiter respectfully.

'How often to you have these assemblies?' Miles inquired.

'Every day we have some sort of assembly on various specialised topics. We have a schedule of assemblies published at the official website of our government. However, these assemblies are often too specialised and only people of certain professions tend to attend, as well as people who are directly linked with the issue. For example we have work safety assemblies where employers and employees who work in dangerous conditions tend to attend. The important assembly though is the bi-weekly general assembly where people can propose policies on anything.' said the waiter explaining as clearly as he could.

'But, wait a minute. Anyone can attend those assemblies, but you only get to speak there on a first-come first-served basis, no? How does that work? How do you avoid clutter?' inquired Miles, suddenly puzzled.

'Ah. Don't worry. We have a small number of great orators who come up with most of the ideas anyway. Apart from these familiar faces, very few people take the podium as a general rule. Most people feel they have nothing to add to the genius and wisdom of these orators so the system balances itself that way.' explained the waiter.

'And suppose you were to take over control of a large area with many many more thousands of people. How would it work then? Surely you can't avoid clutter for ever!' said Miles.

The waiter fell silent and suddenly assumed a pensive

countenance. 'I don't know.' he finally uttered. Silence once again ensued.

Miles realised he had stumbled upon what probably was this system's most crippling disadvantage. It was not scalable. Moreover, the more you get people interested in politics, the smaller the critical mass, i.e. the critical number of people beyond which the system is overran with clutter. As such, the only way for the republic to work on a larger scale would be to have a confederation of them constituting a super-state, just like the communards had done. Sure, technology was aiding the republic in keeping the wheels turning with minimum amount of paperwork and disruption -electronic voting, electronic minuting etc.-, however the problem of scalability could not be entirely solved by it. The fundamental problem lies in the time it takes for a human being to communicate effectively to another human being. Miles saw that first hand. If in the Agora there were 20 speakers of the oratorical prowess of Mr. Ember and Mr. Segner, the assembly would last rather long and the audience would end up bored and tired no matter how important, well-expressed or interesting the subject of the assembly was. At a more general level, the republic was placing too much stress on discussion and debate, and too little on action.

From there, Miles' thoughts wandered to the Commune. There too it seemed that there was too much stress on debating and talking and too little on action, but then in all the other systems he'd seen it was too much the other way. Theoretically, in the old representative system there would be sufficient discussion and sufficient scope for action for a smoothly functional system. In practice it seemed that the system tended to lead to apathy and sink into a state similar to the Royal zone.

'Oh well...' thought Miles. 'In the Commune they have a governing council that can take action with the due urgency if need be so.'

'Say...' Miles addressed the waiter again.

'Yes, sir.' replied the waiter.

'Who actually runs the republic? Day to day.' asked Miles.

'Well, nobody really. We take turns to be in the supreme positions of state power. For example, I can register my wish to be a general, the supreme head of the civil service, or a magistrate of common law. My name will then be placed on a register and then I'll wait for my turn. For general, the rotation is every month, for magistrate, every week, for head of the civil service, every 3 days.' said the waiter.

'But, won't that disrupt your work routine?' inquired Miles.

'Oh yes, it will. But I can't be fired for taking public office. Also, in reality only fairly rich people with a lot of time on their hands take office because all of these positions are not paid; or to be more accurate, you receive 50% of your normal wage from your employer if you are an employee who wishes to take public office and get nothing additional to your regular income if you are an employer.' clarified the waiter. Miles felt headaches were at the horizon, so he stood silent again.

As he learned more and more about the republic, Miles realised that it is a brilliant, but technically unworkable idea. It could never be used for the management of large entities, be they countries, towns, factories or even academic institutions. At least making communism work still did not seem to be outside the realm of the technically feasible. Might be difficult and involve vast amounts of bureaucracy and rules, but it was not technically impossible. The Communes seemed to be somewhere in between. There seemed to be a lot of active participation in government, enough structure to keep the system running -even if just barely enough- and little enough not to create gigantic bureaucratic monsters. Also, in practical terms apathy was not an option. Government was done at such local scale that people could relate to much of it. At the higher level, that of the confederation, it worked like a representative system and national defence, immigration and taxation policy was determined at that level, as well as diplomacy.

All of these thoughts were twirling through Miles' mind when he eventually decided: he would live in the Commune until the crisis blew over and he got a job back in Zone 1. He would share his wealth with the communards and live in a small community based on solidarity, without stress and use the time to think about his life, his future and everything he had learned on the journey around London. The more he thought about it, the more he liked the idea. As the dishes with the food landed in front of him and customers started to arrive, hungry from the general assembly, Miles confirmed it to himself: he was going to live in the Commune along Dr. Stephenson.

With that thought he started munching on his food. It was a bit heavy on the stomach, but tasted absolutely fabulous. For that reason Miles started greedily devouring his food and did not stop so much as to take a breath until even that smallest bits of food were securely inside his stomach. He then completed the meal by wiping himself meticulously, greeting the waiter and departing towards his car that had been just summoned. Once inside the car, Miles gave Hilda the name of the last destination on his counter-clockwise journey around Zone 2 of London: the Commune of Whitton. Hilda nodded in understanding and left south-south-east.

No more than 10' into the journey he was crossing the borders of the republic, back into the bad roads of the democratic sector. A simple show of the pass-card, a polite salute from the border guard and the procedure was complete. On his return leg towards the Commune, absolutely nothing of significance happened. The views were the same, the conditions of the road were the same, the weather was still dark and murky. Only for a brief minute while in Hayes, it occurred to Miles that what all of the systems in Zone 2 had in common, which Zone 1 did not have, was that to a certain degree every system he had seen was able to generate extraordinary leaders; they could all generate administrative geniuses as well as tyrants. On the one extreme in the dictatorships and the communist zone these leaders would hold a lot of power and a lot would depend on their competence, and on the other in the republic and commune these leaders would lead by virtue of their charisma and prowess in swaying people. Only in Zone 1 it did not matter who was in government; money was in actual power.

On the one hand, this state of affairs also meant that all systems in Zone 2 were prone to corruption more than Zone 1. In the Communes, it would primarily manifest itself as demagogy, in the communist sector as bureaucratic inefficiency, in the democratic sector as embezzlement, in the royal zone as nepotism, in the dictatorships as oppression and in the republic as demagogy, just like in the Communes. Of course corruption could take many other forms in all these systems, but these were what Miles saw as the primary sources of corruption in each system. Out of all he'd say that the least likely to go corrupt was the Commune Confederation. Rigged computer voting systems and demagogy were the greatest dangers for the Communes, true, but there seemed to be no such thing as the perfect system and this seemed to be the best compromise. In Zone 1 on the other hand, it was all business, so the system was optimised in an economic sense, yet it was not that corruption had been banished. It had simply been institutionalised and incorporated into the system. Thus it might have appeared that on the outside Zone 1 was the least corrupt, simply because the non-institutionalised, residual corruption was very little, but it had already become clear to Miles that his high-end society was deeply ill on the inside, and currently probably feeling the first serious symptoms of it. Following the contemplation of those thoughts, Miles reclined in the comfortable chair of his car and promptly started napping with a faint, merry snore.

Miles had no idea how long it was since he had dozed off, but when he woke up he could see familiar ground. He was in Hounslow, on the very same road that had led him a while ago -it seemed like an eternity- to the gates of the Commune of Whitton. Nothing had changed. The grass-ridden, cracked pavements and pot-holed streets, the unkempt buildings, the poor people who were wandering along the streets; all were familiar to him. Any minute now he would encounter barbed wire barricades marking the borders of the Confederation and see the guard dressed in the old-fashioned but elegant blue uniforms with the tall hat and the impressive C$_{III}$R badge. Sure enough, back in the distance Miles was able to discern a tall silhouette that could be nothing but one of the Commune's border guards. As the car approached the border, Miles became able to discern more and more detail until he recognised in the guard the man who had first allowed him to enter the Commune. By what miracle of heaven that was possible, Miles had no way of knowing, but the guard was beyond any shadow of doubt the moustachioed man with whom he held the first conversation on the territory of Zone 2; the very same border guard.

The guard on his part recognised the luxurious car from the distance, figured that this could be none other than Miles and waved his hand in a friendly manner, beckoning the car to stop right in front of him. Once that was done he walked to the car to greet the guest as Miles was putting his left foot out of the car.

'My, my, my... You have returned. Welcome back, friend. Formality requires that I run a quick check through your pass-card. I trust you have obtained one by now.' said the guard cordially shaking Miles' hand.

'Certainly! The kind Dr. Stephenson has provided me with one. Here... one moment... there we go.' said Miles taking the special guest pass-card out of his pocket.

'Yes... I see... Everything seems to be in order. Please come in, friend. If you wish to meet Dr. Stephenson, you run a good chance of finding him at one of our local pubs here; 'The Welsh dragon' it's called. He usually dines there, or if not dining, he simply sits in the company of the other elders of our commune and discusses with them; mostly politics.' said the guard after checking Miles' pass-card and concluded his statement with a polite smile.

'Any idea where I could find this pub my good man?' cordially inquired Miles.

'You can't miss it. Simply follow this road straight ahead. At the 3rd crossroads turn right and follow the road until the end. At that very T-junction you should be able to spot the pub fairly easily.' answered the guard.

'Thank you very, very much.' said Miles cheerfully at which the officer of the law smiled and saluted equally cheerfully, yet not completely without formality.

Miles re-entered his vehicle, repeated the officer's directions to Hilda and asked her to take him to the Welsh dragon. She complied and the car started moving once again on the now familiar streets of the Whitton Commune. Shortly he was most likely going to meet a great man again, the ideological father of the Commune, elder of Whitton and a most generous and hospitable host: Dr. Stephenson. And that day's discussion would include a most sensitive matter: his registration as an official citizen of the Commune.

PART III: WAR.

CHAPTER 9: THE 3 ELDERS.

It was getting rather dark as a result of the combined effect of the advanced hour of the evening and the frankly miserable weather. The dark, murky clouds that had marked almost the entire day from the morning, when Miles was in Edgeware, till the present hour, in the Whitton commune had finally decided to act; rain began to pour down in quantities not unfamiliar in the tropical regions of the planet (a thin strip in central Africa that still resisted the relentless advancement of the Saharan desert, a few islands in East Asia and the small chunks of Amazon forest that had escaped deforestation). Hilda was navigating Miles' car towards the Welsh dragon pub where he was hopeful of meeting Dr. Stephenson and talk to him about his registration as a citizen of the Commune.

Before too long Miles was stepping out of his car and with brisk steps heading towards the pub. Hilda knew the drill so she went to park the car somewhere in the vicinity as Miles was accustoming himself to the surroundings of the pub. Rather surprisingly, the pub was pretty full and bustling with people engaged in boisterous discussions amongst themselves. The homely atmosphere of the pub in combination with all this conviviality made Miles feel right at home and with this heart-warming thought he set forth to look for Dr. Stephenson, hoping to find him sitting at one of the sturdy wooden tables of the pub in his usual brown suit with the green cloth over his shoulders.

Sure enough, Miles spotted the man himself, Dr. Stephenson at a table for 4 with two companions of similarly advanced age; it was a silver-headed trio. The Dr. was sitting in the middle of the triplet and had his head bent over what appeared to be his flexible terminal whilst the other two old gentlemen were observing closely the images displayed on the terminal screen. Miles paused for a minute contemplating whether to interrupt the activity of the elders or not and for that brief period he studied the three figures sitting at the table before him. Dr. Stephenson was exactly as Miles remembered him: white goatee, rich white hair and bushy white eye-brows just over his bespectacled eyes. To the left, a rather stockier gentleman with a round, bald head and a couple of white tufts of hair emanating from just above and behind his ears was staring with intense concentration at the terminal screen through his own bespectacled eyes. His glasses were a couple of tiny round lenses, in fact so tiny that Miles was very surprised the old gentleman could discern anything through them at all. He was wearing a fairly thick woollen jumper that was covered by a very old fashioned green vest -also wool-. All in all, he looked like a school teacher. The gentleman on the right was visibly older than the other two and his figure bore a rather striking resemblance to that of Sergey Rachmaninoff. Some people said that he looked like old Prime Minister Gladstone in his later years, but if one of those people was to tell Miles of such resemblance, he would quickly look up the picture of the old PM on the internet and immediately deny that such resemblance existed at all. At any rate, the main difference between the Rachmaninoff look-alike and his other companions lay in his massive spectacles with the thick ivory skeleton. The spectacles' skeleton was painted black and that only served to make them look like a relic from the 1960's, despite the fact that the thick skeleton fashion had returned in vogue for a brief period in the 2030's. This ancient gentleman was wearing a rather elegant black suit, complete with the white handkerchief in the small pocket at the chest, a dark red tie running from behind his impeccable white shirt's collar downwards and a small silvery chain that ran from an anchor point just beneath the spot where the lapels crossed paths to a point below the level of the table; most likely a pocket containing an old-fashioned, but desperately elegant pocket watch.

Upon concluding this examination of the elderly trio and seizing the opportunity that presented itself in the form of a pause in the intense discussion between the three gentlemen Miles decided to step ahead and make his presence known by means of a conspicuous cough. The three gentlemen looked up and at one Dr. Stephenson's countenance was graced by a smile of genuine joy.

'Young man! I knew you would eventually return!' he exclaimed cheerfully.

'You know this man Irving?' asked the gentleman to the left.

'Oh yes. He is a traveller, or rather was for the past few days. I believe that he wishes to join our community.' replied Dr. Stephenson without losing his smile.

'Where is he from? Why does he want to join us?' asked the gentleman to the right.

'I shall explain everything in a few moments. Don't worry Percival. In fact, I believe that the young man himself would wish to talk to us about his adventures too.' said the Dr.

'I shall most gladly do so indeed.' said Miles and proceeded to introduce himself most courteously.

'Young man, you shame us.' said the gentleman to the left. 'Here we are babbling like old owls and you come here and introduce yourself with impeccable manners. Please allow me to return the favour. My name is Roger Dickson, history teacher at the elementary school of the area and one of the 3 elders of Whitton.' he concluded.

'Truly spoken Roger. And I am Percival Latchley, long since retired from the profession of engineer and another of the 3 elders of Whitton.' the man to the right introduced himself.

'And I already have been graced with the good fortune of having made Dr. Stephenson's acquaintance. Nice to meet you all venerable gentlemen.' said Miles bowing respectfully and smiling placidly.

'Please, young man, take a seat.' offered Mr. Dickson grabbing the last free chair that rightfully belonged to that table and dragging it slightly along the floor so as to make it easier for Miles to park his hips on it.

'You are most kind, sir.' said Miles and sat down. He then proceeded: 'Gentlemen, for the past few days I have been on a life-changing journey. I have circled the entire Zone 2 and seen almost all of the political systems in the region in action; talked to people who have to deal with them daily and gathered invaluable information and experiences that will forever live In my memory. Today, I wish to announce my decision to come and live amongst you as one of your Commune, for during my journey I have contemplated long and hard and came down to the conclusion that your system is the best in the region.'

'Is that so, young man?' asked Mr. Latchley. 'How did you reach that conclusion?'

'Well, let me tell you the whole story...' said Miles and set off narrating his adventures to the three elders of Whitton. He mentioned the discipline and militarism of the communist zone, the abandonment and decay of the democratic sectors, the misguided distribution of wealth and immobile society of the Royal sectors, the dreadful sights he'd seen in the dictatorial zone and the dysfunctional freedom of the republic. At the same time he did not forget to mention the positive aspects of each system and attempted to make the most balanced assessment of each system. Then he proceeded to praise the Commune about its genuinely humane solidarity, the spirit of cooperation that micro-communities helped create and expressed his concern about the ability of the Confederation to take organised action and of the Communes to support structures that by nature necessitate that large numbers of people cooperate, for example a united army or the entity that runs the central mainframe system of the Confederation. The elders listened closely for hours as Miles described more and more of his adventures and eventually Miles reached the point in the story where he ends up in the Welsh Dragon pub. At that point, the 3 elders reclined against the backs of their seats for they had been leaning forward eagerly so as not to miss a single word of the young man's tale.

'Most interesting. Very nice journey. I am sort of envious. I wish I was accompanying you.' said Mr. Dickson pensively.

'Think of all those conversations the young man had with inhabitants of the other zones!' uttered excitedly Mr. Latchley.

'Well, quite. I believe we could be here for days on end listening to his adventures and then discussing the content of his conversations and debating on political issues. However, be that as it may, the young man here has reached a conclusion. Namely that he wishes to become a member of our community. I believe that what we should do now is address his concerns about our zone and system of government and inform him of the citizenship registration procedure.' said Dr. Stephenson veering the conversation back towards business. 'We can discuss politics later, as I'm indeed sure, all of us would like to.' he concluded.

'Quite right.' replied Messrs Latchley and Dickson.

'To begin with you must understand that the rule for joining our society is that you need to share your income with the rest of us if it is significantly larger than the average. All your property stays yours. We will then require you to sign a document that confirms your agreement to our rules of citizenship. We will also need identification documentation from your previous location of residence. The implant you carry should provide all the relevant information. We have a very small number of implant readers at our central mainframe centre that can handle that data transfer. Finally since you still are technically a citizen of the United Kingdom -devoid as this notion is of essence nowadays- the procedure should be completed after these simple tasks are completed and you go through a solemn ceremony.' explained Dr. Stephenson.

'Ceremony?' inquired Miles.

'It's simply a short party, so to speak, where you meet much of our small community in person. It's a great opportunity to socialise.' explained Mr. Dickson cheerfully.

'It shall be my pleasure.' assured Miles bowing his head slightly. 'And accommodation?' he inquired.

'For the time being you may stay at a local hotel. After you become a citizen, we can offer you accommodation at some empty apartment of the region. We have apartments allocated for 300 potential citizens. That is why our community may freely accept immigrants until that number of people is reached.' explained the Dr.

'And what if natural demographic shift makes a community grow to over the limit?' asked Miles with genuine curiosity.

'In that case the communities split and we attempt to build more housing. If that isn't possible because of lack of space or other practical considerations we try to encourage people to move to other Communes.' said Dr. Stephenson. 'But our Commune is still young. We haven't got such problems yet. Maybe in the future we get overpopulation and have to squeeze together; who knows? The truth of the matter is that under those circumstances any system would come under pressure, no? Question is how we would cope with it; in fact it would put our solidarity to the test; a very, very hard test indeed.' he concluded talking more to himself than to Miles.

'That would be most dangerous. I can already picture people fighting with each other over living space or some other resource. More oppressive societies may suppress such tensions with their organs of oppression, but here it might descend into chaos. We would have to either abandon our anarcho-syndicalist policies, or perish.' said Mr. Latchley with visible concern.

'Come, come gentlemen! I'm sure people under any system take it rather harshly when the force of circumstances precipitates a drop in their living standards. We can surely show enough solidarity to pull through anything!' exclaimed Mr. Dickson rather optimistically.

'I wouldn't be so certain.' interjected Miles. 'When the situation worsens a certain behaviour is encouraged; that is the 'every man for himself' sort of behaviour, and let me tell you this: people don't take too kindly to it when they see others resort to such behaviour.' he concluded with a shocking dose of realism.

'Quite so.' said Dr. Stephenson with concern. 'And to be frank with you, dear colleagues, I am not entirely sure how our society can deal with such pressure.'

'But... but... all we've fought for!' protested Mr. Dickson.

'What we fought for is freedom. We fought for a society where authority falls together in structures that can be freely composed and dissociated. We fought against ossified authority structures that inevitably slow down and become corrupted with age. Creating an authority whose job is to keep order in society is, of course, possible since people understand the need for protection against crime. However, such authorities of order may not force the hand of society. They have not got the authority to maintain a system nobody wants any more. The people will not stand for it.' reasoned Dr. Stephenson with great concern.

'The people will start committing crimes of desperation as living standards fall and think they are somehow justified in doing so. After all who can find it in their hearts to harshly punish him who steals a bun of bread out of sheer hunger?' added Mr. Latchley.

'That is why I am rather concerned about the long term stability of the Confederation, gentlemen.' said Miles. 'What we see at a personal level will also be reflected in the relations between different Communes of the Confederation. First, some Communes will be hit harder than others. Then there will be calls for solidarity. You can connect the dots after that and see how tensions will arise between different Communes. After that, it's a slippery slope. Relations will just avalanche to ever newer depths.' he concluded arguing rather astutely. An uncomfortable silence ensued.

'In fact, now that I think about it, this problem can be generalised. How can you make sure that the decisions in the Commune will be those that are good for the Commune rather than those that are simply popular?' inquired Miles.

'Ah, that's easy! It has to do with experience. People now take active part in decision making and see what the consequences of their own actions and decisions are. For that reason they show a lot more understanding that you'd think. Also, we have, of course, a constitution which we follow religiously. That way we place some general rules that we have all agreed are good at this point in history, into a 'glass display' so to speak and leave them untouched for as long as they work. For example, our weekly change in council leadership is something we may not change at a whim, but will require a very strong majority to change.' explained Mr. Latchley.

'And even under 'stress' so to speak these rules stand firm and we all have an obligation to defend them.' added Dr. Stephenson.

'Similarly we have rules that safeguard the integrity of the community, condemn crime and generally speaking maintain social harmony. Of course, as we said the police can't force the people to stay united or keep this system unchanged if pressure mounts so much that a large majority demands change, but there are some mechanisms that keep our Communes together and authorities that may act within the boundaries of those rules they protect. Until the people decide to change the rules that is, as we briefly discussed just a minute ago.' completed Mr. Dickson.

'So, unless there is a generalised will for a radical change in system, the Commune is safe?' summarised Miles.

'Effectively yes. You will see that despite the fact that appearances would suggest that we have a radically different and unique system of government, looking beneath the surface revels more and more similarities to other systems. Like the police force, the ability of the state to exercise coercion, more permanent structures of authority. It is only that all these manifestations of state power are significantly weaker than elsewhere...' said Mr. Latchley attracting a poisonous stare from Mr. Dickson. Dr. Stephenson noticed that.

'He is right.' he simply said. The poisonous stare was transformed into one of disbelief.

'However, the other difference is that this state authority is much more accountable and capable of change. After all, when you know your officers in person, when you are an integral part of the decision-making process that generates their general orders, when you an integral part of the system, it is much easier to prevent, or spot or stop corruption and promote cooperation or propose and carry through change.' said Miles vehemently defending the virtues of the Communards' system.

'Thank you, young man.' said Mr. Dickson appreciatively.

'And yet, there still remains the matter of the system's reaction to pressure.' said Dr. Stephenson pensively.

'Well, we all agree that our system is much more resistant to social pressure than we thought, at least?' uttered Mr. Dickson.

'Yes, but how do other systems fare in this respect?' wondered Miles.

'What an excellent idea. Let's discuss the issue by using comparisons.' said Mr. Latchley.

'Young man, you have just travelled a lot, why don't you tell us what you think?' said Dr. Stephenson smiling benevolently.

'Me? It would be an honour.' said Miles and the 3 elders assumed a position that indicated that they were keenly listening.

'Oh well, let's take them in order, shall we? First of all the communist zone. They are prone to destabilisation mostly as a result of their various product shortages and lack of certain liberties, predominantly the freedom to travel abroad. However, under intense pressure the vast bureaucracy of the state would probably turn corrupt despite all the safeguards and herald an era of miserable corruption until the entire structure either collapses under shortage pressure, or is changed by revolution, or is changed from within. So, in essence it can withstand a lot of damage and as a side-effect, outlive its useful life-span by a lot. At least that's the feeling that I get.' said Miles.

'Interesting point of view. Outliving its useful life-span. I never thought about it that way.' said Mr. Latchley approvingly. 'Perhaps some times it is better to let things collapse and start anew. The corrupt monarchy in France of the 1770's, the inefficient Tsardom in Russia of the 1910's and the putrid, stagnant communist parody in the Soviet Union of the 1980's; all prime examples of this idea. What next?'

'As for the democratic zones where the old city councils have been revived in form and function, I see the same problem that brought the demise of Zone 1. Voter apathy. People are too far from power to feel connected to it in any way, so they quickly lose interest in politics and let any clown take over control. Most of the time they elect incompetent fools at the steering wheel, but what if they get an extremist at some point?' said Miles.

'Astute observation, young man. That's how the dictatorship in Harrow & Watford started, you know.' said Mr. Dickson.

'Really? I had no idea.' replied Miles, his chain of thoughts now interrupted.

'Oh yes.' said Mr. Dickson. 'They started as a popular party vouching for law and order in the midst of the chaos generated by the general retreat of the central government. Their ideas for strict policing and an uptight system of Japan-style work ethic appealed to many at the time. Then it started going downhill as the opposition was silenced and policing became more intrusive than most people imagined possible...' he concluded sullenly.

'Ah...' said Miles, following which silence again descended upon the quartet.

'Please do go on, young man.' beckoned the old engineer.

'Ah... yes. As I was saying... as I was saying...' started Miles.

'Voter apathy precipitated the decline of those regions that decided to return to the old system of government.' politely reminded Mr. Latchley.

'Oh yes, that. And, as I was saying the best way I can summarise what I saw in those areas is a number of less successful copies of zone 1, perhaps at an earlier stage of development.' concluded Miles talking about the democratic sectors.

'It is well known that democracies either sink into apathy or vote the means of their own destruction in power. It is a well-known property of democracies.' said Mr. Dickson sagely. Evidently, he was the elder who played the role of the incarnation of idealism.

'And at the next stop?' inquired Mr. Latchley, the elder who represented realism, apparently.

'Next I went to the Royal boroughs of the North, as I already said when I was telling you the story. There, I found out that the way society is structured is rather unfair to begin with. The flow of wealth seems to be directed in a misguided fashion. And well... I think we already know all about autocratic regimes. I don't think I need to comment a lot on it. I'll just say that it is again a system that has the means to greatly outlive its useful lifespan.' said Miles.

'Agreed.' said Mr. Latchley.

'Finally in the republic, I think under serious pressure things would quickly degenerate. The republic's greatest enemies are demagogy and populism. Come to think of it I've sampled a bit of both when I was there.' said Miles. 'Anyway, if under social pressure for change, it would react by giving rise to dangerous factions. People tend to think less clearly when they panic and that manifests itself in voting for parties that the very same people under booming conditions would consider insane to vote.' he concluded.

'Very good observation.' said Dr. Stephenson, the philosopher in the elder trio. 'Anything from ludicrous palingenetic myths to insane claims of messianism tend to be discarded as irrational, ridiculous and even impossible to fool anyone in times of well-being, yet when the situation suddenly worsens and people feel threatened all these blatant lies suddenly represent hope, not folly.' he observed rather eloquently. Miles loved that expression.

'In conclusion, I think it would be reasonable to say that every system has a breakdown threshold, just like a diode or a transistor device. The level of that threshold, its value so to speak, depends on the nature of the system. When that threshold is passed, by definition, chaos ensues. Of course this means that we can compare systems with respect to the levels of pressure that define their threshold, although to me it would be far more interesting to examine the likelihood that these systems ever reach that situation. But that, perhaps, can be the topic of another discussion, if we ever get the chance to talk like this again.' said Mr. Latchley.

'Spoken like a true engineer.' merrily teased Dr. Stephenson in response to which the ancient engineer's face was graced with the quivers of a faint, but cheerful smile.

'That is most true, Irving. I do tend to look at things from a rather more analytical point of view. For example the issue of government stability and system stability in the context of signal processing are not that different from one another.' said the engineer.

'Oh?' exclaimed Mr. Dickson.

'They both have inputs, on the one hand a signal, on the other the geopolitical and social conditions of the time. They both have a structure that bequeaths them with various properties that determine how the input is processed, on the one hand an electronic circuit, on the other a system of government, law and decision-making norms. They both take some time to react to events, on the one hand because of internal system delays, in the other because of internal bureaucratic delays. They both attempt to perform a task, on the one hand to convert an input signal to a convenient output signal, on the other hand to make use of the current socio-political conditions and generate either wealth, or jobs, or a social security net, or most likely a combination of all of the above plus more. They both must control imperfections in the signal, on the one hand noise, on the other hand corruption for example and finally they both go bust if they fail to control such perturbations from nominal running. In fact this point is so crucial that I will give you an example of it. If an amplifier in a microphone-to-loudspeaker design like we used to do decades ago, fails to cancel feedback from the loudspeakers back to the microphone, you get the system in a positive feedback situation that eventually saturates the system or blows it up. If there was no such problem, then any old amplifier would do the job, but in the real world it is there, so you need circuitry that is designed to cope with it. Similarly, communism is a very good example of this in politics. If you assume that people are of an angelic nature, then the system works frictionlessly, but in the real world there will be corruption, laziness etc. so the system must be then designed to take this into account. You see, my esteemed colleagues, some principles are much more generic than we think; often almost universal.' said Mr. Latchley concluding his little speech. The conclusion returned memories of James to Miles' mind. Apparently, he wasn't the only one contemplating what had been just said because once again silence descended upon the party. A couple of minutes later, however, it was broken by Dr. Stephenson who looked at his watch and exclaimed:

'My, my, my. Look at the time.'

It was indeed very late, the elders had to head home and Miles needed at least an evening snack for he had enjoyed no dinner that day. Thus, the elders excused themselves in the most polite of manners and left for their residences, but not before Dr. Stephenson showed Miles on his terminal where to find a good hotel for the next few days, as well as where to go to register for citizenship. Miles then ordered dinner, ate it in peace and quiet and then summoned his car and headed for the indicated hotel to finish his day. It turns out the hotel he was staying at was the same place he had spent his first night in the Commune at. At any rate, after checking in to the hotel, thus ensuring that Hilda had a place to park the car and recharge her batteries, and finally concluding his pre-nocturnal ablutions, Miles fell asleep mentally exhausted, but happy.

CHAPTER 10: COMMUNARD.

The next morning Miles woke up energised. He stretched himself in bed, and promptly jumped out of it in order to dress himself and subsequently go to the bathroom to dispense with his morning toilette. When all was said and done, Miles was ready to head to the local citizen registration bureau and start the citizenship acquisition procedure. He summoned his beloved car and very soon he was on the familiar seats of his private vehicle moving towards Hanworth, where his target bureau was situated. Apparently, the various Communes in the Confederation had a much more elaborate system of distribution of labour that Miles had originally thought. The various Communes in Hanworth were sustaining the citizen registration bureau by providing staff for it and the office serviced about ¼ of the territory of the commune. Of course, the citizens of the Communes of Hanworth had to turn to other communes when in need of, say, a travel agency or any other service that could not be realistically expected to be provided by a different institution for every single commune. Miles began to realise that the way the Confederation worked was different that what he had originally thought. Yes, decisions were being taken at a very local level, with some important decisions being made at the Confederation level, but the economy was far less compartmentalised and far more interlinked than he had thought. In fact, even much of the bureaucracy seemed to be distributed between many different Communes, each specialising in one sort of service. This, of course, implied that the various Communes entrusted to one another very important services. That was quite a show of solidarity, Miles thought. But then again, some of the economic and administrative structures would still have to employ more than 300 people, sometimes a lot more, so it was need as well as solidarity. At any rate, the problem of how these 'large' institutions worked in a system where very a great amount of important decision-making was being made at the very local level was still a matter he had to discuss with one of the elders.

Immersed in such contemplations Miles reached the citizen registration bureau. It was a rather modern building, in so much that it was built no more than 30 years before. So naturally, it was made of predominantly glass, the roof was covered by solar panels and featured a central ventilation shaft that connected a large metal chimney that Miles could see shining at the top of the building to a ventilation outlet that protruded out of the ground next to the building. That was a brilliant piece of home engineering that was fitted to all buildings from the 2020's onwards, although from the 2030's onwards engineers managed to make it much less conspicuous. The principle of operation was simple. The ventilation shaft would begin at the metal chimney, go down through the centre of the building until it went underground, below the foundations of the building itself. Then it would bend and run parallel to the surface of the ground until it was far enough from the building, at which point it bent again and went upwards till it met the vent outlet. During the summer, the metal chimney would get extremely hot as a result of solar activity. Thus, the air in the vicinity of the chimney would expand and rise, pulling air from the vent outlet in, through the cool ground and then through the building. That way the building was naturally cooled during the summer. During the winter, valves shut the system off as it becomes unnecessary, nay, even counter-productive one could say. As for the glass exterior of the building, that was not there for cosmetic reasons either. The glazing was quadruple and in fact only the external couple of sheets of transparent material were actual glass. The outer glass was there purely for safety reasons. The 2nd layer of material, was actually a specially manufactured sheet of nanomaterial that was normally transparent to IR radiation from the sun. Under the application of an electric field, however, it would become reflective to light of polarisation parallel to the electric field. The 3rd sheet of material was similar to the 2nd, but with the structures applying the electric field along them positioned so that the electric fields on the different sheets of nanomaterial ran perpendicularly to one another. Thus, if the electric fields were activated on both the 2nd and 3rd layers of nanomaterial, the glass exterior of the building would reflect all of the incoming IR radiation from the sun. The last layer of material was the inner glass and that was there again for safety, as well as to contain concentrated greenhouse gases that were positioned between the 3rd and the final layers of the glass structure, or 'dome'. Other significant technical details of the dome included the fact that the interior side of the 3rd layer of nanomaterial was coated with a special layer of IR-semi-reflective material. So, IR radiation could come in freely, but find it very difficult to come out exactly because of that semi-reflective material plus the greenhouse gases compressed between layers 3 and 4. Finally, between layers 1, 2 and 3 there was vacuum. Thus, in the winter, the sun would radiate through the deactivated nanomaterial layers, past the semi-reflective layer and the greenhouse gases and into the building, where it would stay trapped and heat up the space. In the summer, the nanomaterial layers would be activated by applying static charges to the capacitors that created the electric fields in those layers, and so IR radiation would all be reflected. As a result the interior of the building would stay cool. During both seasons, the vacuum between layers 1, 2 and 3 would minimise the building's heat losses or gains like the walls of a thermos. Naturally, during the summer windows at the top of the dome and the bottom of the dome could be also opened to create a draft. The top of the dome being lined with shiny steel would act very similarly to the metal chimney of the shaft cooling system and would enhance the draft as well as create a pleasant breeze in the interior of the building during hot days. Finally, potted plants and in some cases roof-gardens attempted to minimise the need for air transfer between the inside and the outside of the building by balancing oxygen and carbon dioxide within the building at least partially like the counterweight of an elevator counterbalances some of the weight of the lift + passengers. With these few systems the building managed to control its internal temperature rather well and at a very low energy cost. A mainframe computer would operate them to ensure they were working optimally for further savings. On an interesting note: some -older- buildings did not achieve the selective polaroid functionality of their dome by manipulating materials through the use of electric fields but by deliberately aligning or mis-aligning disk-shaped polaroid filters to one another. Sure it meant that out of each square element of the dome only the disk that corresponded to the polaroid filters could actively partake in the regulation of temperature within the building, and that at any given time at least one polarisation of the IR radiation coming from the sun would be lost even if the filters were perfectly aligned with each other, but it was much cheaper to implement than the capacitor & electric field solution and had thus been used mostly for buildings of a more advanced age.

Miles approached the energy efficient citizen registration bureau, ceremonially stepped out of the car and asked Hilda to park for a while and then crossed through the heavy double-doors of the glass dome and into the interior of the building. He was met with the sight of a large waiting room with about 20 seats, a reception desk manned by a couple of terminals and a display indicating that no.22 was meant to be heading to the marriages office, no.23 was to be heading to the driving licence bureau, no.24 was to be heading to the pass-card office and so on. Just at the left side of the door that Miles had just walked through there was a machine that dispensed numbered tickets. Miles pressed the button and took one. He was no.32. He smiled as this antiquated system of queuing brought back to him memories from childhood. In the last decade Zone 1 was using implant readers to generate queues. At any rate, Miles grabbed the ticket securely and headed to one of the terminals at the reception desk. A lady's disembodied head was floating on the screen. She greeted him officiously and inquired which service he would like to make use of. Miles replied that he would be much obliged if he could talk about citizenship registration with someone and the disembodied head replied in turn that he would need to go to the citizenship office for that. She then beckoned him to have a seat and kindly wait until the office was free.

Miles thanked her and started walking towards an empty seat when the large display in the waiting room indicated that no.32 was to go to the citizenship office. Apparently all the numbers before him had other businesses to attend to that day. Feeling lucky, Miles followed the signs to the door labelled 'Citizenship bureau'. He entered without knocking, for a small green light on an ultra-thin display on the door read 'please enter', and promptly took a seat right in front of yet another terminal. The disembodied head of a clerk appeared, greeted him politely and listed a number of options for various services that the bureau provided. At the end of the list was the option to speak to a human if none of the other options were suitable for his business. Miles asked for the citizenship registration option and the clerk brought forth the citizenship registration menu. Miles asked to see the 'help' option, which claimed to provide information on the procedure itself and the clerk started talking.

'The first step in gaining Confederation citizenship is to provide the bureaucracy with relevant personal data. We shall need different data for people of different backgrounds. If you have any identification documents on your person, please swipe them at the reader to your left. If you carry an implant, please swipe it at the reader to your right. If you have none, please type in your last foreign address of residence and citizenship.' said the head and paused. Miles swiped the implant to the suitable reader.

'Our system has detected that you are a citizen of the United Kingdom from Zone 1 of London. The system also detects that you are eligible for citizenship in the Confederation. We are ready to proceed to step 2 of your application procedure. Do you wish to do so?' inquired the clerk. Miles replied in the affirmative.

'The 2nd step concerns the rules of gaining citizenship in the Confederation. Please read them at your leisure and tick the box when ready. If you wish to think over the rules for longer, please use your terminal to access them at our website www.confederationgov.gov.uk/ citizenship/ application/ documents/ rules and then return at your leisure to provide an answer. Your session data will be saved for a month.' said the clerk again.

Miles read through the rules of citizenship. They were mostly the same as in the United Kingdom in general, except of course, the rule requesting that any income above a certain level has to be shared with the community, the obligation to defend the Confederation against foreign aggression as well as a few other details, mostly of a bureaucratic nature. Miles quickly read through the rules and accepted. The clerk spoke again:

'Now we are ready for the 3rd step of the procedure. Shall we?'

'Certainly.' replied Miles and the clerk spoke again:

'Now you must choose a Commune within the Confederation that will accommodate you. On this map and list you may see the Communes that have places to offer for you.' Miles searched for Whitton, found it and spelt it out to the clerk, who in turn zoomed into the map on the Commune of Whitton, displayed a few statistics about it and asked for confirmation. Miles did give his confirmation and then the clerk beckoned him to move on to the last step of the procedure: selecting a time and date for the citizenship ceremony. He chose the coming Friday, after the evening assembly of the community. Then the clerk spoke again:

'Thank you very much dear sir. The procedures for citizenship acquisition that have to be made within this office are now complete. You shall officially become a citizen at the end of the ceremony. Until then, please enjoy yourself and have a look at our website www.confederationgov.gov.uk/ citizenship/ guidelines for documents that shall guide you to your new life in the Confederation. These documents include details reports on how the political system works, details on your rights and duties as well as guides on how things work in general in this country. Finally, please take your new pass-card from the slot underneath the terminal screen. This will be your main identification document as well as your main travel document. You may use it to do anything between buying a soda at a vending machine to getting a new job. The aforementioned documents with guidelines to citizenship include more detailed information on the subject. Now, is there anything else I may do for you at the moment?' he concluded nodding with a smile.

Miles replied in the negative, the disembodied clerk then greeted politely and promptly disappeared after Miles returned the greeting. The latter then left the office, pass-card secure in his pocket, thinking how much work and data processing must have been carried out between the moment he swiped his implant at the reader and the moment the clerk announced his eligibility for citizenship. Background checks, criminal record checks, place of residence checks, profession and education checks on his person as well as the comparison of all these results with a presumably vast database that contains the combinations of those variables and many more that make someone eligible for citizenship. All of these were things that as one moved towards the past would have taken increasing amounts of paperwork and human work in order to be processed, but had in the modern world of the 2050's been simplified to an almost completely computerised, automatic procedure. Miles figuratively 'thanked god' for his fortune to be born long enough after the first clumsy bipolar transistors to enjoy the benefits of ELSI (Extremely large-scale integration, the next step after VLSI -very large scale integration-) and CGAI (Computer generated artificial intelligence) technology that gave rise to all those disembodied heads he was so used to dealing with in his everyday life, including Hilda. He was realising that in a very real way computers had been advanced to the point where they could largely emulate humans and communicate with humans just like the said humans communicated with each other. The best attempt to bridge the communication gap between man and machine that far was the robo-scalp (a technological wonder we have already discussed), which scientists were attempting to create in an implantable form with an output only portal that would allow people to directly talk to machines.

With such thoughts about the relationship between man and machine Miles summoned his car and headed to the cylindrical hotel he was staying at. Once there, he headed to the restaurant of the hotel and sat at a small table for two in the plainly decorated main dining area. The restaurant was simple, yet clean, a white tablecloth neatly arranged on top of an old and cheaply made round table marking that the above stated remarks also held for the table Miles was sitting at. He consulted the menu, a piece of laminated paper rather than the usual unrolled terminal screen. After a short time spent considering his options he decided to try the soup of the day with a dish of dumplings, sausages and mash as main. It was too late for mere breakfast, yet too early for lunch, so he thought he'd combine them into a filling brunch and then wait until dinner for his next meal.

The waitress soon arrived and took Miles' order. She then departed and left Miles to his own contemplations. His main concern at the time was how he could get a job and in the event of success, what job that would be. After all, he was a banker by profession, his engineering skills long since forgotten along with all the stuff he had learned to temporarily regurgitate for the purposes of passing exams and progress tests. Miles sighed and decided to turn his thoughts elsewhere. After all he would find something most likely. All he needed to do was go to his room, switch on the terminal there and look for a job at the Commune's website for labour matters, including job openings. He could then presumably browse all job openings and go for a virtual interview once he found something of interest to him. That was the way it worked in Zone 1 and there was no reason he could see why things should be any different in Zone 2. Long time ago, in the 2020's, job interviews were replaced by tele-interviews as teleconference technology became cheaper and more user-friendly. A number of very forward-looking companies first, then a large number of others, mostly involved in electronics and finally the bulk of the companies, all decided to switch to an electronic version of the traditional job interview. Thus the interviewers would be spared a journey to the company's meeting rooms and the interviewee would be spared an often exceedingly long commute with an uncertain outcome. Naturally, all the people taking part in a job interview, even if it was a of a 'tele' nature, had to look extremely formal and presentable and behave accordingly. For that reason people tended to hold their job interviews from the most presentable and tidy room in their residence, or for enhanced credibility and in the name of good impressions, from special job interview studio centres that possessed rooms of various furnishing styles and could be rented by the hour for job interviews. For example an aspiring barrister who did not possess a large house with a sitting area adorned with a fireplace, some random swords, comfortable armchairs and a large, fluffy bear pelt on the floor could easily rent such studio room from a job interview studio centre and use it for seeking a workplace at a respected law firm. Naturally, the same trick could be played with a green screen and graphics, however the real thing always felt more comfortable. At any rate, most people went for the green-screen rooms that were cheaper, but those who aimed high but did not yet possess an impressive enough residence chose the specialised, themed rooms like in the example for the aspiring barrister. Anyone wealthy enough to afford more than that would typically be the owner of a house that was definitely impressive enough for a job interview.

Naturally the job interview itself was not the whole story. Before the interview, the employee had to provide identification information -for example via implant or some ID-card or pass-card- and answer a questionnaire whose aim was to ensure that the prospective employee was indeed interested in the job and at least theoretically able to do it. This was a fairly standard and easy procedure. After a successful interview the candidate was effectively at work. The only thing he had to do was to sign the work contract stating his obligations and since Zone 1 had no labour legislation, that was pretty much the end of the story. Perhaps in the Commune Confederation where there was labour legislation the procedure would not be quite so simple. Miles had no way of knowing. At any rate, his thoughts were at that moment revolving around completely different issues. He was wondering what his new residence would look like, what furniture he should get, if any, what colour curtains to use and other such everyday issues.

While pondering the particularly tricky issue of choosing a colour for his mood lighting in the bathroom his meal arrived. The food was not exactly luxurious, but had been cooked with mastery and spirit and the portion was of a generous size. Miles dove straight on to the soup and started eating with great appetite. The soup was great from the first spoonful. Finely chopped pieces of tomatoes were swimming in a rich, nutritive liquid in the company of small bits of beef, parsley and a hint of basil. The warm temperature of the soup warmed Miles' insides. Once he had eliminated every trace of soup he moved on to his main dish. The dumplings were very filling and had a peculiar texture to them. They felt like they were made out of very pleasantly soft stone and would disintegrate into hundreds of tender little 'chippings' in his mouth creating the impression that he was eating infinitely small, soft granules. Miles liked that texture as well as the taste. The sausages were fried in very little oil and thus had a far less fatty taste but the frying process had been done with care as no part of the sausage was charred or uncooked. Instead it had apparently been fried evenly. Miles appreciated that. Finally the mash was nice and creamy and melted in his mouth. With this overall satisfaction permeating his mind and stomach, Miles thanked the waitress, complimented the chef, paid his bill and headed for his hotel room. During his meal at least, his thoughts were directed at nothing in particular; instead he was just enjoying the food.

Once in his room, Miles sat at the Spartan desk, switched on the terminal and navigated to the government website that lists jobs. He scrolled to the Whitton Commune and found out, not without a slight degree of surprise, that the Commune he was about to become a member of was one of the Communes whose primary goals were to provide staff for the nearby central Condeferation news agency, an institution called 'Kropotkin's diaries'. In the confederation there were no companies, no businesses as such. They were all called institutions. In any case, the 'Kropotkin's diaries' news agency was the official channel of news of the entire Confederation and from what Miles was reading on the net about it, it was held in very high regard for its commitment to pluralism and its coverage of news from many points of view as well as a 'main broadcast' where the news were covered with the utmost possible neutrality and objectivity. That way, anyone listening to the Diaries for about 2-3 hours would get all the news of the day covered from at least 3 'opinionated' perspectives -most of the time mutually conflicting- as well as from one where a conscious attempt was made to strip all opinion, interpretation, speculation, sentiment and spontaneity from the newscast. Miles liked the idea of working for such news agency. A combination of that and the appetite for knowledge that his recent journey had precipitated meant that he was now regarding the job openings for journalists in the news agency as rather appealing career prospects for him. He decided to go for it.

The 'Kropotkins' diaries' website was easy to navigate and quickly he managed to find his way to the careers website of the news agency where he filled in the questionnaire forms, swiped his new pass-card to the terminal reader so that his personal ID information could be transferred to the agency and asked for an interview. The agency's system told him that his pass-card data and the answers to his questionnaire had earned him an interview. He was then asked to choose a time slot for his interview and luckily for him there were two lots of slots every week, one lot on Tuesdays and another one on Fridays. As that day was Tuesday he could go for a slot in the Tuesday lot so he chose that day, asked to be interviewed at 16:45, confirmed the appointment, jotted down the session ID, switched off the terminal and went for a short nap.

Miles awoke in good time to dress himself up for an job interview with the elegant new clothes he had ordered online the previous evening, groomed himself appropriately and headed to the reception desk where the disembodied head of a robo-receptionist greeted him and inquired of the quality of his stay, to which he reported that he was fine and enjoying his stay very much. He then inquired about directions to the nearest job interview studio and having received word that a studio was just a couple of blocks down the road from the hotel he thanked the disembodied head and left at a leisurely pace; after all he had time. Outside, the weather was cold, but the sun was shining. Miles rearranged the collar of his coat so that it better covered his neck and set out on a gentle walk down the street, taking his time to notice all the details of the area. The cylindrical structure of the hotel was the tallest in the immediate vicinity, smaller buildings from the last 30 years to the left and the right of the cylindrical tower. Meanwhile, on the opposite side of the road extended what once certainly was a park, but now was a plantation of Hazels and other fruit trees. People could still walk down certain paths as if it were a regular, public park, but most of the area was reserved strictly for farming activities. Far to the left and the right of the park more buildings could be seen, denoting two more edges of the park's area.

Since time was ample, Miles decided to enjoy a walk through the park. He crossed the relatively traffic-free road and walked to one of the park entrances. He had to, since the park was fenced. The entrance to the park was a rather retro-style metal gate with a large map lying between a large metal sign and the glass screen that protected it. Miles consulted the map carefully and mentally calculated that he had enough time to walk around one of the proposed scenic routes as denoted by a red line on the map, before heading for his job interview. Thus, cheerfully he set off walking amongst the Hazels, whose gigantic stature -maybe 20m tall- was likely to have been the result of genetic engineering. As his shoes tackled the soft, dirt footpath, Miles rejoiced at the sight of fresh, green grass, riddled with clovers and dandelions -although none of them were flowering at the time- and Hazels all around. He kept on walking around the park for a while until the Hazels were replaced by Pomegranates. He turned right at the fork in the road and headed onwards through the Pomegranates. As he continued walking leisurely through the park he spotted some squirrels, brown squirrels to be more precise, on the lush lawn as they were darting in various directions in their usual swift way, stopping at times to raise their little heads and front paws and look around with their beady, black eyes, perhaps scouting for nuts or on the look-out for humans. Soon, the small Pomegranate plantation ended and Apple trees took the lead, creating intricate patterns of light and shadow as their many, many small leaves filtered the sunlight that was descending upon the earth. Some people were playing with their pets -mostly dogs, but also a few cats- in between the gigantic Apple trees, also results of genetic engineering. Apple trees as thick as an old Oak and tall enough to top a 10-floor building.

Genetic engineering, in combination with large-scale experiments on ecology in vast hermetically enclosed and sealed test green-houses, which were completely isolated from the rest of the environment down to the last molecule -as the use of the term 'hermetically' amply indicates-, showed in the 2020's and 2030's that it was possible to create EAEs, a.k.a. Efficient Artificial Ecosystems. The idea was that if a sufficient number of plant species in an ecosystem are genetically engineered so as to make much more efficient use of sun-light, then they could form a new ecosystem that was a more efficient version of the original one. Obviously the energy the ecosystem got as an input from the sun could not really change, however it was 2-3 times more efficiently converted to life. It was the equivalent of taking an old, inefficient, petrol-based car engine from a 1950's car and replacing it with a modern, efficient electric engine, but applied to plants. That way solar energy was used with efficiencies that even green-houses and countless sorts of pesticides of the past could never have achieved alone. Genetic engineering had been the last step in the farming revolution, bringing energy conversion efficiencies close to 95%, i.e. rivalling machines and older solar cells.

As Miles walked through this triumph of technology, blissfully unaware that the very same tree species would have only been dwarves 40 years back compared to the fast-growing giants that biotechnology produces these days, the Apple trees gave way to Plums. Miles continued walking amidst the Plums until he reached a small pond, surrounded by small flower gardens. A commemorative plate indicated that the pond and flower-gardens were there for no other purpose but beauty. That they were left there as a little gift of self-indulgence for the citizens of the various Communes in the region and it commemorated days when the entire park would have been covered by such gardens and water features. Miles walked around the pond looking relaxedly towards the various ducks that were floating in the calm waters. Other ducks had simply parked themselves by the banks of the pond and were blissfully asleep, their shiny green or dull brown heads curled around so that their beaks were buried in their rich plumage. On the footpath joggers and a few cyclists took their exercise merrily and a number of mothers with their children were either walking along the banks of the oblong pond or leaning against the railings that separated the pond from the rest of the park and threw bread crumbs at the ducks below. The picture was completed by a couple of row-boats drifting on the calm waters of the pond carrying couples as their passengers.

Miles eventually walked around the picturesque little pond and started making his way towards an exit from the park. He was naturally heading to the exit closest to the job interview studios. He walked past more refreshing grass and fruit trees such as great Almond trees and charming Sweet Chestnut trees and eventually he reached the exit, where a map similar to the one he'd seen at the other entrance to the park confirmed that he was heading in the correct direction. Then, after a short walk along the avenues of the Confederation he reached the job interview studio centre. A robo-receptionist greeted him and asked how he may be of service. Miles replied that he would like a room for 1hr between 16:45 and 17:45, with a modern office sort of background. Shiny furniture with glass tops, large, leather swivelling chairs, big bookcases with ancient tomes, neatly arranged in order of ascending volume number, a modern OLED desk lamp and the like. The receptionist nodded in understanding, asked Miles to swipe his pass-card to arrange payment and after that was done he announced that green room 201 on the 2nd floor was booked for him at the desired times plus a 5' gratuity time to allow him to set-up before the clock started running nominally and 5' gratuity afterwards to allow him to wrap up any unfinished business gracefully if the interview was to drag on for too long. Miles thanked the robo-receptionist and went past the reception desk to a waiting room where a small terminal screen announced which room was ready for its next user. Miles' number did not appear for another few minutes, during which interval he stared idly at another terminal screen playing a TV documentary on sea manatees.

But the time to get to the interview did eventually come. Miles saw at the display that room 201 was ready for him and in response he made his way there. He entered the room to see a familiar-looking chamber, half painted in bright green and the other half sunk in the darkness. The green part had a rather comfortable chair and a simple desk, intended to let their users sit comfortably and limit their movements so that during the interview their interlocutors would not have the misfortune of seeing them waving a hand through a modern table with a glass top. Naturally, the chair and the desk would be replaced on-screen by far flashier computer-generated versions during the interview. In the dark part, intricate cameras and computer processing units were stacked rather disorderly; clearly that was the 'functional' part of the room. Miles had been in such room before, when he was applying for his plush job in banking.

Eventually, Miles sat at the chair and another robo-receptionist on a terminal screen opposite him (sometimes also called roboceptionists) offered him a few choices of backgrounds. Miles looked at the terminal screen now showing a live feed of himself from the camera combined with a computer-generated background. He examined the image, moved a little to the left and to the right and then requested that the pot of daisies on the desk is replaced by a little miniature statuette in the form of the Statue of Liberty in New York. His next request was that the light was slightly lower in intensity and finally he asked whether it would be possible to add a medium-sized painting of some Japanese cherry branches with a little robin perching on them, to the wall right above his head in between the bookcases. The fact that the bookcases were in the shape of a digital '0', i.e. that they consisted of two large, tall cases running from the floor nearly to the ceiling, connected to each other with a couple of shelves that ran between them aligned with the bottom two shelves and another couple of connecting shelves that aligned with the top two shelves, was something Miles liked a lot. Especially since they left room for the painting above his head and a number of decorative plants behind him -mostly bamboo shoots, very fashionable those days-.

When all was said and done, Miles entered the session ID he was given at the terminal and then sat back in his chair waiting for his interviewers to join the session so that the job interview could kick off. The interviewers did not disappoint him. They were all on time, all 3 of them logging on to the session within a very short interval of a couple of minutes before the clock hit exactly 16:45 and greeting Miles politely before immersing themselves in the activity of reading some non-descript documents until all of the participating parties were ready. Miles took the opportunity to examine his interviewers. They were more advanced in age than he was, but appeared rather relaxed and casual to him, particularly dressed as they were in relatively old, black suits with simple ties of various colours. Other than that air of unusual casualty and informality even, he did not notice anything else of significance about the gentlemen.

Eventually the interviewing trio was congregated and the interview could commence. Miles could see the interviewers in a split-screen on the terminal screen, talking from their offices presumably, at the central partition of the screen the head of the little hiring committee. He spoke first.

'Good evening Mr. Fitzroy. I am Roy Kinnock a human resources assistant director and in this quality I shall be leading the job interview. To my left, and your right, is Mr. Abdul Asif, one of the main editors of our agency and to my right and your left is Mr. Subrahmanyan Sekar, my own assistant in human resources and we are very pleased to meet you.' said Mr. Kinnock.

'Good evening to you too gentlemen. Pleased to make your acquaintance.' replied Miles with the utmost politeness.

'Now from what we can see in the file that was generated from your ID documentation and the questionnaire you filled, earlier today in fact, it is indicated that you are originally from Zone 1, recently became a citizen of the Commune in Whitton, here in Zone 2, and decided to make a career change from banking into journalism.' said Mr. Kinnock.

'That is absolutely correct.' confirmed Miles.

'My first question would be why this dramatic change in lifestyle, if you don't feel that to be a too personal question.' asked Mr. Kinnock.

'It is a personal question, but, I assure you, nothing I would not like to share with you. The truth is that the recent Kinroy bank collapse meant that I was one of the casualties of the wave of redundancies that followed. For some reason that I have a very, very bad feeling about, no other bank has hired me or anyone else for that matter for way too long. This general hiring freeze has lasted so long that eventually I nearly ran out of savings. I then left on my own to travel Zone 2 and see where the best place to settle myself and begin a new life until the crisis is over was. I thus ended up here. That explains why I am here. As for the career change, to be perfectly honest, I was beginning to get a little bit sick of what I was doing at the bank, a mostly relatively mindless tasks during boom times. Also the travelling I've done around Zone 2 rekindled my appetite for learning, travelling and learning the news.' replied Miles with great sincerity.

'That is quite a story young man. It must have been quite a courageous move on your part. I kind of envy your journey too...' said Mr. Asif approvingly.

'It was a bit daunting in the beginning, but then I was just caught up in the journey and the experiences it brought me.' said Miles in reverie. The 3 interviewers nodded approvingly.

'From what we've seen you have an engineering degree, but work experience just in the banking sector. Why is that? Also what sort of training do you have that would help you in a job in journalism?' asked Mr. Sekar.

'Oh. Well, it is pretty standard practice to go for an engineering degree in one of the country's most prestigious institutions and then seek work in the banking sector. In fact where I studied, almost ¾ of my colleagues chose exactly the same path. Most of the others became consultants and a tiny number of them only became actual scientists. As for my training, you are right. I have none that would be useful to the agency, however I am confident that I can learn quickly under training and master both written and oral speech. After all I believe I may assess myself as at least decently articulate in the English language. But above all that, what I believe you might value in me is my will to do this job and my views as somebody who has spent a vast part of his life in Zone 1.' said Miles. Mr. Sekar nodded in agreement.

'In practical terms, this job will mean that you might spend a lot of time away from home. I know you have no family that live with you, however this is still something you must be aware of before accepting this job. Moreover, you may be summoned to cover events in dangerous parts of London, including Zone 3 and that is a very real danger that you absolutely must understand. We take great care that our journalists stay away from immediate danger, but it might get unpleasant at times and we may at times fail to keep you from danger despite our best efforts. Finally, please understand that even thought you will only be technically working for 8 hours a day, 5 days a week, like almost everybody else in the Commune, at times your service might be deemed necessary for more than 8 consecutive hours. You know how events can unfold sometimes. At any rate we shall, of course, pay you extra at overtime rate for such work and try to give you extra time off later on to compensate, but please understand that if the need arises for you to work for more than 8 consecutive hours your continued commitment to your job duties will be extremely highly appreciated. Think of our viewers when you do that. They deserve to know what is going on in the world. How do you feel about these rules? I understand that they may be a little different that for other jobs, a bit harsher, but journalism sometimes requires sacrifices on a personal level.' said Mr. Kinnock with concern, almost paternally. Miles was dumbstruck. He had never seen a job offer with such good terms of labour. In Zone 1 he had no real rights against the company he worked for; only obligations. 5 days times 8 hours with extra overtime pay for any work above that scheduled was something completely new to him. In Zone 1 he was at the mercy of the company and got paid only because he would otherwise not work at all for them, the rate determined by the market and nothing else; no regulation, no legislation, certainly no unions to tip the balance of power in his direction. But engineering graduates who had memorised their lessons well enough to get 1st rate degrees were in high demand and only a plush salary would keep them from going to work elsewhere. For those who could stay at the top of the labour pyramid of London, that was great; for others...

'I... I... I wasn't expecting such a generous offer!' said Miles excitedly.

'What? How?' exclaimed Mr. Asif confusedly while exchanging curious stares with his colleagues. Eventually Mr. Kinnock understood.

'Ah, I see. You are from Zone 1. To you our working conditions must sound like heaven. Right?' he inquired.

'I... Well... Yes. No?' said Miles with confusion and glimmers of excitement.

'Heh heh. Don't worry young Mr. Fitzroy, we are not going to take advantage of you here. We don't do this to anyone. We are all communards.' said Mr. Sekar reassuringly. The other two confirmed with nods and cries of 'That's right.'.

'I am so honoured! I would be most honoured to work for you kind sirs!' said Miles. The interviewers smiled.

'Well, now that we have a basic agreement on the rules of the work and we have satisfied our curiosity about your -excuse the phrase- rather exotic background, I believe we are all satisfied that both you and we wish to continue this interview and look at the details of the job. I won't lie to you, since you agree with these labour rules, which for our country are considered harsh, and we are convinced that you left Zone 1 on a perfectly legitimate reason, as opposed to, well... the result of a heinous crime or something equally sinister I think we are in top shape to move on. Please forgive our suspicions, but we simply cannot take risks, I hope we caused no offence.' said Mr. Kinnock with great sensitivity, almost paternally again.

'I... certainly no offence. You are most, most polite. In Zone 1 interviewers are never even a tenth as polite as you are. I totally understand your position. I would be doing the same in your shoes, kind sir. It is, one could say, your duty towards the company to be absolutely sure of my good intentions. Thank you for your concern towards my feelings though. You could have achieved that background check in a far less delicate manner had you so chosen to do.' responded Miles rather astonished at the politeness of his interviewers. He could see and feel that their politeness was genuine, not mechanical, automatic, and that made him like the Confederation even more.

'Now, if I may ask a question, I would be very interested to know how you would see yourself in relation to your viewers. Imagine for a moment that you are journalist. What would you like to give to your viewers, so to speak?' asked Mr. Sekar.

'I think that the viewers deserve to know what is happening in the world, in fact it does them good to know about the goings on out there...' said Miles waving his hand vaguely towards the window. 'I know it. I can vouch for the truth of that statement as a man who has experienced this himself. I used to be very happy to work for Kinroy bank, go to the tower, click buttons all day buying and selling shares and derivatives and so on, then return home, entertain myself and go blissfully to sleep without so much as a second thought about what may have been happening next door, let alone outside the small part of London that I used to live and work in. But then I travelled, I talked to people, I learned. It has completely changed me as a person. My new knowledge rekindled the feelings of sympathy for the fellow man in me. I began to realise how dehumanising Zone 1 is and appreciate the sort of harmonious society you have here. I am now awake and aware!' he finally exclaimed with passion.

'And you feel that our viewers will benefit in the same way from the knowledge you might give them as a journalist.' completed Mr. Sekar.

'Precisely. For me this job is not just a crusade to self-betterment. It is a mission that carries great responsibility towards my new fellow citizens.' said Miles excitedly.

'Your feelings are amiable young Fitzroy.' said Mr. Kinnock approvingly.

'I have another question.' said Mr. Asif. 'What are your views on time management?' he asked.

'Basically they can be summarised as follows: the sooner I get something done the better. The remaining time can be used to either correct errors made during the process, you know, the kind that usually gets spotted only later on, or to complete other tasks, or to cash as free time. There is no harm in being early, it can only be good.' said Miles simply.

'That makes perfect sense to me.' said Mr. Asif. 'But you must be aware that at times, when events unfold very quickly, you might need to create essays or send in news feeds at a very high rate. Such work cannot by nature be planned and despite your best intentions you might end up under time pressure. You do understand this risk, right?' he concluded inquiringly.

'Certainly. It is part of the nature of the job. What I can do to help this situation is to make sure that all my tasks are completed as quickly as possible so that if a torrent of new tasks precipitates, I have no old tasks to attend to.' said Miles very seriously.

'But this speed must not be at the cost of quality. I don't mean spelling and other trifling things like that. Our software can handle that. I mean creating meaningful articles with organised content and good logical flow.' said Mr. Kinnock.

'Naturally. There is a certain 'quality threshold' as I like to call it. Any work I create has to be above it. In other words I will find it very difficult to convince myself to create a piece of work in less time than that necessary for me to achieve at least that threshold quality.' explained Miles.

'And what if we have events that unfold literally before your eyes, like for example war manoeuvres?' asked Mr. Kinnock.

'In that case the best I can do is to record myself commenting on what I see. In combination with feed from the camera -if available- it should provide enough material a) for the viewers to picture the events themselves and b) for us to process afterwards into a more presentable format. I think that is a reasonable course of action under such trying circumstances. No?' said Miles using his logic.

'That is exactly what we do under such circumstances. This implies that your first attempt quality must also be very high.' explained Mr. Kinnock.

'But we can only test that in action, no?' asked Miles.

'Actually, yes and no.' said Mr Sekar. Miles looked at him with the look of a curious puppy. Mr. Sekar proceeded to explain: 'At some point we shall show you a full-screen video of some rapidly unfolding historical event you might or might not have seen. We shall cut the commentary sound off so that you may comment on the video and its raw sound-track instead. We shall then listen to your commentary and see how good it is.'

'Clever! I'm ready!' said Miles.

'Hold your horses young Mr. Fitzroy. We will get to that point.' said Mr. Kinnock smiling placidly. 'If you wouldn't object to us asking a few more questions until then...' he concluded.

'Please, please, any time!' replied Miles cheerfully. The interviewers seemed like very jolly fellows.

'I have one. As it was mentioned before, you might have to work in dangerous situations, maybe even war zones. You may be asked to do certain things or go to certain places, actions that you might consider not to be entirely safe or reasonable. Other times you may find events unfolding somewhere else than where you've been told to work and have reasonable suspicions that the more senior members of the agency do not know about that. How would you react to such situations?' asked Mr. Sekar.

'Well, short term, I would probably try to stay out of immediate danger. I would not, for example, go to a town square where my handler from central thinks is safe, but I happen to know they just started shelling 2' ago. On the other hand I would go if the handler reassured me that he is absolutely certain that it is safe. I would in such case, proceed with caution, but ultimately reach my destination. So if the information is conflicting: use caution and follow the orders. If I happen to notice that important events are unfolding somewhere else, I would quickly consult with my handler first and act accordingly. After all it may be that a colleague of mine is the covering those events. The handler would know that, surely. In any case I would work with my handler and inform him of any such conflicts or qualms I may have.' answered Miles using his brain to the maximum, an action made visible by him folding his arms and rubbing his chin pensively.

'When you say, 'handler', what do you mean?' asked Mr. Sekar.

'In Zone 1 news agencies have journalists on the field and contacts at the central offices. The job of these contacts is to inform individual journalists of events they gather from other journalists and so help groups of journalists to work together as teams. We call such people 'handlers'.' explained Miles.

'Oh, I see.' said Mr. Sekar. 'Here we call them 'coordinators', or 'team coordinators' to be more precise.

'Oh. I didn't know different agencies called them different names.' admitted Miles.

'They don't exactly. Different countries call them different names. In the Confederation they are 'team coordinators', in the Communist sector they are 'journalist sergeants' etc. etc.' explained Mr. Sekar.

'Oh well, you will get to grips with the specific terminology in no time, I'm sure of that. Knowing mere country-specific jargon terms in advance is not that crucial...' said Mr Kinnock. Then, addressing his colleagues he asked: 'Now, dear colleagues, if you have any other questions, now is the time to ask. Otherwise we may proceed with the video.' His colleagues shook their heads in indication that they were satisfied with the questions they had asked up to that moment and Mr. Kinnock addressed Miles in order to brief him for what was about to follow.

'Now we will show you some raw footage from a historical event and you will comment freely on it. The footage we will show you will pertain to the victory of the Popular Party (or PP) in Harrow & Watford many years ago. Because in those circumstances we would have fully briefed you about the situation and you would have known much more about the conditions on the ground just by virtue of living and working in journalism at the time, we have added little computer-generated name-bubbles on top of various people's heads so you know who is who. I repeat, in a normal situation you would most certainly know those people anyway. The video should last only about 5-10'. Is that all right? Do you still have time in your studio?' asked Mr. Kinnock. Miles looked at his watch and said:

'Ample. We have about 30' or so left I think. I'm ready when you are.' replied Miles.

'First we will show you a 'dossier' with crucial data as part of the film. Please study it carefully in the 2' you have at your disposal as the video will start displaying the raw footage after that time interval has elapsed.' said Mr. Kinnock. Then he looked down towards his desk, said 'Let's roll the movie.' and pressed a button.

The image on Miles' terminal screen was changed, replacing the three interviewers with a piece of paper that simply read:

DOSSIER FOR HARROW & WATFORD ELECTION COVERAGE TEAM.

Location: Harrow assembly hall by the high-street.

Event: Elections for local council 2044 – announcement of results.

Time: 4th of June at 19:00.

Main parties/leaders: Local Tory – Annette Johnson. Modern Labour – Nicolas Chang. Liberal Democrats – Ravi Patnaikar. BNP – Alfred Jobbs. Green party – Elvira Deirdre. Popular party – Alan Woodstock.

Election platforms: Local Tory – Tax breaks for the industry, financial sector and commerce. Cap on immigration to borough. Modern Labour – Tax breaks for the industry, financial sector and commerce. Liberal Democrats – Increased regulation in business, introduction of minimum wage, state-subsidised education and healthcare. BNP – Cap on immigration, introduction of 'Britishness' criteria for immigrants. Green party – Return of state welfare system. Imposition of regulation on businesses with respect to environment, equal opportunities etc. Popular *party – Pledges to strengthen the police by re-creating a council police force to fight crime as efficiently as possible for free. Glorification of the Asian work ethic model.*

Task: Cover the elections as the results of the voting come in.

Special focus: The possible victory of the PP and their unique election platform centred on security. Also: the fact that 3 parties are all projected to obtain similar results, but with the first past the post system only one can win.

Miles had just about enough time to read through the paper, laugh silently as he pondered how confusing these election pledges would have been for someone who was used to more traditional versions of the above stated parties and skim one more time through the page for a quick refresher when the video footage started rolling. Miles was quick to grasp the point.

'Good evening ladies and gentlemen. We are now very close to the moment of truth for the council elections of the borough of Harrow & Watford, very close to the end of this political saga that has seen the traditional parties fight for votes and seats with a relative newcomer, the popular party or PP for short. I am now situated in the assembly room of the borough, as you can see a lovely building, tightly packed with curious citizens who wish to be there for the announcement of the election results in their own borough.' The footage was showing general movement in the packed auditorium of the Harrow & Watford assembly hall but otherwise not much was happening. Miles continued relentlessly: 'We can see that the crowd is quite restless at the moment, people trying to find their seats, others shouting at each other, but no significant activity at the moment. The members of the electoral board are already seated at the long table that has been set up specifically for them with microphones, but they are also absorbed into talking amongst themselves as the actual results are not yet in, in fact even the main candidates are not yet into the chamber.'

Then the noise in the hall increased and some people started clapping as a number of important-looking people started making their way into the assembly hall. Miles did not hesitate to comment on that: 'Oh, and here we have some of the candidates now making their way towards their own reserved seats at the long table. Here we see the leader of the Local Tory party, Mrs. Annette Johnson making her way to her seat amidst waves of applause.' the video was zooming on Mrs. Johnson as Miles was talking about her. 'Now she is taking her seat, waving to her supporters, the local conservatives, mostly wealthy people who stand to gain a lot from her agenda of tax breaks for businesses and have traditionally voted conservative. But, I hear more cries and applauses. That's Mr. Nicolas Chang of the Modern Labour party arriving at his seat amidst even more applauses. Here he is, waving at the cheering crowd of supporters. Most of Mr. Chang's supporters of course coming also from the high business ranks, but also wealthy salaried employees who feel that their companies will benefit from the tax breaks as well as the liberal attitude of the party on immigration. We have heard very often in this election campaign how Modern Labour supporters have repeatedly complained that the Tory policy of capping immigration will impose unnecessary limitations to business activity. In this respect it seems that the Modern Labour party is a true successor to New Labour, which like all other parties, has made its local parties independent and demanded that they change their names for copyright reasons.' continued Miles as the camera concentrated on the Modern Labour candidate. 'Mr. Chang there still waving to his supporters, Mrs. Johnson drinking water and nervously fidgeting, we can all feel the tension in what has been described as an unprecedented, genuine 3-horse race. Literally any of the 3 leading parties could win, something admittedly unlikely in an electoral system that works on the first past the post principle. Now Mr. Ravi Patnaikar and Mrs. Elvira Deirdre are making their ways to their seats. They have symbolically arrived in the same car and are proceeding towards their seats side-by-side as a symbol of their similar beliefs and ideas. Their relatively few supporters are giving them all they have and dear me, ladies and gentlemen, Mr. Patnaikar is most courteously helping Mrs. Deirdre take her seat by drawing the seat for her; a most gentlemanly move indeed although unfortunately even the most honest of politicians are always under the suspicion of acting nobly only for political gain.' said Miles as Mr. Patnaikar was offering Mrs. Deirdre a seat with a benevolent smile on his face, an offer which the dignified lady accepted with a thankful smile. The camera then zoomed at the entrance to the hall where by sheer coincidence the leaders of the PP and BNP parties entered in quick succession. 'And finally the team of candidates is now complete with the entrance of Messrs. Alfred Jobbs of the British National Party and Alan Woodstock of the Popular Party. The hall is resounding with supporters of most likely Mr. Woodstock, who has been faring consistently astoundingly well at pre-election polls in the recent past. Unlike Mr. Patnaikar and Mrs. Deirdre who mostly appeal to the highly educated middle class with their proposals for more government, more social solidarity between people and classes and fairer distribution of wealth, Messrs Jobbs and Woodstock appeal mostly to the lower classes with promises of greatness and independence for their borough, security against crime -a real problem since the organs of justice and enforcement have been privatised- and their hostile stance against immigrants, who according to a large number of people here simply drive wages down and create unemployment amongst their ranks.

Although, perhaps, it is realistic to believe that each society has certain limits and may not accept more immigrants once a certain critical number has been reached -after all most countries limit immigration to a certain degree-, what worries many of immigrant origin in the borough are the measures proposed by these parties, particularly the BNP, to 'encourage immigrants to seek better boroughs to live in' to quote the BNP manifesto for example. People fear these measures might not turn out to be as delicate as they might appear on the proposal papers.' commented Miles while the candidates were seated and fidgeting in their seats. Finally, a little man with an envelope he held high up in his hand entered the room and made his way to the podium, at the centre of the long table. 'And I think we now have the results. The man with the envelope probably carries the final vote count to the president of the electoral committee, murmurs something in the ear of the president.' at that point the president of the electoral committee grabbed a little bell that was in front of him and rang it thrice. He then spoke as Miles fell silent.

'Citizens of Harrow & Watford, I have just received the envelope with the results for the 2044 election for the city council. It will be my honour to announce them to you without further delay.' the president uttered and then slowly took a yellowish piece of high-quality paper from the envelope, held it before his bespectacled eyes, lowered his glasses, for he was long-sighted and then read:

'In last place: Green party – 10.874 votes.
'In 5th place: Liberal Democratic party – 19.278 votes.
'In 4th place: British National party – 59.888 votes.
'In 3rd place: Local Tory party – 105.241 votes.
'In 2nd place: Modern Labour party – 106.386 votes.

'And the winner of the elections is the Popular Party with 110.911 votes.' concluded the president. The supporters of the PP roared in excitement as it became apparent that they had won. But the president wasn't finished yet:

'In light of these results I shall like to call the leaders of the participating parties to address the populace in ascending ranking order.' he said and then proceeded to call the leader of the Greens. She uttered a few words, encouraging her few supporters the privatised educational system had managed to create, to persevere and have hope for the next election, as well as hold true to their beliefs. Next, the Liberal Democrat candidate addressed his own few supporters echoing pretty much what his Green colleague had said. The BNP candidate expressed his satisfaction that despite his party's loss at least a party they can understand had obtained victory. Then, the Tory candidate expressed her dissatisfaction that she had come so close to victory yet lost it and did not miss the opportunity to express her satisfaction that at least Labour had not won. In a similar climate the Labour candidate expressed his own grief that he had lost the election and merriment that the Tories had lost too and by a larger margin. Finally, the winner of the election, the future dictator of Harrow & Watford gave a 2-3' speech in which he glorified the 'intelligent citizens of our beloved borough', law enforcement and disciplined work ethic and made some views on immigration and immigrants public; an act that made it clear that the very same views had been slightly polished and smoothed before being inserted in the party's manifesto. He finished his speech and Miles took it from there:

'And there we've just listened to the post-election speeches of the various party leaders, obviously the big winner here being the PP. The leader of the party Alan Woodstock there repeating his proposed policies for the borough, policies that will now become official government policy. And what a night this is, the PP beating the main contenders for power in the United Kingdom for decades and decades, centuries even. Large, ancient political giants now beaten by a newcomer with a political platform of law enforcement, Asian work ethic and as we've just heard from the leader himself anti-immigration; a lot stronger anti-immigration than the manifesto made clear.' and with that comment the video ended. Following a brief pause during which the terminal screen went black, the 3 interviewers reappeared on Miles's monitor.

'Nice work.' said Mr. Kinnock. 'A bit of personal commentary slipped in there, but with a little bit of practice it will be ironed out. In the sections of the news where you are allowed, even encouraged to say your opinion you may include those, but never in the original, live broadcast. Just telling you as a future note. But, no, very well, very well. Excellent eloquence, excellent flow. Not bad, young man.' he concluded as his colleagues nodded approvingly. 'Anything else you would like to say or comment?' he then asked his colleagues. Mr. Asif nodded in the negative and Mr. Sekar simply said he was covered by his colleague's commentary. Finally he addressed Miles and asked him whether he wishes to add anything or ask anything and after the latter stated that he too was covered, Mr. Kinnock declared the meeting adjourned and asked Miles to be on the lookout for messages at his official email. With that, the interviewers bade Miles a good evening, he returned the bidding and the connection was terminated. Overall it hadn't been a bad interview, thought Miles as he checked out at the robo-reception and headed to his hotel room in the cylinder.

The rest of the day rolled smoothly and uneventfully like a train on butt-welded rails. Miles looked at other job opportunities, dined at the hotel and fell asleep happy. The following day, after the morning toilette and a well-cooked breakfast, Miles went to enjoy yet another walk in the adjacent park, this time with all the time in the world to enjoy himself.

The weather was sunny, making the advent of March evident. Miles thought that it was getting visibly hotter in the fragmented British capital when he realised that it was indeed the 1st of March. It was a jolly day indeed and a very good one for a walk in the park too, particularly since this time around he was going prepared: he had his terminal rolled up under his arm and in his other arm he held a little bag with a couple of traditional triangular sandwiches -cheese & bacon and sausage & tomatoes-. He was going to the little lake area at the centre of the park, sit on one of the benches by the banks of the picturesque little pond and then lay his terminal upon his thighs and read something or other while eating his triangular sandwiches. Said and done he crossed the street with care, walked to the nearest entrance to the park and then past large grooves of fruit tree until he reached the familiar little lake.

At the sight of the calm water and the greenery around him, bathed in the bright sunlight beneath a perfectly cloudless, blue sky, Miles stopped in his tracks, stretched his whole body and inhaled the fresh air with joy. Having completed this manoeuvre, he walked steadily towards an old, green bench and sat there with his terminal screen still rolled but on his lap and the sandwiches just next to him, still in their bag. And for a few minutes, he just sat there, doing nothing. He let the breeze of surprisingly warm air hit his face as he closed his eyes and simply enjoyed the moment. For those few minutes he felt like he could cast away all worry and deep contemplation and simply enjoy being surrounded by such beautiful nature and scenery. The quacking of the ducks at the pond, the idle chatter of the people walking past him alone or with pets, the rhythmical steps of the few joggers all created an atmosphere of pleasant idleness and serenity in which Miles felt really happy to indulge.

Those minutes eventually passed and Miles opened his eyes again, yet he kept admiring the serene environment for a few more minutes. Then, refreshed, he unrolled his terminal and placed it upon his lap. The entire back-side of the terminal, as well as parts of the front were covered in solar cells that could scavenge energy from surrounding light and store it in the terminal's ultra-thin battery. That way he could spend the entire day out reading if he so chose to do, but that was unrealistic. At any rate, he navigated to the Kropotkin's diaries website and decided to have a look at the news.

Miles looked at the news in text, rather than video format. He always preferred to read the news at his own pace rather than watch the video unless a particular piece of news included vital visual information. A quick look through the website announced the main headlines. Apparently there was something amiss in London, in fact not only in London, but all the large urban agglomerations in the entire country. Here is a selection of headlines from that day's news:

> *KROPOTKIN'S DIARIES – HOURLY NEWS FEED.*
> *LATEST NEWS.*
> *HOME AFFAIRS:*
> - *Confederation government pledges to organise referendum on the topic of creating a large university in Ashford.*
> - *Healthcare to benefit from the order of new real-time MRI scanners of heightened accuracy.*
> - *First clinic to implant identification chips to citizens of the confederation inaugurated at Addlestone.*
> - *Confederation army raids small guerilla outpost near the Woking borders. 3 people lose their lives on the side of the army. Number of guerilla casualties unknown.*
>
> *NATIONAL AFFAIRS:*
> - *Communist regional leaders from all large cities in Britain meet with central communist cabinet as a matter of urgency at the Grand Congress in the union HQ tower in Epsom.*
> - *Communist ambassador invites foreign relations commissioner to urgently visit communist HQ in Epsom to discuss defence.*
>
> *INTERNATIONAL AFFAIRS:*
> - *Russian ministry of welfare declares that the demographic situation of the country is 'critical'. Pledge to allow influx of more immigrants and increase parental benefits for families with more than 2 children.*
> - *4 years after reverting to China, Hong Kong becomes increasingly industrialised amidst protest against the environmental harm this might cause. Protests are quashed by the police and 10 protesters are sentenced to hard labour in Xinjang.*

The home and international news showed nothing out of the ordinary, not even the raid in the Woking region was something unusual. However the fact that the communists were moving intensely on the diplomatic front revealed that they were planning something; probably something very big.

After reading through the news he considered important, Miles decided to study the communists a bit more. He could not understand why in the article about the Grand Congress the communist leaders from other British cities were called 'regional leaders' or what their exact relation was to the London communists. He browsed the general knowledge website 'Wikipedia' -now an invaluable source of quick and useful information for the entire world- and found out the article about the British communists. Apparently, the communist sectors of various large cities in Britain were united under the same party and the same leader. Come to think of it Martha, his official escort in the communist sector, had mentioned something like this, hadn't she? The ministries in the tower at Epsom controlled affairs in all communist sectors of the country. The regional leaders on the other hand just made sure that everything is running smoothly and kept corruption in check, like caretakers of the government. According to the article, the total population in communist controlled regions reached as high a number as 7,5 million people with smaller cities in the North and Scotland being controlled by communists to much larger percentages than relatively significantly wealthier London. What's more, in certain parts of Britain coal miners had rebelled and taken control of their corresponding coal mines, converting small towns to communism in the process. Those towns were mainly supported by trucks that provided residents there with supplies from larger centres under communist control.

  Miles now realised that with about 8% of the British population under their control, the communists were a force to be reckoned with. Miles contemplated the possible causes for all this intense activity in the communist camp when a message alert appeared at the corner of his screen. He took note of it but did not otherwise act. He wanted to think about the situation a bit more. The news articles did not specify why the regional leaders were meeting the cabinet, and the ambassador had indeed invited the foreign affairs commissioner of the Confederation for talks centring exactly on defence. At the same time any talk on specific agenda was conspicuously absent. He was thinking that all this activity was rather suspicious, like, perhaps in the event of a war? But no, no. Before wars you usually get all the associated rhetoric. Rhetoric dehumanising the opponents, exalting one's own side, stressing the differences with the opponents and generally getting the populace into a war mindset. Instead, all of this rhetoric was conspicuously absent; if one of course didn't count the constant communist rhetoric against the system in Zone 1. But then, of course, much of that rhetoric was accurate to begin with and nobody in their right mind would invade Zone 1 with its vast wealth and ability to hire very powerful military companies. At any rate, time would probably tell. It is even possible that whatever the communists had in mind, probably a large scale military operation in Zone 3, the other zones of London would be largely unaffected. With this thought he concluded his meditations and took the terminal back in his hands. He navigated to his email and opened the new message. It was from Kropotkin's diaries. They had replied.

Miles suddenly jumped in the air in joy, with the terminal in his right hand and then promptly sat down squashing his sandwiches in the process. He had been hired. The message in short communicated to him the fact that he was very lucky to have been the last person to be interviewed before the deadline for that hiring season (hiring seasons at Kropotkin's diaries last 3 months) so the reply was swift. It also communicated the fact that the interviewers were impressed by the spirit and eloquence he had shown during his interview and welcomed his fresh opinions stemming from his unusual background. As such, the email went on: he had been hired and all he needed to do next was to sign the contract and enter his 'trial & training period'. Miles read in the attached contract that this period was a 1 month period during which he would be training, akin to an apprentice, and eligible to leave the job at any moment he chose to do so. At the end of the month, an assessment would be made on his performance and he would either proceed seamlessly into his regular job, or be given feedback and politely asked to seek further for employment. On this occasion the company would give him a 1-month salary as a form of job seeker's allowance, but that only worked the 1st time someone got declined for a job to prevent people from simply applying for the job seeker's allowance at the end of the 1-months t&t period. Next time he would get 1/3 of a month's salary as a job seeker's allowance. The contract also stated, in different chapters, his obligations towards the agency, the company's obligations towards him ('Wow! They have an entire chapter on the employer's obligations here!' thought Miles), some rules on health & safety and finally technical aspects of the position, such as specific work timetables, exact amount of pay including contributions to the state budget through tax.

Time passed and eventually Miles read carefully through his entire employment contract and ate the squashed sandwiches in the process. The part about his entitlement two a couple of weeks paid holiday every year precipitated yet another cheerful jump in the air. In the end he was asked whether he could possibly start the job from the following Monday, to which he was very happy to agree, as it would give him enough time to install himself to his new home that would be allocated to him during the citizenship ceremony the Friday before his proposed 1st day at work. Thus, completely happy with the contract, he signed it moving his index finger over the smooth surface of the terminal screen in the form of his signature, attached it to a message of his own and sent it back to the news agency. Thereafter, he sat at the bench for just a little longer, enjoying the scenery as before and then he left towards his hotel room.

The rest of the days until the Friday of his citizenship ceremony passed in monotony and quiet. Miles took the opportunity to walk around the immediate vicinity of the hotel and get to know his surroundings a little better, drove around every so often to see more of the Confederation and read the news avidly. The fact that the stories about the defence talks between the Confederation and the communists, as well as the Grand Congress were not followed up worried him gravely, but eventually the festive Friday arrived and for that day Miles could be jolly and forget about the storm clouds that seemed to be descending over the entire country, with a crisis looming and possibly also war. So off was Miles to the little old church in whose basement he held a very interesting conversation with Dr. Stephenson the first time he was at the Commune. He was there slightly earlier than the established time, just in time to see the local council of 10 dissolving the session and commencing preparations for the ceremony. The locals, seated on the pews of the old church like local parishioners had done centuries before them, were shuffling and talking to one another in anticipation of the festive event ahead of them. In that atmosphere Miles entered the old church and shortly afterwards Dr. Stephenson spotted him and waved merrily with his wrinkled hand. Mr. Latchley who was talking to the Dr. at the time turned his head and saw Miles too. In response he waved cheerfully with his even more wrinkled hand and beckoned him to join their company. Mr. Dickson had retired from the council of 10 for the moment, possibly in order to answer a call from mother nature. Miles approached the duo.

'Hallo gentlemen.' he said cheerfully when he was within comfortable talking range of the elders.

'Welcome young man, and congratulations on your successful citizenship application.' said Dr. Stephenson.

'Oh, it was nothing I earned by virtue of my own character or abilities...' replied Miles blushing as he politely declined the compliment.

'Yes, but still it is a MILEStone in your life, pun not intended.' said old Mr. Latchley and chuckled.

'Oh, haha.' said Miles slightly bemused and then realised. 'Ow, I get it now.' he said now amused.

'We are ready for your citizenship ceremony now, young man. Are you?' inquired Dr. Stephenson cheerfully.

'Ready? Was I supposed to have done anything in preparation of it?' asked Miles with a sudden wave of anxiety permeating his words.

'Oh, just psychologically. The ceremony itself consists of a short welcoming speech which I'm probably going to be giving myself, a short speech from you, if you wish to do so, the official handing over of the keys to your new home, which will be shown to you by Mr. Latchley, and then general merriment where you'll get a chance to talk to people and socialise. That last one will really be a very civilised party, so just enjoy yourself and don't feel any pressure.' explained Dr. Stephenson and smiled paternally. Miles sighed in sign of relief. 'May I share your extraordinary story about your fall from Zone 1 and your journey around London with my fellow citizens, in fact your fellow citizens?' asked the Dr.

'Most certainly. I don't want to hide this from anybody. I believe people will find it interesting. It was a life-changing experience and if anybody can take or learn anything from it I will be most happy.' replied Miles.

'Oh, they will. Trust me. The fact that somebody went on a journey of discovery around Zone 2 will open the appetite for exploration and travel in many of our members, particularly young ones. Your tale is an inspiring one young Miles.' said Mr. Latchley approvingly.

'Permit me to be the first one to welcome you to our community, young man.' said Mr. Dickson who had just returned to the company and almost literally oozed relief from his countenance.

'Thank you Mr. Dickson.' replied Miles with the politeness and joviality of a school kid that has just been told he answered well in the lesson.

'Shall we begin?' inquired Dr. Stephenson calmly. Messrs Latchley and Dickson nodded in the affirmative while Miles said he had no objection.

Dr. Stephenson beckoned Miles to sit at a chair right next to his own as he was sitting down himself while Mr. Latchley had already seated himself with his hands crossed upon the table and Mr. Dickson was already seated as well, with his hands crossed and resting upon his rather substantial belly. Miles sat down and pulled his chair forward at the very same time as Dr. Stephenson did. Then, Dr. Stephenson looked to his left and to his right, and satisfied that the group of 4 had all taken their places at the sturdy old teak table he called for the crowd's attention. The citizens of the Whitton Commune seated themselves quickly and the general merriment and variety of conversations going on until that moment faded first into a few dispersed murmurs and then into complete silence. That silence combined with the dim lighting of the ancient structure and the tall arches looming over the church's nave to create a rather eerie atmosphere, whilst the fact that what used to be the chancel of the church, but now hosted the table where Miles was sitting, was lit rather more generously than the nave had the additional effect of making Miles feel in the spotlight. At the moment Miles noticed that the church was lit by holographic fire, emanating from wooden torches that cleverly hid the electronics and photonics that generated them; at least it appeared to be so. In reality the torches also hid arrays of powerful OLEDs that shot light upwards, straight towards the rather Gothic style arches that supported the roof of the old church. To Miles, the whole medieval ambience elicited memories of the Rathauser of Vienna and Munchen that he had visited long ago, as well as the far, far grander cathedral of Strasbourg; very central European.

Nevertheless, all of those contemplations could only last but a few moments before Dr. Stephenson started speaking.

'Fellow communards of our little Whitton Commune. Today is a special day as we are about to accept a new member into the bosom of out small community. I would like to talk a bit about him, with his permission.' he said and Miles smiled politely and nodded once in the affirmative by bowing his head slightly and then returning it to its original position while looking at the crowd. He then resumed looking in the general direction of the speaker. 'Our new member is young Mr. Miles Fitzroy, who you can see sitting just beside me.'. Dr. Stephenson raised his left arm and moved it slightly in the direction of Miles, his hand pointing downwards as if he was attempting to point at his guest with the wrist, an act of the utmost politeness. 'He is a man with a most extraordinary tale. A tale that tells of the tides of fortune, a journey of exploration and the complete change of a man's view of the world.' uttered the old sage as the crowd hanged from his words intrigued. The Dr. continued.

'This, here, young man, is originally from Zone 1.' A wave of murmur swept across the hall like the waves created in wheat on the endless steppes of central Asia by the wind; a wave that filled the hall with astonishment. What could a rich citizen of Zone 1 want here? They thought. 'He is from Zone 1 and used to work for a bank that has now gone bankrupt.' continued the Dr. and the crowd fell silent again, now slightly less eager to comment before they hear the full story. The Dr. continued uninterrupted: 'Originally, he thought he could sit the crisis out, but life in central London is expensive. His attempts to find a job all floundered as the economy in Zone 1 was shocked by the collapse and employers were not keen to hire any more. When a second bank collapsed, he realised that the situation was graver than anyone had thought before, so he decided to come and live here, in Zone 2 until the crisis is over. However, what was initially a plan to weather a financial storm turned out into a life-changing experience. I'll tell you, I met this man on the first day he had wondered into Zone 2. He was so innocent and blissfully ignorant of the workings of Zone 2. Everything was a surprise to him, particularly finding out that Zone 2 is home to a large variety of political systems, living standards and ways of thinking.' Dr. Stephenson made a slight pause at this point and looked left and right at the assembled citizens. They were listening very carefully. The Dr. continued:

'The young gentleman over here...' said the Dr. pointing with his wrist again '...then set off for what he no doubt imagined would simply be a journey not too dissimilar to a trip to the supermarket, or mere house-hunting...' continued the Dr. looking at Miles, who nodded affirmatively. '...and yet turned out to be a life changing experience. In his journey, young Miles saw and learned about and even met people from our own sector, the communist sector, the old-style democratic boroughs, the Royal zone and even visited the republic in Uxbridge, whilst intelligently keeping out of the horrifying, nay surreal, dictatorship in Harrow & Watford and presumably missing other lesser dictatorial sectors.'

'In the end, he decided that out of all the different countries that now constitute Zone 2, he wishes to start a new life in ours.' said the Dr. and a round of spontaneous applause filled the chambers of the old church. It was a civilised applause, one that radiated courtesy. The Dr. continued after the applause had sufficiently died down. 'And here he is now, once again amongst us, in fact once again in my personal company, which is why I can say with confidence that the journey around London has completely transformed him as a man. I can see the change with my very own eyes. He is now much more genuine, aware and humane than he was originally, please don't take offence at this, I mean it as a huge compliment.' uttered the Dr. addressing Miles directly towards the end of his last sentence.

'No, no. I can see it myself. You are absolutely correct.' said Miles showing Dr. Stephenson his palms in what is the international gesture for 'as you say' and 'you are absolutely correct'. The old Dr. continued:

'As such, I am most happy on a personal level to accept a man who has been through such a remarkable transformation into our community, and I hope you will too. I believe that this young man here has only now had the chance to express the humanity, honesty and genuine politeness he always had within him, to the fullest extent. Please welcome to the community, Mr. Miles Fitzroy.' concluded Dr. Stephenson and the room burst into enthusiastic and at the same most amiable applause.

While the applause lasted, Miles thought about something that Dr. Stephenson had said just then: 'I believe that this young man here has only now had the chance to express the humanity, honesty and genuine politeness he always had within him, to the fullest extent.'. That phrase touched a very sensitive cord within him. He suddenly realised his vast transformation over his journey and thought about James again, his views on the human nature. Perhaps if there was a human nature, it wasn't so bad after all, was it? There was good in him and he could see it now more clearly than ever. If human nature doesn't include kindness and altruism, it certainly includes the potential for them. He had to think more about that when he'd have more time though. The applause was dying out in anticipation of the next step in the ceremony and in fact Dr. Stephenson was already announcing that Miles was about to take the podium so to speak. Miles returned to reality fully as the microphone was being passed to him. He grabbed it and spoke:

'Umm... Eeeeh... Ummm... Hallo.' he uttered confusedly. Speaking in front of such different audience than he was used to was far harder than he'd thought. 'Don't be nervous. Just speak from your heart.' whispered Mr. Dickson from behind the back of Dr. Stephenson as the latter nodded in agreement benevolently.

'Sorry, I'm not that used to speaking in front of a crowd that I don't know how formally I should be treating.' started Miles and that proved sufficient to set the train in motion. 'I suppose I can say that I fully agree with Dr. Stephenson and what he said. I can add to the story he just told you my personal perspective and I think I will, nay I should.' he stated confidently now.

'Let's start from the beginning. I can vouch for the truth in the statement that Zone 1 is a dehumanising society. The one-tracked attitude and mentality of everyone and the narrow-minded way in which society in Zone 1 optimises everything for profit are creating a certain sort of people. Perhaps the poor and insecure societies in the ghettos of the democratic regions of London create tough and hard-working people who may not be able to afford the luxury of politeness but will be extremely loyal friends once you are 'one of them'. Perhaps society in the Royal boroughs creates submissive automata that nearly never question the rigidly stratified establishment, but who have refined politeness to a form of art and created an entire culture based on tradition and the establishment. Perhaps society in the communist sectors creates independent and disciplined people, who, however, have to very often keep a lot of their thoughts to themselves. However, in Zone 1, society creates utilitarians and opportunists of the worst kind. Zone 1 is the glorification of competition and natural selection. Zone 1 pits people against each other and creates brutes fit for survival in its own system. That implies making money, a lot of it. Even when people stick together, it is for an ulterior motive, to obtain something down the line. I only recently came to realise how dreadful this is. Even politeness there is fake, spurious, generated as a tool to obtain something in return.' said Miles getting more and more feverish. He then calmed himself down.

'Here, it is different. People here are genuine, and you can't imagine how much I appreciate that. It really means a lot to me. During my journeys around Zone 2 I have had the opportunity to talk to many people living under different systems. Talk to them openly and idly. Learn more about the way they think and act. This has been a real revelation to me. I have learned so much from so many that I could probably write a whole book about it. I learned to analyse problems from other perspectives, and crucially, to put myself in other people's shoes; not literally of course...' the audience chuckled. 'Seriously though, you will simply not believe how powerful this is as a reasoning technique. I came to strongly believe that if people took more time putting themselves into other people's shoes and seeing things from different perspectives, then people would become much more understanding, capable of reasoning and perhaps most importantly, forgiving. After all one who has at least tried to feel what a victim of floods feels when he sees his entire fortune floating down the river, can more easily show sympathy. At the same time, however, it is equally important that we make our own judgements too. If somebody had been robbed by, say, a man of colour and has acquired a misguided prejudice against people of colour, our ability to put ourselves in that person's shoes will certainly provide an explanation as to why the said victim came to be a prejudist, but should in no sane man provide an excuse for that; at least in my opinion, with all its imperfections.

Moreover, it is important to have arguments, yes, however it is equally important to know the arguments of others. By gathering arguments, which can be done only if we are willing to genuinely *listen* to one another, we can very quickly enrich our 'library of arguments' if you'll permit me the rather sloppy expression, and use it to form the basis of our very own cosmotheory, the way we perceive the world and tell right from wrong, acceptable from reprehensible and good from bad. To summarise what is already becoming too long a stop on a topic I intended to spend far less time on, learning about other points of view and genuinely attempting to understand them makes us better people, not just in the form of self-betterment, but also in the form of altruism and 'niceness' to be blunt.' continued Miles as the audience was completely captivated.

'My journey through the various regions of Zone 2 London has given me the impetus to change myself. Make myself a better person. In fact, now that I think of it I'm not certain I could ever return to Zone 1 again.' stated Miles surprising even himself, but also -visibly- the audience. The fact that he was prepared to give away so much material wealth for this absolutely astounded them. Yet it was not that uncommon either. There were many people in the world, even from Zone 1 who had decided to abandon their jobs in finance and seek a simpler life, making a living out of their savings and investments but living in mentally healthier societies as close as France and Germany or as far as India and -mostly rural- Thailand. 'As such, I am most happy to be here tonight, knowing that from now on I am officially a fellow citizen of all of you. I pledge to be a good and active member of your truly incredible society and in my quality as future journalist at Kropotkin's diaries to bring you the news with integrity; if I last long enough that is. Heh. Thank you all for coming.' concluded Miles and a torrent of applause followed. The 3 elders congratulated him on his successful job application whilst applauding him themselves and after a few good seconds of unrelenting applauding Mr. Latchley took the microphone and announced that he was going to be giving Miles the keys to his new home and a copy of the documents confirming his residence there on a small 4TB memory stick, courtesy of the Commune.

Those memory sticks were very handy for handling information portably when a terminal was not readily available. Naturally since terminals and computers were pretty much everywhere to be found, had become nearly as portable as a wrist-watch and certainly as portable as an old-style newspaper -out of paper!-, and were all connected to the internet, use for such devices was little. However, their rather solid and robust mechanical and reliable electrical nature still made them useful for carrying very important documents or backing-up data, just in case. They were made from nanomaterials that were sensitive to light of certain intensity and frequency and contained data in 3D format. When a data bit was written in a 'cell', EM beams from the x, y and z directions would hit the target cell and interferometrically toggle it and only it, by changing the structure of the nanomaterial it contained. This worked because the material would only change conformation if the beam had sufficient intensity to precipitate change. If insufficiently powerful EM radiation hit the cell, then the material would suffer from localised conformational changes and then when the beam ceased to hit it, revert to its original state. However, if enough photons hit their targets at once, the cell would be sufficiently affected to fall into a new equilibrium state. In all honesty, the more intense the beam that hit the cell, the more likely it was to toggle, so it was unfortunately a stochastic process at base. The mechanism was in principle a bit like the photo-sensitive reaction occurring with Rhodopsin in human -and animal- cone and rod cells of the retina, only with this additional source of stochasticity and random errors caused by the fact that the beams used to toggle a certain location in the memory had to cross through many others before reaching their destination. In the case of the memory sticks, the chemical change would alter the optical absorption coefficient of the cell's nanomaterial. By shooting light through a waveguide at a cell and measuring the attenuation at the output the stick would be able to determine whether the cell contained a digital '1' or a '0'. A similar memory stick, older and slower, but a bit more compact, used a different nanomaterial for the memory cell which changed conformation so as to connect or disconnect the terminals of a couple of nano-wires. To read data from this version of the memory stick we would apply a voltage across the nano-wires and see whether the cell was in a conductive or non-conductive state. To delete data from a cell, the specific cell would be bombarded by EM radiation of first one frequency and then another one, again using interferometry to determine the exact target. The first bombardment would change the conformation of the cell's nanomaterial so that it is ready to be returned to its original non-conductive state by the 2nd bombardment. The reason there were two steps needed to reverse the bit writing operation was a result of thermodynamics. The bit writing operation reduced the overall potential energy in the nanomaterial by triggering a conformational change from medium energy equilibrium state A to low energy equilibrium state B. Then, the first volley of energy pushed the material from low energy equilibrium state B to high energy equilibrium state C, where it was ready to collapse back to state B under the influence of the 2nd EM bombardment of the bit deletion operation. At any rate, it was a very high density memory cell which had its uses -in both versions for different applications-. Only problem: it had to be used at a static terminal that was equipped with I/O ports, so it was most of the time incompatible with flexinals.

 Mr. Latchley placed a little, wooden box on the table and opened it towards himself. He then turned it around so that Miles and the audience could see what was inside it. Smooth fabric seemed to cover the interior of the box, which was rather soft, but solid and featured notches specifically designed to hold a key and a memory stick. A commemorative brass plate also on the interior of the box simply read: 'Welcome to the Commune of Whitton. May you live in harmony here.'. It was a very tasteful little box that was. Mr Latchley then took the box in his hands again so that the open side of it now faced away from him and presented it ceremoniously to Miles, who was sitting to the immediate right of Mr. Latchley. Miles took the stick and the key itself, a card with an RFID chip, and bowed respectfully towards the old engineer amidst yet more applause. Back in Zone 1 doors at private residences also opened with RFID chips, but every door also had an implant reader so access to people could be granted without the physical transfer of a key being necessary.

 Shortly after the key was in Miles' hands Dr. Stephenson placed the microphone closer to him and announced that it was time for partying and the staff unveiled a large number of tables at the sides of the church that were previously covered by white tablecloths, only to reveal a buffet of various miniature pastries, sandwiches, fruits, small items of confectionery, most with chocolate, and light refreshments. Miles stood up, following the example of the 3 elders and the audience who were making their way towards the buffet. The rest of the evening went on smoothly. Miles met many of his new neighbours and fellow communards. As expected, it was the most extrovert and sociable ones that he made an acquaintance with, more introvert members of the Whitton commune preferring to keep more to themselves, express themselves laconically and open up to the newcomer in time. He met Mr. Patel from the corner shop and his lovely wife, a nurse at the local hospital in charge of coordinating the robo-nurses and making sure they were in working order. They were a very open and straight-forward couple; genuine people, thought Miles. Then he met Miss Amina from the local restaurant, an excellent chef specialising in Arabic and Indian food, and her colleague, Monsieur Le Brun, who specialised in European food, both from the west of the continent, and from the east, both of them lovely people. No matter how advanced robots became, when it came to cooking there was always a need for a good chef. Afterwards he made the acquaintance of Mr. Engelbert from the bus institution that operated public transport in the entire confederation and was head quartered in a nearby commune, a mechanical engineer originally from Germany, capital chap. And generally, as the evening went on he met more of his future neighbours and fellow citizens. At the end of the evening and the close of the party, when most guests had already departed, Miles made his way to the exit as well and just before walking under the large, arched door of the old church an officer of the law saluted him and greeted him with a 'good evening'.

'Good evening.' replied Miles. 'Can I help in any way?'

'Actually I'm here to help you.' answered the officer.

'Help me? What for?' asked Miles curiously.

'Don't you need to find your new home?' inquired the officer opening his hands in the international gesture for 'isn't it a bit obvious?'.

'Oh yes, of course!' realised Miles. 'Let's go by car. I have checked out of my hotel earlier today so all my belongings are now in the car.'

'Makes sense to me.' replied the officer. 'Please, after you dear fellow.' he concluded bowing respectfully.

'Certainly!' replied Miles and led the way.

Hilda had parked the car in the very immediate vicinity of the old church so the two men walked up to the vehicle. Once inside, the officer gave directions to Hilda, trying very hard to hide his curiosity and amazement towards the advanced AI of Miles' car mainframe. The new apartment was not particularly far away from the old church. In the small commune, nothing was. After all there are tower blocks that house more than 300 people. Finally, the car stopped in front of a fairly modern tower block. 5 floors, a lot of glass on the outside, central ventilation, windows made out of quadruple glazing for more efficient heating during the winter, OLED lighting everywhere of course, walls with turf stuffing in between sheets of concrete, water recycling systems and the like all included. Of course Miles had no idea what was waiting for him in the apartment yet. He descended from the car and the officer followed him. He then took a little travelling suitcase he had procured in the communist sector for the purpose of placing inside it the growing number of things he acquired as his journey went on; a few new clothes, new toothpaste, a shaver, since his own one was back at his place in central etc. As he started carrying it towards the entrance to the building the officer stopped him.

'Please, allow me. Today is a day of celebration for you. I shall carry your little bag for you.' he said at the height of politeness.

'You are very kind, sir.' said Miles thankfully and bowed with respect.

The two of them then made their way up the stairs to the last floor of the building. The lifts could have been used, but people who could use the stairs tended to actually use them out of concern for energy saving and as a good exercise. Finally, the two men reached the desired floor, navigated the rather long corridors of the building, the officer first, Miles following closely behind, until the officer suddenly stopped in front of the door that bore Miles' apartment number: 509. He then turned towards Miles, gently touched his suitcase on the floor, by the door-frame and saluted saying:

'Welcome to the commune young man.'

CHAPTER 11: LEARNING TO FILL THE PAGES OF KROPOTKIN'S DIARIES.

Miles thanked the officer for his kindness and as he left, placed the key-card in the slot of the reader that covered the locking mechanism of the door. A little LED shone green for the briefest of moments and a clicking noise announced that the door had been unlocked. Miles opened the door to his new home and as the large wooden door slowly pivoted upon the sturdy and well-oiled brass hinges without so much as a little screech, the apartment revealed itself to Miles.

The main entrance led directly into a large sitting room, already furnished with an old sofa, by the looks of it quite soft and comfortable, a large carpet with an intricate pattern akin to those often found on large Persian rugs, a tall lamp that simply consisted of a supporting pole and a globular OLED, a tall bookcase that was sturdy, simple and completely empty, a shorter cabinet that seemed to belong to the same set as the bookcase, the cabinet featuring two large drawers and two small ones above the large ones and a little round table with 3 chairs arranged around it. Behind the sofa was a large window and what appeared to be a balcony. As for where the entrance to that balcony might have been, it was not entirely obvious. Finally, a large light in the shape of a spherical sector adorned the ceiling, a light switch and dimmer was to be found on the immediate left of the main entrance, and on the left and right walls of the sitting room there were doors leading elsewhere in the house.

Miles chose to explore the right side first. As he entered through the door he found himself in a tiny room about 1,5 by 2 meters. In the space between where he was standing and what must have been the wall separating his apartment from the hallway outside there was a little shoe rack and a hanger bar where he could hang heavy coats. A couple of hat hangers were screwed into the walls left and right and a small and very tall basket presumably would hold umbrellas. If he wished to keep going right, Miles had to open yet another door and he did. That door led to his bedroom. The bedroom was at a corner of the tower block, and as such it had a couple of windows, each on different walls. A large, double bed stood, just under one of the windows, in the alcove created by the presence of the small 1,5x2 room, which took away a portion of the area of what would have otherwise been a rectangular bedroom. At the far corner of the room, a door led to the balcony. Under the other window and facing the bed and the door through which Miles had just walked into the room, was a short and long, empty bookcase with a few closed shelves at the right end of the complex. Standing against the right wall was a large triple wardrobe with doors out of thawed glass surrounded by a metal frame. Just behind the door to the little room and to the right of Miles was a little round armchair and an even smaller round table. Up on the wall next to the wardrobe on the side of the armchair there was a strange metal rail that was bolted vertically and ran from near the floor all the way up to near the ceiling. Miles had no idea what that was, but could fathom a guess. On that rail one could attach a special frame that could hold a terminal screen. When in use, the metal frame could travel up and down the rail, tilt upwards or downwards, yaw towards the wall or towards the wardrobe and fold or unfold the terminal screen. Miles could easily picture himself sitting in the comfy armchair, snacks on the little table, keyboard on his lap, surfing the net. Hell, there even was a tiny little shelf sticking out of the wall just to the right of the armchair that was perfect for use as a mouse-pad; if you were right-handed obviously, which Miles felt thankful of being at that time. Light was provided to the room by a strange collection of OLEDs on the ceiling that were crafted in the shape of planets that can be found in the solar system and radiated light at the specific planetary colours. At the centre of the ceiling was a large, disk that probably represented the sun and was presumably there in the case the inhabitant of the bedroom simply wanted bright, clear, natural-looking light. Finally, curtain bars were installed at each window and even at the door leading towards the balcony; a sturdy yet simple door which consisted of a metal frame and mostly quadruple glazing.

Having acquired a complete impression of this part of his new home, Miles walked back to the sitting-room ready to explore the 'left wing'. Upon crossing the threshold of the sitting-room door, Miles found himself in a small hub corridor, barely 2x1m -with the long side parallel to the corridor outside the apartment- that featured 4 doors, one for each wall. One he had just arrived through, the one to the left was revealed to be a small general-purpose storage cabinet where he could place anything from DIY tools to onions and garlic, the one to the right led to the bathroom and the one ahead he decided to explore later. Thus he entered the bathroom. A toilet was sitting by the door, a sink was next to it and a bathtub was lying against the wall behind which there certainly was the balcony. Above the sink was a small cabinet for storing various items of everyday hygiene with a mirror for a door. High above the bathtub a short but long rectangular window with a thawed mural representing a robin on a cherry tree -Japan style- was letting enough natural light to come through into the bath whilst preventing light from coming out of the bathroom with sufficient clarity for people outside the building to be able to clock embarrassing details of Miles' body. Artificial lighting during the night could be provided either by a bright yellow OLED panel fitted on the ceiling, or by a number of dim, blue OLED disks arranged on the floor at the corners where 4 floor tiles met together. The walls also featured pleasant to the eye pale grey tiles with a lone strip of florally themed coloured tiles running along the perimeter of the chamber. Those tiles were also coloured in pale colours and thus didn't stick out to the eye or become tasteless. Finally, there was enough space in the bathroom to fit a decent-size combined washing machine and drier. Satisfied with the bathroom Miles returned to the little hub. He pressed the switch he thought was for the bathroom lights and a small disk-shaped light inside the little hub came on. Miles smiled at the cute little light and decided to play with the lights later. Thus he switched off the lights in the bathroom by hitting the correct switch this time, let the little light in the hub on so he didn't have to rely on light from the sitting room while crossing the last door of the hub and confidently stepped into what proved to be the last room of the apartment: the kitchen. He switched the lights on just as he had done in the other rooms he had visited thus far and looked around. Right in front of him was a large empty space that could easily host a fridge and a freezer. To the left was a little wooden table of a rather Spartan nature and a couple of equally simple wooden stools. Far above them stood a coat hanger board that would presumably normally host kitchen aprons. To the right was a small, narrow corridor formed by the double kitchen counter flanking it. The counter was made of pressed wood but was covered in a tasteful shiny black surface. A double sink stood on top of it and not much else though Miles could easily picture both counters covered by various appliances like a blender, a microwave oven, a toaster, a kettle or even a rice-cooker or a bread-baker. On the counter opposite the sink stood the only other element of the kitchen that occupied counter surface: the cooker. It featured 4 heating elements of various sizes -as was the tradition- and underneath those it hosted the oven. Above the cooker stood a cooker hood. Beneath the surface of the counters, any space not occupied by the sink, the cooker and the embedded dish-washer was either a drawer of sorts or a cabinet of sorts. Above the counters any space not occupied by the cooker hood was also transformed into some sort of cupboard. Lighting was provided to the entire room by a long rectangular strip of OLEDs although special smaller lights were fitted just above the sink, on the bottom surface of the cooker hood and on the ceiling in a sparse pattern for when the kitchen is meant to be only dimly lit. Finally, at the end of the corridor between the counters was another door that led to the balcony, similar to the one in the bedroom.

Thus Miles finally exited to the balcony. He could see little but the street below and the neighbouring buildings, most of them shorter than the tower-block he was in. Various lights could be seen in the distance, but nothing significant, not even the few tall buildings of up to about 30 floors that sprouted sparsely and populated the dark night sky with their lights. He could not see Zone 1. That was behind him. Miles scanned the horizon for any landmark he might recognise until he spotted that there actually was something of significance he could make out. The weather was slightly foggy so he struggled to recognise it at first, but then he realised that the skyscraper he was seeing far south-east was the government tower in the communist sector. Thereafter Miles turned his attention to the balcony itself. He flicked a switch that stood just by the side of the balcony door on the inside and a small array of little disk-shaped pale yellow OLEDs started shining, bathing the balcony in a very smooth and pleasant light. The balcony was empty and only about 1,5m wide throughout its entire length. The railing of the balcony was simply a concrete wall -optimised for minimum heat transfer with the environment- and the roof was again quadruple-glazed glass. Similarly the roof and the railings were connected to one another by quadruple-glazed windows so in effect it was more like a green-house rather than a balcony. Miles walked along the balcony from end to end and re-entered his new home satisfied. It was small, it did not include expensive stuff like a wardrobe chamber, but he could imagine living comfortably enough in such place. The commune, after all was not such a bad place to live in.

  Overall, he was happy with the place; an apartment that normally 2 people would share. Yes, it did not have glowing tiles in the kitchen and the bathroom, tiles you could activate by touching them and change colour by placing two fingers on each tile and turning them either clockwise or counter-clockwise, or placing 3 fingers on one tile and rotate to change the colour of all tiles on that side of the wall simultaneously. Yes, it did not have a human-like AI mainframe and a dressing chamber. Yes, it did not have small ventilators that blew hot air across the bathroom floor and dried it after a particularly messy bath or shower. Yes, it did not have all the most modern energy saving and water recycling technology installed, and yes, the floors in the living-room and bedroom were not equipped with moving, rotating elements that allowed the user to switch between a soft 'lotus effect' carpet, thick mink fur or wooden parquet floor textures at the press of a few buttons or a verbal command to the mainframe. However, be that as it may, that apartment was more than many people had in the commune, by sheer virtue of its relative youth. Miles was genuinely lucky to have been allocated such good quarters.

  Miles returned to the living-room and sat on the sofa. He'd have to procure furniture and the like fast. He unwrapped his terminal screen and logged on to his email account. Quickly, he noticed that he had a new email from the housing committee of the Commune. It welcomed him to his new home, relayed to him a few technical details about the building including its energy efficiency rating, accurate area, date of construction and generic information about its previous owner, apparently a medic who had moved to a different Commune after getting married. Finally, the email notified him that he could link his terminal or any terminal screen to either of the special sockets in the living room and the bedroom and thus connect to the apartment's mainframe, whose CPU was hidden away in a cupboard under the sink. If he wished to access the mainframe, it was always far more convenient to do it through his terminal, the email clarified before communicating to him his new resident login details. Satisfied, he saved the details from that crucially important email in a file on his new memory stick, along with the documents confirming his residence at that place and set off looking for basic furnishings and appliances. Thankfully, in the commune -just like in the communist sector- such services that required the physical presence of the client when they were being carried out (for example installing a new fridge, buying a new wardrobe, going to the doctor for an appointment etc.) were open on 'weekends' as the people of Zone 2 seemed to call Saturdays and Sundays, when everybody else was at work. Instead these services were closed or partially open on Mondays and Tuesdays when most people who were likely to need them would be at work anyway and have limited opportunity to make use of them. Museums and libraries also operated on this principle and generally, the timetables of various enterprises, whether state-owned or private, were agreed in such way with the mediation of the commune councils and the confederate parliament that they tended to be open when they were most likely to be needed open. All of this timetable staggering, of course, occurred within the limits that prescribed 2 days off each week on average per year and 8 hours shifts a day for almost every working person etc. etc. Miles figured that it would take him some time to get used to the peculiar labour legislation in the Confederation, but he rather liked it as a whole.

Said and done, over the next couple of days Miles added possessions to his new home. A combined fridge-freezer, a new terminal screen with the special add-on that allowed it to use the convenient rail in the bedroom, a combined washing machine and drier as well as some most convenient kitchen appliances such as a toaster and a kettle to begin with. All in all, by the end of Sunday, and before his first day at work Miles had a fully furnished and equipped apartment. He even went for a drink at the local pub with one of his neighbours, Mr. Cho Huang, an old antiques salesman. The two of them decided to sit down at a quiet corner of the Welsh Dragon pub and enjoy some British ale called 'Red Star' made in the communist sector of Glasgow. They then talked a lot about their lives. Miles told his new neighbour more details about his story, Mr. Huang expressed his admiration towards the young traveller and then told him his own story. How he emigrated from Hong Kong long before the turn-over to China, how he had ended up in the Commune by sheer chance from the times before Zone 2 was split in different countries, how he chose to stay having taken a liking to the new system even though apartments were nationalised on paper and how he chose to enter the world of antiques out of a sheer love and yearning for the past. His parents were also merchants and shop owners back in Hong Kong, selling amongst other things also antiques and thus he learned to appreciate the ancient. Then they started talking about themselves, Miles talking about his shattered beliefs in the free market, his new experiences and so on and Mr. Huang about him being a Buddhist as well as his satisfaction with the commune system.

'I think the commune system is great because it makes good people.' said Mr. Huang sipping his red ale.

'How do you mean exactly?' asked Miles.

'See, the commune system makes people stick together. Solidarity keeps it together.' explained Mr. Huang and he was right.

'So people basically are placed in an environment that encourages them to be nice and helpful to one another.' reasoned Miles.

'Yes. That's right. That's why the commune makes good people. People know if they're good they'll bee rewarded. Eventually it becomes nature.' added Mr. Huang.

'It becomes nature? Isn't that a bit of a paradox?' asked Miles facetiously, but also quite seriously beneath the surface.

'Why paradox? That's no paradox. Nature is nothing, nature is made in the process.' said Mr. Huang who despite expressing himself fairly simply, had mastered English grammar very well.

'Made in the process? Isn't our nature something we are born with? Something that compels us to act in certain ways?' asked Miles.

'No no no...' said Mr. Huang. 'You have choice, right? They have choice, right?' he said waving vaguely towards the other guests of the pub. 'So long as there is choice and different people make different choice for same thing, nature is not compelling.' explained Mr. Huang disarmingly simply and effectively.

'Demonstrably.' agreed Miles.

'Human nature is not good or bad, human nature is just human nature. We build it.' argued the old man.

'Surely not entirely.' retorted Miles.

'Foundation is there from birth, that's what nature is when we are born.' replied old Huang.

'But if the foundation is there, then doesn't that mean that the building can only be built to a certain specification?' inquired Miles curiously.

'No no no... What about choice?' retorted the old man.

'All right, the building can then be built to certain specifications with some choice like how you paint it.' said Miles again bordering on the facetious.

'Hehe, no no no...' repeated Mr. Huang with a chuckle. 'You underestimate choice. Choice is a lot more than you think. How many floors to build? How many windows per floor? What do you put in each floor? Do you put elevator?' argued old Mr. Huang.

'All right, perhaps the building was a bad example...' said Miles but Mr. Huang interrupted.

'No! Why? Building, good example. If you don't like building think of it like a sheet of paper. Or, I know. I'll give you both examples!' exclaimed Mr. Huang and paused in anticipation of his interlocutor's reaction. Miles nodded assent without hiding his curiosity. Mr. Huang considered this -quite rightly- as licence to explain further.

'You see, human nature is like a building foundation. The foundation can only handle some weight, so you can't build forever. The foundation is only of certain size, so you cannot build too wide. The foundation limits you, but from there on the choice is yours. In the piece of paper example human nature is like a blank sheet with few lines drawn on it. The lines are there, but will they be part of a steam engine when you draw around them, or will they be part of a lychee leaf? You have choice, but the paper size limits you.'

'But in both cases there is more to it than just that. The foundation forces you to build upwards rather than underground and the lines on the paper already inadvertently fill your head with ideas for sketches that could make use of them, no?' argued Miles.

'Clever young man!' exclaimed Mr. Huang. 'That is exactly so. Both give you a small starting... starting... platform, that's part of the limit. But a lot of choice is still there!' said Mr. Huang. Miles nodded in sign of deep contemplation. Perhaps it was so. Human nature is like a blank sheet that imposes limits people may not cross and upon birth it starts with some initial 'drawings' on it, such as the instinct for survival, hoarding, eating etc.

'And practically, how do you capitalise on your freedom of choice? I mean how do you break out of those initial limitations, or rather the inclinations, not limitations?' asked Miles.

'Ah, good question. The more fundamental an inclination is the more difficult to break from it. But people do it, young man. People do it. In the monasteries of Tibet and Nepal and India Buddhist monks live... eh... live... voluntarily a simple life. It is not easy to shake off greed or will for wealth but people do it. Will to live is more difficult to lose. I mean THE will to live.' said Mr. Huang simply.

'So it is a bit like a potential field then. Your nature lays an 'easy' track for you that you may follow and be a simple-minded, selfish hunter-gatherer but with increasing effort, one may depart from this track and achieve more with his life.' reasoned Miles.

'Good way of thinking about it.' agreed Mr. Huang. 'That is why attributing all things to fate is wrong. As wrong as attributing everything to choice.' he concluded.

'So basically, to return to our original argument under the light of our recent discussion, what society does, or rather can do, is skew this potential field in one direction or another. For instance here, the potential field is skewed so that people learn to appreciate solidarity. Oh, now I see the full implications of what I was saying at the citizenship ceremony when I was talking about the sorts of people that various zones produce. They were far deeper than I thought at the moment...' exclaimed Miles thinking aloud more than talking to someone.

'Yes, but at the same time if a system assumes it can change that field too much and works on the assumption that the field is indeed as wanted, it fails.' added Mr. Huang.

'True. You can't build a system assuming that everybody has lost their will to live. Society can only influence people so much, the rest of the change coming from within. The farther away from the natural path society tries to 'operate at' the more difficult to do so, the more deviations in the form of people who have not been sufficiently influenced to conform to the new pathway of society. That is why in a society where crime is discouraged you have more criminals than you have good people in a society that encourages crime. By extension the same can be said about other character attributes.' argued Miles.

'The principle is correct, but it is not so simple. It is easier to make the wrong choice than to make the right choice.' argued Mr. Huang. 'So people in criminal society can't survive if they are good, but people in good society can survive if they are criminal.'

'True, but this is included in what I said about being closer to the 'original path'. No?' retorted Miles.

'Not only. There is also the fact that building is harder than destroying.' argued Mr. Huang simply.

'Entropy...' uttered Miles abstractly. 'In practical terms it is more difficult to do the right thing, as if nature or the universe conspires against you. It makes it much more difficult to shift the path towards what we generally call 'good' or 'constructive' rather than towards the opposite. That is certainly an effect we must take into consideration!' exclaimed Miles.

'Human nature doesn't try to lead us to our worst, but our worst is often the easiest to deviate to.' summarised Mr. Huang very succinctly.

'That's it! We have found out the shape of the function that determines a man's personality! You start from birth and as time moves on you have a valley whose bottom denotes the path that human nature at birth makes it easiest to follow. The precise location of the valley is influenced to a certain degree by the structure of society. The slope climbing towards 'utter evil' is less steep than then one climbing towards sainthood. Finally, if the valley as determined by the original human nature is very different from the one determined by society, then the latter one is inevitably weaker and as such many people jump back into the their natural one. And all of this, of course, ignores higher order effects.' reasoned Miles, sounding increasingly more like James. Mr. Huang kept sipping his ale while struggling to follow his interlocutor's complicated 'mathematisation' of the argument.

Afterwards, they switched to more everyday topics until the end of the evening out when Miles returned to his apartment and fell asleep very happy.

As the following day dawned upon him, he woke up energised and excited about starting work as a journalist. He made his way to the central building of the news agency by car, asked Hilda to park nearby and take the car for a recharge if possible and headed for the main entrance. Once there, he headed for the reception desk on the ground floor. The reception area was, in fact, not exactly in the main building of the agency, but in an extension built in front of the building in the form of a half-cylinder topped by a glass dome in the form of a quarter-sphere. During summer that sphere let sunlight through (in the visible range of the spectrum) creating a very nice visual effect. During winter it still let sunlight through but was not nearly as impressive. The floor was made out of a shiny red mosaic dotted with small black, yellow and white stones, with thin strips of white marble segmenting the surface of the red milieu into large rectangles. The reception desk was made of a metal skeleton and thawed glass and along the walls of the chamber abstract paintings hanged idly while large potted plants grew at each corner of the neat chamber. At the far side of the chamber were a couple of doors, one either side of the reception desk, presumably leading into the main building whilst at the ceiling above, just where the glass quarter-sphere dome met the concrete base upon which it was standing, an entire row of thin and slender, transparent, conical crystals with their side slightly concave hanged down towards the floor like very smooth stalactites. The row of 'stalactites' was spanning the entire length of the concrete support that kept the weight of the glass dome under check and the effect that those tightly packed crystals had on the room at day was to give it a very 'icy' air. During the night small but very bright OLEDs were lit up inside the cores of each crystal and provided a very impressive artificial illumination pattern to the reception chamber. 'How simple yet beautiful.' thought Miles. 'In Zone 1 they would have been made out of real crystals, perhaps even artificial diamonds.' thought Miles. The science of creating artificial diamonds had been perfected resulting to a slight drop in diamond prices in recent decades. Either way, the banks of Zone 1 could most certainly afford it. They had enough money to make landscaping their primary expense, even above staff costs, if they wanted to. But of course the largest expenses for banks were and were going to be the bonuses of the very high-ranking section of staff. With these thoughts Miles approached the reception desk where he was greeted by a robo-ceptionist.

'Good morning.' said the robo-ceptionist girl bowing her head Japan-style.

'Good morning.' replied Miles, and before the robo-ceptionist could continue he stated his business: 'I actually got hired as a journalist. It is my first day at work... My name is Miles Fitzroy, by the way.' Miles explained.

'Of course. We've been expecting you Mr. Fitzroy. Please make your way through either of the doors behind me and navigate to the 3rd

floor, office 312. The lifts are just through the doors behind me and so are the stairs. The way to each office is clearly sign-posted. And of course, good luck with your new job. We hope you enjoy.' the roboceptionist concluded with a charming smile.

'Thank you.' replied Miles and headed off.

He quickly crossed the threshold of the door to the left and found himself in a foyer which was carpeted in a plush, yet not expensive-looking red carpet with thin yellow lines about 3cm away from each verge i.e. where it met walls or doors. There were more potted plants here and there, simple but functional OLED lighting along the ceiling and not much more. A wide staircase covered in the same red carpet was heading upwards towards the next floor and mid-way it split into two branches, each leaving in its own direction and spiralling up towards the next level for the remaining ½ of the distance. To the left and the right of the stairs Miles could see the doors to a couple of elevators. He opted for the stairs and after the brief moment he spent looking around, he headed up. There was nothing of particular significance to see as he ascended towards the 3rd floor. Just corridors with doors either side. Eventually he reached the 3rd floor, followed the signs that led him towards the correct office and reached a door with a small brass plate that read:

'Simon Thompson. Journalist. Daily politics section.'

Miles knocked at the door and upon being asked to enter he did. When he opened the door he saw a simple, small office furnished with little more than a couple of chairs for guests, Thompson's chair, a bookcase overflowing with notes and sketches and a messy desk that housed a terminal screen and lots and lots of sticky notes, each filled with scribbles, one more incomprehensible than the other. The man himself, Simon Thompson, was sitting at his chair talking fervently on his mobile phone, or more likely his job's mobile phone. Landlines had become a bit of an obsolete fashion over time and everybody was simply issued a mobile phone for work that satisfied just the most basic functionality of a mobile phone: the ability to talk and be talked to, stream a live video to the listener while talking (good for explaining things visually over the phone) and being able to receive the same service. Anything more was really superfluous and could easily be covered by a flexinal. Not that the functionalities of the phone itself could not be covered by a flexinal either, but a mobile phone enjoyed better mechanical robustness, was cheaper and therefore an ideal choice for an employer who wishes to equip all his employees with a means of effective communication. At any rate, Thompson was in the middle of a conversation about news from the confederation government central that a national emergency had been declared and the government was mobilising the troops and increasing enlisting rates for the army. Miles stood by the door at first, and then, when beckoned, sat at one of the guest chairs until Thompson had finished his call and addressed him.

'Whew! That was quite something! Let me tell you something, I don't usually start my day with a call from my coordinator about such big news. Simon Thompson's the name. You must be the new fellow.' said Mr. Thompson.

'I... well... yes.' answered Miles slightly startled by Mr. Thompson's flamboyance. 'Miles Fitzroy at your service, Mr. Thompson.' he finally managed to say, composing himself.

'Glad to meet you Miles. You can call me Simon. I'll be your mentor for the first difficult month and generally show you the ropes.' Thompson said. Miles smiled very, very slightly curling his lips.

'Are you American by any chance?' he asked.

'Why yes, how did you know?' asked in turn Mr. Thompson.

'Just a guess. Right, to business. What do we do today?' inquired Miles.

'Today we go outside the building that houses the confederation parliament and try to get hold of the news as they unfold. We damn well weren't expecting them to come down to a resolution as important as this one. Come on!' said Mr. Thompson as he was beckoning Miles not to fall behind.

'Now listen kid, and listen well. Our coordinator is getting the team together, we now go downstairs and meet the guys in the truck. They'll take us to where the action's happening and then you watch me and learn.' continued Mr. Thompson as the two of them were heading down the stairs. At the same time Miles was smiling covertly and trying to contain a lustful laughter. Mr. Thompson seemed like quite the figure.

'OK.' Miles finally said.

'We won't be the only guests at the table there, son. There'll be others too. Colleagues from our own news agency trying to interview the outgoing representatives and competitors from other news channels. We don't engage them and they don't engage us as a rule. No need to. You stay behind the camera and watch what I do.' further explained the flamboyant reporter.

'Understood.' confirmed Miles.

Before long they were in the TV van along with the cameraman, the sound assistant, a make-up lady, the administrator working the mainframe of the van and another reporter whose job was to attempt to interview the outgoing representatives. Miles positioned himself next to his mentor and the make-up lady and when all passengers had been seated Mr. Thompson shouted 'Roll it!' and the driver set off like a raving lunatic who'd been given a super-car for a present. The make-up lady started putting make-up on the face of the interview reporter in the moving van, a feat which amazed Miles to the very utmost. He seized the opportunity that arose from the silence in the van to ask Mr. Thompson.

'Mr. Thompson...'

'Cripes, call me Simon, kid. We're all in this together now.' interrupted the flamboyant American.

'Err... Sure thing... Simon. I was wondering how we know that there has been such important decision at today's confederate parliament sitting.' inquired Miles.

'Well, parliament here's open. There's live cameras in it and everything. We have people at the agency who monitor what's happening there live so that we know whether there's any breaking news occurring or not. When we got wind that the president of the parliament has called an emergency vote on urgent troop mobilisation after talks with the ambassador of them reds we pounced at the news realising we'd caught ourselves some big fish.' said Simon.

'Ah. That also explains why we can still make it there and report on the news before all the representatives are back home drinking a cup of tea.' reasoned Miles.

'Got it in one kiddo.' replied Simon and once again Miles fought long and hard to hide a very, very cheeky smile and perhaps a chuckle.

The van kept running at insane speeds along the streets of the Confederation and long before the time when they were at parliament square in Weybridge the make-up lady had performed her task admirably well. She had even asked whether the young gentleman needed a make-up to, but Simon replied in the negative. Then, while Simon was getting all painted up and ready with the help of the make-up lady the other reporter told Miles that it would be nice to make formal introductions, but the urgency of the situation forbade such luxury. He apologised for that promising that on the way back, when the van would presumably be moving at a slower pace they could all formally introduce themselves to him. Miles then replied that he fully understood the situation and was by no means offended by what others might take as a breech of protocol, but he himself understood for what it was: reasonable behaviour. The other passengers, who were following this brief exchange of words nodded agreeably and said 'Thank you.' as the van continued speeding towards the parliament.

Finally, the van reached its destination, the back doors opened and the crew exited in a hurry. The reporter responsible for the interviews started running towards the gates of the parliament building from where representatives were already beginning to emerge. It seemed that the resolution for mobilisation was the last item on the agenda, which was rather strange considering the fact that it was only about 09:45 AM. Miles later on asked why that was the case and Simon replied: 'What planet are you from? The parliament has been in assembly discussing this matter over the entire night. This is the end of a solid 24hr session! They didn't just come in a decided to vote on the matter just like that!'. The sound man and the cameraman both rushed towards a spot from where the parliament could be seen with the clarity of a tourist attraction in a post-card and deployed all their equipment. The make-up lady was on stand-by with random accessories used to make a man more presentable -taming the hair, erasing wrinkles, making the skin less prone to reflecting light etc.- and Simon groomed himself while taking up his position in front of the camera. Shortly before going live Simon advised Miles to unroll his terminal and watch the news there to see how what he did was transposed into the live broadcast. Miles agreed with the great idea and soon enough he was watching Kropotkin's Diaries live.

Before we dive into the action, let us set-up the scene by describing what Miles could see before his very eyes at that very moment. In front of him was the confederate parliament, a new building in the peculiar shape of a pyramid. The pyramid was supposed to represent the fact that power stemmed from the people, which is why the assembly chamber was on the ground floor and why there were not steps leading up to the pyramid from the street level, but rather a single step leading down. Of course we can claim that the building was in the shape of a pyramid, and technically speaking indeed it was, however it consisted of a couple of pyramids in reality. An external one that handled ventilation and crated a very nice visual effect, and a smaller one on the inside, about 80-85% of the size of the external one, that was the actual building. The internal pyramid also had an exterior made out of glass -a symbol of transparency- and only the inside walls of the various offices along the external sides of the pyramid were made out of an opaque material. This created the impression that inside the small pyramid there was yet another one, slightly smaller. Of course, all the calculations had been done before construction to make sure that the extra heat losses precipitated by the increased surface area that the outer pyramid was presenting to the environment would be compensated by heat from sunlight during the day and similarly that the glass exterior of the actual building was also helping run the building's air conditioning system on less energy. In other details, the apices of the two pyramids were connected together by a glass tube that could only be part of the building's central shaft cooling system. An additional clue indicating that this was the case was given by the metallic top of the large, external pyramid. The floor between the internal and external pyramids was covered in something very shiny that looked like a dark, black mosaic with shiny chippings of stone here and there. Naturally from the distance we was at Miles could not discern that much detail. All he could see was a very black surface that when at the correct angle with respect to the sun shone at an intense golden hue. Around the pyramid there was a large plaza littered with greenery and flowers. The plaza placed at least 80m distance between the external points of the pyramid and the neighbouring buildings, and hosted the ventilation shafts that kept the parliament col at summer. Overall in size, the pyramids were not excessively large. In height Miles could count 8 floors to the apex of the internal pyramid and the inclination of the walls was about 45°.

With this view and under an 85% clear, blue morning sky Miles saw the following at the screen of his terminal. In the main studio of the agency (the KD agency as Simon called it in short) the familiar face of one of the news announcers was apologising for the interruption in the service to bring some breaking news. This was the exact transcript of the newscast that followed:

'Dear listeners, we are sorry to interrupt this morning's 'Tea with Nigel' program to bring you a breaking news bulletin. We have just received word that the confederate parliament has voted 302 to 199 in favour of the urgent mobilisation decree proposed by president Shinjiro Imada. As a result, the Confederation is now officially in a state of high alert and troops across the sector are beginning to mobilise. We have no details as to where this activity will concentrate, but we have gathered so far that the mobilisation is coming at the original proposal of the ambassador of the people's republic of Anglia, who according to reports, has asked the Confederation to be ready for large scale military operations should anything happen in the next few days. We will now go live at the gates of the parliament as the 24-hour marathon session that decided upon mobilisation is drawing to a close and the representatives of the communes are beginning to emerge.' said the main reporter and then addressing Simon Thompson, who appeared in a small, separate frame within the screen so that he looked as if he was behind the reporter, he continued: 'So, what is the atmosphere there Simon?'. Simon replied as Miles was watching him closely:

'Well, David, as you can see behind me the representatives have just started making their way out of a battering session discussing effectively whether the country should prepare for war based on the warnings of an ally. We have no idea yet how specific the information conveyed by the Anglian ambassador to the foreign commissioner was, or in fact any of its contents, however one thing is for certain, and that is that the representatives have had a very long round of discussions over the course of action that should be taken.'

'Indeed we have seen a session that lasted far longer than what we are used to seeing. We also hopefully have contact with Jemil who is trying to convince some of the departing representatives to talk to him. I believe we have audio contact with Jemil. Jemil, how is the situation there?' asked David Ramsay, the main news announcer for that newscast.

'It's hectic here, David. Lots of tired faces coming out of the pyramid, most of them also burdened by worry. I have managed to talk to Mr. Ivan Ravinsky who's representing a group of Communes from the largely affected border region of Woking. In fact he is standing next to me right now.' said Jemil and pictures of Jemil and Mr. Ravinsky appeared on the screen just next to the main announcer and below Simon's frame. Jemil continued: 'Mr. Ravinsky, can you tell the public why the session deciding upon the matter of mobilisation came down in favour of putting it into motion?'

'Well, the information from the ambassador was very worrying and a number of us were of the opinion that it is better to be safe than sorry, whilst others insisted that since our own government sensed absolutely no danger from outside our borders we should not mobilise until we have at least some evidence of a necessity to do so.' replied the representative chosen by a group of 15 Communes in the region to speak for them in the confederation assembly.

'What was the information from the ambassador exactly, if you are allowed to tell us Mr. Ravinsky?' asked Jemil.

'I am allowed to tell you much of it. Basically the ambassador said that within the next few days the communists were planning a large-scale military operation in Zone 3 which could potentially incite unpredictable violence. Naturally, we tried to persuade them to use a more peaceful approach, but they are adamant that very soon a great opportunity for resolving conflict in zone 3 will arise and they are ready to take it. In fact they asked us to honour our alliance and aid them in the impending campaign saying that in the case of military assistance being granted to them, the Confederation stands a chance to expand its territory into Zone 3 and help people who are currently suffering in the chaos that reigns there.' said the representative.

'That is incredibly important news.' exclaimed Mr. Ramsay. 'So effectively the communists are planning a vast raid on Zone 3 in the near future?' he asked of Mr. Ravinsky and he replied:

'That is the feeling that I get although of course they didn't specify very clearly. So far the whole operation seems a bit vague. They seem to be waiting for something. Some 'opportunity' of sorts that they don't specify.'

'Would that be why the assembly seemed slightly reluctant to give a definitive answer very quickly to the ambassador?' asked Jemil.

'I believe so. If we have clear evidence of danger we could have simply voted upon the issue quickly and gotten our troops ready for battle as soon as possible, but as I said, in the absence of concrete evidence or even a concise plan of action that I'm guessing the communists have probably been preparing for quite some time now but are not willing to disclose to us yet, we were not able to cast aside our doubts and simply follow. Either way, in the end the ambassador convinced us. After all the communists have been good allies so far and would not risk their diplomatic reputation by providing us false information or creating an embarrassing situation for us. In any case, they have already fully mobilised in the past few days. This delay between their and our mobilisation would indicate to me that they probably waited to ascertain something before telling us that it is very likely we will need to mobilise because some event of heavy significance is about to be precipitated.' added Mr. Ravinsky.

'And when do you suspect we will be hearing any updates from either them or our own government?' asked Jemil.

'Well, I don't rightly know. However the cabinet are looking closely at the matter. We have agreed by vote in the big plenum that if the communists declare war the cabinet should automatically assume the power of the dictate, i.e. that all its decisions for a 3 month period will become mandatory once voted upon by the small plenum alone.' said Mr. Ravinsky as Miles was wondering what the big and the small plena were and whether indeed the Confederate cabinet was indeed just a consultative body that issued optional directives to the various communes during peacetime. It was, as he was going to find out. To begin with, because of the large number of communes, in the parliament every 15 communes on average were represented by one representative from one commune -in rotating order- thus creating a so called 'small' plenum in the parliament and a 'big' plenum of all the communes. In normal times of peace the cabinet could only apply compulsory legislation that had been voted upon by the big plenum of the communes, not just the small plenum of the parliament and the small plenum could only pass optional directives. Generally, the big plenum was summoned sparingly and only decided of very important issues like war and peace or vast projects etc. In times of war or national emergency, the big plenum could invest the cabinet with new powers that would allow it to act solely on voting activity in the small plenum, effectively turning the Confederation into something similar to an old-style representative democracy for a short while. All this was explained to Miles later that day by his mentor. On a side note, for matters too big to affect only one commune, but too small to affect the entire confederation, temporary regional councils could be formed and invested with powers akin to those of a 'confederation within the confederation' at the unanimous vote of the member communes with an interest in that matter and that new body would stay there as a structure until the matter was resolved, after which point it would be dissolved. It was all in the spirit of devolved and flexible authority that the communards valued extremely highly. At any rate, Miles had little chance to ponder over the issue for too long at that time since the newscast hadn't really stopped.

'Any other measures you have taken today?' asked Jemil.

'Yes, as a matter of fact.' asnwered Mr. Ravinsky. 'We have all booked rooms in nearby hotels so that we may quickly be summoned in parliament for debating or voting if any emergency occurs. I mean we of the small plenum. The situation is most worrying; most worrying indeed.' concluded Mr. Ravinsky ominously.

'Thank you for your time Mr. Ravinsky.' said Jemil.

'No problem. Glad to be of service.' replied the representative and left.

'So, what do you make of this situation Simon?' asked Mr. Ramsay.

'Well, David, we've heard the man. The big plenum was summoned by electronic voting during the marathon parliament session and agreed that should there be a declaration of war in the next few days the small plenum will assume powers akin to those of the house of commons a few decades ago when the United Kingdom was a representative constitutional monarchy in substance rather than just on paper. We've heard that the members of the small plenum will be staying around in case they are needed. To me all of this indicates that the representatives are marred with worry. The fact that this mechanism that was designed to allow the Confederation to deal with crises is being used for the first time ever is most probably adding to the stress that the representatives feel. So, all in all, it is a worrying situation, which however we can only counter by keeping our cool judgement.' said Simon.

'Indeed so. Any more thoughts from you, Jemil?' asked Mr. Ramsay.

'Not much to add to what my colleague has just said. I can just say that if war does occur, the vast war machine that the communists have been fervently building up pretty much since the foundation of their sector is probably going to be doing most of the work, in my opinion.' added Jemil.

'Indeed the communist war machine is a lot larger than the confederate militia, and probably also better equipped. Thank you for watching dear viewers, we will update you with more information at our regular news broadcast at noon and again at 9 o'clock and issue more emergency bulletins if any breaking news appear on the horizon.' said Mr. Ramsay and the regular TV broadcast resumed.

Miles rolled the terminal and Thompson along with the rest of the

TV crew made their way back to the van. On the way back to the studio Thompson, with the help of the other passengers, explained to Miles the complex power structures that operated at the top of the confederate government and how they manage to pull the entire country together when the need arises, but remain largely inactive when there is no need for their intervention. After the explanations had ceased, Miles introduced himself formally to the other crew members who did the same for him. He learned that the cameraman was Mr. Chris O'Brien and he would be working as part of Mr. Thompson's team, the sound specialist was Craig Johnson, also member of 'the Thompson team' as he called it, the make-up lady was Missus Barbara Wilkins and worked again with Thompson on a permanent basis, the other reporter was Mr. Jemil Umbangi, a very esteemed colleague of Thompson who worked with him on a non-permanent basis and the administrator was Mr. Yusef Abdel Amindullah and was again a permanent colleague of Thompson's in what he jokingly called 'the A-team'. Miles would be working with them for quite a while, at least a month before being promoted to a full-fledged member of staff and possibly starting to go on his own missions.

After these sundry introductions and shortly before the van pulled up at the news agency's parking lot Miles asked Thompson why the cameraman and sound specialist were centred upon him at the pyramids rather than at the man who was doing the interviews and Thompson replied that if it was centred at the man with the interviews his own impact upon the broadcast would have been far, far smaller and seemed superfluous. At any rate, the news agency had never had to react so quickly to anything before so in the future they'll probably be using a bigger van with a cameraman and sound specialist for each reporter on board.

That question being answered the crew descended from the van and each headed in their own directions. Miles followed Thompson to his office. Just outside the door, Simon pointed towards another door next to the one leading to his office and said:

'FYI, that's where you'll be working son. But for now, just follow me and watch what I do. I'll explain as we go.'

Miles agreed and followed him to the office. There he watched Thompson writing an article for the next day's internet feed as he informed him that the live feed was written by other people within the agency whose job was to take the important bits out of what the journalists were saying during live broadcasts and put them in written form as quickly as possible on the net. Miles then watched as Thompson sent the article for editing elsewhere within the agency and then preoccupied himself with observing his mentors preparations for a possible broadcast later that day with a guest from amongst the ranks of the parliamentary representatives, as was requested from him by his coordinator. Soon, it was lunchtime and the two of them headed towards the agency's canteen where the watched David Ramsay repeat a polished-up summary of what had been breaking news a few hours earlier, to the public. After lunch, preparations for the guest interview continued as Thompson's handler informed him that a willing representative had been found to do the show at about 17:00 and for about an hour. As such, Thompson completed his preparations quickly and when the time arrived, he went to the make-up room and emerged fully groomed again to meet his guest. The 17:00-17:50 show was mostly a repetition of what had been said that morning, with the representative giving a few more graphic details about the proceedings of the marathon session, a few more details about the communist ambassador's exchange of words with the foreign affairs commissioner and generally adding more detail to the already known general story. Short intermissions for content that mostly advertised opera performances, theatrical shows and concerts and included public service announcements, allowed Thompson and his guest to take breathers, drink water and adjust themselves and their microphones more comfortably before resuming their interview. Finally, at 17:50 the show ended and Thompson was given the green light by his coordinator to go home. As he was wearing his coat in his office he addressed Miles:

'You see son, this is what a busy day looks like. You are lucky, or unlucky to have started working for us on a day packed with important news. Something tells me that we should be getting used to this regime of work...' he said wearily, but above all else worriedly. He then continued after a brief pause: 'Come, it's time for us to head home. You've learned a lot today. On the way back watch the news that's about to begin in...' he looked at his watch. '...2'.'.

Miles nodded in agreement and departed for his car with his mentor. On the way towards the entrance Miles summoned his car using his beacon. Thompson noticed and said:

'That's a damn good ride you must own. Just in case you didn't know, you may now park at the agency's car park. Since you gave your identification at the job interview data about your car registration plate has been passed on to the agency and you now by all means must have access to the car-park.'

'Oh. Nice! Just like in Zone 1 then.' said Miles and smiled.

'Oh well... I said just in case you didn't know, didn't I?' asked Thompson smiling in return. Then as he made his way towards the car park and his path with Miles split he added: 'Take care.' to which Miles responded with 'Good night Mr. Simon.' and then departed.

On the way back to his new apartment he followed his mentor's advice and watched the news. Again a refresher of the noon news but with more details and a few extracts from the show where Thompson hosted a representative of the parliament. Eventually the news bulletin ended and Miles reached his apartment. He dined simply with an ill-cooked meal -no robo-butler to do that for him in the Commune- and some soy milk with cereals, concluded his evening ablutions and went to bed after setting the alarm clock on time for him to be at work punctually on the morning of the next day. And as he fell asleep, a smile quivered on his lips. It was the unmistakable smile of satisfaction, the result of a fruitful day.

CHAPTER 12: WAR CORRESPONDENT.

The next morning Miles woke up cheerfully and proceeded to dispense with his morning toilette. After eating a couple of scrambled eggs on toast for breakfast and drinking a bit of water to keep himself well-hydrated Miles left towards his new workplace. Once in the correct vicinity, he instructed Hilda to park the car within the limits of the agency's car park if possible and then entered the building. He bade good morning to the robo-ceptionist who responded with an equally polite good morning and informed him that there was mail for him. Miles asked for the mail and obtained his new badge. A name-badge that carried his name and position within the agency, as well as his picture and an identification number and bar code, while an RFID chip was hidden inside. The robo-ceptionist explained that it was tradition that the first day at work counts as orientation day and only the 2nd day is considered the first 'real' day at work. Of course the 1st day was also paid. It was just the tradition in the commune that each employer would give each new employee one day to 'adjust to the new environment' as elementary courtesy. The communists had taken a liking to the idea and adopted it for themselves. At any rate, Miles received his badge and went straight to the office of his mentor without forgetting to thank the robo-ceptionist.

She was just a computer simulation, but her reactions, her near ability to express feelings, made Miles feel her as a human being deserving respect. Just seeing her virtual face smiling after him being polite to her made him feel right. After all at what point does a simulation of a human being becomes such a faithful representation of an actual human being that we can assume it has feelings? So what if in our human brains signals are transmitted electrically from cell to cell in the form of 1s and 0s generated by neural cells via weighted averages of 1s and 0s that serve as inputs to those cells, and in the form of 1s and 0s generated combinatorially by various circuits in an electronic brain? If we simulate suffering and happiness too closely, don't we end up creating them in a very real sense? Qualitatively there is no difference between the faithfully simulated suffering of a robot and that of a human. To illustrate this we can take examples: If we create a robot whose brain perfectly simulates a human brain and appearance perfectly simulates a human body is its suffering real? If we make the body evidently robotic but we keep the humanoid brain, is its suffering real? If we replace the brain with a slightly different model is its still suffering real? How different should the brain be to make its suffering a mere simulation like the clumsy graphics of dying people in action games of the previous century? Miles had never given too much thought to those questions. He just followed his heart, which told him that he should be polite and affable to the robo-ceptionists, robo-butlers, robo-nurses and other such humanoid robots that populated the Earth alongside humans, but often on a different plane.

At any rate he reached the office of his mentor and found him making himself comfortable after having presumably just arrived himself. He had brought himself a cup of tea and encouraged Miles to make one for himself if he wished to do so. After Miles came with a mug full of tea for himself, Thompson told him that to start what he hoped would be a more normal day he would scan through the news feed coming directly from the councils of the various communes and temporary 'super-communes' that fell under his jurisdiction and look for any important political news there. The feed was enormous. Hundreds upon hundreds of news being emitted from the press officers of each commune in a strict headline-summary-body format. Thompson would scan the feed reading the headlines. Any headline that looked promising would be transferred to a special folder. Once the feed had been exhausted, Thompson would look into the folder with the promising results and start reading the summaries. If those were promising they'd go into yet another folder. At the end the ones in the last folder of the chain would be read and maybe a story would come out of them eventually. Then, messages from press offices of other public organisations such as hospitals would be searched for interesting information with the same system. Finally, a multitude of viewer calls would be screened for any interesting information, particularly information that the afore-mentioned offices would very much like to hide from the public. That would last until 10:30, so for just 1hr and 30'. Of course at this job Thompson was helped by other employees of the agency who screened such information during the night and alerted journalists if something interesting was going on even by waking them up from their night's sleep if necessary. Information coming directly from journalists who happened to witness an event while off-duty or simple information gatherers that were employed specifically to monitor potential sources of news were handled by the same people as well. After 10:30 Thompson had to help David and his team assemble the news at noon by passing them the information he had gathered thus far. Then he'd work on any shows he'd have to do later that day or even later that week, if any, or else continue the search. In 'low seasons' without many extra shows the workload would drop significantly, but in 'high seasons' it could get pretty busy, Thompson explained to Miles.

Said and done that's exactly how events unfolded until lunch. During lunch Miles and Thompson watched the noon news where some political analysts from the confederate president's advisory board had been invited to discuss the situation regarding the mobilisation decree issued the previous day. After lunch, work resumed with more searching for news and a small draft article for the next day's internet feed on how a commune in Molesey had passed a new rule stating that bigamy was no longer illegal so long as all parties involved consented in being part of such relationship. The article commented on the historically more than averagely liberal ideas of that particular commune and expressed interest in seeing how the experiment would turn out to work in practice i.e. whether it would lead to more people living happily in relationships that suit them and their particular tastes. It argued that morally speaking, if that is what everybody involved wishes, they are all consenting adults and nobody is getting harmed, then why not allow such relationship? Miles, when asked by Thompson, expressed his opinion that he had never given too much thought to the matter, but was curious to see what was going to come out of it.

The day would have then passed in relative quiet had the anchor from the communist sector not brought in some urgent breaking news. Thompson was informed by phone from his coordinator and was asked to pass on the information to Miles and prepare for action. The scene was very dramatic. Thompson was working on his article about the council that had legalised bigamy and Miles was looking from behind his shoulder trying to learn the procedure he used to write it when Thompson's phone rang. He answered:

'Hallo. Thompson speaking.' Pause. 'Yes. What's the news?' Another pause. Seconds later the aromatic cigarette in Thompson's mouth fell on the table. It was a cigarette made out of a specifically bred in the 2020's artificial plant called 'Doctor's flowers' that when burned emitted smoke that was very beneficial to the function of the lungs freshening the breath of the inhaler. It was also pleasantly scented. It helped lung cells stimulate surfactant production in patients with cystic fibrosis too. At any rate, the cigarette fell on the table and as Thompson was picking it up he uttered extremely disturbed: 'Bull****!'. Miles could hear vague noises coming from the telephone indicating that the coordinator was saying something akin to 'It's true I tell you!'. Thompson continued speaking on the phone: 'Yes, I'll tell him too.' Pause. 'What do we do next? Head for parliament again?' Another pause. 'Yes, yes. Understood. We'll do exactly so.' Thompson hung up.

'What's happening? What's happening?' inquired Miles full of curiosity.

'You know what my coordinator just told me?' replied Thompson by means of another question.

'What?' asked Miles.

'He literally said: drop everything you're doing, the communists have invaded Zone 3 with a force of 10.000 ground troops and half of their artillery, tanks, ground troops armoured transporters and battle droids.' replied Thompson.

Battle droids were what was replacing the traditional soldier. A traditional soldier was equipped with a lot of gadgets that allowed him to see farther and better than normal people, hear only what was important, communicate with his team easily and eliminate targets as well as bearing an exoskeleton that granted him super-human power from a large battery. For relatively little extra money a battle droid could be manufactured. It had the same capabilities as a traditional soldier, only more accurate at targeting and was remotely controlled by soldiers stationed in a large, underground control centre. Tanks, of course already had such systems and so had artillery so both those units left to battle unmanned -the latest models at least-, being given life via a remote control. To help them there were smaller and cheaper 'house-keeping robots' that, for instance, loaded shells into the artillery cannons. All those units were controlled remotely by controllers who now had the additional benefit of a large terminal screen displaying vital combat information coming from their colleagues and superiors, all to themselves and goggles that allowed them to feel as if they were right in the middle of the action with the boon of being able to switch perspectives at the click of a button. One minute they were watching the action through the rear hatch of the tank and the other they were watching it from on top of the tank, from 'camera 2'. Same principle applied to the battle droids and the artillery where special software could lock-on to a target selected by the controller and work out the values of all the technical parameters for the set-up of the cannon/gun so that the shell would hit bullseye. Meanwhile the controller was a highly trained individual who had to be able to judge and react quickly to the changing situation, follow orders coming from above and be perfectly able to move his hands about with mechanical accuracy so that he could hit the right switches at the correct times. The ingenuity put into developing the cock-pit of, say, a battle droid was remarkable. For instance, the goggles that the controller wore had 3 modes of operation. Normal view where they could simply see their surroundings, tactical mode where they could see the action unfolding right before them and strategy mode where they could see on a map what their colleagues were doing and orders being issued by their officers displayed graphically. Then another example is the tactical mode itself, where the system could detect movement of the controller's head and amplify it by a bit more than a factor of 2 while yawing. As such by moving his head across an arc of slightly less than 180 degrees, a controller could look all around the battlefield much more quickly than a mere human could ever do. The examples, of course, abound. We shall simply limit ourselves to describing one more at this stage: most of the controls were actuated by buttons an levers since very often the time necessitated to utter a command for the speech-recognition software was too slow. Nevertheless, there were still commands that were activated upon speech-recognition so that they keep the hands of the controller free for other, more urgent commands. The distribution of commands between the speech-recognition and button/lever systems had been optimised after a long process of trial and error and fine-tuning. Finally, lots of the basic commands of the battle droid had been simplified, for example the movement of the unit was controlled by a joystick, and a few nearby buttons and sensors on the legs, all hiding the mechanics of moving the battle droid completely from the controller, instead mapping the final results to intuitively sensible actions of the human controller in the 'hot seat'. At the end of the day this created a new model soldier. One that no longer had to be a paradigm of physical fitness, but mental fitness. A good military controller would be able to act quickly upon a torrent of received information from the tactical mode and over his ear-phones (that would be not only orders, but also ambient sounds, although orders were prioritised), toggle to strategy mode, assess the situation and incorporate it into his actions and planning at the blink of an eye, and never use the normal mode of the goggles because he could find the buttons for each action blindly, much like a good pianist knows how to hit exactly the right keys and configure his hands and fingers to create the correct musical intervals on the piano without having to look at them. That's why Thompson, an amateur pianist, used to call soldiers the 'musicians of death'.

At any rate, it seemed like many musicians of death would be performing that day and onwards according to Thompson's coordinator. Miles could hardly believe it:

'So, this is it? It's war?' he asked.

'Yes sir-ee.' replied Thompson trying to pretend to be more cheerful than he was.

'And our instructions are? Are we going to parliament again?'

asked Miles.

'No.' replied Thompson very sombrely. 'Jemil is going there... Listen, I don't know how to tell you this kid, but we are going somewhere where ever I don't have much experience. We're going to the battle front covering the news from the communist army camp. We'll shortly be issued bullet-proof vests, large signs saying 'Press, don't shoot' and good old-fashioned Teflon helmets.' he continued.

Miles was dumbstruck. 'We're war correspondents then?' he managed to utter in the end.

''fraid so sonny.' said Thompson. 'Now compose yourself, as you say here in England. Get ready to go to war. We'll be given a chance to stop by to get supplies on the way there so don't bother with that. Just make sure you're hydrated and have had a good meal before we go. Nobody knows how long until our next meal.' he continued relentlessly.

'Supplies?' asked Miles.

'Yes. Toothpaste, toothbrush, towel, razor and the like. We'll probably be living at a relatively nearby hotel in the beginning and get to the front by car, but if the communists push deep into Zone 3, which I suspect they will, we'll end up following them in a tent.' clarified Thompson. 'Now go! I'll meet you in 30' at the reception area from where the two of us, as well as the rest of our crew will set off towards the front. We may not have had to cover war news before, but we have been preparing for the eventuality. We have procedural protocols that prescribe what we should do.' he explained further and once again encouraged Miles to go. But Miles still had a question.

'One minute. Why would they invade now? Why today out of all days?' he asked, hoping for an answer.

'I don't know... I don't know...' said Thompson prodding the terminal screen with his finger frantically in the process of looking for the most recent news on the internet feed. And then, it appeared: 'Aha!' he said. 'I think I might have found the answer. Look at this.' he concluded.

Miles approached the terminal screen and looked at the headline that Thompson's long index finger was pointing at. It was from the economic section and read:

'Mornington savings 3rd bank to collapse in Zone 1. All banks rush to announce cost-cutting measures and seek aid of the Bank of England. Official UK government states that it is a matter for the private sector to solve for itself and declines to intervene.'

Thompson was quick to make ends of the connection with the communists' actions: 'If Zone 1 is in 'cost-cutting' mode...' he started.

'...they will be reluctant to hire a private military company to confront the communists even if they hurt their interests quite badly.'

completed the sentence Miles who had been equally quick to spot the connection.

'You're sharp as a razor son.' said Thompson. 'Now go get ready. The clock is ticking.' he concluded.

Miles complied and left. 'The communists must have had information that something like that was about to happen. They must have known that the collapse of Mornington Savings was imminent and that it would precipitate a wild reaction from Zone 1. They were waiting for it ready to push the invasion button at the very minute the collapse became public.' thought Miles. 'They must have a formidable espionage network.' he reasoned. 'Although in Zone 1 money can easily buy anybody, so it's not exactly as hard as the pentagon to break in, is it?' he reasoned further.

Letting those dark thoughts aside for that moment he stepped up his pace and walked briskly to the canteen where he consumed some sustenance and drank to his heart's content before heading down towards the reception area. He lived too far to be able to make it to his place and back in good time, so instead, he went to the reception area and walked right through it and into the street looking for a local supermarket where he could easily buy the necessary supplies. Luckily, just across the street there was such business -a mini-market- and Miles got the supplies indicated to him by Thompson without failing to notice that the cameraman who had accompanied him the previous day at the parliament of the confederation was also present at the scene, evidently having figured out that buying the supplies on the spot was better than lugging them all the way from his place.

When all was said and done Miles was at the reception area where the cameraman, and the make-up lady were already waiting. Thompson appeared soon afterwards and a few minutes later but still before the pre-determined time the sound specialist arrived as well. Thompson declared his satisfaction with his team and gave the signal to go. Miles inquired about the administrator and Thompson replied that he would already be in the van by the time they joined him. Thus, with all queries answered and all problems resolved, the group made its way towards the car park where the van was conveniently pulling up just in time to encounter them. The door opened and the administrator beckoned the team to get in quickly. The 'A-team' did not hesitate for a minute.

Once inside the van, the team started strategising, or at least tried to do so while the van started racing again on the bumpy roads of the Confederation.

'Dear fellows, I'm afraid this is rather serious business.' started the administrator. 'We are going into a war zone, most of us, if not all of us for the first time ever. More experienced anchors from war zones around the world are all busy, so I'm afraid it is all down to us...' he explained as an introduction which nobody wanted to hear. He then continued: 'On the bright side, it should be decently safe. We will be official detaches of a governmental news agency in a foreign country and official guests of the army. They will most certainly warn us of any danger and provide us with advice, as is the protocol; of that I am certain. The communist army's press office should also be of service, in as much as providing us with their side of the story and advising us against getting into trouble while in the war zone.'

The rest of the team felt slightly comforted by this revelation although clearly by the looks on their faces, they were still reserving a certain amount of doubts. The administrator continued: 'For the purposes of granting us access in their camps, barracks and other areas that are normally restricted, but we as members of the press shall need to cross through or visit, we have been issued with passes that prove our identity to the communists. I'm going to hand one to each of you. Once we reach the first destination, which by the way is a communist barrack in the region of Leatherhead, we shall present these passes to the guards who will then alert their own press office. After that, we shall hopefully be issued with communist zone passes, which we can treat as our journalist, professional ID-cards whilst being the guests of the communist army.' he explained while handing out the cards. Miles took his one and examined it. It had a picture of him, his Commune pass-card number, an RFID chip inside and a few more bits of information written on it.

'All clear, boss.' said Thompson. 'Now what do we do once there? Do we start covering their preparations for war?' he asked.

'What preparations? Their troops are crossing the borders in mass as we speak. We will only be visiting the barracks to sort out the identification administration. After that we are going straight to the battle zone.' replied the administrator. Silence ensued.

'Presumably the communist journalists are already there covering the story, no?' inquired the cameraman.

'Yes, and I have been watching them on this screen while waiting for you.' replied the administrator while pointing at a terminal screen behind him. It was part of the van's equipment.

'What have they been saying?' asked Thompson.

'Well, there seems to be chaos out there, but they are doing well. That's what the 'Worker's Bulletin' is saying at least.' uttered the administrator.

'Worker's bulletin?' interjected Miles.

'It's the main newspaper in the communist sector. You will eventually learn all this stuff, don't worry.' said Thompson.

'Do we have any more specific information?' inquired the sound specialist.

'Well, the communists are saying that their army is pushing into Zone 3 along the entire border. That is to say the Whitebushes-Dorking-Horsley line is being pushed outwards. They indicate that a force comprising 10.000 ground troops, battle droids, tanks and artillery is currently on the job and express their confidence that within a day they will have pushed the line by up to 5km. Other than that, it is mostly about troop movements that the army press-office chooses to disclose, some stories of human interest, interviews with military personnel and politicians and a certain amount of war propaganda.' replied succinctly the administrator.

'And what do you reckon?' asked Thompson.

'Good question. I think that the communists are going to push really far unless someone intervenes.' replied the administrator.

'Like who?' asked the sound specialist.

'Like hired troops on behalf of Zone 1.' said the administrator.

'Don't be ridiculous!' uttered Miles suddenly, startling the make-up lady, who was sitting right next to him. 'Look at the news today! Mornington Savings has collapsed, most banks have announced cost-cutting plans and asked the Bank of England to step in.'

'I think the youngster here has a point.' agreed Thompson. 'Zone 1 has no money to hire goons to kick the -let's face it- quite powerful communists.' he explained.

'They've been preparing for it. For days, perhaps even weeks.' added the make-up lady referring to the communist invasion.

'I think more. I think it's been months. In fact, I think it's been since the 1st bank collapsed.' said the cameraman.

'What makes you think that?' asked the administrator.

'Well, they've always been very secretive, so if they were going to be preparing for it we wouldn't have known anyway for one. They've always wanted to expand their borders but could not do so because of the risk of war against Zone 1, so they have good motivation to leap at every opportunity for another and finally, the fact that the timing with respect to the 3rd bank collapse and the announcement of cost-cutting measures in Zone 1 was so perfect. They must have spies in Zone 1.' said the cameraman very darkly.

'I was thinking along the same lines.' chimed in Miles. 'That would explain also why they alerted the Confederation a few days in advance and insisted on mobilisation without being too specific about their information and sources...' he concluded. The team nodded silently.

'Do you reckon that the communists have an extensive espionage network through Zone 1 then?' asked the sound specialist.

'I think so. I was thinking only earlier today that in Zone 1 you can get anything for money. I believe even espionage is not in any way morally reprehensible or illegal. It's just another business.' said Miles.

'Really?' asked the administrator. 'That's quite disturbing.'

'Oh well... It just makes it easier for them to have spies in Zone 1. Much easier than having spies elsewhere.' stated Miles very neutrally.

'Elsewhere? Other independent parts of Zone 2?' asked the sound specialist.

'I have a feeling that yes.' said the cameraman even more darkly. 'Perhaps even in our sector.' he concluded with gravity.

'Surely spying on your allies is something that is generally and widely accepted as a rather unfortunate reality.' said Miles.

'That's true, but I fear that there may be a little more to it than that.' said the cameraman mysteriously.

'What do you mean Chris?' asked Thompson.

'I mean that if in the next few days you see very intense communist activity in other parts of Zone 2, don't think it's a spontaneous miracle.' said O'Brien the cameraman without really explaining much.

'You're not suggesting...' said the make-up lady with surprise.

'Yes... They have enough agents inserted in neighbouring sectors to precipitate a change of regime.' said the cameraman worried.

'Nonsense!' discarded the administrator.

'Even if that was the case, the communists are our allies, we shouldn't have much to worry about, no?' said the sound specialist. Silence ensued as nobody wanted to confront him for fear of appearing to be impolite.

'Whatever the situation, the one certain thing is that we will have a lot to report for the next few days.' said Miles.

'I reckon that within a couple of days this big push will be over.' said O'Brien the cameraman. 'Don't get over-excited' he concluded.

'What makes you think that?' asked Yusef the administrator.

'Within a couple of days the communists will have probably achieved all their strategic objectives.' O'Brien explained calmly.

'Which are?' asked the Make-up lady.

'You tell me.' said O'Brien. 'What strategic objectives can you think of south of the communist sector? I'll give you a clue: there's 2 of them.'

'Gatwick airport.' said Miles.

'Yes, and?' asked O'Brien. More silence. Finally the make-up lady broke it:

'Oh, come on. Tell us!' she asked him with a gentle prod.

'Well, to be fair this is not a single place, it's more general and I'm referring to open farmland. After all, the communists would love access to open farmland so they can grow their own food without having to import from elsewhere and cultivate their own public parks. It all makes sense, because both objectives would have been deemed worthy of defence from the perspective of the large financial conglomerates of Zone 1 for Gatwick airport and by the large farms of south England for the farmland.' said O'Brien.

'But the large farms are not involved in the crisis.' argued Mrs. Wilkins, the make-up lady.

'Ah, but how would these farms, or rather farming corporations, fund a defensive campaign against a powerful army of communists?' asked O'Brien.

'Debt? Oh, I see.' said Thompson and everybody realised. The capitalist economy had historically relied upon and been financed by debt for far too long. Nobody would give a loan to even a large corporation if the purpose of the spending was to finance an expensive war campaign against a powerful enemy.

One major problem with the system was that it encouraged the accumulation of debt. It is the classical game problem. If I take a loan and get a temporary competitive advantage over my rivals, I win. If I don't obtain the advantage, I'll have a hard time repaying the loan. If I don't take the loan I run the risk of being overtaken by someone who has taken a loan. That's how businesses and entire countries have been reasoning for nearly a century. The other major problem of the system was its inherent instability. Increased economic activity generated by the loan money circulating into the economy pushed the economy into growing more, albeit on an artificial basis. On the other hand if the economy was on a downturn, debts remained unpaid, forcing banks to stop issuing more loans or even pushing them to the brink of collapse. As such, the existence of extensive lending-borrowing mechanisms served to amplify any natural growth or shrinkage in the so-called 'real' economy. Thus, debt-driven growth and prosperity bequeathed artificially high living standards to the people living under this system (i.e. nearly the entire world of the early 2050's), at the cost of stability.

Looking at the transition between periods of boom and bust, we can set up a system that is growing moderately and follow its progress. The healthy growth gives confidence to businesses that they will be able to repay loans in the future, so they obtain loans for the aforementioned reasons. This amplifies the growth as that loan money is invested in more productive capacity and employment. With more growth, comes more optimism that future loans will be repaid with ease, so more loans are issued. Eventually, the market saturates and growth begins to level off, however, the loans have not necessarily been repaid by that time. Thus, banks end up with more bad loans in their hands and start issuing new loans with more difficulty. Businesses that are in genuine need for loans are now not being serviced, perhaps even pushed to bankruptcy. The slowdown is amplified and eventually a crisis may be precipitated. Quite worryingly, this meant that even banks that had been lending -quite prudently- only to healthy businesses and healthy (or as it was proven, merely healthy-looking) banks risked being taken down by the collapse themselves, since even the best of businesses and banks will eventually be touched by a global crisis. It's only a natural chain reaction.

In the modern world, however, the governments of most countries around the globe had legislated against excessive loan-taking, had imposed heavy capital/loan ratio limits on their own banks and all held large funds intended to stop a new crisis from precipitating. These measures were taken following the 2008-2011 crisis along with many others including a world-wide limit on bank bonuses that the United Kingdom opted out of, helping create Zone 1. These limitations on banking activity and the prudence of governments to act anti-cyclically with respect to the natural world economy tides (i.e. spend more in times of slowdown and save in times of boom) had helped create moderate, but robust and continuous growth in the entire world for 4 uninterrupted decades. By monitoring increases in labour productivity -the heart of sustainable and real economic growth- governments tried to estimated the 'real' growth rate of the world and attempted to adjust their spending and loan-taking so that their own countries didn't fall far behind their 'real' growth rate, but nor did they exceed it by too much.

It seemed like a good plan, but the British opt-out and subsequent dismantling of all legislation that businesses saw as harmful to themselves, led to an underground loan market whereby businesses that wished to play dirty could open a subsidiary office in the UK, take loans without any limitation other than that imposed by the banks themselves and pass that money to the parent company. On the overt side of the business, British banks involved themselves into all the normal and perfectly legal activities of the banking sector, that is, lending money to other governments and foreign businesses within the limits of the foreign countries' regulation. For that reason governments of very powerful countries like China, India and America all held loans from those banks in total sums of trillions of pounds (although the loans were not always denominated in pounds). Similarly vast conglomerates of industry (Euromotors corporation, Rusky Neft I Gaz, Kali IT systems, US Army civilian research labs etc.), commerce (All American Supermarkets, Sparmarkt AG, Tokaido Booeki etc.) and agriculture & mining (Societe Nationale des Fermiers Francais, North American Cotton Company, China Mining International, Russkie Iskopaemye etc.) were hugely indebted to British banks on a fully legal basis.

Miles brought the team back to reality:

'Excuse me if I'm being thick, but aren't we supposed to have crossed the borders by now?' he asked.

'Oh no.' said Yusef, the administrator. 'We are not going to cross the borders at Kingston, we are going to cross farther south, just after Cobham.' he continued and then looking at his screen: 'In fact we are approaching the border right now. We should, in fact, be descending for border control very shortly.' he concluded.

Sure enough not a couple of minutes later the van ground to a halt and the team descended, ready to be subjected to the border control procedures. The procedure was exactly as Miles remembered it from his first journey to the communist sector. At the end, they were given their armed escort and with his help they navigated to the barracks where they were meant to contact the communist army's press office and obtain their ID-badges. The guard went at the front of the van and sat next to the driver, so the group of journalists remained at the back of the van in exactly the same formation as before. The way between Cobham and the Leatherhead barracks was a lot shorter so the journalist team reached the barracks quickly without having engrossed themselves into any deep conversation this time. The van thus, promptly stopped at the gates of the Leatherhead barracks and the armed escort handled the formalities. In response, the barracks guard returned to his post where he informed his superiors of the journalists' arrival over the army's official messenger software interface and asked the escort to convey to the journalists news that the press-office lieutenant would be with them shortly.

Indeed, few minutes had elapsed when a rather short middle-aged man with fairly little black hair and little round glasses approached them briskly. He was uniformed in a typical green uniform, used for official business. The epaulettes on his shoulders indicated he had achieved the rank of lieutenant and his rather reddish face that he had probably jogged a good part of the way. In his hand he held an envelope.

'Good evening comrades.' he announced cheerfully. 'Sorry to keep you waiting. I was detained. A lot of work at the press-office you see. A lot of unexpected work I should say.'

'Oh, don't worry. We totally understand. It's not like there are such major combat operations every day.' said Yusef sympathetically.

'Thank your for your understanding. Now, to business. I have this envelope here for you. I'll open it for you... Just give me a minute...' said the lieutenant while carefully tearing open the envelope. 'Here we go.' he exclaimed after opening it fully. The officer then proceeded to grab the contents and present them to the journalistic team.

'The folder contains a few very crucial objects. Your journalistic ID passes to begin with and a mini-terminal screen connected to our own servers through which you will be able to communicate with us at will.'

said the lieutenant.

Terminal screens were beautiful achievements of engineering and even supported sound. The power and hardware needed to emit a bit of light and do some processing had been miniaturised to the point where terminals effectively ran on the bare minimum power needed to power the screen & speakers and communicate with the outside world. The processing was done at static servers elsewhere in the network effectively meaning that the terminal screen was just a touch-screen with an antenna and some speakers and used external modules to complete any tasks that were not related to the user's eyes (or ears) or communication to those modules. Another clever trick in the screen mechanism was absorbing all ambient light possible and using the resulting energy to adjust the brightness of the image at a very reduced power cost. Thus, if a user set a certain comfortable screen brightness level in absolute darkness, the terminal would 'memorise' that setting and then attempt to adjust the brightness of the screen dynamically as a function of incident ambient lighting so that the image would retain its clarity under any circumstances. When it came to sound, there had to be some sort of vibrating membrane capable of moving enough air about to create an audible effect. Such membranes had been successfully integrated in to the terminal's slender and flexible design, courtesy of nanomaterial engineering. The speakers were typically a couple of small disks at the top corners of the terminal screen. The material there was engineered so that under the influence of an electric field all its elementary cells would attempt to 'curl up', a bit like a mimosa flower after being stroked. The combined effect made the entire disk move up and down in accordance to the electric field applied to the speakers, thus creating sound. The microphone worked on the basis of the same principle. On an interesting side-note, terminals could not integrate the functionality of a webcam because of the absence of a decent, integrated lens.

For the audio system to work, the speakers and microphone had to be perfectly flat. That, however was no problem because the flexible terminals were also made out of nanomaterials with interesting properties. In fact, the skeleton structure of the nanomaterial screen consisted of nano-structures that had a property similar to those in the speakers, namely that under certain circumstances they would curl up. However, in the case of the skeleton structures, it was mechanical pressure that made them roll-up in conjunction with an electric field. To be more specific, the skeleton's nano-structures had two equilibria. A low energy equilibrium in the curled-up state and a higher energy equilibrium in the flat state and they tended to assume either one state or the other, and nothing in between (the high energy barrier in between the equilibriat states was very high). For that reason, the terminals were either flat open

-as the speakers wished it to be-, or rolled-shut. Clever engineering meant that users had to put effort into triggering the 'roll-up' or the 'flat-out' reactions of the terminal. That prevented accidental opening and closing of the screen. Naturally, heavy speaker, antenna and screen use all together could quickly deplete the small batteries that were integrated into the terminal. For that reason terminals were very aggressive energy scavengers, but also had a port that allowed them to recharge at the mains. The terminal that the lieutenant handed over to the journalists was a very small and versatile version of what Miles and everybody else owned. A version optimised for low power consumption and versatility rather than image or sound quality.

'Now I'll hand over the passes.' the lieutenant declared and started calling the journalists by name one-by-one. When all the passes were handed over he inquired: 'Who is in charge of the expedition?' at which Yusef the administrator pointed towards himself. The lieutenant handed over the small terminal to him and said:

'Then you are in charge of the terminal. Unroll it and you will be taken to its interface. No need to log on. You should already have a message with your next instructions. And now gentlemen.' he said addressing everybody. 'May I interest you in some refreshments? Or would you rather make haste towards your next destination?' he concluded invitingly. Yusef looked at his team. They had that unmistakable look on their faces that indicated they were craving some refreshments but knew that work had to come first.

'I'm sorry, we haven't got time for that I'm afraid. There's rapidly unfolding events out there and we need to bring them to our viewers as quickly as possible.' Yusef replied in the end.

'Pity, but I understand your position. Good luck comrades.' said the lieutenant, saluted and left as the journalists returned to the van.

Once Thompson-team was inside the van and the armed escort was sitting next to the driver, the van set off; quickly. Nevertheless, the van driver was a real artist with the steering wheel. The traction control systems also helped keep control of the old van, of course, and under the combined effect of human mastery and machine support the van moved fast without causing too many objects -or people- at the back of the van to shift positions rather unfavourably. Finally, the smooth and well-maintained roads of the communist sector also helped.

At the back of the van, team Thompson engrossed themselves into debate once again:

'This is a nifty little terminal.' said Yusef holding the terminal flat open.

'How cute!' said Mrs. Wilkins, the make-up lady. Then she quickly added: 'In Japan they call this sort of cuteness 'kawaii', or 'kawasa'. It is a very very good term to describe my exact feelings for this little terminal, but sadly we have no direct translation of this concept into English.' She always had a passion with Japan and had even learned the language a little. Her anime-themed purse alone, featuring a small cat amongst others, paid ample testimony to that fact.

'Roll it up, please Yusef.' said O'Brien looking darkly towards it.

'Why?' asked Yusef very curious as to the new tide of darkness that had suddenly possessed the normally grumpy and grim cameraman.

'It's safer that way.' O'Brien said, not sounding very convinced about that fact himself. Thompson sensed that something was amiss and addressed Yusef:

'Just do it. Please.' he said curtly. Yusef now positively intrigued, rolled it up indeed.

'Now can you two tell me what's wrong with that terminal?' he asked.

'That terminal is not just for us to keep contact with the army and their press office.' said O'Brien darkly with a rather unpleasant frown on his face. Thompson pressed him for more details. O'Brien explained: 'They are also probably using it to track us down and listen to what we say.' he said very morosely.

'Oh for god's sake...' exclaimed Yusef and started unrolling the terminal again. O'Brien grabbed him by the arm.

'All right. Don't believe me. But even if you don't believe me, heed my advice. Be very careful of what you say when the terminal is unrolled and in general.' he said and let go of Yusef's arm. Yusef, on the other hand, looked at O'Brien with curiosity for a minute, uttering nothing as if attempting to make up his mind about something. When he finally did, he spoke:

'Meh. You're being too suspicious. Don't buy too much into all that conspiracy theory malarkey. Either way, the communists are our friends. It's not like we're asked to cover the news in Harrow & Watford or anything...' he said reassuringly. O'Brien frowned unpleasantly and shrugged his shoulders as if saying 'suit yourself'.

'Ugh...' said Miles trying to attract the unwanted attention upon him and then defuse it by opening a new discussion. 'How about confederate involvement in this campaign?' he asked.

'Well, the communists wish to fight with the Confederation as their ally, that's for sure. It gives them some extra fire-power, although not too much and keeps the warring gangs of Zone 3 as well as rivalling armies at bay or at any rate, at least busy.' said Johnson, the sound specialist who usually liked to keep quiet.

'What rivalling armies? Who else is out there?' asked Miles slightly confused.

'Currently nobody. But there is always a possibility that either Zone 1 mobilises a military company to defend their interests or that another major player in Zone 2 steps in. Both very unlikely, I admit, but having the Confederation at their side the communists are making it even more unlikely.' said Johnson.

'Must be a dreadful place this Zone 3. I've never been there.' said Miles reflecting upon the abnormally high military activity that seemed to be unfolding in the region.

'Well, Zone 3 does live off the chippings that fall off from Zone 2 dear. Just like we live off the chippings that fall off Zone 1.' said Mrs. Wilkins addressing Miles.

'Well, if Zone 1 then wants to defend its interests, all they have to do is replace all their communist workers with others and that will force the communists to capitulate.' reasoned Miles.

'Ah, you see, the communists have been making vast efforts to break their dependence on Zone 1 so they play with slightly different rules. They even negotiate with Zone 1 on a different level.' said Yusef.

'Ow? How is that?' asked Miles.

'Well, to begin with they have a far smaller portion of their workforce employed in Zone 1 than anybody else in Zone 2 has. They have formed an industrial base over the years and are now beginning to be seen as an industrial powerhouse, even abroad. The communist-controlled regions of the country include mines which extract many minerals they either need and use or can export, as well as power plants that provide energy to most of the country. Those, and the various companies they have bought abroad finance them with their profits, but the power plants also give them political capital. They keep Zone 1 running. That's why it is in nobody's interests to attack those power plants. By making themselves the major providers of electricity in the country, they have secured their power plants against any attacks. Either way, they have permanent garrisons at all large power plants and if anybody attacks those plants, special embedded explosives they planted all over them will make them explode, thus making any mission targeting those power plants a suicide one -and therefore a very expensive one too-. Furthermore, they have set up their own basic arms industry and can manufacture at least ammunition in war quantities and processed food and clothing for their population. Finally, the Russians declared that they like them and cooperate with them tightly.' explained Yusef.

'The Russians?' asked Miles. 'Why?'

'The Russians have had experience with communism before. Despite the fact that in the end it failed them, it still made them a respectable superpower for as long it lasted, albeit at a terrible cost. As time progressed and the people who lived during those days became fewer and fewer and all that was left was the memories of glorious socialist construction whilst the memories of goods shortages and political persecution vanished. To be honest, with their current form of autocratic half-state, half-private capitalist system that they operate they are not too far from the communists here ideologically either.' explained Yusef patiently.

'Still though, China dislikes them and so does the USA.' noted Thompson.

Indeed China, holding a policy of aggressively trying to impose the free market everywhere in the world was bound to be hostile to the communists. To that end they found an ally in America although the fact that China didn't like to follow the free market like it was demanding from others but preferred to lock its internal market to foreign competition didn't ring a good bell with the Americans who failed to remember how nice it all was when they were doing the very same to everybody else but were now on the receiving end of the 'free market paradox'. India on the other hand was mostly neutral in terms of foreign policy and simply tried to forge business relations with whomever was in power at the time. So long as they could be left alone to hate their Pakistani and Bangladeshi neighbours they were fine. Finally, continental Europe, poor and powerless, still had a residual instinctive fear of communism even though politically they were probably closer to the communists rather than to the current masters of Zone 1. At any rate, apart from the Russians, who were actively supporting the communists, no other country had expressed any views on the situation or made any moves. Miles stated it:

'At any rate, no other country -apart from Russia- has commented on the situation. I guess it remains to be seen if anybody will.'

'Assuming there is no foreign intervention, the communists have little to fear from Zone 1. It has just occurred to me that even if Zone 1 decides to exclude communist workers from their workforce, that will simply translate into a shortage of labour for them and drive the wages of the other workers from Zone 2 higher. So, boom! Both lose. In any case, even if the communists take over control of Gatwick airport, if passenger flow remains mostly undisrupted and they keep running the business normally, Zone 1 has no economic reason to be afraid. On the contrary, maybe the communists will build some decent public transport to Gatwick, perhaps revive old railway line.' said Thompson pensively.

'It makes sense.' said Mrs. Wilkins. 'In the end their competition spirit will be their undoing.' she said confidently referring to Zone 1.

'You mean their intense rivalry and selfishness destroys their unity and now they'll have to face judgement for that?' said Miles refining the sentence a bit.

'Yes. That.' said Mrs. Wilkins.

'Well, that's what happens when you turn your soldiers into part-time employees. Having a standing army at all times is generally good in terms of prudence. Even in the worst of economic stringency, a certain weapons stockpile is present and the country is defended, whereas now, with the crisis the defensive capabilities of Zone 1 have been completely pulverised, vaporised, eliminated.' said O'Brien gesticulating intensely. At least his mind was now no longer dwelling on the argument he'd had with Yusef.

'Wasn't it Lenin who said that the capitalists will sell to the communists the rope with which they are going to hang them? Well, it seems that instead they seem to have sold the scissors which would have allowed them to cut loose. Heh.' said Johnson with a chuckle.

'Nicely put dear!' said Mrs. Wilkins with a little giggle.

'Seriously though. How could they ever be so short-sighted?' asked himself Yusef.

'Well, if you were a businessman, a big CEO, and they told you: What would you say if the government disbanded the entire army and replaced it with a group of contract soldiers, hired out from a company. In return you will get a tax reduction of 10%. What would you say in response?' asked Miles.

'I'd say that it's madness and that we need an army to defend ourselves.' said Yusef straightforwardly and completely honestly.

'Well, you see, the leaders of the various banks and insurance companies of Zone 1 replied along the lines of the 'when are you going to start selling then?' sort of reply.' said Miles.

'What were they thinking?' asked Yusef.

'They were thinking that nobody is going to invade anyway and that even if things go wrong they can get together with a social mediation company or the government, agree on contributions to a war fund and then hire a military company to quickly deal with the issue.' said Miles.

'And it didn't occur to them that there might not be any money.' said Yusef reproachfully.

'Ah, here's where things get interesting. It didn't occur to them that there wouldn't be any money while they were presiding over their respective banks.' said Miles.

'So what you're saying is that it was a short-termist issue.' said Thompson facetiously.

'Laugh all you want but the CEOs and presidents of the various financial conglomerates in Zone 1 stay, on average, only about 4-5 years at the same company and then they leave to occupy a position elsewhere, often in a different country altogether! For that reason they have no need to feel any attachment to any nationality, people -as in the population of a country-, company or even cause. For them the point is to make the company before whose steering wheel they are sitting as profitable as possible during their tenure at the wheel and reap the maximum possible bonuses in return. In fact, the only thing which prevents them from draining the companies so much that they bleed to death after their departure is the fact that they then need to find a job elsewhere and nobody would hire an executive that behaves in such way like nobody would hire a doctor who leaves a trail of corpses behind him.' said Miles with resentment.

'It's all part of one gruesome optimisation process along the profit variable...' said O'Brien with disgust. 'Bloody leeches.' he continued with an evident desire to spit.

Silence followed O'Brien's remarks. The minutes passed, each of them bringing the team closer to the war zone. Thompson veered the conversation towards business again.

'Now, Miles, and in fact everyone. This is a big, big story. It's the big fish as we say in America. Our actual coverage of the story will be part of it. Writing articles for the internet columns of our newspaper will also be part of it and then there are lots of side-stories that can be generated from our experiences. There will be interviews, memoirs, first-hand accounts of the war zone. That's why I and Miles must as part of our job keep daily diaries detailing our experiences and minuting our conversations. I would recommend the rest of you to do the same. You never know. Maybe they'll end up on the newspaper or even in a book, if good and plenty enough.' he stated emphatically.

'Cracking idea!' exclaimed Miles. The others seemed equally enthusiastic.

'That'll be something to read to my grandchildren.' said Mrs. Wilkins.

'Or turn into a book: How I remember the war.' said Yusef placing his right hand on his chest and gazing upwards as if he'd spotted some sort of insect on the ceiling of the van. A pose he presumably thought was what a world-class classical poet would assume before being immortalised in a bust sculpture.

'It'll be interesting to read when I'm much older.' said Johnson.

'It might be what shifts my career from behind the lens to in front of it!' declared O'Brien.

Generally, Thompson's idea seemed to excite the crew. He smiled in acknowledgement of this fact and continued talking business:

'Our next stint will be at the 18:00 news. Until then we gather information and try to organise it. If we see anything extremely important happening we contact HQ and maybe we'll end up with a breaking news bulletin on our hands. Is that fine?' he asked and looked at everybody in the team. The team nodded affirmatively in return and Yusef and Miles both said 'Makes sense to me.'. Thompson nodded in turn with satisfaction, but before he could move on to his next point Miles interrupted as if he'd just though of something.

'Wait a minute...' he said raising his arm with his index finger pointing towards the ceiling, a little like a kid who wants to ask his teacher a question in primary school.

'Yes. Question? Out with it!' said Thompson.

'I was thinking, when we reach the battle zone whatever we see and record will be the first scenes from the battlefield for our own news channel. Surely that is breaking news, no?' inquired Miles having in mind all the occasions when he'd seen breaking news with 'first images' from various battlefields of the Earth, for example the Korean wars in the early 2040's that ended up with North Korea attempting to launch nuclear missiles on South Korea, having their plan foiled by the common so called Northern-hemisphere Anti-ballistic Missile System and ending up being bombed by tens, if not hundreds of nuclear missiles from Russia, the United States and Japan. For the record: The NAMS project was a massive defensive project in which the United States, the European Union, Russia and Japan cooperated to create an anti-ballistic shield with nearly full yield. Completed in the 2030's it was a miracle of technology and was aimed primarily against possible attack from China, the new superpower, as well as to prevent rather small, but very, very insane nuclear powers like North Korea, Iran and Israel from doing anything stupid.

Back to the present, Thompson had also seen many such breaking news bulletins, including the Korean war one and fully understood Miles' concerns. He smiled, let out a hearty laugh and said:

'Oh shucks. You are quite inexperienced, aren't you? It's all right. You will learn. The thing is that you always, and I mean always, process the images you are going to be sending to the public, one way or the other. It's got nothing to do with crowd manipulation or anything. Let me give you an example. Suppose we do reach the battle zone and the first images we see have nothing special because the defenders have surrendered. Do we show our spectators normal buildings, or do we ask the army to show us, for example columns of war prisoners or piles of captured weapons? There may be a significant delay between the first images from the battlefield and the first images from something genuinely interesting. Another example. Suppose, heaven forbid, that when we reach the battlefield we are greeted with scenes of unimaginable horror; carnage, death or worse. Do we show those images, or do we simply report from within a military tent and show the people the preparations of the army while limiting our coverage of the battlefield to softened descriptions? You catch my drift now son?' said Thompson and Miles began to realise how much more there was to journalism than he'd thought. What ended up on the public's terminals was the end result of a meticulous and refined process. Miles, thus, nodded in understanding, Thompson returned the nod and moved on.

'Now, Yusef. Update on what our own channel is doing?' he asked more in the imperative sense of the sentence than in the inquisitive. The administrator turned around his swivelling chair and checked the terminal screen. He manipulated something on the dedicated touch-screen of the van's elaborate terminal with his index finger and quickly enough the live feed broadcast from the Kropotkin's diaries TV station, news division filled the large view-only terminal screens of the van. Yusef then turned back to face his companions and exclaimed:

'Yep. Same as before. Mostly interviews with political advisers from parliament and a lot of 'panel talking'. Now I think David is hosting a parliament representative, a political advisor and a politics professor from the communist sector over a teleconference.' he said calmly.

'Shall we listen in for a little while, just to get up to speed?' asked Thompson.

'Certainly.' said Yusef and cranked up the volume. The voices of David Ramsay and his guests started resonating in the van as the team watched in silence. David was speaking at the moment:

'...as a result of which you, sir, are expecting that Gatwick airport will be under communist control within a maximum of 3 days, if I'm not mistaken. Is that a statement you would agree to Mr. Telemann?' he asked the parliamentary representative (sometimes called simply MPs).

'Oh definitely. The show of force we have seen on the central news agency of the communist sector certainly lends credit to this projection. By Thursday night Gatwick will likely be under the control of the communists. However, the question is not so much when they will gain control of the airfield, but how long it will take them to mend the war damage and how they will operate it later on. For the time being the communist army press office is refusing to disclose any potential plans they have for the future of London's main airport. The most they were willing to disclose just earlier today was that they are not sure whether they will end up controlling the airfield and that until then any talk about its future is an exercise in futility and pointlessness. It remains to be seen, but I think we can say very confidently that everybody expects the communists to take over control of Gatwick certainly by the end of the week if not Thursday.' said the MP factually.

'And how do you judge this situation Mr. Antonetti? You are an advisor to the foreign commissioner of our government. Do you feel that communist success is so certain? And if you do, do you have any worries about the future operation of the airfield?' asked David Ramsay.

'Well, Mr. Ramsay, I must say that if we lend credit to the images the central news agency of the communist sector, the Workers' bulletin, is transmitting these days, then it seems that communist tank and battle droid forces are sweeping the sector encountering more surrender than resistance and the people of Zone 3 seem to be greeting them with cheers of joy. Images from combat and helicopters seem to confirm this information. Of course, we in government are also being kept up to date by the army command liaisons that also inform our own top brass about the situation and help coordinate the battle action over the next few days. As such, we are fairly confident that the communists will indeed take over control of Gatwick airport and consider it as a foregone conclusion. The communists have no reason to lie about the situation to the commanders of an allied army. As for the operation of the airport, I'm confident not only that the communists will have it up and running very quickly, but also that they will do a good job of running it well. They are not telling the general public because they want to avoid embarrassment in case they somehow fail to secure the airport, but they have plans for its future operation; plans that they have shared with us. So, I just want to say that if the communists do take over control of the airport, its operation is not only going to be secure, but also improve dramatically in all likelihood.' said Antonetti, advisor to the foreign affairs commissioner.

'This now puts forward some very interesting questions regarding the near and far future. First let's talk about the near future. Mr. Antonetti, Mr. Teleman, could you tell us anything about the mobilisation process and the involvement of our own militia to the ongoing battle operations? Next we'll go over to you, professor Joran with another important question. Apologies for the delay.' said David managing to keep excellent balance between his guests. The professor nodded in understanding and then the MP and the political advisor politely encouraged each other to speak first. In the end the MP gave way first and agreed to speak first with a graceful thanking.

'Well, Mr. Ramsay, my view is that our troops... at least a section of our troops should be already battle-ready. We, the Confederation, as you know, also have interests in Zone 3. Much like the communists we would like access to the farmlands around London so we don't have to plough our public parks with tractors, and also very importantly we have a political agenda. We wish to bring peace and attempt to convert the anarchic sectors of Zone 3 to our Anarcho-syndicalist method of government. Then they can choose whether they like it or not, whether to change it or not and whether they wish to join the Confederation or not. I would expect that within the day, or the latest tomorrow morning, we'll be summoned to parliament to approve the commencement of battle operations for our own militia and confirm some strategic objectives. Moreover, if need be so, the military airfield we control at Heathrow can be used by the communist helicopter and VTOL (vertical take-off/landing) air-force if need be so.' said Telemann as factually as possible. Heathrow airport that he referenced was once the main airport of London, but as the city grew around it eventually it became too central to be of any use. It was shut down in the 2030's and Gatwick, Luton and a new airport at the outskirts of Chatham were all reconfigured so that they could take the extra capacity. London city airport had similarly been shut down and quickly converted to office buildings. Back in the 2030's the government and city of London authorities financed one of the last large public projects in the UK and built extra fast underground train links from the airports to central London at Waterloo, Victoria and Kings-Cross/St. Pancras stations. No airport was more than 25' by train from central London, which made sense. Now most of that network lay rusted and disused. Heathrow, meanwhile, after being shut down was abandoned for a long time and then, when the Confederation was formed, it formed the basic airfield for the Confederation's small helicopter air-force.

Back to the present, Antonetti was giving his own views on the matter of possible battle operations of the Confederate militia:

'Mr. Ramsay, I'm very much inclined to agree with Mr. Telemann. Very shortly we should commence operations in the vicinity of our own borders and start pushing into Zone 3. I have very little to add to what Mr. Telemann said apart from the fact that these operations will not only help us secure our own borders from their usual exposure to raids from various gangs and factions of Zone 3, but should also stabilise the region and create the conditions for real economic growth in Zone 3. It is, in fact, high time that the dependence of outer London upon the core loosens.' said Antonetti.

'Very interesting answers gentlemen. Answers that create more questions. Professor Joran, two questions for you. First of all, how do you see this shake-up in the geo-politics of London developing in the future and affecting the rest of the country? Second, how do you think the economy will be affected for various regions of the capital? There have been concerns expressed from our viewers, as well as from various Commune elders that in a globalised world we will never be able to produce anything that is either good or cheap enough for other countries to buy it so we can get foreign currency in exchange and import what we may not produce ourselves.' said David Ramsay and Miles thought immediately: 'Damn good questions...'. The professor was only happy to answer.

'Very good questions...' said the professor. 'Heh' thought Miles, amused by the coincidence. The professor continued: 'First let's look at the politics, but be warned that the replies might take a very long time to fully unfold.' he said warningly.

'It is all right. We have time. These are extreme times and we have chosen to dedicate a lot of time on our news feed. Please carry on professor at your own leisure.' encouraged Ramsay.

'Very well, I shall. Politics. It is no doubt evident that the crisis in Zone 1 has tremendously weakened their position in the power pyramid of the United Kingdom. As such, they have no longer the power to defend their interests, such as Gatwick airport or finance their clients with loans to help them defend their own interests. This is seen by the communist government as a golden opportunity to turn the tables. The government reckons that if they seize the opportunity to acquire land and strategic resources or infrastructure, even if the crisis is overcome at some later point in time, hiring a military company to take back those acquisitions from the well-defended communist sector will still be prohibitively expensive to be worth the effort. Moreover, by seizing the airport they hope to increase the dependence of Zone 1 upon them, like they have already done with the power grid. In many ways, the communists' rather militant approach to... well to everything really has had the unexpected benefit of giving them a position of unusual power towards Zone 1. It would not be an exaggeration to say that Zone 1 depends on the communist sector more than it depends on anyone else.' said the professor.

'Thanks for the commercial.' said Telemann.

'I thought you'd think I was merely being an instrument of propaganda... I'm being perfectly honest with you. That's why propaganda doesn't work. When things are genuinely going well, nobody believes it either.' said professor Joran indignantly.

'Apologies, professor. At any rate, if you are indeed right, history will prove you right and that's what really matters.' said Telemann apologetically.

'Please continue professor.' beckoned Ramsay. The professor nodded assent, coughed in a very 'old sage' sort of fashion and continued speaking:

'Politically, the balance of power between Zone 1 and the rest of London will shift radically. The balance of power between the various regions of Zone 2 will also shift radically. We will see the communist sector gaining a lot of area and population, we will probably also see the Confederation benefit from increased power as a result of the alliance with the communists and, of course the military actions of the confederation itself. As for the rest of the country, we can expect the other communist zones to benefit from the increased power their comrades will be enjoying here in the metropolis. We might even see military operations commence in other communist zones around the country, although nothing on the scale we are witnessing in this part of the country.'

'And economically?' asked Ramsay.

'Economically, there are a number of important points, in fact 3. The primary sector of economic activity already under communist control, the communist industry and the Russians. The primary sector will provide the communists with ore and food, as well as give them a number of resources they can export for foreign cash. The various mines of Britain will play a vital role in creating a new British industry. In turn, this industry will provide goods that would have otherwise been imported from abroad. This will have a double effect. First of all the citizens of the communist-controlled regions would have access to a secure stream of vital products, that's the positive effect. The negative effect is that these will be produced in the communist sector at a far higher price than they would have been produced in China or other so-called 'labour dumps'. In effect, the communists decided to trade away some 'living standard' in the form of cheap goods, in exchange for more economic self-sufficiency. Finally, the Russians will play a key role in maintaining trade-relations and sustaining the freshly expanded communist sector.' said the professor.

'Professor, if I may.' said Antonetti and after receiving the full attention of the professor he continued: 'How about debt? And how about keeping the economy running long-term?' he asked.

'Well, in terms of debt, the communist sector has always been very risk-averse, so there is very little of that, most owed to the Russians. They've been financing the communists with their oil, gas, diamond and uranium money since very close to the foundation of the sector. As for long-term economic progress, the secret is expanding the communist zone as much as possible, ideally until it covers nearly the entire country and forming a network of exclusive trading partners that is large enough to be self-sustainable in the theoretical case of isolation from the rest of the world trading system.' said the professor.

'Impossible!' exclaimed Mr. Telemann.

'Not impossible, but very difficult to achieve. Ideally the communist system would work fairly well in a vast union of countries, the size of a large continent; large enough to be fully self-sufficient on everything. Otherwise it becomes extremely difficult to sustain this artificially high living standard. Everyone must become a 'cheap worker' so that the products made in the communist sector become sellable abroad and foreign cash comes in; cash that as we said can later be exchanged for what the sector cannot produce itself. In fact, for that reason the exchange rate between communist sector pounds and other currencies is different depending on what is being traded. Once things stabilise, of course, activities like tourism will also start bringing in foreign currency and there is always foreign aid, but the bulk of the economic activity can probably be seen to follow the rules I've been talking about just now.' concluded the professor.

'Well that means some arduous diplomacy and an insecure future down the road for the communist sector. Meanwhile, closer to the present, the economy can probably keep running on the output of the mines and power plants and the generosity of the Russians.' said Ramsay. The professor nodded assent.

'In any case, we should perhaps leave the philosophical conversation for later and concentrate on the present state of affairs...' offered Mr. Telemann.

'I think we have indeed been rather drifting farther and farther from the topic.' agreed Ramsay before continuing: 'Back to the nearer future, I would like to ask all of you what you think the near future holds for the people caught up in the action, those in the areas immediately affected by the military action, the people in the areas now being controlled by the communist forces. Are there any plans for them? Professor?' asked Ramsay.

'I'm not entirely sure. Anything I can say will be mere speculation. I believe that there are plans to provide them with emergency food and medical supplies, as well as erect temporary accommodation for those who have either lost their homes as a result of the military action, or simply had no real shelter even before the military operations.' said professor Joran.

'Mr. Telemann?' asked Ramsay.

'The communist government has provided us assurances that affected civilians will be taken care of in a humane way and...' said Telemann but he wasn't destined to finish his sentence. As Mr. Telemann was uttering his last few words, Ramsay placed his left hand on his ear-piece and interrupted:

'Just one minute, Mr. Telemann. I'm receiving news that just as we speak in other urban communist sectors the various red armies have begun pushing into their respective 3rd zones. In Glasgow communist forces from Clydebank and Paisley, their Glasgow strongholds are pushing west towards the new airport at Greenock. In Leeds-Bradford, the push is towards the southern Zone 3 regions since communist-controlled regions in that city complex lie at the diametrically opposed part of the city with respect to the airport and they'd either have to crush through the local Zone 1 to get to it, or through their Zone 2 neighbours. Finally, in Manchester where the airport is very close to the communist zone, the army has besieged and isolated all terminals of the airport and is currently preparing to match on the airport itself. These are breaking news, reported by the Worker's bulletin Glasgow, Leeds-Bradford and Manchester divisions respectively. In other sectors across the country there seems to be very little activity apart from a generalised alert in the ranks of local militias. Professor, we see a push towards airports in general. Are the communists attempting to achieve what we all think they are?' uttered Ramsay.

'If you are thinking that the communists are attempting to secure all main airports so that they can create a secure internal system of air-lifts, then you are probably correct. This will reduce the dependence of the communists on foreign businesses and will increase the dependence of Zone 1 on the communists, as I have said before...' said the professor. Thompson had heard all he needed.

'I think we catch the drift. Seen enough. Now let's switch to the London Workers' bulletin and see how they are reporting on the situation.' he said. Yusef nodded and switched channel. A very well groomed and officious newscaster appeared on the screen, a small image next to him with pictures of a non-descript urban landscape with smoke rising from between the buildings. In the background behind the news anchor, an image of Epsom at night with the government tower mostly lit up was creating a nice and reassuring backdrop of serenity to what could, quite unfortunately, only be described as grim news. He was relating the situation to his viewers:

'...in the affected areas. Army engineers are now arranging the delivery of emergency food, water and medical supplies and have earmarked some of the captured public parks as areas where local residents may receive these supplies. In the very same parks, tents are beginning to be installed in anticipation of waves upon waves of refugees who have lost all shelter. Vans equipped with loudspeakers are making these facts publicly known in the affected areas as we speak and buses with civil engineers are touring the area surveying, estimating damage and helping plan the future of these new regions. It is a flash operation.

Meanwhile the general secretary of the party and the minister for defence have both commented that the result of this campaign 'simply must be success' and then proceeded to qualify the statement by saying that they will consider the campaign a success only when every street of the newly annexed areas is safe and secure, every citizen has a job and generally the new territories are fully incorporated into the administrative and economic structure of our people's republic. 'The restoration of food, water and electricity supplies, of course, are self-evidently crucial parts of the plan and no success can come forth without fulfilling these tasks.' characteristically said the minister for defence.

Sources from the army press-office confirm that trucks carrying barbed wire, heavy machine guns and temporary barricades are already moving into the newly acquired areas and setting up blockades in an attempt to compartmentalise the new areas and thoroughly clear them of arms or remaining pockets of militant resistance, as well as prevent possible foreign invasion in areas that have already been cleared. No foreign military action has been yet reported in response to the big push towards Zone 3, however the army press office stated that the military is adamant about making sure that the line of assault is kept defendable and that at least one fall-back line is maintained at all times. General Marburg has further commented that...' said the newscaster of the Workers' bulletin before Thompson interrupted:

'I think that's enough of the Workers' bulletin as well. If there is anything important that happens, I'm sure Aisha will tell us.' said Thompson as Yusef cut off the sound from the terminals again.

'Who's Aisha?' asked Miles with curiosity.

'Oh, that's right. We didn't formally introduce you two, did we? Aisha is our coordinator. For the most part she is a disembodied voice in our earpieces but I have met her in person and she is a lovely gal; not to mention an excellent professional.' said Thompson. 'I will introduce you to her in person at some point. I promise.' he continued winking in a friendly fashion.

'Just one little point.' said Miles again.

'Yes?' asked Thompson.

'The news of coordinated war activity starting simultaneously in Glasgow, Leeds-Bradford and Manchester as well as the heightened state of alert of all communist militias nationwide was rather breaking news. Shouldn't our coordinator... you know... have called us about it or something?' he inquired. Thompson smiled with that countenance that unmistakably said 'you're so inexperienced, but you will learn in time, son' but it was Yusef who replied:

'She did.' he said pointing towards his own earpiece. An earpiece he hadn't removed during their entire journey. He continued explaining: 'She has been filling me in with critical information on the go non-stop. Well, I say non-stop, but breaking news don't just occur every second of every minute of every hour. Let's just say that I've been keeping my ear to the ground for anything interesting.' he concluded.

'Ah, I see. And you didn't want to say anything because we were already watching it on the terminal screen.' added Miles.

'Indeed. I texted her my thanks for the information through our messenger from this here terminal...' said Yusef pointing at the touch-screen terminal that was used as the input to the terminal complex of the van. '...and also told her we are, in fact, all watching David announcing the breaking news.' he completed his explanation.

'Ow. I see. Makes sense.' said Miles and just as he did, a voice was heard from the little wireless that connected the back of the van to the front:

'Prepare yourselves, we are reaching our destination within 5'.' said the driver laconically as well as curtly. The team scrambled to get ready as everybody was checking that their equipment is in position. Yusef glanced at the little terminal the lieutenant had given him and opened the message with their next instructions. He read it to the team:

'Your next instructions are to head to the Whitebushes area and follow regiment 4 as attaches. They shall provide you with the necessary protection and the press-office attaché shall let you know where you may go safely and where you should keep out of for your own good health and safety. Your armed escort will be briefed about your missions and shall follow you wherever you go. Please remember: Once you have established contact with regiment 4, they shall indicate where you may or may not go for the rest of the day and then you are free to cover the story as you see fit. Should the situation change for any reason whatsoever, your escort shall be alerted and you shall receive a message at your special terminal. Should you require some aid with your coverage, such as a helicopter journey, or -heaven forbid- help while under attack, please contact regiment 4 through this terminal. The contact information for the person in regiment 4 responsible for journalists in the regiment's area of operations has now been added to your contact list on the interface.'

Yusef had just finished reading the instructions when the van stopped and the driver gave the green light for the reporters to descend. Sure enough, the rear door opened and out came the team. The armed escort had taken care of the administration so the van was not delayed at the gates of the Whitebushes barracks at all. In the courtyard, a sub-lieutenant who introduced himself as Jeffrey Moore of the 4th regiment press office imparted with them that he would be the person that they would be contacting through the small terminal for the entire duration of their attachment to the 4th regiment. He then proceeded to invite them inside the main building of the barracks. The team followed.

Shortly afterwards, the team were in a medium-sized room with a large, modern table 3x4m and simple, padded chairs all around it sitting beside sub-lieutenant Moore and his personal adjutant. A window was presenting a view of Whitebushes before sub-lt. Moore closed the curtains and switched on a little light, barely strong enough to illuminate the entire room. Sub-lt. Moore then spoke:

'Gentlemen, comrades, please pay very close attention to the information I am about to impart with you. Your safety will depend upon understanding it. The army asks all journalists to be given the so-called

LOE, standing for Limit Of Exploitation, areas in person on a holographic desk to make absolutely, 100% certain, beyond any doubt that everybody understands where they are supposed to go and where they are supposed to keep away from. This information will be passed on to your terminals once I finish my presentation, so you can consult the map on your terminal and check whether you are within your LOE or not at the flick of your index finger. For now, please turn your attention towards the desk.' he said and manipulated something at the interface of the holographic desk that was simply a terminal embedded in the body of the table, just before the seat where sub-lt. Moore was sitting at the time. For every seat at the holo-desk there was a mini terminal screen, but for the moment only the one used by sub-lt. Moore was active.

In response to sub-lt. Moore's manipulations, a 3D image of a cityscape appeared hovering a few centimetres above the surface of the holo-desk and the small light of the chamber dimmed until it eventually went out. The figures of buildings, trees and other objects appeared on the holo-desk in a pleasant, pale blue light. Darker blue shades denoted the edges of objects so despite its intricate complexity the image was very clear to see. Miles remembered the holographic systems at the Royal Zone and realised that this was very similar in function. Sub-lt. Moore swept his hand across the hovering image and spoke again:

'This is the map of the area my regiment is operating in, and also covers the region of our sector where the barracks are. First let me show you what the image looks like normally.' he said and started pecking intensely with his finger at his terminal screen. The image turned from the bluish colour it was into the true-colour representation of the area. It was just like having a model of the zone right in front of them. Mr. Moore continued: 'In the army, we normally prefer to look at the image once in true-colour and then switch back to pale blue so that we can then selectively highlight points of interest. I shall follow the same procedure here. But first, a little bit of landmark spotting.' he said raising his arm slightly and shaping his hand into the 'human pointer' form, i.e. all fingers folded in except the index, which was left straight as a ruler. Mr. Moore dropped his finger over a large building complex with a number of tarmac courtyards and a fence all around, towards his end of the table. 'This is where we are now. Whitebushes barracks.' he said and without any other utterance he moved his finger towards the other end of the table until it stopped exactly over what could be nothing more than a large white wall. 'This is the wall constitutes the official border that's separating us from Zone 3.' he said and without any further utterance his finger started tracing a very precise trajectory over the dilapidated, poorly-painted and often ruined buildings that lay beyond the wall. 'This region is where we operate today.' he said and then explained further in his officious, military style: 'The way our army works is in waves. I believe you will see more of it in action for yourselves as you cover the story, but I may as well give you a brief explanation of how the system works. It shall help you realise why you may be placing yourselves in danger if you veer outside your LOE zone. Right. Waves: there's 4 of them. The 1st wave is the 'steamroller'. Our main and best equipped military force. It crushes resistance ahead of it. If it can't do it, nobody within this country will be able to. The operational zone of the steamroller is where the heat of the action is. It is where you are most likely to end up injured or dead. Being inside the LOE of the steamroller means there are no guarantees for your safety and is thus expressly forbidden. The LOE of the steamroller is also secret, so we will never tell you exactly where it shall operate, however be certain that the off-limits zones for you will always include the entirety of the steamroller's LOE. Clear?' said Mr. Moore and looked around in anticipation of many nods of understanding. He received those nods and continued: 'The 2nd wave of the force is the 'sieve'. The purpose of the sieve is to sweep very thoroughly through the regions over which the steamroller has gained control and clear them of any residual resistance, arms and militants. This zone is also dangerous, although probably not as life-threatening as what you'll find in the steamroller LOE. I am not going to go into the specifics of how we can do such thorough job in clearing behind the steamroller partly because it's secret and partly because you won't be interested in trifling details. If you wish to report something to your viewers simply say something generic, for example that the thorough clean-up can be made because the overall area of the campaign is reasonably limited and the campaign is paced at a rate that makes such efforts realistically achievable without holding the rest of the campaign efforts back by too much. More importantly, you are not allowed in areas where the sieve operates as they are not considered secure. We will not tell you exactly where the sieve operates, however, the limits of its LOE again are guaranteed to be inside the forbidden zone for you. Finally, some people refer to the sieve as the 'broom' so now you will know what they mean when they refer to it thus. Understood?' asked sub-lt. Moore and once again waited for signs of his interlocutors' understanding. The team nodded and Mr. Moore carried on: 'The 3rd wave is the emergency fall-back area, a.k.a. the 'shield'. That area is not entirely off-limits to you, however, if you enter it, be ready to retreat if you hear the alert sound coming from your small terminal. Please unroll the small terminal and I shall show you what the alert sounds like.' said the officer and Yusef did as he was asked to. Mr. Moore played a bit more with his desk terminal and a loud sound akin to that used by trains as whistles was emitted from the small terminal. The sound was quite deafening and must have had a draining effect on the power supply of the small terminal. The siren sounded metallic, rasp and sharp and came in 3 intervals of about a second with ½-second pauses in between. Once the terminal fell silent again, sub-lt. Moore resumed his speech: 'This is what it sounds like. Because the terminal makes a supernatural effort to be loud, and trust me, if gunshots start raining you will need it to be that loud, it drains it battery very quickly. If you are in the shield and hear the siren, you absolutely must retreat and evacuate back out of the shield as soon as possible; also you must get back to safety and recharge the small terminal. Why, you ask? Because the shield is the belt upon which we shall fall back if we are attacked by powerful forces that destroy the steam-roller, or if our 'sieve' discovers a very powerful pocket of resistance they cannot contain by themselves. At any rate, the shield is a fairly safe area, but always runs the risk of suddenly becoming active. For that reason whenever you are in the shield you must carry your terminal with you fully unrolled. Clear?' asked Mr. Moore and the interactive ceremony was repeated yet again. Once all the nods from the team were in, Mr. Moore went on to clarify the last wave: 'And the 4th and final wave is the 'aid' wave. Everything in that region is considered safe and aid workers should already be in operation in those zones. You may wander about freely there and interview people, but please consider who you interview. Don't interview doctors for example if you can see that they are too busy and generally please use discretion, courtesy and common sense in your coverage of the operations. The final point I'd like to make is that there is one more siren sound you need to know about. Ready? Here we go...' said sub-lt. Moore and pecked on his terminal screen with his index finger one solitary time. The room was filled by an alarming noise that seemed to constitute of a superposition of the previous siren sound and the shrill clash of metal against metal at high frequency, much like in a century-old alarm clock; the type that used to feature two 'Mickey-mouse ears'-shaped bells on them. The siren went on for 5" and then it fell silent. Mr. Moore explained: 'This alarm means that the shield has been breached and you must evacuate as far away as possible. Understood?' Nods all around.

Following that little speech and siren display there was a short pause as the journalists tried to remember everything that had been said. Sub-lt. Moore interrupted their contemplations: 'All the information is on the terminal, including today's map. You may revise the briefing at your heart's content later. Remember: there's a reason why having this terminal with you at all times is obligatory and why outside the 'aid' zone you must keep it unrolled on a permanent basis. As for more generic information, if you wish to visit other zones, special permission may be granted to you and you may be able to visit the 'sieve' under heavy escort, but I wouldn't recommend it. Entering the steamroller zone is expressly forbidden under all circumstances.' said Mr. Moore factually. He then continued: 'And the last thing from me is your actual daily briefing. You will receive one of these every day at 09:00 sharp, with possible revisions later on if we believe that the situation has changed too much to stick to that plan. Keep your eyes on the terminal for messages carrying updates to the daily zone regime. Now, a few words about the briefing. Every day we shall tell you which area belongs to which zone and where you can go if you wish to resupply with sustenance, refreshments or anything else you may need. So, to business: here is today's map.' said Mr. Moore and the hologram turned pale blue again. Mr. Moore then started manipulating his terminal screen frantically while explaining: 'At the moment we are here...'. The building of the barracks turned white on the map. 'Your supply centre for today is here...' an area in a park beyond the wall was painted white. 'Today's aid zone is this...' the area between the wall and about 1km into Zone 3 turned bright green. 'The shield region that's within your LOE is here...' a strip stretching all along the eastern border of the aid zone where it met parts of Zone 3 the communists had decided not to invade and then followed the southern edge of the aid zone shone orange. The shield was between 200-300m thick. '...and everything else is off-limits to you.' concluded sub-lt. Moore and every other part of the map that represented territory outside the communist sector turned red. Mr. Moore wrapped up the meeting: 'And this is today's briefing. Now you may either choose to make your way directly to your next supply point, or start wandering about and report on what you see straight away, or resupply here. We have a small canteen where you may eat and drink, lavatories are just a corridor away from that canteen and if you need anything else I'll try to procure it for you.' said Mr. Moore with a polite and benevolent smile. The team looked at Thompson.

'Thanks a lot chief, but we have to get going. We have already missed a lot of the action. Offer much appreciated.' he said and the A-team suddenly felt a bit more B-class. But at least nobody had to answer any urgent calls from nature, so the team could leave at once without any real calamity befalling the party. Thus, the communard journalists bade their officious and polite host goodbye and headed back to the van, where the driver and the armed escort were browsing something at their terminals and had engrossed themselves into what appeared to be some sort of jolly banter. Upon clocking the approach of the journalistic team, they rolled their terminals and assumed a less relaxed position in their seats, geared towards functionality rather than comfort. In the process they saluted the approaching team with waves of their hands, a salutation that the two journalists and their entourage returned with equally convivial waves of the hands. The driver released the rear door of the van, the jolly team ascended into the vehicle and soon they were all heading south towards the border with Zone 3.

The short journey towards the war zone passed in silence as Yusef had activated the large on-board camera and was streaming the live feed into the terminal screens of the van. Naturally, everybody was looking at the images transmitted from the camera in anticipation of seeing the walls separating the communist sector from Zone 3 and their anticipation was not frustrated. Within a few minutes of departing from the barracks the walls appeared in the camera's field of view, with their full accessory additions of barbed wire and sentry towers. The van stopped right before the gates leading to Zone 3 and the armed escort from the communist zone handled the administration. Before long, the gates were opened and the van crossed into Zone 3.

'I think we should congratulate ourselves now, team.' said Thompson.

'Why?' asked Miles.

'Because now we are truly war correspondents!' replied Thompson with a wink and then turned his attention to the images displayed at the terminal screen. The first images of Zone 3 Miles had ever seen.

CHAPTER 13: FIRST IMPRESSIONS OF THE WAR ZONE.

The images on the terminal were quite disparaging. The buildings were fairly modern, as London had only recently extended that far from the centre, but the smashed windows, worn-off paintwork and general grimness they exuded made Miles' heart sink. Every now and then there would be a building or another that had clearly suffered a direct hit from a projectile, but to Miles it seemed that the overall sullenness associated with these buildings pre-dated the invasion. The streets were in ruin, grass growing from every crack in the mostly unused roads. The lamp-posts, rubbish bins and benches that had survived the invasion of the steamroller looked in dire need of a paint-job and general repairs. The pavements were dirty and unkempt, full of rubbish, empty shells and every now and then piles of generic debris. To complete this picture of desolation, the few people that had either mustered the courage or were forced by need to leave their quarters were dressed in very, very ordinary clothes with no signs of any significant consideration for fashion or general appearance -creases all over shirts and trousers alike were ordinary-, in fact, they looked extraordinarily like the destitute immigrants that often attempted the crossing from continental Europe to wealthy Britain, or even worse, engineers. The proliferation of nanomaterial suits was zero and even the quality of the fabrics exhibited by the inhabitants of Zone 3 indicated that their attires dated back to times when the norm in textile technology was nothing more sophisticated than mixing cotton with polyester (no lotus-effect fabrics or the like and even very little satin or silk).

The sky above was clear as the sun slowly descended far towards the West, bathing everything in a life-lustre light, which was, however, beginning to show the first signs of yellowness and herald the advent of that day's twilight time interval. The shadows of the dreary buildings in Zone 3 were beginning to elongate themselves under the rays of the falling sun while the southbound road ahead grew increasingly dark as it was slowly overtaken by the advancing shadows. Far ahead, a few trees indicated the presence of a park, most likely the park where the first supply point of the advancing communist army was set up. That supposition was enforced by the fact that the few people that were wandering the streets of war-torn Zone 3 were scurrying wearily towards the park, possibly in search of food & water, medical or less likely, other supplies.

'What do we do now?' asked Miles.

'Let's head for the park that Mr. Moore indicated on our map. The place is called Salford Refugee Camp, it is our resupply point and what's more, there will likely be some activity going on there as we speak. We will probably end up interviewing some refugees, if we are lucky also some army officers. We still need to do the 6 o'clock news, remember? That's in only, what, 1 hour or so, no?' said Thompson and without waiting for a reply he continued: 'After that we probably just rest and digest the news of the day as it will already be dark. We may be asked to go out at a high point on some building and show footage from our night-vision cameras, otherwise it's beer and banter till night.' he concluded.

'Ah, nice. So, no pressure.' said Miles with relief and relaxed by sitting fully back in his seat and crossing his arms behind his head. Everybody else in the van smiled in response.

'What?' said Miles unfolding his arms and looking at his colleagues in surprise. 'What?'

'It's a joke.' said Yusef. 'We'll have to find a vintage point somewhere and set-up a camera just in case anything of significance happens. We need to be on the job when the news is happening. There won't be any rest for us for a while now!' he explained. It was now Yusef's turn to be the butt of the joke as everybody else smiled at the prospect of interpreting some of his more unfortunately expressed points in a rather less refined fashion.

'Ow...' said Miles, suddenly worried. Smiles started appearing all around again. Miles pouted, curling the left side of his lips by engaging the muscles in his left cheek. His countenance was saying 'Seriously guys...'. Thompson explained:

'Nah, in reality it's not as rosy as just getting off the hook right after the 6 o'clock news, and neither is it as bad as spending nights upon nights sleepless. In all honest reality what is probably going to happen is that we will be scurrying around much of the day in search of news, but we won't simply be scurrying around aimlessly. The army's press office will show us what they want to show us. It is in their interest to get good publicity and if they think they have something spectacular they want the public to see, they will get in touch even in the middle of the night. If we get wind of anything interesting that is going to happen, then we may need to sit long hours in the dark and cold waiting for it to happen.' he concluded.

'Makes sense, but doesn't that mean that they will get to 'guide' us into showing on our screens more or less what they want us to show?' inquired Miles.

'That's true, but remember that we are their guests and they are our hosts, so we have little choice as such. Meanwhile, nothing stops other people, e.g. residents of Zone 3, from coming to talk to us with what they think might be interesting stories, or us going to them for that matter. We will not be entirely left to the mercy of the army press office.' explained Yusef.

'That's much more satisfying.' said Miles happily as the van kept moving towards the park.

Eventually, the driver found a parking slot in the region designated by the army as a dedicated parking lot for the press and the team descended again. Yusef stayed in the van, scanning other newscasts for anything related to their story and worked to that end in close cooperation with the coordinator of the team back at the agency building. The rest of the team, and their armed escort were greeted by an army officer upon entering the temporary camp set up by the army. He requested to see their journalist ID documentation and once happy that they were genuine journalists with a genuine armed escort, he downloaded on to their small terminal a map of the encampment indicating where the supply point was, where the emergency hospital was, where the refugee tents were etc., saluted them and beckoned them in while not forgetting to tell them that they are welcome to roam the camp freely and speak to people freely, so long as they don't interfere with the pressing duties of the medics or the administrators of the camp -or any other member of staff for that matter-. The team thanked him politely and proceeded into the encampment.

'Where to now Mr. Thompson?' asked Miles.

'Ah... I told you to call me Simon... Anyway, we'll have a quick tour of the facilities and see what we should be putting into our part of the 18:00 news. There's too little time for a drink now, we must be ready for the news, our viewers won't be waiting. Let's head to the refugee tents first. Of course, the rest of the team can go to the supply point. We will be touring the camp alone.' said Thompson.

'Why?' asked Miles.

'Because for the time being we only need to make a reckie of the encampment. We will have our microphones with us so we can record any interesting conversations we hold for articles later on. The 6 o'clock news we'll probably do live here, on site.' Thompson said and then addressing the rest of the team: 'Right team. 45' break. See you exactly here at 17:45. Be ready.'

Said and done, O'Brien, Mrs. Wilkins and Johnson went for a break at the supply point while Miles and Thompson headed for the refugee tents. As they were walking on the ill-ploughed furrows of the park Miles thought he should strike conversation:

'Listen, uh... Simon.' he said.

'At it kid! What's the question?' asked Thompson gleefully.

'I was wondering... you've lived in the Confederation for a long time, no?' inquired Miles.

'Nearly 30 years.' replied Thompson.

'So tell me, the Confederation works in small cells of 300 people at most.' said Miles.

'Yes, that is correct.' confirmed Thompson chiming in.

'So, how do large structures work within the Confederation? Our agency surely employs more than 300 people.' observed Miles.

'Clever kiddo. Truth is that larger organisations within the Confederation have always had to work more or less as they work anywhere else. Once you get above that magic 300 threshold, the solidarity created by the tight personal relationships generated by micro-communities begin to wane. Beyond that, even we in the anarcho-syndicalist sector acknowledge the need for some rather more permanent structure of authority. The big difference is that every year we hold company-wide elections for the top brass within our news agency.' said Thompson raising his index finger and nodding as if to ask whether Miles was 'catching his drift' as he'd put it.

'Elections? What top brass?' asked Miles astonished. For him the only power within a company were the stockholders and the CEO and his immediately subordinate few.

'Look, you're from Zone 1, no? There, companies are owned by stockholders who eventually vote for their governing boards, boards which choose the CEO and top officials, who in turn choose those below them and so on. Here it works roughly the same way, but the people working for the company get to vote for the board.' said Thompson.

'But that would be a financial disaster, no? What is to stop the companies from being ran to the ground by an overly self-indulgent work-force?' said Miles posing a very, very hard question.

'Ah... a very interesting question which can be generalised to something a lot more fundamental. Every organisation is led by people with certain tenures and certain motives, and these people have certain personalities and certain competences, which they may mobilise for different reasons. The question now is who do you give authority to? Obviously, if we keep the conversation general, the person in power should have the necessary competence, be moved by the correct motivation and be given enough time to carry his projects through, but not so much as to consider himself immune from scrutiny for too long. Finally, the personality of the person and particularly charisma and integrity will also impact their performance, as well as the performances of their subordinates. So... how do you make sure that the people in charge have all the right qualities, are motivated by the correct things and spend exactly the correct time in office?' said Thompson without really answering Miles' question, but certainly putting it into context and posing a very interesting rhetorical question. Thompson continued:

'Truth is, it is very difficult to do that in practice. Give all the power to the stockholders and you end up with profiteering. Give all power to the workers and you lose the connection to your clients; you get an overdose of self-indulgence. Give all power to a ministry and you end up with a pen-pushing system that works more to generate numbers than anything real, and can you blame them? The government can't be everywhere so they have to reduce themselves to measuring various performance metrics. To complicate things even more, what is the objective? What should the economy work for? What are the right qualities?' asked Thompson rhetorically and then continued again:

'Let us say that a decent goal for a national economy is to achieve this variety of sub-goals: Provide goods to as many people as possible, distribute them fairly and not too unevenly, make sure the aforesaid goods are of good quality, spur growth in productivity and technological advancement and achieve everything above sustainably.' he said and paused to think a bit. 'There may be even more, but this should illustrate the complexity of what we are talking about.' he uttered and continued pacing. Miles followed. Thompson went on with his contemplations aloud:

'So can we motivate a group of people with exactly the right competences in exactly the correct direction? Hmm... I think not. It is, after all, very difficult for a stockholder to care for the environment when turning a few baby seals into cosmetic products will fill his pockets to a greater extent than refraining from that practice. What's almost as difficult is for an environmentalist to care about profit. So, what if you put a number of conflicting groups together and ask them to compromise? Well, this is Britain so you'll get civil war within minutes, so putting the conflicting parties together is not enough; you must play 'dirty' so to speak and force them to compromise. The way to do this is to appoint someone as the president of the debate, the speaker, the coordinator and of course, he must be a diplomat of great skill. Then, make sure that the fruit of compromise tastes sweet and the fruit of conflict bitter. For that reason we have fairly large company boards that consist of people elected by the workforce, people elected by viewers via an online personalised poll, people whose emoluments are linked to the financial health of the agency and so on. All these people are rewarded for different things, however the president, or presiding council is rewarded as a function of a combination of these factors and stand to lose a lot if any individual factor is dragging behind...' said Thompson oratorically.

'Lagrange multipliers.' uttered Miles, but Thompson didn't hear and continued instead, as if uninterrupted:

'For that reason the presiding council has access to many, many ideas, but has to choose very wisely and balance the conflicting interests out.' concluded Thompson.

'And who sets up the parameters? The goals?' asked Miles with interest.

'The Confederate government.' replied Thompson. Miles smiled and declared:

'So the communards are a little bit communist at heart, no?'

Thompson was slightly taken aback by the remark but then thought about it. And then he thought more about it. In the end he realised that his young colleague was absolutely correct. The communist economic management system was based on the same fundamental principles, only adapted for use in a much more heavily centralised country and with bureaucracy that had evolved into a form of art. A bit of a black, art, admittedly, but art nonetheless as the communists sometimes liked to say jokingly. At the same time Miles was lost in his own contemplations. Thoughts about the universality of the fundamental principles of cosmos that James kept going on about were being recalled from his memory. Set the potential field properly and the ball will fall in the correct minimum. How true that is in everything and everywhere.

Nevertheless, after a few minutes of intense thinking Miles got headaches again and decided to stop thinking about it. Thompson looked far more relaxed as well, so presumably he had abandoned his high intellectual pursuits under the same mental stress.

'Oh well, that's roughly how things work. Then, there are many details as well. For example if somebody works in a company whose products they use, do they get a vote as a worker and one as a consumer? If a company is very labour-intensive and has very few institutional customers e.g. 2 or 3 foreign companies and another couple of local institutions, but employs thousands of people how should the votes be counted? And I'm afraid at this point much of this still works empirically rather than analytically. Nevertheless, the general recipe is to give about equal standing to clients, workers, profiteers etc. And that I think is as much as I can really tell you about it...' said Thompson and went silent. Miles nodded in understanding and kept silent as well.

That conversation had seen them through to the refugee camp. It was a very organised array of special quick build – quick reset tents made out of tough air-tight nano-fabric with chemicals inside them. The user would squeeze a capsule until it popped and a so-called 'slow release explosive' would combine with a dense solid and release gas. That gas would inflate the tent to its correct rough shape. A variable number -depending on tent size- of external, spiky-ended poles defining the edges of the tent would then be easily pushed into the ground and be anchored within it to give the tent a bit more structural stability, whilst simultaneously a variable number of internal spiky-ended poles (seen from the inside of the tent only) would be again driven and anchored to the ground to give the tent a better foothold, so to speak. When the time came to remove these poles, they had to be pushed further into the ground so that their spiky ends would fold in, a button had to be pressed which would keep the spikes retracted and then the poles could be easily removed. Then, a valve would be opened and the gas from within the tents would be released. Subsequently the tents had to be sent back to the manufacturer or a special workshop where their chemical bags were replaced. Naturally, in windy environments the internal poles could be set-up first, even though that required some experience before it could be done properly.

Inside, the tents were rather homely in so much as they were well-insulated thermally and since the material was burn-proof and water-proof and had special holes that could accommodate chimneys and zip-up windows the users inside could easily light their gas or hexamine stoves without fear of suffocation. Those tents were truly engineering masterpieces. Extremely easy to set-up, slightly more time consuming to deflate and fold back into place, their only weakness was that when hit by bullets they'd pop, although if all the poles were properly fitted that wouldn't bring the whole structure down on its residents. As for their ability to withstand attacks from wild animals with sharp claws -the kind you find in god-forsaken places of Africa and Asia where people are in dire need of emergency shelter- it was perfect. The nano-fabric was so tough that it could withstand anything. Even attacks by rogue elephants, although there were so few elephants left in the world that that was no longer a realistic fear. At any rate, such emergency tents were the standard tools of various peace corps that operated in war-torn parts of the world, the various internal emergency services that operated in areas of their respective countries that had been hit by natural calamities and a variety of advancing armies in war theatres world-wide, who were seen to have a responsibility towards the victims of their own war.

Back outside Miles and Thompson walked between the tents amongst various refugees who had trusted the communist loudspeaker messages and sought shelter at the supply point, as well as military personnel intended to keep the peace and enforce law and order. Far ahead and slightly to the right a moderately tall chimney was smoking dark, heavy smoke and soot. It was the chimney of the crematorium that had been hastily assembled at the camp, burned the dead and turned them into electricity; anything to help the dire situation. Slightly closer to the two advancing journalists, a sort of 'town square' amidst the tents had been formed. The army had brought tanker trucks with clean, potable water and had set hastily a corresponding number of 'tapping stations', which were nothing more than a few simple, mostly metallic structures normally towed behind the water trucks. The station was connected to the truck through a thick, flexible, rubber pipe which eventually distributed the water that was inside the truck's cistern to about 10 faucets arranged in groups of 5 side-by-side. The faucets were pretty low so that the system was kept passive and the need for a pump eliminated. This system greatly helped distribute water much more quickly and avoid long queues, unlike years ago when all there was was the water truck and a soldier straddling its top whilst distributing water by sinking a mug into the tank, or, if they were lucky, had a solitary tap at the back. At any rate, there was a long, but fast-moving queue in the vicinity of the tapping stations as the army had set-up a common-feed queuing system. Refugees were lining up with old kettles, pots and glasses, hoping to have a drink while soldiers -one at each tapping station- were calling 'Next!' whenever a position at their own tapping station became free. That's what allowed the queue to move on not only with great speed, but also in perfect order.

'Golly!' said Thompson. 'Look at all these people! Being so close to suffering makes you appreciate your own well-being, no?'

Miles remained silent. His mentor was right. Seeing people in such dire straights with one's own eyes could never be replaced by images via a terminal screen. What he was witnessing first-hand all around him had a profound effect on him. He wanted really badly to somehow help, do something. He imparted that thought with Thompson. The latter, in turn, smiled and spoke:

'There is good in human nature after all, no? Your intentions are admirable. At the same time I believe there is very little we can do apart from bring the plight of these people to the spotlight of our viewers at home and abroad. The army has everything else sorted, at least for the time being. You saw the water queues. All well-organised. There is probably a similar queue for food supplies or for medical assistance.'

Miles nodded in agreement and moved on alongside Thompson. Their steps eventually took them past the food queue and into the temporary hospital that was located in a large emergency tent. Rows upon rows upon rows of stretchers were populating the entire floor area of the tent, with the exception of those spots that were reserved for various, easily foldable medical cabinets or the few desks that handled the administration and logistics. Doctors were tending to patients who were suffering from a variety of ailments ranging from fever to severe injury from bullets. At the back of the tent, those latter patients constituting more serious cases were being treated by a combination of doctors and surgical robots that were either in the regular service of the military medics or had been temporarily detached from civilian hospitals in the communist sector. Above all else, one thing was certain: the hospital was home to many, many sad faces. Both journalists noticed that fact and Thompson commented on it very obliquely:

'I think that we should probably show our viewers the water queue instead of the bed matrix of the refugee camp hospital. We can, and in fact should, comment on both, but showing our viewers something less depressing might be for the best...' he said hesitantly.

'I agree. Showing other people's pain is probably a little distasteful.' said Miles and then changing the subject, he continued: 'Now shall we go and see the POW part of the camp, or should we return to the drop point and meet the rest of the team?'

'What POW part of the camp? POWs are kept elsewhere and we are not allowed access to them, ostensibly for our own safety, but probably because their treatment is far less kind than for the general civilian population. No, we're going to the drop point now. The newscast at 6 must not be jeopardised.' said Thompson and as Miles nodded the two of them left towards the entrance to the camp.

The team was already there and waiting. O'Brien spoke first:

'So, where do we go for the broadcast now?'

'We decided to have it just a few minutes walk in that direction...' said Thompson pointing towards the 'camp square', '...by the refugee tents and the water distribution system.' he completed his statement. The team nodded in understanding and they all left together towards the pre-determined spot.

Thankfully, despite the queuing there was enough space in the camp square for the journalistic team to set-up stall and carry on with their work. As the sun had already given its position of predominance in the sky and the moon -a beautiful crescent on what was promising to be a very clear night- assumed the position of dominant celestial body, the cameraman set-up his professional camera on the tripod without forgetting to light up the powerful lamp it carried. Thankfully, signal processing in the vastly advanced and highly automated cameras that professionals used meant that there was no longer a need for a lighting expert on the team. The cameraman could handle the few lighting controls that were still left in the care of humans. Alternatively, for larger events, the van had a camera with more powerful lights, small flood-lights in fact, that could be controlled by the administrator from within that van. Powerful computers housed at the news agency would carry out the computationally intensive signal processing real-time and automatically correct the raw footage coming out from the camera for optimal contrast, brightness, and ultimately viewing quality. The make-up lady powdered up Thompson's face so that no embarrassing reflection would be seen from his skin while the sound-expert was setting up stall too. Now, the camera had advanced sound recording systems itself and could clear the signal automatically through advanced signal processing. However, the sound-expert had a new weapon in his arsenal: the long range directional microphone (LRDM in short, but often jokingly called the 'lard-um'). The LRDM had no vibrating parts at all, which probably comes as a surprise from a device that is supposed to record vibrations in the air. Yet, it needed no vibrating parts because it featured a laser beam fascicle and a pixelised laser detector instead. The beam fascicle would be pointed towards a target surface that could be as far or close as necessary. So long as that surface vibrated in response to air-vibrations i.e. sounds, the nominal path of any incident beam fascicle would be subject to perturbations as well. In more detail, the beam would auto-focus on the target surface and as a result a pattern of reflected beams would return to the detector. If that surface then vibrated, its reflectance towards the laser beam would change as a function of the particular phase in the vibration cycle. As such, changes in the intensity of the reflected beam pattern would be generated and received by the detector, which in turn would be able to recreate the vibrational pattern that created those changes in the first place as sound and then pass that signal on to a loudspeaker. With proper signal processing it could even be configured to only retain information in the human speech range of frequencies (about 1-5 kHz) or any other frequency band of interest. Naturally, the surface upon which the beam fascicle fell would determine the efficiency of the system since rougher surfaces would tend to reflect less of the radiation back to the microphone's detector. Also, the consistence of the material of the target surface would determine its susceptibility to respond to air vibrations, so harder surfaces responded worse and in consequence be usable only ins rather short ranges. Finally, natural scatter through the air would further decay the signal. To try and at least counter the heavy dependence of the device upon finding a surface to 'listen on' that was perfectly suitable, the microphone possessed a 'barrel' with lasers of varied frequencies that would be reflected more efficiently by surfaces of different roughness. The trade-off here was that the longer the wavelength of the beam, the better it was reflected by smoother surfaces, however this also meant that its resolution was lower because it would be less sensitive to the vibrations induced in the material and also because if the surface that one was attempting to 'listen in' on was not perfectly facing the microphone, the device couldn't exploit the roughness of the surface to recover at least some of the signal. At any rate, the mechanism was highly complicated, suffered from high signal losses, particularly at high ranges and, as could be expected, the choice of laser wavelength, beam intensity and all of the signal processing had to be carried out by the computer inside. The sound expert could tweak performance and had to use his experience to find 'good' surfaces to home on. For that reason, the microphone actually looked a lot like a rifle and had a variably magnifying scope so the sound expert could more easily identify the type of surface he was homing on. It goes without saying that similar systems were used by intelligence services around the globe since window glass was an ideal material to home on when using that system. At any rate, for that part of the report it was unlikely that the sound expert would be needed, however he was present, just in case.

When all was set-up, Yusef established the connection to central and Aisha notified David Ramsay that the Kropotkin team in Salford (at the Northern part of which the park was situated) was ready for connection at any minute. Thompson assumed his position and told Miles to, again, watch and listen closely since it was very likely that he was going to be appearing on TV to present a report later that day. With those words the cameraman gave the signal that they were 3, 2, 1 seconds away from going 'on hold' and everybody fell silent. 'On hold' meant that the connection was on stand-by, ready to go live as soon as the newscaster back in central referenced them. Miles unrolled his terminal and tuned in to the Kropotkin news. The theme tune and video of the Kropotkin newscast was playing. It was a surreal string of animated cartoons that looked like they had been cut-out from ancient newspapers and referenced important news of the past 20 years. The music was an excerpt from Shostakovich's 8th quartet. After the short introduction David Ramsay's familiar figure appeared on the screen with a radiant smile. He addressed his viewers:

'Good evening everybody. In the news tonight, we have a look at the situation at the war front in the communist sector, the preparations for war at home, the council that legalised bigamy, sports news, the cultural review for this week's performances and finally the weather report.' he said. In the Confederation, this had come to be the formal format of the news opening sequence: the main news along with the standard ending sequence. Why that happened, nobody could tell exactly. Ramsay continued:

'At the front lines, the war waged by the communist forces against gangs that have been terrorising Zone 3 for years seems to be swinging decisively in favour of the communists as their forces reach Horley, barely 1km from Gatwick airport. The overwhelming numbers and coordination of the communist war machine makes this more or less a 1-horse race as rebel forces mostly retreat or surrender with few pockets of resistance to slow down the march of the red army. As a result, large parts of the armed forces are engaged in so-called 'sweeping' operations intended to ensure that areas recently acquired are entirely clean of militant presence. So far there has been no diplomatic activity as the rest of the world has not yet commented upon the situation, with the exception of the Russians who voiced their strong support of the communists and their mission to pull Zone 3 out of the dark ages, according to Russian foreign minister Andrei Tarchenko.' said Ramsay and the screen was filled with images borrowed from the TASS agency showing Tarchenko speaking in Russian with subtitles underneath. He was saying:

'The Russian government fully supports the communist allies from Britain in their mission to pull Zone 3 out of the middle ages. This is something that should have happened a long time ago with the contribution of everybody in the fragments of British society. With the old balance of power Zone 3 was merely a war theatre, a war arena and a buffer-zone to prevent Zone 2 from rising to rival Zone 1. Now, at least somebody in Zone 2 may rise and defend the interests of the weak. We have full confidence that the communists are capable of balancing what can only be described as a frightfully unjust situation.' concluded the minister and David Ramsay reappeared on the TV screens to continue commentating:

'Russia is up to date the only country to comment on the situation. Meanwhile in the territories that have been occupied, the communist army has been setting up refugee camps. Let's now join our journalistic team, who I'm being told have reached the Salford camp in safety (Yusef had informed coordinator Aisha about that).' he said and the image of Thompson appeared on the TV screen as the connection went live.

Ramsay now referred to Thompson:

'So, let's hear what our journalist on the field, Simon Thompson -good evening- has to say about the situation, Simon?' he said passing the ball on to Thompson. The experienced reporter did not hesitate to reply:

'Good evening David. The situation here seems to be difficult, after all it is war, but the camp seems to be well-organised and so far we haven't seen many supply shortages here.'

'So what can you tell us about the state of the refugees and their numbers? Do you notice a lot of activity?' inquired Ramsay.

'What we are seeing here is that most of the tents are rather full, at least from what I could make out when passing by the open flap-doors of the neatly arranged tents in the encampment. The hospital also seems to be bristling with activity although how many patients are military and how many civilians we can not tell. The refugees look rather quiet at the moment. Efficient common feed queues are set-up to ensure proper water and food supply distribution and the officers manning the camp are making sure people are treated as efficiently as possible. Of course, there is still space left for more newcomers and we don't know whether in the near future the incoming refugees will eventually begin to fill the encampment above capacity. The true test of the organisation of this whole undertaking will be when and if that moment arrives. As for activity, it is rather brisk, but seems to be very well-organised, as I said. You can see behind me refugees queueing up in an orderly fashion in order to get water supplies.' concluded Thompson answering all the questions. The camera zoomed slightly towards the water queue.

'Indeed so Simon. After all, just like the power grid or public transport, this system will be judged by its ability to respond to peak demand, not just average demand. Thank you very much.' responded Ramsay and Thompson replied:

'Thank you David, good evening.' and the connection went back on stand-by. Ramsay continued his newscast while Thompson relaxed a bit. He knew that he might be called back into the newscast at any moment.

'So we have seen that there is still military activity in the affected regions of London yet at the same time the red army is making huge efforts to begin restoring normalcy to the newly acquired and secured regions. This is what Reginald Dalston, minister for defence in the communist sector commented on the situation:' said the reputable newscaster and the screen switched to some footage of the communist minister speaking before a multitude of journalists by the entrance to the Epsom government tower.

'The rebuilding of the newly acquired parts of Zone 3 should begin within the next day if we don't get any nasty surprises. It is important to understand that the people of Zone 3 are our comrades, people we share a lot in common with, and at the same time people who have been neglected and abandoned by what used to be the British government for too long. There has been a lot of talk about invasion recently, but what people surely must see is that this is no invasion. It is not the conqueror taking over control of the conquered. It is the one brother finally finding the strength to join the other brother in the struggle for emancipation. These people will very shortly be naturalised as fellow citizens of our sector. They will enjoy exactly the same rights and be subjected to the same obligations as their comrades who have been living here for longer. Finally, it must be said that these people will once again be cared for by their government. With time they will obtain jobs like everybody else and integrate themselves into a much more caring and safe society.' said the minister and the camera cut back to Ramsay.

'Well, we never know. In the end history is what judges success and failure. It remains to be seen whether the communists can integrate such large regions under their control smoothly. So far the regions now controlled by the communist forces contain an estimated population of roughly 700.000 souls. Food and clothing supplies will sooner or later begin to grow scarce as the proportion of 'new' citizens over 'old' citizens increases. In any case, the ministry for agriculture, also responsible for food supplies in the communist sector commented that the military operations have been planned for long and that calculations showed that the food supply situation was not going to get out of control, but refused to give details on the exact nature of their calculations. At the moment it is estimated that...' said Ramsay before pausing abruptly and pressing his earpiece deeper into his ear. Thompson did the same whilst Miles -also equipped with such ear piece this time around- listened in to Aisha speaking. The contents of her curt monologue were soon to be echoed on TV by Ramsay. Meanwhile the connection to the Thompson-team went off. Aisha knew they were done for the evening and could go resupply. Thompson, who had been listening to Ramsay through his earpiece all throughout -despite the fact that his own microphone was off- fully relaxed, so he went straight to Miles curiously trying to see what was going on. O'Brien and Johnson joined them. The make-up lady had been quietly watching the news from over Miles' shoulder so she hadn't missed anything. Thompson placed his arm over Miles' shoulder and leant against him. O'Brien did the same and when Johnson did exactly the same Miles collapsed under the weight and the entire team -except Mrs. Wilkins and Yusef-. While the 4 colleagues were still on the grass, one over the other, Ramsay started relaying the message they'd just heard from Aisha to the public.

'Dear ladies and gentlemen, I'm receiving some breaking news from our anchors in the democratic sectors near Croydon and Bromley, just east of the communist sector. It appears that masses of people, followers of the communist parties in their respective regions are now taking to the streets and marching towards their council authorities. Apparently members of the respective police forces are amongst their ranks. Let us connect to our news anchor in Bromley, Tanya Fiodorova (Her full name was Tanya Fiodorova Lobatchova). Tanya, can you hear me?' asked Ramsay.

'Yes, I can hear you David, but it is very noisy here and I'm speaking to you through my little personal microphone so the sound quality on your end might not be that good.' said Tanya explaining her predicament.

'We can hear you clearly enough Tanya though there does seem to be a lot of noise over there. Can you tell us what is happening there at the moment?' asked Ramsay.

'It is very difficult to say David. What I can see around me are protesters waving red banners and placards in support of the military action, calling for solidarity with the communists and for government change. At the moment the crowd is marching towards the city council of Bromley shouting slogans. To this moment we have met no resistance from authorities.' said Tanya Fiodorova.

'What are the protesters chanting? Can you read to us any of the slogans they have displayed on their placards or repeat some of their verbal slogans?' inquired Ramsay.

'Certainly David. Currently the crowd is chanting 'down with the council, workers of the world unite' whilst their placards are reading things like 'democracy has failed us, bring change now', 'down with the council, all power to the workers' and 'support our comrades in their efforts to liberate Zone 3 from the capitalist yoke'.' said Tanya Fiodorova.

'Ah, it is 1917 all over again, eh? Or 1989 in reverse.' commented Ramsay and then continued: 'Thank you very much Tanya and good evening. Keep yourself safe there.'

'Thank you David.' replied Tanya and the floor was back to David Ramsay.

'We'll keep you up to date with events as they unfold. Next, the army in our own confederate sectors has been mobilising fervently and there is widespread speculation that military operations in the adjoining Zone 3 sectors could begin imminently. The militia refuses to officially comment on the situation, and quite understandably at it since any such information should be kept secret or the health of our troops might be put under serious jeopardy. Once again, we shall keep you informed of events as they unfold. For the time being we have no more information of military activity from within our own sector. On to a slightly lighter topic now, a Commune in Molesey has legalised bigamy in a controversial vote that...' said Ramsay and the team finally condescended to rise up to their feet again.

'Hmm... It seems that the communists have a very extensive subversive network as well as a very extensive espionage network. Mark my words: within days other sectors will also be troubled by communist revolts.' said O'Brien.

'Subversive network...' sneered Thompson dismissively. 'Has it not occurred to you that maybe the communists enjoy genuine support around Zone 2?' he asked.

'It's possible.' admitted O'Brien. 'In fact most likely there is a combination of genuine support and subversion working in favour of the communists as we speak. But yes, you are right. They are very likely to be enjoying genuine support at the moment. After all, communism thrives where people are very poor and well-below average income. Once they cross average income, however, they tend to change their political views. People become communists only if they have nothing to lose or stand to gain a lot from the redistribution of wealth that communism promises.' he concluded, not without a fair drop of bitterness in his voice.

'Presumably that explains why ardent communist youngsters who idolise Che Guevara during their university years grow up to be well-groomed insurance salesmen who vote Tory.' said Mrs. Wilkins half-seriously, half-jokingly.

'You may laugh, but that's the way I think it works.' said O'Brien.

'How very cynical. I applaud.' said Miles. 'Has it occurred to you that some people may actually believe in communism genuinely? Purely on principle. After all unlike fascism, communism isn't pure evil. Fascism was created for evil and that's why to this day it remains the ultimate symbol of odiousness. Communism, on the other hand, has been accepted over time as an experiment that went out of control. It's no longer a dirty word either, like it used to be right after the collapse. It is very possible that genuine support for the ideas behind the experiment has been rekindled. Not that I necessarily support those ideas, but let's think about it logically.' said Miles.

'Interesting thinking.' replied O'Brien. 'Perhaps you are right. But I still think that it is more about opportunism than principle. I have never seen a rich communist.' he concluded stubbornly.

'That's because genuine communists are very unlikely to pursue a career in investment banking and be ruthless enough to make it to the top. There may not be rich communists, but not all poor people who believe in communism believe in it out of opportunism either. There is genuine, grass-roots support I think. After all communism by its nature prohibits its believers from accumulating obscene amounts of wealth.' interjected Yusef.

'Meh.' said O'Brien. 'You may be right, but still the fact that principle and morality are luxuries we maintain only for as long as we can afford them doesn't change. People will resort to cannibalism to survive if necessary. It's human nature.' continued the stubborn cameraman.

'Interesting point.' noted Miles. 'Actually your argument is powerful, but only partially correct. It's not human nature, it's human inclination. The instinct for survival is extremely powerful; the most powerful human inclination in fact. However, as counter-examples I can give you names of people who died defending a faith, a political system, protecting family or clan etc. etc. So people may or may not overpower this natural inclination for survival if they feel they have a good enough reason to do so. On the other hand, there are more inclinations into 'human nature'...' said Miles making quotation marks in the air with the index and middle fingers of both his hands. '...such as the inclination to belong to a group, the inclination to accumulate and hoard material wealth and objects that represent it or the inclination to build a family. All of these are less powerful inclinations that more people manage to overpower, however they are still there. The inclination to belong to a group explains why religion has not been wiped out with the advent of the age of reason, however atheists and agnostics exist, as well as people who do not define themselves by the group they belong to. On the other hand, this inclination is what largely keeps the Communes of the Confederation together. On a different note, the inclination to build a family and have children is also strong, which is why everywhere in the world there has always been a looser or stricter notion of family. However, in medieval Arabia polygamy was the norm, in modern Europe monogamy is the norm. So, human inclination allowed both to exist, but within each example society, medieval Arabian and modern European, the tendency for polygamy or monogamy has been monolithic, which means that social pressure has played some role there, and it overpowered whatever the inherent human inclination is on the subject... But I digress. What I mean to say at the very end is that principle can overcome many, many human, natural inclinations, of which the inclination for survival is the most resistant to being overpowered. As such, principle is not an empty or hollow notion. There is a lot more to it. I hope I have demonstrated this to your full satisfaction.' concluded Miles. He had indeed changed a lot since he was an up-and-coming investment-banker in Zone 1. The rest of the team looked at him, including the cameraman but said nothing. After a short silence Thompson started clapping his hands. The other members of the team started applauding as well, with the exception of O'Brien. He said:

'Young man, you have wisdom beyond your years. You are probably right, but you will excuse me if I take some time to myself to think about what you just said. That will keep me busy for a while.' he uttered ending his sentence with a smile -rarely seen on his countenance- and a polite nod of the head. Silence ensued once again. Eventually Thompson broke the silence:

'Now back to business, I was thinking perhaps we should find a vintage point of observation and see whether we can discern anything interesting happening in the 'steamroller' zone that sub-lt. Moore was talking about.' he stated.

'Makes sense. Depending on the number of explosions we can discern from our vintage point we can make a judgement on the intensity of the combat.' logically concluded Miles.

'But how do we know where to find such observation point?' asked Mrs. Wilkins; a very real concern.

'Who has the small terminal?' Thompson asked he after blinking in response to Mrs. Wilkins' remark, as if suddenly awoken.

'Why, it is Mr. Yusef dear.' replied Mrs. Wilkins.

'Right, he can drop a line to the army's press office. I'm sure they know this area really well. If they find a suitable point of observation, they are as good as certain to impart that information with us.' said Thompson unrolling his terminal and starting to type his instant message to Yusef. Then, having finished with the typing he rolled his terminal back and addressing nobody in particular he exclaimed:

'Right, team. 15' break. Let's go to the supply point, eat something, drink something, freshen up and then prepare to go to the vintage point, if any. Otherwise we'll just start work on our articles for tomorrow straight away.

A loud cry of 'Horray' resounded and the team headed towards the supply point. Once there, they all had a quick sandwich (or two) from the automatic dispensers and enjoyed some hot tea with milk -except Thompson who'd rather have coffee-. Other journalists, aid workers and military personnel populated the tables at the supply point and in general the atmosphere inside was tense as a result of all the military action that had been going on, yet the signs of relief coming after the conclusion of operations in that particular region were beginning to make themselves felt. Finally, the supply point tent was also filled by the aroma of hot soup, which helped people release their stress a lot.

After what can only be described as a very fast, but filling meal enjoyed in the good company of one another and livened up by idle banter, Thompson unrolled his terminal in anticipation of finding a message from Yusef with instructions on how to get to a good observation point. Indeed Yusef had replied. The communist army's press office had indicated an old 15-floor tower-block not very far away from the park as a good candidate for an observation point. They had added a slowly blinking red dot on the map at the small terminal to indicate the exact location of the edifice. Thompson quickly keyed in a message of thanks to Yusef and announced that the team was on its way to the van. Thus, the journalists and their entourage scrambled and made their way to the van where the driver and Yusef were waiting patiently. Once inside and with the sundry salutations properly dispensed with, Mrs. Wilkins opened a small cabinet at the back of the van and took out a change of clothes for everyone that had been befallen by the misfortune of falling on the grass back at the camp square while watching the 6 o'clock news. The affected parties changed clothes with all due haste and placed the dirty clothes into a laundry-bag that was going to be dealt with at the supply point's launderette.

Eventually, the van reached the tower block and the team descended. A couple of communist guards had opened the door of the block in anticipation of the journalists' arrival and were guarding the entrance against any rogue activity that might endanger the residents of the tower block. The armed guard saluted his colleagues and took care of the administration. Soon the journalists were inside the tower block and heading up towards the roof of the building. To the great disappointment of O'Brien they had to take the stairs because nobody knew whether the power supply would be clement enough to stay on for the entire duration of a hypothetical elevator ascent and the stout Irishman made sure that his grief was widely known by uttering a very long string of words that are rather unfit for publication. In his defence though, they did have to carry quite a serious amount of equipment up the stairs.

Once at the top floor, the armed escort unlocked the rooftop door with the aid of a key he'd borrowed from the guards downstairs. He then beckoned the team to step through and on to the roof with a pleasant smile on his face. The team stepped through, each member saying 'thank you' as they passed by their official escort. Once everybody was on the hard surface of the block's flat roof the escort shut the door gently and the team started setting themselves up. The folding chairs were unfolded, the acoustic equipment was deployed, the camera was set-up on its tripod, looking in the direction in which any potentially interesting images were anticipated to appear and everybody sat down. The team had kindly brought an extra chair so that their armed guard could take a seat himself, a thought that the man highly appreciated. And then they all sat in silence. The two journalists just by the solid concrete railing of the building, one across the other, and the rest of the team with the armed guard sat in a circular configuration a bit farther away from the railings, deployed a small OLED lamp, unfolded the blankets Mrs. Wilkins had carried from the van on the way up and placed a couple of thermos bottles at the centre.

The sky was already dark and clear. The moon was shining brightly over the war-torn sector and a multitude of stars from nadir to zenith spangled the entire sky. Other than the rustling of blankets that was emitted whenever a companion tried to reach for a thermos, seat himself more comfortably or engage himself in any physical activity it was completely silent. Towards the far side of the building, the skyscrapers of Zone 1 could be seen glittering with light and closer by, the government tower of the communist sector rose like a column of light with its red, blinking lights pulsating serenely and solemnly. Towards the near side of the building there was nothing but low rooftops and very little lighting. Far, far away a string of aeroplanes could be seen on their approach to Gatwick, creating a moving chain of red & white lights that grew larger as the aeroplanes approached Gatwick's 5 runways (pairs of parallel runways running East-West and North-South and a diagonal one, mostly for emergencies) and eventually landed on the partially visible runways of London's main airport; the rest was hidden by buildings that blocked the view.

Once Miles absorbed all that imagery he turned his attention to Thompson, who had unrolled his terminal, and asked him:

'What do we do now then? Wait for something interesting to happen?'

'Basically yes, but I'd suggest that in the meantime we work on our reports for tomorrow's web-page update. I'll make one and then you make one as well. In the end we'll compare versions and see how publishable what you produce is. It's all part of the learning process. If our versions are significantly different but both publishable we may as well ask that they are both published in a new column we can name something like 'The war from within' or something of the sort. I'm sure the editors will sort something out if we both produce interesting essays. My advice is, be eloquent and if you want even poetic, but don't over-do it. This is after all a news-feed, not a literature club paper. Above all else be honest and try to be objective and indicate whenever you are stating an opinion rather than simply factual information.' said Thompson. Miles nodded in understanding and unrolled his own terminal but typed nothing. Instead he fell into deep contemplation.

What do the people of this sector think and feel about the communist assault? Do they want to be annexed to the communist sectors? Do they feel freed or do they feel like they have just changed masters but remained slaves? Is this military action justifiable? These were all questions that had been tormenting Miles ever since a conversation struck such a tangent for the first time back when he was still touring Zone 2, in the Royal Zone in fact. Thus far he had looked at the issue from the point of view of the invader/liberator. But what about the point of view of the conquered/liberated? Miles racked his brains to find an answer and finally he came up with a general idea:

Societies are much like systems of thinking, cosmotheories. You start from a base of arbitrary assumptions and then you define a set of rules. Once you set-up the rules and base, the functional basis of the system is in operation and you may use your rules on your assumptions to start generating logical conclusions. The only thing you need to make sure if you want to have a viable system is that none of the arbitrary assumptions and logical conclusions either contradict each other or invalidate any rules. Geometry and a lot of mathematics was built that way, but the concept is far more general. So long as a system is self-consistent, it is incredibly difficult to be influenced by external argument. For example, a fairly self-consistent system may be as simple as the following collective of propositions:

1. Assume – God X exists.
2. Assume – The holy scriptures of religion X are genuine and fully true.
3. Assume – Full faith in religion X is the only way to reach god.
4. Rule – Anything contradicting the holy scriptures is untrue.
5. Rule – Religion X is unquestionable.

Under this system, a person who holds it true will form a self-consistent, nearly impenetrable shell that operates on these principles. They will reject anything that contradicts their religion by definition and accept anything their religion says as true. If their own religion has internal inconsistencies in the holy scriptures, then they will be ignored, rationalised or attributed to the mysterious nature of god because of the assumption that the scriptures are by definition true and the rule that they are unquestionable. Perhaps this example is overly simplistic, but the principles are generic. It will be very difficult to punch a hole in this system because any attempt to do so will crash against clauses no4 and no5. Thus an argument presented to an adamantly religious person by, say, an atheist will be perfectly valid under the assumptions and rules of the proposer, but completely invalid from the point of view of the listener. Similarly the reply from the listener will probably hit an equally strong brick wall on the proposer. For that reason, the best bet to change the listener is to attack his assumptions or rules in a huge effort to shift the system from its foundations. Logically that is impossible under the rules of the system, however, this simplistic system is likely not to be the only self-contained and self-consistent system in the person's cosmotheory. It is likely to co-exist with others so long as the conflicts it creates with its co-habitant systems are either unknown to the person or deliberately ignored. However, so long as that system is not 100% dominant and doesn't define its holder alone, there will be room for questioning despite clause no5. This questioning will come from another system maintained by the same person; a system that has the power to challenge our model system. This explains why debating often works on people who are undecided because their 'allegiances' are split between rivalling systems or because their own systems are by nature very open to the concept of a 'system update', and why it doesn't work on people who have been entirely dominated by one self-consistent, but also self-sealing system like our simplistic example. How useful is each person's system going to be? Impossible to tell unless we define goals for each system. Thus we may add some clauses to our original system that include goals, in our case just one:

6. Goal – The goal is to have faith in religion X in order to gain eternal salvation.

Now we have created a system that is also very good at fulfilling its own goals. Thus, the believer will have the comfortable and happy feeling that he is achieving his goal on a constant basis. How useful is this system? Biologically speaking, not very. It will not help the believer put food on his table. Psychologically it is a very effective painkiller and motivator and may be of crucial importance in somebody's life, for example give someone the necessary mental strength to overcome a very big obstacle or difficulty in one's life.

Along similar lines of reasoning, science as a system is the exact opposite of our simplistic religious system. It is extremely complicated, very open to update, does not proclaim to hold any absolute truth, but preaches disbelief in its own self -the 'True only so long as it's not proven wrong' tenet-, has no goal per se, compels people to question everything and everyone, has almost no use whatsoever in helping soothe emotional pain, but is extremely useful when it comes to survival, or more generally, when it comes to the struggle of man to manipulate and control nature to his own advantage, mainly through engineering; the executive arm of science. Do we need both? Depends on the person. Many people have satisfied themselves with science alone and form the group of rationalist atheists. Few, have satisfied themselves only with religion. Most believe in both, each for different reasons and to varying degrees. Science provides them their daily meals and fancy terminal screens and religion provides them their daily dose of mental harmony.

However, things would have been all fine and dandy if it all stopped there. No person is an isolated individual, except the lonely hermits of the wilds. Holding beliefs that vilify those who don't hold the same beliefs (like many religions do), nullify those who aren't contributing to one's happiness (as extreme utilitarianism might do on occasion) or otherwise create tension, may lead to conflicts, often very, very bloody, with such illustrious examples as the crusades, or WWII and concentration camps. As such these systems of thought will also be defined by their ability to form peaceful relations to one another and coexist.

Taking this line of thought and applying it to societies we can see that all the points made about self-consistency, goals, assumptions and rules, as well as relations between systems also apply here. Perhaps this should not come as a surprise since societies generally are formed by systems of government, which stem from systems of thinking. Societies must be based on 'core values' that are widely accepted and maintain social cohesion. They must have rules that are equally widely accepted as just and morally correct. These must be self-consistent or unrest will be generated. After all it is difficult to live in a society that vilifies wealth but has a ruling elite of obscenely rich rulers and everybody in that society wants material wealth advancement. And finally, they must all be able to co-exist with one another or tension and maybe conflict will eventually occur.

Taking this and applying it to the present situation Miles figured that it was impossible to argue whether the communist military intervention was right or wrong. To argue so would have to be clarified by revealing the selection of thinking system that led to that conclusion from the given premises. For many people, living in a more or less homogeneous society that is self-evident. The system used to reach conclusions X was THE system; the one they live in. Thus, realistically speaking the bet was to eventually convince the people that were soon to become citizens of the communist sector to switch -if necessary- to a system that justifies the military action and accept it as something good. Considerations of nationality, religion, previous history and living standards have traditionally been key to the eventual outcome of such campaign. It is what made the difference between the cheers of the German reunification in 1990 and the boos at the Czechoslovak split in 1993. On this occasion, most of those factors seemed to benefit the communists, so Miles figured that in the end, history would remember this as a liberation war or a reunification that involved the clearing of rebel presence in the Zone 3 regions and not as an invasion.

Putting finger on terminal Miles penned down these thoughts into an article and showed it to Thompson, who by luck had already finished his own article and was engrossed in proof-reading it. Thompson read it and smiled.

'Impressive.' he said. 'Not exactly hot-off-the-press news, but I think we can publish this in our 'Opinions column', but you will need to proof-read it before that at least once. Very interesting ideas. Now read mine.' he concluded and passed his terminal screen to Miles.

Thompson's report was exactly that: a report on the situation and what he'd witnessed in Zone 3 that day. Thompson commented on that once Miles made it clear that he had read the report and handed back to his mentor the terminal screen:

'So you see, the difference is that my report is a narration on exactly what I've seen, whist yours moves on an entirely different level that has to do with philosophy more than anything. I want you to know that they are both very good material for different sections of our news apparatus. Now you've shown to me that you can do this high level sort of work. Next article show me that you can also do the low level work. It should be a breeze for you. You are learning very fast. Well done.' said Thompson patting Miles on the back before continuing:

'Don't worry. In this month we will go through all the types of articles together and tomorrow I want you to do an 'offline' reportage, that is to say, we'll tour around the area and report & record what we see. Then at the 6 o'clock news probably, our reportage will be broadcast, hence offline as opposed to live. When you feel confident about your offline reportage quality I'll let you do a live newscast.' concluded Thompson smiling benevolently.

Having seen not much interesting while they were working on their reports, the journalists sent their articles to their editors and coordinators and decided that it was probably time to head back. They notified the other 4, who were now sitting on the roof-top with their legs crossed and played cards under the moonlight, and the lot of them headed down towards the van. Before long, they were at the supply point, in the sleeping areas of their allocated tents and were all attempting to sleep.

CHAPTER 14: TECTONIC MOVEMENT.

The next day the team found out in an email sent to them late at night why the previous night was so quiet. The communists were engaged in so-called 'silent operations' all night and had advanced a lot, taking by surprise vast numbers of militants in the process. After ceasing operations for a few hours, the militants outside the affected regions eventually dropped their guard and sniper teams along with elite troops went building-by-building clearing them of enemy presence as silently as possible. This had the advantage of creating the impression that Gatwick airport was not going to be affected by military action for quite a while, so the company running it had ordered its employees to either go to work next day or lose their jobs. For that reason, the airport was fully operational that morning, however, the communists had it surrounded by elite troops and the steamroller was not far behind, ready to completely engulf the airport into a pocket. Aisha had sent that message at the crack of dawn to Yusef, indicating that there was no need to hurry and wake up the team since the red army press-office was going to notify them anyway when Gatwick fell -or was about to fall- under communist control. Instead she advised that the team kept reporting from behind the front-lines and keep their eyes peeled for any unexplained military activity. She finally noted that the army's press office had declared it would announce all journalists whenever they had anything spectacular to show in relation to Gatwick airport.

As a result the team woke up refreshed and ready for action, and immediately knew that soon they would have to cover the Gatwick airport story; see how the communists handle its capture. The fact that the communists were going to capture the airport was now beyond any doubt. Just as the team was having breakfast, David Ramsay was announcing in a breaking news bulletin that the CEO of the South British Airports Corporation (S-BAC) in control of Gatwick airport declared that unless Zone 1 put a lot of capital in hiring a private military company to confront the communists, Gatwick was all but lost. Shortly afterwards and as the team had concluded breakfast, another breaking news bulletin announced that Zone 1 corporations declined to help in view of the recent bank collapses and the cost-cutting schemes they had announced. To put more wind in the sails of the communists, some big CEOs in Zone 1 announced that they had contacted the communist government about the possible future of Gatwick airport and had received assurances that the airport would remain open with minimum possible disruption for travellers, and that the communists would take over control of operations and perhaps even cut the prices charged to aeroplanes using the airport, in order to spur partially privately financed growth in the region. They added that those assurances made them happy about the situation and that it was nonsense to spend money to fight a powerful army just for Gatwick when Luton, Stansted and Chatham airports were still fully operational and could easily handle passenger traffic from Gatwick in the wake of the dip already caused in flights due to the crisis. Finally, the Russians re-iterated their support towards the British communists and offered support in the form of medical, food and fuel supplies, whilst press-releases from other countries that had been made overnight indicated that China, India and the United states considered this a minor regional conflict that is not worthy of attention, more for the purpose of stopping curious journalists from knocking at the doors of their foreign ministries to ask for their opinion on the matter. The EU expressed concerns about a possible humanitarian catastrophe in the region and offered some aid in the form of medical and food supplies, followed by

Japan. Other major powers such as Indonesia and Brazil completely ignored the events.

With full knowledge of these events now, the journalists of the Kropotkin team went to the information centre of their allocated supply point at 09:00 sharp, where, as promised, they were given their daily LOE briefing in person by a uniformed officer. Other journalists were also present at the briefing, which was kept -oddly enough- brief. No real opportunity for socialising arose since immediately after the conclusion of the briefing all journalists went on with their business. The Miles and Thompson combo was no different. They now knew what their LOE was and more importantly, they had been allocated a new supply point. The red army had cleared enough area for the next supply point to be in South Horley. The journalists were also told at the briefing that they could move quite freely around their LOE, which now had been significantly extended, but they were advised to spend the night at the 2nd supply point where press tents had been set-up for them, just like the ones they'd spent last night in at their present location. Thompson and Miles conveyed those news to their colleagues once they had all gathered at the van -all packed and ready- and the driver 'hit the road' as Thompson liked to say.

The idea now was that they would look carefully outside through the cameras as they were making their way to their new supply point and report back to central their assessment of the damage. Most likely they were also going to stop on the way for a reportage, if they found anything of significance. Said and done, the team looked at their terminal screens closely, scrutinising the passing images, streaming from the van's roof camera, for anything of interest. As a result the van was silent, but the atmosphere reverberated with intense concentration. Finally, shortly after their departure, Mrs. Wilkins asked:

'Is it just me, or does every building we pass by have a graffiti 'x'-mark by its entrance?'

'Holy...! I think she's right!' said Thompson.

'Astute woman.' said Yusef appreciatively. 'Should I ask the army's press office what these marks are?' he continued, unrolling the small terminal. Upon receiving positive nods from all around, he did exactly that. Barely a couple of minutes later the reply came. They were marks inflicted upon the buildings by the army's civil engineers and were meant to represent the state of each building. In fact, they were marks very similar to the ones used in quake-ridden countries after a particularly powerful earthquake. A red cross meant the building was to be immediately demolished because it was unstable, unsafe, or simply too old and of too little historical value to be repaired from whatever damage it sustained and it was better off simply being re-built. A yellow cross indicated that the damage was repairable and comparable in advantage to rebuilding. It also meant the building was safe and could sustain people temporarily, but would eventually require major repairs. A green cross indicated that the building that bore it was definitely safe and structurally secure and the undoubted recommendation was that it should be repaired.

Upon hearing those news, Thompson asked the van driver over the comm-link to drive around the general region amidst the ruins for a while. Miles was suspecting what the purpose of such manoeuvre might be, and indeed his suspicions were soon confirmed as Thompson expressed them explicitly:

'Right, for the benefit of our new team-mate let me explain clearly what we are about to do. We have driven around for a little while to get familiar with the area. Now, remember that charred building we saw just earlier?' asked Thompson. Nods all around. 'We will show that as an example of the hell of war, but then we will show others as demonstrators to the fact that most operations in this region seem to have been of fairly low intensity. Yes, you guessed right. We are doing a short reportage here today.' he continued before concluding: 'And today's reportage will be carried out by our new team member.'. Thompson presented Miles to the rest of the team, as if for the 1st time, and Miles received handshakes and advice like 'don't be nervous, you're not going live anyway you can try as many times as you like' and peps like 'you'll do fine, I bet'.

Said and done, a few minutes later the van stopped and Miles descended, followed by Thompson. He was equipped with a microphone on the left lapel of his suit and was then curtly briefed by Thompson:

'Report what you see. Make every word count. Make every word have meaning. Make sure you stand in the right position and the camera shows images that count. Remember we can make it so that we display images without you in them while you talk, but it is good to have at least a few, say 10% of the reportage with you in it. You get to decide what gets shown where. You have 15' maximum. We can edit it and shorten it later if need be so.' he said in a quick-fire fashion. Miles gently nodded affirmatively at every sentence as he was having make-up applied on his face by Mrs. Wilkins. Then he stood in front of the camera, making sure that the said camera could capture his image as well as the charred building behind him and started breathing rather more heavily than normal.

'Are you all right?' asked Thompson. Miles nodded affirmatively rather nervously. 'Don't be nervous, we can try as many times as you like... well, within reason. Obviously we can't spend 5 hours here.' reassured him Thompson. Miles nodded again, slightly relieved at the thought.

'Ready?' asked O'Brien. Miles nodded again and O'Brien gave the signal that they were seconds away from filming. Miles mustered his thoughts quickly and upon O'Brien's signal, he started:

'This, is what London's Zone 3 looks like. Dilapidated buildings with smashed windows, grassy, cracked roads, few solitary vehicles from other times, that somehow still manage to carry their owners about the rather depressing surroundings. For years this region has been home to the destitute. Those who were too far from the rich centre to be able to commute back and forth and earn a decent living from the bread-crumbs falling from above, or too far to be integrated into the societies that have emerged in Zone 2 after the complete collapse of the central government's real authority. For most of us, Zone 3 is a region known as the source of border unrest and the home of ruthless gangs; a region where the rest of London chooses to wage its proxy wars in.

However, being here changes one's view of things. Seeing people scurrying to get supplies from the refugee camps the army has set-up makes one realise that even here there is human life, life not so different from ours. This is no longer a faceless zone of conflict, it suddenly all becomes much more personal.

The advent of the war has had a strong impact on the already pretty dreary surroundings as we can see. The workers' army engineers have already earmarked buildings with crosses in an attempt to start rebuilding. Green for repairs, yellow for major repairs, red for demolition. There is little doubt that the building behind me bears a red cross by its entrance. It's charred remains, a strong reminder of the disaster that war brings wherever it goes.

However, there are glimmers of hope even in this situation. Despite the fact that a handful of buildings have obtained large numbers of bullet-holes, the intensity of the military operations in this war theatre has been very low compared to what we tend to see in other war zones. Meanwhile, the communist army is operating refugee camps with clockwork precision and discipline. So far the victims of war have found shelter, food and medical assistance, but the question is for how long the communist sector of London will be able to provide such assistance to everyone.

Finally, the communists seem to have found a strong ally in Russia; a country that supplies them with fuel, food and medical supplies. The EU and Japan have also chipped into the humanitarian effort and have sent food and medical supplies as well.

For now...' Miles started walking slowly towards the camera. '...we don't know whether everything that is happening in London's outer ring is for the better or the worse. All we can hope for is that the future will bring the people of Zone 3 better days under the red flag of communism. A flag which will nearly certainly soon wave over much of

Zone 3 of London.' said Miles and indicated that he had concluded.

Thompson was very happy and clapped his hands in support of his colleague. The rest of the team followed suit in a polite show of support. Thompson then addressed Miles:

'Have you been thinking about what to say for a while now?' he asked.

'Well, I've been thinking about what to say since I found out I'd be doing the reportage. I first made a generic skeleton in my mind and then I sort of decided I'd talk about the items in the skeleton in order. Introduction to Zone 3, the feelings it elicits for us, the effect of war on the Zone, the efforts the communist have committed into ensuring civilians don't suffer, the situation abroad and a little conclusion with a hopeful message.' replied Miles.

'Well done.' said Thompson. 'Now I want you to go over your dialogue and decide what images to put where. You'll love the software we have fort that job.'

'Nice.' said Miles smiling with satisfaction.

'I'll be damned. Say what you want about the communists, but I have to admit that they have taken good care of the victims of war from what I could see.' said O'Brien. 'Of course, all of this could just be a charade...' he continued.

'Oh, for god's sake...' said Mrs. Wilkins. 'Yes, they do tend to have an unhealthy obsession with monitoring their own people and sometimes imposing very indirect restrictions on freedom of speech, but they are making an honest effort. This is not Stalin's Soviet Union. This time around they are making a sincere effort not to repeat the mistakes of the past. Give them a chance, darling!' she uttered slightly upset.

'I supposed you are right...' grumbled O'Brien. '...but if we witness with our own eyes the situation spiralling out of control in the future don't say I didn't warn you!' he concluded. Miles thought that careful and sceptical procedure was probably the best way. After all why should the communists not be given another chance after so long? Perhaps they have learned from their mistakes in the past. But what if they didn't? It was imperative that this time they got it right.

With these contemplations still swirling in his mind, Miles ascended back in the van and the driver set off southwards again. Now, the team circled up again to watch Miles piecing his first reportage together on the software Thompson was so proud of. As Thompson unrolled his terminal he asked O'Brien whether he'd been busy and O'Brien replied:

'Certainly chief. I've been taking shots that might be useful for such eventuality, just like I always do.' Then Thompson addressed Miles:

'We've been a bit unfair on you to be honest. Normally for a reportage we plan a skeleton like you did well in advance, then film what we think is relevant while writing the actual lines we are going to be reciting. We asked you to do this more or less impromptu as a test. Very good, very good.' he said with appreciation and added: 'You have a knack for this, you know it?' Miles smiled and thanked his mentor.

The terminal was now fully unrolled and Thompson had kicked off the user interface of the software. He loaded Miles' recording on, pressed a few buttons and the software re-created Miles' speech in text form. Thompson began explaining:

'First, you'll have to split the text into paragraphs and edit anything you believe has been misspelled.' he said. Miles did exactly so.

'Next, split your text into regions where you want the same continuous footage to show. Here, use this tool. It's rather unimaginatively called 'Continuous footage border tool'.' continued Thompson. Miles did as he was advised.

Now, place images to the sections you just created, and you're effectively done with your 1st draft.' finished Thompson.

Miles added video footage with the help of O'Brien to the sections he had just created while the rest of the team remained silent. For the introduction he used some older footage of Zone 3 that was available to download from the agency's archive. For the emotional part, he used images that O'Brien had taken of people walking about the refugee camp, minding their own business and children playing in the furrows of what used to be a field, but was now just the camp. For the part detailing the impact of the war on Zone 3 he used various 'moving images' (very short footage) of buildings featuring bullet-holes or signs of explosion damage (collected from the van's camera on the go) and then longer videos taken from the van that showed buildings with crosses of various colours by their entrances passing by. Also the part where he was referencing the building behind him was showing him talking in front of the said building. The part that was dealing with the situation in the refugee camps, perhaps unsurprisingly, contained snippets of video taken by O'Brien while he was roaming around the camp. The part describing the international situation was featuring a map of the world with Russia, the EU and Japan highlighted in different colours. Finally for the conclusion of his report the images showed just him walking towards the camera. Once done he showed the fruits of his efforts to his colleagues. He received accolades from his team and Thompson commented:

'Not bad. Not bad at all. Now make any changes you think should be made and I think we are ready to send it to the editors. They will then edit it and return you a copy for quality checking. If you are happy with their changes and believe that none of the material or information is missing or distorted, you confirm that it can be published and that's it.

Alternatively, if they are very unhappy, they'll ask you to submit another draft, but I don't think that's going to happen. You've covered all that's essential in quite a balanced way, I think.' concluded Thompson. The draft was sent and the team turned their attention to the road ahead.

It seemed that that day was going to be a busy one. About 20' later, Yusef announced that Aisha was telling him there is going to be a breaking news bulletin within a minute or so. He followed the coordinator's advice and switched the terminal to the Kropotkin channel. Sure enough, not a minute had passed when the theme music and video for the news section played on the TV, interrupting the normal flow of the schedule (Tea with Nigel was the unfortunate programme yet again). David Ramsay appeared on the screen and started his broadcast:

'Good morning viewers. We are interrupting this programme to bring you breaking news in relation to the progress of the war. Generals of the Confederate militia war-command have just released a press-statement declaring that large-scale military operations have begun beyond the borders of the Confederation with Zone 3. Confederate forces are heading West towards Farnborough and South-West towards Guildford. At the present time we have no additional information about the troop movements, but we shall keep you up to date with news about the progress of the front as time goes by. Thank you for your attention.' he said concisely and 'Tea with Nigel' reappeared on the terminal screens of the van.

'Well, let's hope that our militia has success of similar magnitude to that enjoyed by the communist army.' said Yusef.

'Unlikely. Maintaining discipline in the militia has always been the weakest point of our system. Strong authority and orderly subordination don't go down well with the Commune system.' said Thompson. Although, to be fair, the chain of command was far more strongly influenced by relations of respect between the troops: Each small group would appoint a leader every year. Each group of leaders would appoint their next in command and so on to the top. At the staff HQ level, elected members would stay in their positions until the confederate parliament decided otherwise. Naturally, elections were suspended in war-time except in the case where a person in command fell in action and so did his designated successor. In that case, the people in the same 'leader' group as the deceased -e.g. all of the same rank- would vote quickly on a successor. The problem was that despite the fact that the confederate militia fought with a lot of passion, generated by the respect and recognitions towards the elected commanders, there were always those who had voted against the current commander. As such, maintaining harsh discipline within the army had proven to be very difficult.

'You reckon we will be crushed once out in Zone 3 and away from our familiar Zone 2?' asked Miles.

'Probably not. We may have trouble with military discipline, but the gangs that lurk outside are far worse.' reasoned O'Brien.

'Either way, if we stall, the communists will come to our rescue. They will not be happy, but they will come to our rescue.' said Johnson with a care-free air.

'I concur.' said Miles. 'The communists have precious few allies in the region, or the country even. By which I mean we are their only real ally nation-wide. They would be rather annoyed to lose us as allies.' he reasoned.

'Not quite so.' said O'Brien darkly and everyone looked at him startled.

'No more conspiracy theories, will it be darling?' asked Mrs. Wilkins.

'Not this time. Hear me out and then make your own judgement based on what logic tells you.' said O'Brien. A pause ensued while O'Brien was looking around. Noticing that everybody was listening carefully he continued: 'The reason the communists traditionally only controlled about 10% of London is not just that London is richer and traditionally more right-wing, but also that many of their supporters have been convinced by our anarcho-syndicalist system. They might have a secret grudge against us...' he concluded as the countenances of everyone present were filled with disbelief.

'The communists are our allies.' said Johnson.

'That's even worse. It means they can not use their position of military strength to engulf and assimilate us. They have no casus belli against us.' reasoned O'Brien.

'Therefore?' asked Thompson.

'Therefore, I don't know. Therefore, they might not rescue us if we completely screw this campaign. Therefore maybe they seek to subvert us instead of using force.' said O'Brien even more darkly.

'Just relax...' said Thompson dismissively. 'Even if it happens, what can we do about it? We can't start hammering the communists on our news while they are our formal allies and very, very real hosts.' he continued.

'No need to do anything. I'm not saying living under communism will be particularly bad. We'll get used to the shortages and being watched eventually... I'm just saying we should be mentally ready for the change if happens.' said O'Brien overtly bitterly.

'Heh. Of course not. Being watched all the time and having to deal with constant shortages is not so bad, no, heavens no!' said Thompson mockingly. 'What about the fact that everything seems to work there? What about the discipline and order that permeates their society? What about their impressive public infrastructure, social care and comparatively high living standards?' he argued.

'Is it worth giving up privacy and standing in queues? In fact, forget the queues. It is worth giving away privacy and living in constant fear of arrest?' asked O'Brien.

'Gentlemen, gentlemen!' interjected Miles before things got nasty again. 'We could sit here and argue for hours whether the communists respect privacy and/or arrest people indiscriminately and for political reasons. I'm the first one to declare I don't know, and I've been there before. The impression I'm getting is that they are trying not to repeat that mistake again, but in reality...' Miles shrugged his shoulders. '...god knows.' he finished dramatically and then continued before people could interrupt him: 'The more important question is whether we believe it is right to give away rights in exchange for living standards, or for that matter security or anything else.' he said trying to deflect the conversation towards a more generic topic.

'Liberties are supreme!' declared O'Brien.

'Yes, but we limit them as part of being members of a society!' contradicted Thompson and the conversation went down that road. Miles was filled with recollections about similar thoughts he'd had during his journeys. He had concluded that in the end it was a matter of preference so he was confident and content to let the two battle it out on a far less political issue, hopefully with far less emotional tension. Indeed, at the end, after what seemed to be an endless conversation the two men decided to agree that they just prefer the rights/duties balance to lie at a different points and finally the van went silent. For quite a long time nobody said anything, enjoying the relative silence, punctured as it was by the ramblings of the slowly moving van (due to rough roads). At the terminal screens, more images of war-torn Zone 3 were passing by. Miles noticed that as the van was moving deeper into Zone 3 the buildings slowly got more modern, but also more dilapidated. That made sense. The farther away from the centre, the more recent the construction effort was, but also the farther they were away from Zones 1 and 2. Despite the poverty in Zone 3, truth is that some residents of Zone 3 maintained business relations with Zone 2 and created a small economy around the borders. It was as Miles had said in his reportage: the people living farther from the centre largely survived on the left-overs of the people who lived closer to it. On top of this, the intensity of recent combat operations seemed to increase as well with travelling farther away from the centre. That also made sense since more poverty led to more unrest and more militancy. That's why the density of charred buildings increased as time went by. As for the non-charred buildings, they looked as if they were completely abandoned to begin with, windows broken and replaced by sheets of metal, doors forced open, paint worn off, all forced upon them long before they were filled with bullet-holes. The very small number of ill-looking, poorly dressed people on the clearly unmaintained streets, the increased mounds of debris here and there and the destroyed little signs of civilisation -rubbish bins, benches, lamp posts etc.- combined with the ghostly impression of the apparently empty husks of the various buildings to create a terrifying impression on Miles; like what he had seen upon entry in Zone 3, only twice as intense this time.

At the end, the van reached the next supply point. The procedure was more or less the same. The team were greeted by the guard, toured the camp -nothing significantly different compared to the previous camp except the different layout- and headed towards the supply point to regroup and prepare for the noon news. Yet it was not meant to be. While heading for the canteen at the supply point, Thompson was called on his phone. It was Yusef, and he was asking them to return to the van immediately. He said that he had important news from the army's press-office and that he was going to call everyone else as well. Thompson replied that he was on his way and that Miles was with him at the moment, so he didn't have to call him as well and then he hung up. Next, he proceeded to explain the situation to his companion and the two of them made haste towards the van.

The team didn't take too long to assemble and once everybody was seated and listening, the van was already on the move and Yusef began explaining what he had just learned:

'I have just been contacted by the army's press-office. They marked a tall building on the map for us and instructed us to go there at once if we wish to see something interesting. They recommended we take a high magnification camera as well and said that their guards will be at the building to open the door for us.' he said without pausing so much as for a breath.

'Anything else?' asked Thompson.

'They also said we wouldn't be the only journalists in that building so we should hurry.' explained Yusef.

'Ow...' said Thompson. 'Well, we are making our way there as quickly as possible. Right. Did they say what we were meant to see?' asked Thompson.

'No.' replied Yusef. 'They said it is secret until it occurs, but also that when it does it will be obvious.' he concluded.

Everybody understood and the van went on. Shortly before 11:00 the van pulled up by a tall tower-block. As before, the journalists had to make their way to the 15th floor on the stairs, prompting yet another torrent of rather strong oaths from O'Brien. Right behind them was the van of the Royal Herald from Enfield, covering the news for the Royal Zone. The journalistic teams rushed to the roof of the tower block and without so much as a pause for a breather they set off to set-up their stalls. On other tall tower-block rooftops in the area other journalists were also setting up stall, but Thompson and his team neither knew of this, nor did they particularly mind. The rooftop was full of red-faced journalists and their equally red-faced teams as the clock struck 10:55. Thompson instructed Yusef and his team to be ready because he sensed that a breaking news bulletin was brewing. Yusef agreed and informed Aisha immediately. The two of them then set-up the connection on stand-by, summoned David Ramsay to the studio and had him prepared for TV. The clock indicated 10:59 and everything was ready. David Ramsay, Aisha, Yusef and above everyone else Thompson were all at the height of tension, not to mention O'Brien who was tirelessly scanning the horizon for any activity and Johnson who had a hunch that whatever was going to happen was going to somehow be connected to the airport and therefore was trying to home on to a suitable surface at the airport just 2km south-west of their location.

The clock struck 11:00 and the tension was so thick it could have been cut with a knife. Nothing happened. Journalists, cameramen and sound experts were nervously sweeping their surroundings looking for anything that might be noteworthy. Judging by the similar levels of tension amidst the journalists from the Royal Zone, they also did not know why they had been summoned by the army press office. 11:01. Still nothing 11:02. Nothing. 11:03. A scream pierced the air as the cameraman for the Royal Herald pointed his finger towards the airport and said: 'Look! Look!'. Everybody on that rooftop immediately turned their heads and eyes towards exactly the indicated point and saw what was happening. Thompson shouted in his microphone: 'Breaking news!' and the connection went live. Miles had his terminal unrolled and watching the Kropotkin channel. As expected, the theme tune and movie for the newscast replaced the normal TV broadcast. Thompson who had just been linked straight to David Ramsay muttered a few phrases before O'Brien indicated that transmission was about to begin. Seconds later the terminal screen featured David Ramsay and Thompson in a vertical split-screen. Ramsay started off:

'We are sorry to interrupt the normal flow of the schedule. We have just received news that the communist army is now marching upon Gatwick airport. Simon Thompson is there, in the area, right now with a view of the situation. Simon?' said Ramsay and passed the ball to Thompson.

'Indeed David, just seconds ago we saw the first signs of the communist army marching upon Gatwick airport. You can see behind me...' said Thompson pointing towards the airport as O'Brien zoomed towards the grassy 'buffer-zone' between the airport and surrounding residential areas. '...large numbers of battle droids, supported by tanks and followed by ground forces are now in the buffer-zone between the runways and the terminal buildings of Gatwick and surrounding regions, completely enclosing London's main airport into a massive pocket. I'll tell you David, we were invited to watch the operation from here by the army's press-office, however we don't know any details yet. We don't know how the communists intend to deal with the situation, the staff, the airport guests or indeed the airport itself. All we can tell now is that the army is advancing towards Gatwick along the entire perimeter of the airfield.' concluded Thompson.

'Do we have any sounds from the airport Simon?' asked Ramsay. A slight pause ensued as Thompson was listening to Johnson talking to him through the ear piece.

'Our sound expert here tells me that we have nothing of significance. He has managed to lock-in at a sentry tower around the airport, but is getting no sign of any gunshots or anything similar.' said Thompson.

'Any violent activity in the region, such as explosions?' asked Ramsay.

'No, so far nothing of the sort. In fact, it's been so quiet it might as well have been a military parade.' said Thompson.

'And what are we seeing now Simon? Is it what I think it is?' asked Ramsay.

Thompson looked at the terminal screen Mrs. Wilkins had placed open in front of him on a little tripod, as part of her duties. He looked at it and saw what Miles was seeing. O'Brien had diligently zoomed into a couple of guard towers at the near side of the airport, which he predicted would be hit first by the armies of battle droids. As a result, he was ready to film the images of the guards manning the airport's defences waving the white flag of surrender that appeared soon after. Ramsay had clocked that fact as Thompson was still talking.

'It seems that the garrison of the airport is surrendering, presumably intimidated by...' answered Thompson but that's as far as he got before Johnson cut his microphone to replace it with what his long distance microphone was transmitting at the moment. It was a robotic voice, coming -presumably- from one of the battle droids:

'Drop your weapons, open the gate and come out with your hands up and you will be treated kindly.' it said.

The white flag stopped waving and was instead latched at the window of the sentry tower that had summoned its services, in indication that the plea for mercy still stood. The guards dropped their weapons on the grass in front of the tower and because the said tower was at the near side of the airport, O'Brien could capture everything on his camera and Johnson could hear everything with his long distance microphone loud and clear.

'The airport guard is now surrendering and opening the gates to the advancing armies of battle droids.' said Ramsay as the heavy gates of the airport began to open.

At this point, it must be said that Gatwick airport was defended by a concrete wall against incursions from Zone 3. An elevated highway left it and led all the way to central London crossing safely above Zone 3 and the democratic sectors of Zone 2. Launching a ground-based invasion from the highway -which had no on-ramps all the way to central- was as difficult as just trying to jump over the wall instead. That explains why the communists did not bother attacking the highway. At any rate, disturbing the highway prematurely would cut-off passenger traffic between the airport and the city, which was not the objective of the communist army.

Back to the present, the heavy gate was now wide open and the armies of battle droids and tanks started pouring in, in a very orderly formation. They were not fighting their way to the airport, they were marching their way in. On the elevated highway, helicopters of the communist air-force landed and blocked all traffic. Ramsay commentated all of that with the help of Thompson who added a few words here and there when he thought it necessary. About 5-10' passed as the troops were now marching upon the airport from every single gate. Apparently there had been no resistance anywhere as the guards determined that it was better to surrender than face certain death in the face of far, far superior forces. The entire communist steamroller was concentrated on the airport as operations in all other battle-front sectors had been suspended. Finally, the troops entered the terminal building and attempted to calm down the crowds of tourists and businesspeople that had been trapped there. The glass shell of the shiny, new terminal buildings at Gatwick airport offered a clear view of what what going on inside. Terrified travellers and non-armed staff lay on the floor between the rows of padded metal seats with their arms spread while armed personnel was being restrained and taken away. Younger -mostly female- travellers were weeping, trying to suppress their natural reaction of screaming in horror. They had all heard stories of the communists' ruthlessness after all. O'Brien snatched the opportunity to film it all and Johnson hurried to lock-on to the glass exterior of the building. Johnson's microphone indicated that the heralds the army had brought were ordering everybody to lie down and wait to be searched for weapons.

As the time-consuming operation of searching travellers and staff for weapons continued a couple of other things happened. First of all, the incoming aeroplanes that were beginning to queue up on the inbound taxing strip were now being dispatched by the army. Passport control and luggage control was under the control of the army and incoming passengers were channelled through a secure corridor to a different exit than usual where they embarked in light, armoured cars that shuttled them back to the communist sector from where they could make use of the underground railway, taxis or other means of public transportation and connect to other sectors. Secondly, troops had made their way to the control tower and announced that the entire staff had a choice of either working for the new, communist management and bringing their families to live in the communist sector, or staying on until someone could replace them and then leave towards their families.

Once those operations were completed, the inbound passenger traffic had been restored and the control tower was under the control of the army, a press-release from the staff HQ of the communist army was broadcast making these facts public. The announcer also declared that it was the ambition of the army to security-screen all outbound passengers, board them into the grounded aeroplanes and hopefully resume a partial outbound service in the near future. He also thanked the air-traffic controllers who out of a sense of duty towards those on-board the various aeroplanes heading towards Gatwick decided to keep working until interrupted, which the army did not do for more than a few minutes and only one person at a time. Funnily enough, that was not mere propaganda. Air-traffic controllers knew that if they did not direct the aeroplanes safely to the runways they'd be forced to land elsewhere and potentially crash with dire consequences. As such many of them did stay on at their posts and kept working diligently exactly out of a sense of duty.

Clearly, events had been unfolding in very quick succession that day and before Miles could notice, the clock struck noon. Ramsay noted the fact and informed his viewers that it was time for the 12:00 news. He also imparted with his viewers the fact that if there were any more critical updates to the situation at Gatwick, there would be either more breaking news bulletins or dedicated sections in the 6 o'clock news and the 11 o'clock news summary. Finally, he iterated through the other stories of that day thus far. The news stories revolved mainly around the fact that the International Red Cross had sent a small group of medics in the communist-controlled areas where they were helping the army provide medical assistance to those affected by the war and that brigades of construction specialists from the communist heartland had begun rebuilding Zone 3 according to new standards.

Team Thompson listened to the noon news all the way until the sports section and then packed-up and set off towards the van again at a relaxed pace. The Royal Herald's team was already gone. Once in the van the team started discussing ardently about the situation. Thompson speculated that there would be nothing important enough to warrant another breaking news bulletin that day but that at the 6 o'clock news they'd probably find out more details, such as whether the communists managed to fully restore air traffic, what happened to stranded travellers and staff etc. O'Brien did not miss the chance to speculate that shortly the communists would be in control of the elevated highway as well and that their economic collapse was inevitable since their mines, i.e. what was producing their only significant export were not going to be able to sustain such increased population with their profits. Johnson argued that given the meticulous planning of operations that far, the communists surely had a plan for the economic development of the new regions. Miles agreed with Thompson and added that he was expecting that whatever plan they had would involve international companies, probably in the service sector. Mrs. Wilkins argued that given their history it might also involve science and industry. After all the communists always stressed the importance of pushing research and having a home-grown industrial base. Once that conversation was over, Thompson started talking business again. His advice was that they should put together a reportage from all the data they had gathered that day. Miles received the additional task of writing an article for the next day's web page. All the talk about political speculation, how the communists would handle the airport etc. etc. made time fly as the van returned to the new supply point that the military had indicated on the map that was available at the small terminal.

Back at the supply point, the team lunched together. Even Yusef was with them, as opposed to eating in front of his terminal in the van. Of course, he was available on the phone for his coordinator to contact in case anything important happened. Amidst all the friendly banter and cordial exchange of impressions about Zone 3 thus far, Miles made a rather striking comment:

'I just realised something strange. There seem to be no elderly people around here. Why is that? Where are they?' he asked. The others looked at him unsure of how to respond exactly. Finally, Thompson answered:

'Kid, I don't know how to say this... There are no elderly people around here. There is no healthcare system here. Life expectancy is in the 50's.'

'My god...' said Miles.

Medical science was very advanced in terms of technology, however the persistent problem was bringing that technology to the patients. Since about the 80's-90's medical technology had been advancing at a very fast pace; so fast that the economics behind public healthcare were falling behind. Vast and extremely complicated scanners like the real-time MRIs they only had in the most advanced hospitals in the world and personalised robotic medical assistants were good examples of this problem. For that reason medical research, traditionally split between preventive and palliative, was now being binned into 5 categories:

- Preventive medicine: Attempting to prevent the spread of disease -as traditionally-.
- Palliative medicine: Attempting to cure disease -again as traditionally-.
- Functional medicine: Attempting to prolong the useful lifespan of the patient -that during which the patient may carry out work-related tasks-.
- Longeve medicine: Attempting to prolong the lifespan of the patient regardless of whether that lifespan is useful or not.
- Econometric medicine: Attempting to reduce the cost of medical care.

There were very good examples to show how medical science advanced on all these fronts. The greatest achievement of preventive medicine was the universal vaccine. A sample of the subject's stem cells would be taken and with that blueprint, memory B and and memory T cells would be generated by manipulating the differentiation process of the stem cells. Those lymphocytes would then be exposed to a vast variety of diseases, acquire immunity against all of them, and be injected into the subject to grant him immunity against a very extensive mixture of ailments. Sometimes, with slight alterations to the DNA of those bred cells, their functions could be augmented and enhanced. Perhaps sharing the pedestal of fame with the universal vaccine, was the genetic pre-screening of all infants that were born in a hospital as mentioned before.

Palliative medicine's greatest achievement, on the other hand, was the invention of nanobotic injections. Nanobots would be engineered to disguise themselves as B or T cells of the body and perform functions similar to those of B and T cells, only much more efficiently. For example the problem that the natural human immune system had in dealing with the HIV due to the virus' ability to survive the attack of the antibodies was solved when nanobotic drugs were invented that would lock-on to the virus and physically tear it apart, much like the Pyruvate Dehydrogenase Enzyme Complex tears apart Pyruvate to create Acetyl CoA. The RNA of the virus would also be bound by the drug and disintegrated. A mechanism akin to that of the mitochondria -In principle.

It had its own ATP-synthase and pump molecules and all the associated paraphernalia.- would generate the necessary energy to activate the drug. With just the correct dose of the anti-HIV drug the virus could be kept under control if not killed completely with extremely small chances of disease recurrence. When the drugs were no longer needed, a special substance would be injected into the patient's blood-stream and cause the nanobots to disintegrate in very fine parts, fine enough to be eliminated through the kidneys, along with the substance that caused the disintegration in the first place. Unfortunately such drugs worked well for blood-borne diseases, but if the danger was elsewhere, such as in the neural cells -poliomyelitis-style diseases-, the situation was slightly more difficult. For that reason, when damage was unavoidable, palliative medicine brought in the other big weapons it could wield: stem cells and genetic therapy viruses. Just like in the 90's when the first genetic therapy treatments were created, the so called 'positive viruses' would infiltrate their target cells and either bestow upon them some sort of immunity, or fight a negative virus, or even provide immunity against some virus (that last one was in the sphere of preventive medicine). Thus, when treating a disease that worked like poliomyelitis the first stage of the treatment would be to grant immunity to all nearby cells in the affected region by the insertion of positive viruses. Next, the virus was left to run its course, impeded by the various positive viruses in action in the region as well as the interferons of the natural immune response. Finally, stem cells would be called into action to repair the damage, even if it was in neural tissue. Finally, limb-regeneration techniques with the aid of stem cells and neural stimulation techniques to restore damaged limb functionality in victims of paralysis also fell within the realms of palliative medicine.

Functional medicine was preoccupied with topics like slowing down the wastage of blood vessels, stopping neurodegenerative diseases and generally stopping the ageing of the body and brain. Nevertheless: the clean-up of blood vessels from deposited fat -particularly in the coronary arteries- and various techniques used to prevent the brain from degenerating itself, which might be seen as fitting under the jurisdiction of functional medicine belonged to the realm of preventive medicine. Most of the solutions in the domain of functional medicine were linked in one way or another to stem cells. After all, what better way to 'keep the body young' than actually keeping the body literally young by introducing fresh cells into it? Cells engineered to behave 'young', as well as being given special abilities. For example myelin cells were engineered to resist against inflammation, which seemed to prevent the demyelination, so characteristic of multiple sclerosis. By balancing the imbalances in the biochemistry of the brain and slowly replacing the 'old cells' with 'new and improved cells' little by little, medics managed to greatly extend the useful lifespan of the human brain. Nevertheless, by a certain age the natural degeneration accelerated so much that even the improved cells could no longer be injected at a sufficient rate. Similarly for degenerated blood vessels, once damage occurred stem cells would regenerate the artery or vein with full levels of elastin -as opposed to the elastin-poor old cells-. Experimental therapies were attempting to coat the interior of all blood vessels from the aorta to the tiniest of capillaries with a temporary 'fixating material'. Due to the natural narrowness of capillaries, vasodilating agents made sure that they stood vastly dilated for the entire duration of the treatment. As such, red blood cells could still slip through the capillaries despite the layer of 'fixating material'. The purpose of this layer was first to provide a base for the stem cells that would in turn create the new artery lining and second to slowly consume the old lining. The fixating material was, of course, able to carry out diffusion just like the walls of the capillaries; it was -after all- made out of a very specialised nanomaterial. Other incredible properties it had were that it could only form a molecular mono-layer of which one surface would latch on to the old artery lining and the other would simulate the environment felt by the basal side of arterial lining cells as well as possible. These properties allowed the material to be injected into the patient in a fairly large quantity where it would automatically form a uniform mono-layer over the entire -or almost the entire- inner surface of the blood system, suitable for the stem cells to settle upon. At the same time the fixture would start consuming and dissolving the old arterial lining. For that reason the stem cell injection had to follow immediately after the fixture material was given enough time to settle (about 2' to circulate through the entire body a few times). The following 12-24 hours the patient would suffer from hypo-tension, increased breathing rate because of the temporarily reduced efficiency of diffusion between lungs and blood and between blood and organs and generally had to be kept under very close monitoring. Following that re-adjustment phase the whole internal lining of the patient's blood-system would be completely renewed.

  The so-called longeve medicine would mainly revolve around life-support systems that kept people at the very brink of death alive, whether in a coma or fully operational. Despite the fact that it had its uses, mainly in applications where people had to be kept alive at any cost until they reached a point where other types of medicine could work their magic, it was probably the least funded branch. Naturally, the most obvious application where longeve medicine was needed was in emergency care, accident response units etc.

  The final category of econometric medicine was pushed extremely hard since it addressed the fundamental problem of modern publicly funded medicine, namely the gap between the available and the affordable. Its most illustrious achievements were a very wide range of personal, portable, implantable or semi-implantable bio-sensors with the capability of either administering treatment (in the form of chemical or electrical stimuli for example) or advising the patient to administer treatment to himself. Their natural counterparts were a range of consumer-grade medi-kits that allowed patients to actually administer treatment to themselves, a very good example of which were the various 'easy injection' kits that helped patients administer fairly pain-free injections to themselves.

All these incredible advances in medicine resulted in significantly longer lifespans all around those parts of the world that could afford them, as compared to a few decades earlier. As such, relatively wealthy places enjoyed very long life-spans. Zone 1 of London and the other -smaller- financial paradise, Hong Kong, enjoyed lifespans in the region of about 100-102. The EU, Japan and a few other places like Russia, Australia and New Zeeland and -despite rather incomplete statistical data- the communist sectors of the UK hung about in the 90's, the US with their entirely private medical insurance system were trailing behind in the 80's along with China and a few others who simply could not afford a much more lavish medical system for everybody. India, the Middle East, North and South Africa and Latin America were hanging in the 70's and as traditionally, the middle part of Africa along with Afghanistan and a few other hell-holes ranged anywhere between the 60's and the mid-30's. An interesting effect of this situation was that in the advanced world most of the population would be considered 'old' back a few decades. In many countries more than ½ the population was over the age of 45. The age of retirement also shifted as a result of the climbing lifespans, resulting to retirement ages in the region of 82 years, although for the sake of completeness it must be noted that this change was precipitated also to offset the 'higher education effect', namely that people had to spend a longer time in education before getting into the labour market. The advancement of technology meant that in those times a PhD could only be started after a very long undergraduate degree consisting of 5 years of general learning and 4 years of 'specialisation'.

At any rate, Zone 3 seemed to be in the same tier as the god-forsaken countries of Africa, when judging by the life expectancy indicator. The constant state of war did not exactly help, and nor did the extreme poverty that was visible wherever the journalists went. Miles was extensively briefed on the dire situation of healthcare in Zone 3 by his better informed colleagues. Nodding in understanding he remained silent contemplating the sheer dreadfulness of knowing that your lifespan is going to be 4-5 decades shorter than that of people living often within visual range of your own dwelling. With those sad contemplations, a little more of the already meagre portion of naiveté left inside him, died. An uncomfortable silence ensued and Thompson broke it with his suggestion that the two of them take a tour of the refugee camp and assess the situation after the occurrences at Gatwick airport. Specifically, he was interested in seeing whether the infrastructure at the camp could deal with the increased numbers of refugees. After all, everybody was expecting that after annexing populated regions containing more and more and more people, the communist sector would eventually feel the weight of having to maintain and supply them.

Thus, Thompson and Miles set out to explore the camp. Apart from the fact that the tents they were passing by seemed to be more packed and that the queues for food and water were significantly longer, there didn't seem to be any signs of the situation exiting from under control. The army seemed to maintain the sort of clockwork order that the journalists had witnessed first hand at their first supply point in Salford. Having assessed the accommodation, food and water supply situation the two journalists consulted their map and prepared to head towards the encampment's hospital when Thompson was summoned by Yusef again. Yusef was asking him to consult the Kropotkin channel on the news as there was a fresh breaking news bulletin to be broadcast within seconds. Thompson immediately unrolled his terminal and quickly tuned into the channel operated by the agency he was working for, just in time to see the end of the theme clip. As David Ramsay had finished what was already an incredibly long shift, his fellow newscaster Eberhard Schultz appeared on the terminal screen instead. He announced the contents of the breaking news bulletin with his usual grave tone, accompanied by an equally solemn and grave countenance, itself accentuated in sheer gravity by Schultz's silver hair and small round skeleton-free glasses. These characteristics combined with his old age to create a picture of unparalleled amiability. His words to the communards were:

'Good evening viewers. We apologise for this most regrettable interruption to the normal flow of the program, but we have just received word from our anchor in Bromley that following uninterrupted rioting in the democratic sector of Bromley, communist rebels have overpowered local authorities and stormed the council building. Minutes ago they have forced the council to sign its own resignation and installed their own rebel government in replacement of the old one. Simultaneously, the local TV station has also been overtaken by rebels and is currently transmitting the message that Bromley is now a communist state seeking annexation to the communist sector of London. So far we have had no reaction from the communist government in Epsom yet, however the general belief is...' said the venerable old man and then sombrely grabbed his earpiece and listened to it closely for a few seconds before resuming:

'I have just been informed that the press-office of the communist government has just released a press statement publicising the acceptance of the annexation of Bromley and informing the public that a battalion of combined battle droids and infantry had just crossed the border to 'safeguard peace and order' in the tumultuous sector. We have no information on whether the rebellion in Bromley was committed with the support of the main communist sector, however what we do know is that within minutes of the publication of the resignation of the council of Bromley and the installation of a communist government the border battalion that has just been mobilised crossed the borders. We are now joined by our news anchor for Bromley, Tanya Fiodorova who will describe the situation on the ground in more detail.' he said as the screen split and Tanya's beautiful figure appeared on the screen.

She was a woman of rather short stature, but with a countenance of iron will that one would expect to find in only the most legendary of women. In fact, she looked like she came straight out of a 1920's Soviet propaganda poster (an 'Agitka'). Long, dark hair woven together artistically in an intricate braid all around the top of her head, strong chin, pointy nose and a large pair of rectangular, skeleton-free spectacles described her face and head. She was dressed in an elegant yet simple dark green dress with a large brooch made of a silver skeleton with intricate patterns made out of very fine strips of silver and a large amber stone in the centre, which appeared to be containing an unfortunate ant inside it. She spoke just like on the radio broadcast before: curtly and confidently although now that her voice was combined with her appearance on the terminal screen miles could feel the full force of her character emanating through the screen. Tanya wasted no time in describing the situation:

'Well, Mr. Schultz, the situation here is actually not as chaotic as one might think. After a night spent protesting, the communists decided to storm the HQ building of the Bromley council and take it by force and the populace have reacted rather apathetically to the development. We all know that in the democratic sectors only a tiny percentage of the population ever votes and that in most sectors, such as Bromley, the communist party has been outlawed. It seems that the fair numbers of communist protesters are enough to overturn the government here because any detractors to the communist cause either do not possess the necessary numbers to stop them, or simply don't take enough of an interest in politics to mobilise themselves.

Now as you can see behind me, communist rebels have taken over the council building and have hung their hammer, sickle & molecule flag as well as a variety of banners out of various windows of the building. Here we have one saying 'Victory belongs to the proletarians and the intellectuals' and another one declaring that 'British socialism must operate united – union with the communist sector here and now'. The local channel keeps broadcasting news about the situation at the borders where the communist government of Epsom has sent a battalion of battle droids and infantry, and at the heartland where protesters revel in victory.

The mathematically precise timing of the revolution and the border crossing of reinforcements from the main communist sector as well as the level of organisation of the protesters seems to indicate that the communists are very likely to have been supported in their endeavours to seize power by the secret services of the communist sector. Whether that is true or false and whether this turns out to be a blessing or a curse for Bromley, it remains to be seen. What is certain at the moment is that the people I can see on the streets right this instant, and there are a fair number of them, seem to rejoice in the knowledge that now they are citizens of the communist sector of London.' she concluded sternly.

'Thank you very much Tanya.' said Schultz and the entirety of the screen returned to him alone. 'Before we leave you, let's just review a few basic statistics about the communist sector and Bromley. Bromley contains about 1,2 million people, is one of the poorest sectors in Zone 2 and is economically heavily dependent on labourers who toil in Zone 1 and bring money back to Zone 2 to move the local economy. Geographically it extends in a rough quadrangle between Croydon, Sidcup, Sevenoaks and Redhill and shares an extensive border with the core communist sector between Croydon and Redhill. This now means that the communist sector of London currently encompasses areas that contain 4,4 million people, of whom 2,2 million live in the core sector, 1 million people live in the newly acquired Zone 3 sectors and 1,2 million in Bromley, which although not yet under the military control of the communists is widely expected to be fully protected by a battle droid and infantry garrison within hours. We shall keep you up to date with events as they unfold either through more breaking news bulletins or through our regular news broadcasts, the next one being aired at 6 o'clock later today. Good evening.' said Schultz and the normal flow of the TV program resumed.

Thompson and Miles looked at one another. Thompson spoke first:

'You know what this means, right?' he said.

'Oh yes. It means more pressure on the communists. They now have to take care of as many people as they originally housed in their core sector. Their invasion must be nearing to its end.' said Miles.

'Yes... and that. But I was thinking more of O'Brien boasting about his evidently correct speculation that the communists are maintaining an extended subversive network in London. We'll never hear the end of it!' Thompson exclaimed in reply and raised his hands distressingly towards the sky. Miles chuckled.

'Oh well, what does it matter?' he said. 'What matters now most is that the war is probably reaching an end and we'll be able to return home soon. I give it another day or so and we'll be home.' argued Miles.

'You have a point there kid.' said Thompson and Miles suppressed another urge to chuckle. 'More to the point, lets start working on a short reportage for the 6 o'clock news. This time you have 2 hours to produce it and I recommend you concentrate mainly on the capture of Gatwick airport, but also devote a small portion to the situation within this camp.' Thompson continued veering the conversation to business again. Miles nodded in sign of understanding and the journalists returned to the supply point where Miles started thinking about his reportage, Johnson and Mrs. Wilkins were filling their daily diaries and Thompson engaged all his mental constitution in the task of ignoring O'Brien's gloating jests. Shortly, however even those two decided it was time to get back to work, so Thompson engrossed himself into the activity of writing some articles and O'Brien went back to filing the footage he'd collected by placing each video snippet into meticulously categorised folders.

In this busy atmosphere time went on until it was time for the 6 o'clock news. Miles' reportage was long since ready and submitted and it was to be broadcast that evening as a piece of newsreel, announced by Schultz. The team watched closely every single story related to the war without forgetting to cheer and applaud when Miles' newsreel was broadcast. The first important news story was the fact that at Gatwick airport the communists consolidated their control as well as seizing all aeroplanes belonging to the British 'South East English Airlines' (SEE airlines) company, repainted them with their own banners and started their own airline under the name 'Red Star Air'. The fact that struck Miles as strange was that the communists had sent a small contingent of people abroad to be trained as civil air-force pilots about 6 months ago -as Schultz was saying-, which was back when they had no such thing as a civilian air-force. This reinforced Miles' suspicion that the communists must have known that a crisis was aloof and had planned the seizure of Gatwick and other airports around the country, all well in advance. At any rate this meant they had the manpower to run a small airline. Military engineers were more than capable of servicing the aircraft. On the other side of the runway, a contingent of air-force personnel had also been sent abroad to be trained as air-traffic controllers so that communist forces could resume the operations of their various freshly-acquired airports without delay. This amount of planning also showed the attention to detail the army had committed to the operation since so long as one was in the advanced world, pilots and air-traffic controllers were not strictly necessary to run airports and aircraft. Within North America, Europe including the whole of Russia, China, Japan, South Korea and Australia & New Zeeland all major airports as well as the vast majority of minor airports were equipped with computers that could coordinate traffic within a 25km radius and automatically land and launch the aircraft. In mid-air, the on-board aircraft mainframes would monitor traffic in a 200km radius and cooperatively adjust the course of their respective aircraft, much like the ancient TCAS system, but instead of in a consultative role, now in a decision-making role. For those reasons, pilots were only needed under two circumstances: either the plane was in some sort of emergency that the automatic systems and even the AI could not cope with, or the aeroplane had to land at an airport that did not possess advanced enough computers (like most airports in Africa for example) or on rough ground. In that case, the AI worked cooperatively with the pilot to land and take off the machine. On the traffic controller side, they were needed very heavily in badly equipped airports, but in well equipped ones with all the modern electronics their tasks mainly revolved around monitoring the system and intervening in an emergency. For example the recent military activity around Gatwick was something the control-tower AI was simply not designed to cope with, putting Gatwick's air-traffic controllers under unprecedented strain. At any rate, the military decided to take no chances and be fully staffed to run the airport even in an emergency (Did this foreshadow more military activity? Wondered Miles.).

  The story continued though as the recent decision to found 'Red Star Airlines' integrated well in a wider plan of the communist economy. The government in Epsom realised very quickly that isolating the local economy could not lead to prosperity. It was absolutely imperative that the sector traded with the outside world in order to import everything that couldn't be manufactured, extracted or grown at home. For that reason there was a pressing need that the communists either exported something back or somehow got hold of foreign exchange. Miles had already discussed this problem and knew that the communists were operating lucrative mines to counter the problem. Now he was finding out that Epsom was also beginning to branch into the services sector. Apparently Epsom was already operating a large international bank that lent money to businesses abroad, they were planning to raise the bank's capital, had placed a bid for a major foreign transport company and finally they were also seeking to expand the communist sector's domestic internet and telecommunications business in the rest of the country, as well as abroad. Naturally, these were not all spur-of-the-moment moves precipitated by the military operations. The communists had been operating businesses on the free market for years (electricity and mining being the foremost examples), but their activities were mostly centred on Britain. It was only in the past few months that a drive for internationalisation of the communist foreign business machine seemed to become so dominant in the economic agenda of the Epsom government. Once again, this fact made Miles certain that the communists had spies in Zone 1, had seen the crisis coming months in advance and were doing their utmost to prepare for large-scale military operations and the incorporation of large areas of Britain into the communist sector.

Miles could easily see the benefits of operating a vast sovereign fund to compensate for an economy that is simply not geared towards competitiveness in trading, yet is at the same time too small to manage and get by without any trading activity whatsoever. The profits in foreign currencies flowing in from across the globe would be used instead to supply the communists with what they needed and keep their economy artificially supported on a home-grown industrial base that would otherwise stand no chance against international competition (mainly from cheap China). The main drawback of this approach was also very dire, however. By operating companies abroad the communists became prone to political pressure as governments could freeze vast amounts of assets at a terrible cost to the government and people of the sector. Epsom was trying to counter this problem by investing in a large variety of very essential businesses in a number of countries. Thompson, when asked about the subject at a later date, told Miles that the communists were operating power plants in Germany, Japan and Iceland and were engaged in joint ventures in China and Russia and that's all they had money and time to buy in the past decade or so that they have been in existence as a de facto sovereign entity. Thus, freezing communist assets was going to create large disruptions in the host country and was much more likely to be avoided, particularly in Iceland where most of the electricity was generated in communist-owned generators. These businesses were ran with an obvious eye for profit, as that's what powered communist imports, but also with great care for customer satisfaction as Epsom believed that if they ran their foreign operations responsibly towards their clients and society as a whole they would be gaining brownie points with local populations, who would later support them if their government decided to freeze their assets for political reasons.

Economics aside, the 6 o'clock news steamed on relentlessly to the next story forcing Miles to carry out some of his contemplations about the economic relations of the Epsom government with the outside world at a later stage. The next story Schultz was talking about was the resumption of military operations in Zone 3 after the suspension of aggressive activities whilst Gatwick airport was being overran. The communist army's 4th regiment had reached the outside of Crawley and had thus hit upon the edge of London whilst regiments 1, 2 and 3 were pushing towards the edge of Zone 3 as well, probably in a bid to consolidate the dominion of the communist sector all the way to the edge of London on the Crawley-South Guildford line before the day was out. Regiment 5 was sending forces to Bromley to consolidate the situation there and the remaining few regiments, whose numbers the communists were no disclosing were stationed inside the core communist sector on high alert (they were regiments 6, 7 and 8). At the same time, confederate troops were slowly pushing their own fronts against heavy resistance and had reached the Ascot-Bagshot-Fox corner line incurring some losses on the way. Finally, having concluded the war-related part of the newscast Eberhard Schultz made the following comment that Miles remembered for a very long time:

'Thus ladies and gentlemen, we are witnessing change on a large scale these days in the balance of power not only in London, but across the country. Over the last 2 days we have noticed very strong tectonic activity in the geopolitics of Britain one could say. Whatever the outcome one can be certain: whether you live in a commune in Staines, a modern apartment in Belgravia, or temporary shelter in Zone 3, you will be affected one way or another.'. Miles then realised more than ever that he was living in times of great upheaval. And he also loved the phrase 'tectonic activity in geopolitics'.

The rest of the day was spent, once again, working with just one interruption for a breaking news bulletin at around 22:00 announcing that the communists had reached the edge of London and that the eastern edge of the front kept advancing over the farmlands of the English countryside southwards towards Brighton. The communists refused to publicise the strength of the force that was heading south, but agreed to state that the rest of the army was now tasked with securing the outer London borders and clearing the newly acquired areas of any resistance. Miles thought that that was an interesting strategy and immediately realised -just like everybody else- that the communists now wished to gain control of Brighton harbour. Yet, he was too tired to contemplate any such mentally taxing subject with all due concentration. He thus bade the rest of his team good night and sleep well and headed for his allotted bunk, promising that they would have a chance to informally discuss Epsom's decision to keep pushing the invasion despite annexing vast territories that would be very hard to supply.

CHAPTER 15: ENDGAME.

Next morning Miles was woken up by a sun-ray that was making its way through the window of the tent and straight to his face. He languidly shuffled in his bunk and turned around so that his back would face the rising sun. However, the little hand-held mirror he had placed by his bedside reflected the sun rays back to his face. Disgruntled, he arose from bed and proceeded to dispense with his morning toilette routine. Following that he started browsing his terminal in an attempt to kill time since he was by then, fully awake.

A quick look at the news from around the world showed that beyond the national borders of the United Kingdom there still was a very conspicuous silence about the situation in London and the other cities, in so much as there were -naturally- broadcasts detailing the incidents at Gatwick airport and short newsreels with regard to the humanitarian situation, however governments did not seem to be in a particular rush to comment on the situation. In their defence the situation in the Middle East was of greater concern. In a move that astonished the entire world, the government of Israel declared the middle-eastern crisis over as Israel now controlled the entire territory claimed by the Palestinians, in the only way that a country can genuinely control territory. It could claim that a vast demographic majority of people in the affected region defined themselves as Israeli citizens. Apparently, the colonisation strategy that the government in Jerusalem had been pursuing for many, many decades did pay off in the end. The former Palestinian residents had been either exiled or killed in military attacks intended as retaliation against the few terrorists that somehow still managed to slip through the extremely tight defences of the 'already integrated regions'. Much like in the conflict between the government forces of Morocco and the Polisario front, Israel raised a succession of defensive walls that would separate the core and 'integrated' parts of the country with the 'not integrated' parts. Anybody crossing inwards had to submit to a fast-MRI scan that would reveal absolutely everything they carried and would -as a by-product- perform an MRI upon the person revealing their internal physiology. Automatic pattern-searching algorithms using associative memory cells would detect any 'non-physiological' object completely automatically and then generate a list of found items for the guards to see. A typical traveller might have a list that looks like this: Shirt, belt, watch, trousers, underwear, sock x 2, shoe x 2, terminal. Its only weak point was when it came to complicated objects like the watch. If would either fail to recognise the watch as a full entity and list it as a collection of anything up to a few thousand parts -for antiquated analogue watches- or if something was hidden inside the watch it would fail to recognise it as a separate object. The Israeli military figured out in the end that the best way to avoid risk and confusion was to ban watches from entering the country through those defensive outposts. At any rate, this line of defences advanced deeper and deeper into what used to be Palestinian territory each year as, by the means described above, the people who defined themselves as citizens of Israel became an overwhelming majority along the advancing 'front line'. Naturally, people who were born Palestinian were never given a chance to become full Israeli citizens in the sense that is implied under this context.

On a related note, headlines were being made by Israel's latest assault on Iran. Over the past 2-3 decades Israel had been assaulting Iran on a regular, nearly weekly basis with military jets and missiles provided to them free of charge as part of the US program that was intended to recycle rather than scrap obsolete armaments that once belonged to the US air-force. The armaments provided to Israel were still very competitive in comparison to what was considered state-of-the-art elsewhere in the world, and as a result Iran never stood a chance. Instead it was a large country covered in smouldering ruins. The great mosques of Isfahan, the graves of the Persian emperors and even the ruins of old Persepolis had all been ravaged in the regular bombings that bashed the country. The rest of the Arab world was no better as Israel took care to bomb Syria and Lebanon as well at regular intervals. All of this was the apotheosis of a miserable failure and refusal on all sides to reduce political tensions. All sides were so passionate about the truth in their beliefs that they were completely blind to the valid arguments of the other side, as well as to the failed arguments on their side of the table. The best example was the situation in Israel and Palestine. As time went on, the solution of forming a bi-cultural society where lineage did not define its citizens but merit did became so outlandish that nobody even considered it as a realistic possibility. The same principle could be applied to all conflicts in the middle east where unreasonable hatred seemed to fuel most of the crises. Most certainly the hostility boiling violently in the region was by no means explicable by the mere conflicts of interests in the region.

In other international news, a scientific expedition had been sent into North Korea to investigate how the flora and fauna had been affected in the decade following the country's complete nuclear annihilation, a terrible event that shocked the world back in 2041. They were going in a specially constructed vehicle where they could find safe shelter for long enough to perform essential tasks such as eating and drinking; tasks very difficult to perform while wearing a very thick rad-suit.

With those news, Miles got bored. There never seemed to be anything positive in the news anyway. At the bunk above his, Thompson was beginning to wake up himself. He jumped down from his bunk as quietly as he could, stretched himself properly and upon seeing Miles was already awake bade him a very drowsy sort of 'good morning' that Miles heard as a sort of 'gmaaahhh'.

'Sorry, what?' he asked.

'I said good morning.' said Thompson composing himself.

'Ow, hehe. Good morning to you too.' replied Miles cheerfully.

Thompson smiled and proceeded to the allocated chemical bathroom for the tent. Wonderfully elegant, its toilet contained genetically engineered micro-organisms and nanobots that would disaggregate human waste into basic atoms and molecules and create a mixture of useful elements. Both the nanobots and the microbes used sugar as a power supply and worked very quickly with the aid of enzymes. At the end, a featureless aqueous mixture of materials would be extracted and centrifuged, the various separate materials isolated and the process of recycling completed. Naturally, the bathrooms did not only contain toilets but also running water -from a tank above- and a little mirror for shaving.

Having made use of all these facilities Thompson returned to the tent where the rest of the team was sleeping, collected the others and together they all went to receive their daily briefing. Interestingly enough, the officer in charge imparted with the gathered journalists and crews that the daily briefing would this time include a few extra bits of information as the combat operations were going to be occurring in the open field. Many an eyebrow were raised at that announcement as every single man (and lady) in that room had exactly the same thought: 'Yes, the operations will continue southwards. Must not forget to report that.'. Thompson looked briefly at Miles, who nodded and both men knew they were thinking the same. The officer went on to explain that there would be another supply point in Crawley, at the southern edge of London. If they wished to see any of the action, they were allowed to travel on the old motorways and whatever A-roads were still open and maintained, but were sternly warned to keep permanent track of their exact location on the map in order to avoid entering prohibited areas. Finally, they were told that veering away from the roads was at their own risk, as the army could not guarantee there would be no mines laying around. Finally, the uniformed officer showed them the exact map with the colour-coded zones, a significantly larger map than usual that included mostly farmed fields and forests. Upon glancing at the geographical map it became apparent that while everybody was sleeping the communist army had made significant advances to the South. The agrarian towns of Burgess and Hassocks had been captured although journalists were not allowed South of Burgess. As for where the 'steamroller' was, nobody had any idea, and presumably that's exactly how the communists intended to keep it. The officer went through all the other maps -various holographic versions etc.- making sure that he wouldn't mention any strategically important details, saluted at the conclusion of his speech and dismissed the journalists, himself departing towards his own office.

The Thompson team left towards their van and shortly they were all seated in a circle, as usual. Thompson declared his intention to visit and create a reportage about the situation in the villages of Britain. The news was greeted with a great deal of excitement as the majority, if not all, of the people on the team had not been to the countryside for at least a decade. That could easily be explained by the fact that there was pretty much nothing of particular worth to see in the British countryside since the decline of tourism, itself precipitated by the retreat of state power, and the transformation of the vast majority of the once picturesque fields, villages and towns of Britain into miserable and under-run agropoles. People tended to leave those places to find better jobs in the large urban agglomerations of the British isles and those left behind were either enjoying their pensions or working for some large agricultural company that exploited the wealth of British soil. The increasing automation of agriculture meant that those jobs became scarcer and scarcer over time, causing even more people to head for the cities.

After a considerable amount of time crossing through the southern rim of London and rolling past the vast terminals of Gatwick international airport with their shiny metallic skeleton and large windows, the van started going through areas where the houses were modern, but small, sparse and fairly simply built. Old petrol stations, motel-restaurants and lots of old and disused warehouses for the light industry intertwined with the sparse, low buildings. There would be a high-street here and there with some depressive little shops and obvious signs that it's seen better days, a very small number of tower blocks here and there, clearly out of place, and all around small houses in a dreadful state of decay with overgrown gardens and very often broken-down vehicles from another era in the driveway. Even farther away the buildings grew even sparser and yet more dilapidated with lots of green, open spaces between them until the road straightened, the ambient vegetation became more dominant and the first moment since the beginning of the journey when the team could see no building anywhere arrived. The terminal screens inside the van were showing images relayed directly from the camera atop the van and everybody stared at the views in silence. The vehicle was sweeping past low hills and shallow depressions where pine, elder, hawthorn and hazel bosks with rich undergrowth mixed with arable fields and grassy meadows. A small herd of cows was grazing in the distance, enjoying the bright sun whose rays were reaching the ground unhindered, except in the few places where they were weakened by the presence of thin, fluffy clouds that could be seen here and there against the very blue background of the sky. At intervals the van would pass under high-tension transmission lines belonging to the power grid and the van's passengers would see the regularly spaced high-tension wires extend from pylon to pylon farther and farther away until the intricate steel structures of the towering carrier pylons became just smudges between the green of the Earth and the blue of the sky. Yes, the trees here seemed tiny and unimpressive compared to the genetically engineered groves of fruit trees that could normally be seen in the parks of Zone 2 and commercial tree orchards, yet the team thought of them as much more natural than the monster-trees that provided them with nutrition. Even Thompson and the others who had lived in the Confederation for nearly a decade and had not had many chances to see an unfarmed bosk in a normal park for many years were all old enough to remember what a normal size tree looked like and what size of flora a real public park used to host. For that reason the effect of seeing these trees was to soothe the souls of the van's passengers; somehow seeing all that reassured them that everything was going to be all right. Miles wondered what the children of Zone 2 would say if they saw such trees. Having only seen real trees in the giant size of what was growing in the parks of Zone 2 how would they react to normal-sized trees? Trees that took many decades to grow to a modest size, not genetic mutants that were built for a specific and perfectly legitimate purpose but grew to a monster-size within at most a decade.

His contemplations were interrupted by the images at the terminal screens again. The van was now crossing a heavily forested area. Miles asked Thompson with a whisper, as if not to disturb the tranquillity and silence that permeated the van:

'May we stop here for a while?'

'Certainly.' replied Thompson and indicated his intention to Yusef, who then spoke to the driver about it. Thompson did not ask why the stop, he didn't need to. He was just as eager as Miles to get out of the van, breathe some fresh air and step on the unpaved and uneven ground, walk amongst the trees and all the little critters that populated the forest and feel his trousers brushing idly against harmless bushes as he walked past. The rest of the team exhibited similar yearning and silently thanked Miles for proposing the stop. The van shortly stopped on a piece of fairly flat grass, just off the road, and everybody descended, including the driver and the armed escort. Thompson declared:

'Let's take 20. It is definitely worth it. Our reportage won't be any better if it comes 10' later, but it will certainly be done with more inspiration if we take a bit of time to gather our thoughts.'

The team nodded silently and they separated. O'Brien and Johnson left together in one direction, the van driver and the armed escort said they'd be in the region, but would not wander off outside visual range of the van, Mrs. Wilkins and Yusef left in their own direction whilst Miles and Thompson departed in yet another direction. The two of them started walking amongst the trees and past small undergrowth that consisted mostly of bracken, ivy and grass with the occasional dandelion and mushroom here and there and even rarer, but rather menacing agglomerations of stinging nettles and bramble. The sun was partially blocked by the thick layer of leaves growing on the trees above and occasionally some grey squirrel would leap across their path, stop a few meters away from the advancing journalists, look at the unfamiliar as well as peculiar strangers with its beady eyes,shake its little nose and then dart off either directly away from them, or up some nearby tree. Meanwhile, the silence in the forest was broken by the steps of the advancing journalists. Most often this corresponded to the sound of grass being stepped upon, less often the characteristic sound of a snapping twiglet. From the distance, the chirps of various birds -robins, nightingales and the like- would also punctuate the otherwise silent forest. Finally, at rare intervals a random gust of wind would shake the leaves of the trees gently and create a very discrete and pleasant rustle.

The two journalists advanced for a few minutes saying nothing, until Thompson broke the silence:

'You know what?' he said relaxedly.

'What?' asked Miles calmly.

'Being here makes me feel funny. Pleasant, but funny. I just can't believe we are a few miles away from an international airport and a few more miles away from a vast metropolis. This place is so, virgin and natural. Being here makes me think a lot. Think of where we came from as a species and where we've come to. Makes me wonder where we are going. Makes me consider the complete incongruity and difference between a world like this...' he said waving with his hand all around him. '...and a world of metal, silicon, glass and nanomaterials.' he concluded.

'Indeed.' replied Miles. 'The scientifically generated environment we live our daily lives in is geared towards satisfying our every need and wish with incredible efficiency. Yet somehow being here, in an environment just like the one our great-great forefathers have lived in somehow makes me feel at peace. If we consider the fact that this is an environment where the laws of evolution kill the weaker, temporary weakness -for example in the form of disease or injury- is not treated with medicine, but very often met with death, there are no luxuries such as modern plumbing and immediate access to information over the internet, and sustenance has to be earned by force, it is quite something to feel so inebriated with serenity under the circumstances.' he concluded. Thompson nodded in assent.

'Yet despite all of our technology and advancement we are still not happy. It might sound silly, but I can hardly ever achieve such peaceful state of mind as when I'm here. No matter what I'm doing. It might sound cliché, but this inevitably brings to my mind the question of whether we are really heading in the correct direction. Technology is a very powerful instrument that amplifies human activity, but with it we also willingly amplify the effects of our actions and inadvertently amplify human emotions alongside. Just like a simple lever amplifies the strength of a man to that of ten, technology can amplify the effects of war -look at North Korea- or character traits such as megalomania. Where is the limit? Are we really going in the right direction? At the moment there are biological and nuclear weapons whose effects are comparable to the Terran globe in magnitude. Weapons that can wipe out a substantial amount of life or create craters we could easily see from orbit respectively. Similarly, our collective behaviour as a human species has effects of similar magnitude in a vast variety of spheres of activity. The best example is global warming. Now, in 2051 we have enough data to look back upon our history and determine that yes, within the statistically significant margins we can confirm with at least 95% certainty that it is our activity that caused the climate shift over the past few decades. Back 40 years when this possibility was all the hype we had no such solid evidence and no self-respecting scientist could declare we did without a disclaimer. However, that was never an excuse for not increasing our energy efficiency, recycling more and generally striving to achieve equilibrium with our environment and achieving sustainability. Sadly, people didn't take the message and that did affect all of us. But I digress...' said Thompson pensively, arguing with himself more than talking to his colleague. He continued: '...The point is: do we deserve the hard-earned ability of wielding such incredible power? Do we have the responsibility we need to wield it in a way that will not condemn our future? What is the limit of our powers?' he finally uttered.

Miles thought about those contemplations for a while. Indeed technology was no longer a bonus brought about by human thought. A just reward in a 'game of Darwin' and a means of survival. It was a powerful weapon that handed over to the human race the complete domination of the planet over all other life forms. With those thoughts the two journalists kept on walking in silence until they spotted something shiny amidst the woods. They approached and realised that what they were seeing was the reflection of the sun on the calm surface of a small lake. The lake was so small the journalists could see all of it and realised it was no more than the size of a football pitch plus a little. At either end of the slightly wonky, zucchini-shaped lake there were small creeks; one, the inlet, the other, the outlet. Trees surrounded the entire lake at a few meters distance from the shore. In between the grass and flowers slowly gave way to mud. Unfortunately there was no imposing alpine mountain-range behind to serve as a majestic background with towering, snow-covered peaks and rugged, rocky slopes, but the perfectly calm surface of the water, broken here and there by little expanding, circular waves and covered in parts with water-lillies was enchanting enough as it was. The circular waves were created by fish that curiously poked the surface of the water from underneath. This picture was completed by the distant sound of a little, short waterfall just where the inlet met the lake.

Thompson and Miles stood by the shores of the lake at a distance that guaranteed their shoes were going to stay mud-free and just breathed in the scenery. Neither of them said anything for a few minutes. Finally Miles spoke first:

'I was thinking... The limit of our power is always the amount of energy we are using. I now realise to its full extent that every society is defined and limited by the amount of energy it can exert its command over. With enough of it we can do anything. Probably even bend time and space itself. For that reason it would probably be no exaggeration to use the consumption of energy as the main metric for the degree of advancement of a civilisation. How many Joules per capita do we consume on average? How many kWh do we generate in a year? Thus, the limit you seek is the physical limit imposed by the unbreakable rules of the universe and thermodynamics, the limit that tells us how much energy is physically possible for us to extract and wield. For example, the limit of sustainability is the point at which we begin to consume more energy than the rest of the universe -mainly the sun- provides us in net terms. If we exceed that limit, then we may extend our civilisation by millennia by tapping into fossil fuels, nuclear fuels, geothermal energy and all the rest, but we'll be living on borrowed time. As for the question of being worthy of the power, only your views on human nature and humanity as a whole can answer that.' concluded Miles and silence ensued once again, in so much as only the small waterfall and bird chirps were audible. Thompson nodded slowly and apparently absent-mindedly even though he was listening carefully and the two colleagues stood like that for a while longer.

The geothermal plants Miles mentioned were true wonders of technology and it is worth examining how they worked. Originally, a suitable location would be chosen. Depending on the country, that could be more or less rewarding. Then a large industrial building would be built upon the target ground for the purposes of housing the initial drilling equipment first and the energy-producing machinery next. Typically at the centre of the installation there would be a large patch of earth without a floor. That was where the drilling was going to occur. The drilling equipment itself was then positioned at the centre of the target patch and a 4-head milling head was lowered into the earth. Its purpose was to drill a super-deep borehole that could easily reach 70km in depth if necessary, so depth was not an issue. Once the meticulously calculated depth was reached, a very large explosive device was lowered at the bottom of the pit. After the device was securely sitting on the ground, a metal tube -hollow but with sealed ends- was lowered into the centre of the pit, the borehole was hermetically sealed, and a nanomaterial was injected into the said hole in gaseous form. The material was specifically engineered to be denser than normal earth and cling onto the surrounding soil or rock with incredible affinity. Once settled upon every available surface it would latch on to it tightly and grow forming a regular lattice, a little like a silicon crystal undergoing Czokralsky growth but on the inside and outside of a couple of tubes rather than just the outside of one. Injecting the nanomaterial in liquid form was not advisable since it could lead to the collapse of the floor and create an artificial volcano as the red-hot magma would blow the whole set-up to smithereens. At the end of that process, the net effect was that a large tube of earth had been replaced by a very tough nanomaterial with a tubular core of very precisely specified diameter and a huge explosive device at the bottom. At that point the construction of the central pit was nearly complete. Following that, 6 similar pits would be constructed all around the central pit, but the nanomaterial used this time around as a filler would be geared less towards toughness and more towards thermal insulation. In essence the central pit was surrounded by an array -often double-layered- of thermal coats. These would not go as deep as the central shaft, but would follow it down to about 1-2km before the bottom. After -or during- the construction of the side-pits, a tube that was engineered to withstand huge temperatures was created and connected to the tube at the central shaft. Its purpose was to channel cooled-down magma through the main heat-exchanger of the turbine and into a large tank where it was kept into a highly viscous state. As the magma cooled down at the bottom of the tank, it would solidify and be cut by special diamond-tipped knives. That is why beneath the bottom of the tank there was an entire robotic workshop dedicated to slicing off the solidified magma and sending it away in the form of solid blocks. Once a full layer of magma was removed, special flaps lining the tank at a very specific distance form the bottom would retreat into their notches and allow the highly viscous material to drop down in the place of its solidified predecessor and wait for its own solidification. Naturally, the bottom of the tank was compartmentalised in relatively small 5x5m squares. Above the tank there was another heat exchanger with water feeding the turbines. That was the core of the design. The shafts that were drilled around the central one, however, played another role apart from simply insulating the central well. Their secondary role was as heat exchangers since after so many kilometres of ascent the incredibly hot magma would eventually leak a lot of heat into the surrounding environment -despite the thermal insulation-. At the point where the side-shafts became hot enough for commercial exploitation, heat-exchange tubes were added that helped cool the magma enough to make it harmless to the infrastructure of the power plant. To put it simply the magma was robbed of just enough energy on the way up to make it just cooler -by a safe margin- than the engineered limit of the piping system. Naturally, a lot of the nanomaterial towards the bottom of the borehole and all of the central pipe encased in it were melted by the rising magma, but that was normal. The internal diameter of the nanomaterial close to the top of the central shaft had been calculated very carefully so that given the pressure coming from underneath a very well-specified flow-rate of magma would be achieved. Finally, the last couple of details completing the picture of the power plant were that a huge, concrete lid with the same nano-engineered coating as the pipe that led the magma to the core heat-exchangers could be lowered upon the central shaft to shut down the plant in an emergency. Restarting the power plant after the lid crushed everything underneath it was no simple task, particularly since the seal was never perfect and an additional ring of the same material had to be quickly applied on the crushed complex after the activation of the emergency alarm. The other point was that -as might have been guessed- the large explosive charge at the bottom of the main shaft was what eventually connected the shaft with the magma cavity. If that didn't work the engineers were better off drilling again nearby, but with experience and improved geological survey methods they had become pretty good at making the plant go on the 1st attempt.

To aid a little further with the intuitive understanding of the power plant, the main principle could be expressed so: In effect engineers were creating an artificial cavity that brought magma much closer to the surface of the Earth, but due to the temperature gradient on the way up it was below the maximum temperature that could be handled by the nanomaterials and high-melt-point alloys of the time. That cavity then, featured a very precise aperture through which the half-cooled magma could flow in a controlled fashion -an artificial volcano-. Finally, it would be sent through a series of heat-exchangers and settle in a tank where it would cool on the way to the bottom, eventually solidify and finally be removed in small, solid pieces.

On an interesting side-note there was also a 2nd way of building such power plant with different benefits and drawbacks. In the 2nd method, the milling head would have the explosive charge already incorporated into the area just behind the milling tip and the central shaft it used to extract and clear the excavated material would be itself used for the flow of magma after the plant was completed. As the milling head went down, nanomaterial as described before was poured, this time in liquid form, and that process continued till the desired depth was reached. One benefit of this solution was that there was no seal required while the nanomaterial settled. Another benefit was that as the milling head dug deeper and deeper, the pressure of the earth that kept magma at bay would be gradually replaced by pressure from the poured in liquid, thus the borehole could be dug deeper before it had to be sealed and filled by the nanomaterial. As a result, the explosive charge used to connect the tube with the underlying magma could be smaller. The main drawback was that the milling equipment used to create the borehole in the first place was sacrificed in the process.

Thompson and Miles eventually realised they were running out of time so they turned their backs to the lilly-ridden pond and headed back to the van hastily. Once back in the metal can again everybody looked refreshed and soothed. The driver stepped on it and the van headed farther South. After more rustic and natural scenes the journalistic van entered the town of Burgess. It was a very sad little town that had evidently seen better days. Its population of barely 5000 souls was just as much as was needed to man the nearby farm and livestock fields and control the robots that took care of the menial work: sowing, reaping and the rest for farming, feeding, milking etc. for husbandry, tree-carers that helped maintain forests and even little humanoid robots that were tasked with entering the nearby forested areas and picking mushrooms. Naturally, this included the people that ran the local economy, stores etc. In any case, it was clear that the town had once been far larger -as evidenced by the vast number of empty dwellings- and its population was dropping almost every year as a result of technology and investments in mechanisation and automation made agriculture more productive. In theory that freed working hands for more challenging jobs with the net result of increasing world-wide average productivity and in times of boom indeed it did as a rule. However, in times of bust the grim reality was that these people were left unemployed and indeed the ranks of the populace of Zone 3 had been growing steadily, reinforced by newcomers from the depopulated English countryside. They left for London where the prospects were to share an apartment or house with way more people than it was designed to hold and then either forage in the parks, fight with the various gangs, or profit from the war economy. What they left behind were ghost towns and villages. Indeed many a town like Burgess had seen their electoral rosters shorten and even more villages had been completely abandoned.

The passengers of the van, as well as the driver and his new buddy from the communist zone, could see this with their own eyes. The road leading to the city centre itself was verging on being of 'decent' quality, but many side streets lay abandoned, grass growing through the cracks in the asphalt and the pavement tiles. The buildings to the left and right were similarly abandoned and exhibited all the traditional signs of neglect and decay: broken windows, worn-off paint, the occasional collapsed wall, entrance hall or destroyed balcony railing. All the little details that also made a city a city were in equal disarray: broken benches, bent and broken lamp-posts, long since worn-off parking lines along the sides of the road and markings indicating which lane to use, disused traffic lights, destroyed of missing traffic signs; the lot of them. On top of everything else though, the complete absence of people was the most unsettling factor. It was a ghost town, at least far away from the centre. As the van neared to the centre of the city the state of the buildings and streets became slightly -not much- better. People appeared and even a very small number of private vehicles. Most importantly, tractors started appearing here and there. The heavy agricultural equipment -robots, combine harvesters, mobile multifunctional agricultural units (MoMAU) with the ability to sew, water, harvest etc. and the rest- was stored in huge sheds near the fields where it was meant to be operating, same for equipment related to husbandry, and all those sheds were connected to the rest of the world through rough dirt roads. People in Burgess sometimes had to visit those places to either assess the situation on site, or commit emergency repairs or any other conceivable reason. For that reason a private company was hiring out tractors and even offered some tractor-buses for those times when groups of people had to visit a specific place. Those tractors and tractor-buses could move easily in most of the fairly easy, rural terrain usually associated with the South of England and were an efficient means of transport that eventually caught on. After all, despite the expense of operating them, when people needed them, they needed them badly and would pay enough for their services to make the business profitable. As for transport within the town, the only alternative seemed to be using the two limbs at the bottom of a human being that's standing the right way up. If for any reasons the townsfolk wished to leave for a different city -for example a business trip or family visit- they had to hire a car or taxi or take the weekly bus to London or Brighton. Very few were lucky enough to afford a car and many of those who did owned old bangers.

At the very centre of the town, an old cathedral and a short high-street were all little Burgess could show. Once again, most shops were closed and in fact appeared to have been closed for years. Few unkempt trees were adorning the pavements and in general the entire area still seemed very eerie to the visitors. Thompson proposed they keep driving around for a while to explore. The team agreed and the van set off in a random direction. During the tour the journalists saw a couple of schools, one that appeared to have been recently operational and one that had evidently been closed for years, what used to be the town hospital, now a large empty husk of a brutalist, strictly functional building, the small clinic that replaced it and not much more of any particular interest. Mixed with all this scenery was always a discrete but ubiquitous military presence as the communists had stationed a small infantry company in the town as a garrison and were running an evacuation service whereby people that wished to receive assistance could leave for the refugee camps set-up in London.

Having seen all this Thompson asked for the van to park somewhere in the vicinity of the high-street. The driver entertained that request and the team descended from their beloved van. Thompson did this reportage himself. He planned it, showing Miles a few interesting tricks along the way, drafted it -again with Miles looking over his shoulder-, rehearsed it a couple of times and then off he went with it. His reportage covered fully the descriptions made above about the ghost-town of Burgess and also made a very interesting observation: 'It seems that we live in that uncomfortable interval of time between when agricultural work was labour-intensive enough to sustain villages and when it becomes fully automated. We live in that time when agriculture is a chore that is executed by a community that is too small to be fully functional on its own.'. In other words, it had become a very important task which became too expensive to execute properly: the natural ground for a state subsidy. After all is it not the task of the government subsidy to maintain alive a process or company or anything that generates a benefit that is either too long-term to be exploitable in business, or bestowed upon others rather than the operator? Of course, Thompson's reportage also covered that specific point. Following the reportage, Thompson proposed that Miles mobilise his eloquence to write a small article about the experience in the forest and then write a factual article corresponding to the reportage made. 'You must be able to do both and switch immediately from one 'poetic' to 'factual' mode instantly.' reminded him Thompson as he 'showed him the ropes'. Miles coped with both tasks admirably. He was genuinely enjoying his work, which is more than what he could honestly claim back at the bank.

At any rate, the workload that day was significantly lower than usual. Nothing dramatic to report, nothing that would make it to a breaking news bulletin. Thus after a relatively relaxed day, the team returned back to their supply point in Crawley where they toured the camp, watched the news at 18:00 and after concluding work fell asleep in a now all too familiar tent.

    The next events were all significant, but there was no occurrence on a personal level that needs to be described in detail. Thus a summary of these events is enough. The next day the communists reached Brighton and 'liberated it' according to the spokesman of the MoD at Epsom. With that the war ended and the well-armed communists ended up controlling 3 major airports in the UK (Gatwick, Manchester and Glasgow), two main seaports (Brighton and Glasgow), a significant amount of farmland and forests and populated areas enclosing about 16 million people, or about 17% of the country. The Confederation on its side eventually also managed to take control of its corresponding part of Zone 3. However, that was not the end of the story itself. In the days following the war, a massive reconstruction effort began. The aggressive economic policies of the communist sector and the sovereign enterprises and funds they had created helped quickly improve living standards in the newly acquired regions (Bromley and the new sectors of Zone 3 in London for example), while at the external front it turned out the communists had rigorously and patiently built a vast subversive network with roots in every part of the country -and unbeknownst to many, even abroad-. In many parts of London and indeed the country, people began warming up to the communists. More mines and even farms now rebelled against their masters and declared allegiance to the communists. In the democratic sectors of London, the various communist parties became legalised, if not already legal, for fear of following the fate of Bromley and once legal they gained significant support and swept the floor at following elections. As such, in time and with almost each passing election the map of London turned increasingly red. The newly converted boroughs quickly merged into the main communist heartland and immediately received aid, albeit not as much as Bromley and Zone 3 had enjoyed in the beginning as even the communist economy had trouble coping with such growth in population. The small pockets of resistance to the communist expansion were treated in different ways. The republic of Uxbridge eventually voted communist and the sector was incorporated into the heartland, but the various small dictatorships that ended up as enclaves in a communist ocean were crushed mercilessly. The best example was the 'Holy Kingdom of Brentwood' where a fanatically fundamentalist Christian government had been set that brought the country back to the 50's (1950's that is) or on the other side of the disk the 'Islamic republic of Slough', an equally insane fundamentalist regime. The Royal zone and the dictatorship of Harrow & Watford stayed in place for the time being because the communists were arming themselves for a final showdown. They were expecting to eventually make Zone 1 pay for its arrogance.

    Indeed, all this time Zone 1 watched with increasing alarm the situation at the outer sectors but never moved because the communists had become too expensive to confront unless the matter was extremely urgent and important. At the same time the collapses of banks and insurance companies continued for a couple of years at a greater and greater frequency until eventually the rot spread so far and deep that it was officially announced: 2053 was going to be a recession, if not even depression year -not that there was economic expansion for the two years preceding it anyway, thought Miles-. Too much of the financial sector had been taken down by the crisis and now the domino effect had spiralled out of control. It was exactly the moment the communists expected, but we will see more about this shortly and in more detail. Outside Britain, banks that had played by the rules and hesitated to lend to reckless City bankers did well. Unfortunately for Zone 1 those included most national banks in the world. For that reason, bankers abroad were rubbing their hands at the crisis in the UK as they knew that despite the hiccups they'd experience as a result of disruptions in world lending, their banks were strong and prudent enough to not only weather the crisis, but also cover the market vacuum that the collapse of London and the other Zone 1 sectors in Britain would leave behind. As such, the major powers such as China, India and the USA remained decisively silent on the situation whilst Russia increased its support for the communist cause. Everybody knew that if Zone 1 collapsed, trillions of debt would be magically wiped out at the stroke of a pen. Sure, the global economy eventually started suffering at around 2052 under the effects of the tighter lending from the UK, but the solid framework developed by the other nations of the world (rescue funds, making sure that their own banks only lent safely etc. etc.) had kept it going forward despite the problems. As such, it became very clear that Zone 1 was getting closer to its ultimate demise.

On a personal level, Miles became a full-fledged journalist and started covering stories on his own. He got a new team standing by his side, with his own van, administrator, make-up lady, sound expert and cameraman. Every now and then, when something significant happened, he teamed-up with Thompson and his colleagues and covered the events in shifts. As such, he never really lost contact with Thompson, O'Brien, Johnson, Mrs. Wilkins and Yusef. In fact, very often they all went out together on social events and as time ground on the two journalistic teams got to know each other, as was very often the case with the teams working for a fresh journalist and his old mentor. Meanwhile, he never forgot Martha and kept talking to her over the internet. With his external knowledge of the news he could provide Martha with a different perspective on the news than the usual party line she got from her local media. However, unlike what was expected, the communists did not make any attempt to restrict information on TV or the internet so she still had access to foreign news agencies if she chose to listen to them. At any rate, speaking with someone face to face (or screen to screen) is always different to simply reading news, so Miles was helping Martha a lot simply by keeping personal contact with her.

In his spare time he typically went back to his apartment, that he had fully grown accustomed to, and engrossed himself in reading, surfing the internet -mostly for news from abroad- or simply immersed himself in a hot bath. Perhaps the bathtub here was no hydro-pool, but it was still decent size and he could always add some bubble gel and enjoy a relaxing bath. Sometimes he'd even take a terminal with him. A special version with no external ports, small and additionally processed so that it would be water-proof. It seemed to be designed exactly for this kind of occasion, yet it was originally designed to be used by people who were drifting helplessly in the ocean as a result of a ship-wreck. It's GPS capability allowed users to know their exact longitude and latitude, which they could then communicate to rescuers through the internet since a massive effort to bring internet to every corner of the planet -including the poles- meant there was network coverage everywhere on the surface of the globe. Anyhow, Miles had also acquired a taste in classical literature, becoming a member of the local library -fully electronic- and downloading or just simply accessing online freely various e-books. Whichever way one took it, Miles got used to his new life in his little Commune. The only problem was that as time went on and the crisis in Zone 1 deepened, more and more people lost their jobs and that affected Zone 2 as a whole very heavily, except of course the communists who had apparently broken almost free of their dependence on Zone 1. Nevertheless, the Confederate parliament had also taken a few steps to try and activate the local economy and make it less dependent on Zone 1, most notably they offered a very streamlined bureaucratic system to companies that wished to settle in their sector and even started repairing roads, sharing infrastructure with the communists etc. In essence the Confederation was becoming a bit like continental Europe in terms of ease of business and that kept them afloat. The increased size of the Confederation also meant that by necessity the system became more complex to run, despite the benefits it had for the economy. Yet the Confederation soldiered on and seemed to successfully become a more and more defined political entity that was not overburdened by its dependence on Zone 1.

Eventually, on a summer night in June 2053, all news agencies in the world noted that Zone 1 was collapsing economically due to the mountain of bad loans they had issued. The event that triggered that disparaging broadcast was nothing short of the collapse of the Bank of

England itself. Over the years the BoE had become the largest bank in the world and it was deeply involved in slowing down the rot and maintaining order in the beleaguered financial sector, but the increasingly spreading corruption in the system had ended up bringing down even this giant. Apparently, the communists once again somehow knew about this since the army's press office announced to the Kropotkin news agency that if they wished to be amongst the first to see some serious action they should send a journalistic team or two to the central barracks at Epsom. Remembering the last time the communists had invited Kropotkin journalists to their sector the journalists could certainly not complain of being summoned unnecessarily, they sent Thompson and Miles there together with both their teams. Why they didn't just send one team, nobody really knew. The communists had certainly recommended two but for what reason, nobody knew either.

It was in that climate that the two journalists met again in the morning after that fateful evening of June 2053. They greeted each other cordially and summoned their vans. Thompson's van arrived first, he boarded the vehicle, uttered a quick 'See you later kiddo.', winked and shut the door. The van then left and Miles' van arrived shortly afterwards. He boarded, greeted his team and the van left, following in the tracks of Thompson. Soon afterwards the journalists were crossing the borders to the new and extended communist sector. The usual ceremony took place whereby everything and everyone was searched extremely meticulously and an armed escort boarded each van. With those procedures completed the journalistic convoy continued its journey, which was concluded rather uneventfully upon their arrival at the Epsom central barracks. Once again the journalists and their corresponding teams were issued with journalistic ID cards and given their first briefing. This briefing was very different than what both Miles and Thompson had gotten used to during the events of 2051 in so much as this time the army was going to take care of the journalists, transport them in armoured vehicles and take them where they were instructed. In essence they were the 'intimate guests' of the army this time and they were going to be under their command this time. The army reassured them that this was not to restrict their journalistic freedom but to take them exactly where the main action was to occur. Finally, they politely indicated that food, drink and accommodation would all be taken care of by the army.

Thompson didn't seem to particularly like the idea of a golden cage but he eventually figured that 'what the hell, they must have their reasons'. After the briefing the journalistic teams made their way to the courtyard of the massive barracks complex, where they were boarded into armoured vehicles. The vans were to remain parked at Epsom until the return of the journalists. As such, Yusef remained at Epsom and was going to be kept in direct contact with his colleagues over the internet, on a channel operated by the army. Similarly, Miles' team administrator stayed in his van but kept in regular contact with Yusef as well, not just to assign each other shifts and the like, but also for a friendly bit of banter every now and then. In the armoured cars, the members of the various journalistic teams were wearing their bullet-proof jackets and helmets as indicated to them by the soldiers that escorted them. This was serious business. Unbeknownst to the journalists, this time they had been awarded the extremely rare honour of accompanying the 'steamroller' into operations, which explained all the safety measures. It also explained why they had fully armed soldiers guarding them whilst the border guards they normally associated with travel in the communist sector remained with the van drivers and the administrators back in Epsom.

In this atmosphere of general uproar the armoured vehicles departed. From little hubs made out of extremely tough but transparent nanomaterials the passengers of the said vehicles could see outside with a limited field of view. Various cameras that littered the outside of the sturdy military vehicle channelled their images into the mainframe, which in turn synthesised them into a full 360 image spanning the top-bottom range of angles from a zenith of 90deg to a nadir of about -45deg. The 3 soldiers inside the vehicle were tasked accordingly: One person would sit in front of the large terminal screen where the driver in a normal vehicle would probably sit. Typically with one hand he'd control the movement of the machine by manipulating a joystick while with the other he'd caress the touch-screen and shift the image feed as convenient. A little red spot at one discrete corner of the terminal screen would immediately centre the image from the driver's terminal feed to the main axis of the armoured vehicle. At the seat next to the 'driver' there was a similar set-up, however in this case the 'co-driver' was actually the gunner. His responsibility was to scan around for targets, lock down on them and then eliminate them. His terminal screen was therefore configured slightly differently than the driver's. The gunner would use one hand to manipulate the image on his terminal screen, eye-tracking devices -ancient but very efficient technology- would understand what object he was looking at and encase it in a red bounding box if they were not recognised as friendly, and green otherwise, and once the gunner was satisfied that he had successfully locked on to a valid target he would use the other hand to squeeze buttons on a funny-looking device. The device with the buttons looked a little bit like an old grenade, plump and round and was tied to the gunner's hand by means of a Velcro strap. To each finger corresponded a button, activating different things. For example the thumb switched the terminal screen's view from normal to night-vision to x-ray vision etc. The index and middle fingers activated the heavy and light guns of the machine and the other two fingers controlled other parameters such as the communications channel the gunner was listening to or repeating the standing orders in a loud and clear voice. A good gunner could operate those buttons like a pianist who plays etudes every day can operate a piano keyboard. Finally, the 3rd member of the crew was there simply as an escort to the journalists. Normally, such armoured vehicles would be used to transport infantry troops and would carry up to 10 soldiers each. However, in this case these vehicles were used specifically to carry journalistic teams and left ample space for all members of the team and their camera, audio and all sorts of equipment, so despite the fact that there were only 5 passengers in the vehicle (excluding the two at the front operating the machine) it was not far less crammed than it would have been with a full crew of 10 soldiers on board.

    A very long terminal screen inside the passenger area of the armoured vehicle spanning all 5 pairs of seats could be lowered from the ceiling much like traditional rolling presentation screen. On that, soldiers could either review their orders, look at images coming live from the outside of the vehicle or simply entertain themselves if they were allowed to do so -more commonly after the end of a mission-. At the moment it was simply displaying images from the outside for the benefit of the journalists. The military personnel within the vehicle already knew their orders perfectly well, so there was no reason to disrupt the journalists from their work. Miles and his team in one vehicle and Thompson and his team in the other were all looking with curiosity at the images transmitted from the exterior of the vehicle. At the bottom of the terminal small mini-maps showed the exact location and bearing of the vehicle. With a few calligraphic finger wags along the surface of the screen the mini-map could be magnified to the detriment of the main image (grabbing the corners and stretching), moved around (touching a point towards the centre of the map and moving it along) and zoomed in (touching a couple of points and pulling apart) or out (reverse process for zooming in). The map indicated that the vehicle was following the old A24 towards the Merton border post. Shortly afterwards and as the armoured vehicle was about 3km away from the border post, the driver of the transporter veered off the A24 and started following side roads instead. This most curious behaviour was quickly explained when Miles pointed out that if one looked between the buildings towards the A24 one could see rows upon rows upon rows of armoured vehicles just like the one they were riding that very moment. They were covering all lanes in both directions and were positioned so precisely as to resemble a parade formation. The vehicle with the journalists continued under the perfectly cloudless June morning sky on its way farther North-East. Soon, the endless rows of the BMP-style vehicles were left behind, only to be replaced with endless rows of battle droids, arranged in the same fighting formation. As the vehicle was passing fairly nearby the droids, Miles realised that this was the first time he had ever seen such war machine from close by. He noticed that the droids had some sort of transparent capsule stuck between their 'heads' that carried all the armament and sensors and their 'legs' that carried all the weight. Apart from a small section of the part that connected the head to the legs that obviously carried wiring and maybe more, the transparent capsule seemed empty and by all means a waste of space. Miles inquired the escorting soldier about the practical use of that empty chamber. The soldier shook and shivered at the question and reluctantly imparted with the journalistic team that somebody had the bright idea of adding that capsule for 3 reasons: To give the droid more height, to give it more structural stability and to enclose prisoners within so that anyone striking down such droid would risk killing a compatriot or even a comrade in arms. Miles and his team also shook and shivered at the revelation too and then resumed watching the scenes unfolding outside. As the vehicle neared the border at Merton the droids got replaced by battle-tanks. Massive, monstrous tanks that were armoured like a shellfish and armed like a tiger. Apart from their fighting capabilities (which sometimes included anti-air defence) the tanks were similar in construction and shared a lot of their electronics with the BMPs and the battle droids so there is not much additional information about them to describe here.

    Finally, after an interesting journey that included seeing that large parade 'in reverse' that is to say the military units stood still but the spectators moved past them, the gunner addressed the passengers and simply said: 'Look straight ahead, 12 o'clock.'. Miles rearranged the image on the BMP's terminal screen so that all the passengers could see straight ahead. A very tall white structure that spanned the horizon from left to right, towering over the Victorian housing below could be clearly seen. It was enormous. Boasting a height equivalent to 15 floors, it absolutely towered over even the wall that Zone 1 had erected. The reason for that was neither megalomania, nor pride. It was simply a matter of being able to mount surveillance equipment on top of it and monitor activity inside Zone 1 very, very carefully, just like the Royal Zone generals monitored their troublesome neighbours in the West, as well as preventing Zone 1 from doing the same to the communists. As the BMP approached the wall more and more, the detailed structures at its top could be seen more and more clearly. Guard towers were placed at even distances along the very top of the wall and seemed to carry all sorts of antennae and electronic equipment on their roofs. There was barbed wire all along the top of the wall to prevent anybody from landing on its verge from a helicopter. Massive flood-light pairs stood below all the funny antennae, one pointing inwards, the other outwards. Finally, a little to the left, where the A24 was presumably intersecting with the wall, huge, very wide and evidently very heavy metal gates barred access to the land beyond. The BMP continued nearing the wall and eventually it stopped right at the foot of the imposing structure, just by one of the guard towers that hosted the huge hinges of one of the heavy gates. The journalists and their escorting soldier exited the BMP. The first impression of being at the very foot of the wall was akin to that felt by someone standing at the foot of a hydroelectric dam. The wall's smooth, curvy, impeccably white surface raised from a solid, underground foundation, pierced through the grass and continued upward till it ended in barbed wires. If there was a guard tower above, then as the wall got thinner farther up, the cylindrical piece of beton-arme that sustained the guard house started protruding more and more prominently from the main structure of the wall until it spread out radially and formed the floor of the guard house. Thoroughly impressed by the wall, Miles and his team were escorted to a door by its side. The door led past the guards and through a tight, but adequately lit tunnel into the concrete, cylindrical structure that stood below the guard towers. It quickly became evident that the cylinder was hollow. Towards the left, a metal staircase commenced and spiralled upwards whilst at the centre, a metal cage channelled the elevator up and down. The elevator was summoned and the team entered it. It could easily handle the weight and volume of the 5 people riding it plus all their equipment. The guard pressed the button called 'Toggle' and the elevator started moving upwards as the counterweight behind it did the opposite. Interestingly enough, the elevator only had 3 buttons: Toggle, Alert and Talk. Since there were only two levels, the toggle button was all one needed to change the state of the elevator. Alert and talk fulfilled the functions they usually did for the past century and ½.

Details aside, the 5 people reached the top of the wall shortly and exited into the guard house. As the elevator was rotating gently on the way up, its riders exited it facing the North. The guard house was prismatic in shape with a nonagonal base. The walls were entirely made out of bullet-proof, semi-transparent nano-materials so people could see out of it, but not inside it. A small antechamber marked the termination of the large staircase the they'd seen at the bottom of the tower and another antechamber marked the beginning of a smaller staircase that led farther up, presumably to the equipment on top of the tower and was meant to be used by maintenance crews. In the main area of the tower, a circular corridor encircled the elevator shaft and the antechambers, as well as a small restroom an a tiny kitchenette with a small fridge, a microwave oven and a sink. Clearly the people who manned the tower were not meant to stay there for short intervals of time. At those sides of the prismatic guardhouse that intersected the main communist wall perpendicularly, small staircases led a few steps lower to closed doors. Of those doors one connected the guardhouse to a similar adjacent one by means of a tunnel made through the wall structure while the other one connected the said guardhouse to the other adjacent prismatic guardhouse through a bridge-tunnel that crossed over the gate and was made out of a metal skeleton and a semi-transparent nanomaterial screen. To complete the picture, the outer rims of the guardhouse were littered with electronics, screens and all the rest. In fact, the windows of the prismatic structure could immediately be transformed into monitors. That property was used particularly at night, when the normal daylight image of Zone 1 was replaced by a night-vision image that directly corresponded to the day-time one. Guns, hidden inside the wall pointed towards Zone 1 and were ready to strike under guidance of the operators at the guard tower at any time. The system used for their control was an eye-tracking & ball one, similar to what the BMP was equipped with.

  At that moment it was day, so the journalists could see to the north the skyscrapers of Zone 1 and marvelled at their grandeur. However, as Miles was still admiring the view of Zone 1 under a clear -gosh it was nearly noon- sky in the company of his sound expert and make-up artist, the cameraman glanced back towards the communist sector and exclaimed 'Goodness gracious, what does all this mean?'. The others turned around and realised what he was looking at. Below the majestic sight of the Epsom tower, the university complex and a few other huge skyscrapers that had appeared in the communist sector since Miles last visited, the perfectly straight A24 could be seen for miles and miles, all the way to the roundabouts around the Epsom tower. Its 8 lanes (4 in each direction) were completely filled with armed vehicles. It was nothing the journalists couldn't have guessed given what they had witnessed on the way there, but seeing all those troops amassed together in one extremely long line was quite a sight. The team did not hesitate to start unpacking their cameras, microphones and make-up kits, but the escort stopped them: 'No.' he said 'I have a better idea.'. The team looked at him peculiarly but he winked and beckoned them to go towards the door he was just opening. It led to the connecting bridge that lay above the main gate. From there the cameraman could have an equally good view of the situation in the communist sector, but if he so chose to, he could immediately flip the camera around on its tripod and start taking images of Zone 1, its wall and the 200m buffer zone that was left between them: an area that had been flattened and covered in grass by the communists. The cameraman asked the guard why he had to be able to cover the buffer zone but half-way through his question he realised the answer. The unthinkable was happening. He communicated that to Miles who promptly asked the guard whether he was allowed to broadcast the fact in a breaking news bulletin on the spot. The guard nodded in the negative, showed his military watch to Miles, tapped it with his index finger and simply replied: '5 more minutes.'. Miles looked at his own watch and realised it was 11:55. The communists wanted to start their invasion at noon, evidently. Miles had no idea why so late, but the government knew that once through the gates of Zone 1 resistance would be minimal. Nobody in Zone 1 had enough money to mobilise a force large enough to stop the steamroller quickly enough. Not any more at least. So what the government was after was a collection sensational images that would serve as incredibly effective propaganda abroad and in other places of the UK. That's why they chose their invasion timing with an eye towards optimal lighting for broadcasting.

The next few minutes passed in silence and tension. The escort kept checking his watch more and more frequently and that behaviour was apparently contagious as Miles and everybody else on the team did exactly the same. Even the sound expert was feeling the tension despite finding out that his long distance microphone was useless from within that tube. 11:57. The escort started fidgeting and notified Miles that he could now start his breaking news report. 11:58. Miles and his cameraman started looking at the troops for any signs of motion or life even as the connection was being set-up. 11:59. Connection was established, the normal flow of the news was interrupted and a huge swarm of helicopters took off from within the communist zone. The cameraman was capturing all this on film and the tireless staff of the Kropotkin news agency were bringing everything to the screens of the public. David Ramsay, who was on shift for the noon news, announced the breaking news bulletin and passed the ball to Miles who was 'on the ground'. The latter then started commentating intensely. At the same time Thompson was also connected to the breaking news bulletin and his images appeared below those coming from Miles' team in a split-screen mode.

At 12:00 he was interrupted by a very loud metallic voice coming from the guard towers and an infernal rumbling coming from below. What was happening below was that the heavy gate started opening whilst the voice coming from the guard towers announced slowly, clearly and very ceremoniously: 'Guards of Zone 1, attention!'. The cameraman quickly turned around and started filming the Zone 1 wall. Through the fully transparent windows of the Zone 1 towers sudden animosity started making itself evident. A strategic zoom-in revealed that the Zone 1 guards were now fully concentrated on the happenings in the communist zone. They were watching the gates open and listening carefully, although in disbelief. The metallic voice continued: 'Behind these gates there are 4 divisions of the Red Army and above these walls there is a full airborne battalion of the Red Air-force. Surrender now and open the gates, or face the consequences.'. In the meantime the animosity in the Zone 1 side grew as the guards scrambled, the gates opened fully and the metallic voice said: 'Look before you at what you are pitting yourselves against if you decide to resist.'. The guards stood frozen and perplexed as they witnessed the massive show of force that the communists were putting on. Very shortly the smaller gates of Zone 1 were opening too as the communist tank force started spilling through the communist sector gate and into the buffer zone. In the meantime, Miles' team was capturing everything through the lens of the camera and commentating at intermittent intervals with Thompson who was also somewhere nearby. Then, Miles saw him. Amidst all the tanks and battle droids there was one military vehicle that was different from all the others. It seemed to be a modified BMP where all around the top side of the vehicle there were more nano-engineered windows that allowed journalists on board to have a 360-view with their cameras. Due to the relative vulnerability of the vehicle, it was always escorted by stronger units. At any rate, judging by the images broadcast by Thompson's team, the man himself was on board that very vehicle watching the invasion from the very tip of the spear; the steamroller itself.

After Thompson passed through the gates of Zone 1 and into the rich core of London, he caught the ball from Miles and started playing the role of main commentator of the breaking news bulletin. It was good teamwork. Eventually, Miles stopped commenting altogether, his cameraman zoomed on to the advancing military columns in the direction of Zone 1, deactivated his personal microphone and asked the guard: 'Now what do we do?'. The guard replied that whenever they are ready, they may proceed to the 2nd part of the tour, which would involve them leaving the defensive wall. Miles thanked the guard, activated his microphone again and pushed a little button that was hidden in his jacket pocket. Once pressed, the button activated a little red light below the image coming from his team's camera and channelled to the feed before Ramsay's eyes. Ramsay, in turn, noticed it and gracefully announced that Miles had something new to add to the story. Miles thanked Ramsay for the granted time and apologised to Thompson for the interruption and explained that his team was ready to move to their next destination according to the military. Ramsay understood and once all the greetings were dispensed with, the connection to Miles was closed, his team packed up and they all left; back into the guardhouse, down the lift and eventually in the BMP once again.

The vehicle then left and headed away from the advancing military columns, back towards the interior of the communist sector. Meanwhile, Thompson was sending impressive pictures of Zone 1 where traffic stopped before the military column, prompted to do so by the loud horn of the tanks at the apex of the invasion. That left the military column advancing freely through the streets and avenues of Zone 1, carefully avoiding any unnecessary damage to parked vehicles, buildings or other street features, but crushing mercilessly all traffic-calming measures in their way. A few times, the column split as military units were diverted to the left and to the right so as to cover the most city area they could as swiftly as possible. Thompson's cameras were capturing all the action as well as the surroundings that consisted increasingly of Victorian housing along the usual luxury cars, extremely well-dressed people, modern lamp-posts (they seemed to be designer-made) and huge advertising electronic billboards on every privately owned surface whose owner had consented to the erection of such boards. Every now and then the column would pass through a local high-street where extremely flashy and luxurious, well-stocked shops, mostly with high-end products and expensive-looking restaurants invited customers by putting up a show of flamboyance, much like a peacock with a fully unfolded tail or some tropical bird in the process of courting. Even life-like android robots in the form of attractive and extremely neatly clad ladies were waiting at the doors of the shops, bowing respectfully at the incoming customers and with a big smile uttering 'Welcome.' Japan-style. Glass and extremely well-shined metal dominated the façades of most shops, with artistically positioned OLED panels in various shapes, sizes and colours creating a very professional and attractive atmosphere that the owners hoped would induce customers to consume more. During the entire journey, the skyscrapers clustered tightly around the City, Canary Wharf and less tightly in other areas were steadily becoming larger and larger. Thompson was certainly not short of material to show.

As the military procession continued advancing deeper and deeper into the very heart of central London without so much as a single gunshot being fired, Miles and his team were making their way back towards the interior of the communist sector, as we already know. Shortly, the reason for travelling in that direction was revealed: the team reached a helipad where a medium-size transporter helicopter was waiting for their arrival. The armed escort handled the administration of allowing the BMP trough security and into the premises of the small helicopter base and soon everybody was working frantically to load all the journalistic equipment to the helicopter. The armed guard helped with the task and very quickly everything was in order, the passengers were sitting securely, the equipment was also securely stored and the pilot got the go-ahead for take-off. Miles, now in control of the small terminal traditionally given to journalists operating in regions where the communist army operated, decided to take a look at it just in case there were any updates to the situation. Apparently, while he was covering the news from the suspended bridge at the Zone 1 – Communist London walls he had received a message. The message imparted to him what he already knew, namely that he was able to head to the Sutton helicopter base (so that's what it was called) where a helicopter would be waiting for his team, and then continued to inform him that the helicopter would fly over a pre-determined trajectory around London, specifically to the Merton gate and then into the very heart of central London, Zone 1. Miles read further that he could cover the events he found interesting either using the glass floor of the helicopter (looks like it was specifically modified for the benefit of the press) or through the rear door that was normally reserved for parachute drops, fast roping missions and loading/unloading while the helicopter was stationary on the ground. Upon reaching the end of the message (a number of safety instructions in the case of using the rear door), Miles rolled the terminal again and looked at the interior of the helicopter, stopping for a few seconds at the glass floor that now offered a nice view of the Sutton helicopter base and the rear door that stood firmly shut. That quick set of glances made him realise how helicopters had been mostly unaltered for over a century in basic form and function. Indeed all that had changed was the efficiency of the engine, the quality of the avionics and the destructive power of the weapons -for military helicopters-; yet the basic design and its traits of good airborne mobility at a relatively low cost had remained the same.

Not in a position to carry out such meditations due to the job at hand, Miles instructed his cameraman to prepare the camera as he was expecting that there would be interesting scenes to be seen below. Indeed before long the helicopter was over the Merton gate where the column was still spilling through the wide-open gates. From his vintage-point in the helicopter Miles could see very clearly how the military train was making its way towards Lambeth, with branches veering off towards Richmond and Wandsworth. Towards the East and towards the West, it seemed that the other gates had also been breached, although by smaller units than the impressive assault force that was at the moment parading towards Lambeth. The helicopter followed the route of the large assault force while the cameraman was at the very back of the helicopter looking forward through the glass floor of the helicopter. The camera was pretty much stuck to the floor of the helicopter so that it could capture images farther to the front of the helicopter despite the natural downward pitch of the flying machine.

The view was majestic. The roofs of the old Victorian houses and the newer residential and commercial developments were covered alike in solar panels, solar panels that were reflecting the bright sunlight in various directions, every now and then the helicopter passing through the exact path of one of the reflected beams, temporarily blinding any of its passengers unfortunate enough to be looking at exactly the wrong spot at exactly the wrong time. To the left, Richmond park and Wimbledon common park were offering a brilliant view of greenery amidst the low buildings that surrounded them whilst ahead of them the massive skyscrapers of central London were towering above the old city. Farther ahead, the river Thames could also be seen snaking its way across the heart of the city and growing wider and wider as it made its way towards the East. Finally, a careful glimpse towards the West revealed the location of the beautiful royal botanical gardens at Kew, with their picturesque gardens and Victorian glass houses. Although they were too far for Miles to see all that detail with his own eyes he could easily rely on his memory to reconstruct the beautiful surroundings at Kew gardens in his mind. Despite the majestic view, the helicopter steamed on without a pause until it overtook the advancing military column (roughly above Clapham by then), veered sightly to the left and headed towards Westminster. It was not long before the helicopter crossed the river Thames from far above, to fly over the very heart of London. The houses of parliament, the historical Battersea power plant (both now shopping malls), St. Pauls cathedral -farther away-, Tate modern gallery, Buckingham palace, the eye of London and many more tourist attractions were now visible through the glass floor of the helicopter.

Once almost directly above Westminster, the helicopter pilot addressed his passengers: 'We are now over Westminster. I would advise you to have a look at the main roads leading here from the outer parts of the city. See if you can spot anything unusual...' he concluded mysteriously before explaining: 'That's what my commanding officer is ordering me to convey to you.'. Clearly he was simply executing orders that were given to him without being explained in any significant detail. Miles and his team decided to follow the advice, so they all knelt on the floor and started looking over London for anything unusual. Their armed escort smiled at the thought that they looked a bit like pigeons in public parks that were just given some old bread by some old lady sitting on a park bench. Nevertheless, that search proved fruitful. The sound specialist suddenly shouted: 'Look! Over there!' while pointing with his finger somewhere far away. Almost at the same instant the cameraman indulged into a similar set of actions, but pointing in the opposite direction. Miles struggled a little to see what they were pointing at, but then realised: They were looking at orderly columns of traffic that could be nothing else but more army units entering Zone 1. Since the communists had taken over control over the vast majority of the democratic sectors around Zone 1 they now enjoyed the benefit of being able to attack Zone 1 from almost everywhere around. The part bordering with the Confederation was covered by the massive column that entered through Merton while similar arrangements had been made for the region that bordered the Royal boroughs. So, both his colleagues had spotted such advancing columns in different parts of the city and did not need too much time to spot even more. The images captured of the large column advancing towards Lambeth would be good material for a reportage later on, but the images of vast numbers of military units converging from the entire city to central London were definitely breaking news quality.

Thus, preparations for a quick connection to the main studio were made. Miles and his make-up lady prepared him to appear on TV if need be so -although given the conditions in the helicopter and the fact that the images of interest would be down through the floor he would probably opt not to appear on camera-, the cameraman set-up his tool of the trade as stably as possible and was connected with the helicopter pilot through the comms to ask him whether he could slowly spin the helicopter in a 360 so that he would be able to capture a full panoramic view with his camera over a timespan of about 2-3' -the pilot cooperated gallantly-, the sound expert started recording the sound of the helicopter blades so that he could 'teach it' to a special sound filter that could then remove that specific sound component from the transmitted voice message and the administrator back in Epsom handled all the additional administration linked to setting up a breaking news connection whilst another one -Thompson's- was already active.

The electronic filter that the sound expert was setting up was simply a predictive filter that took a sample of a periodic signal, registered it, detected the periodicity of the signal and averaged all of its periodic cycles to create an 'average signal cycle'. Then, the sound expert had the option of removing that component from the soundtrack he captured, leaving only useful signals such as the voice of the TV presenter, and other noises which may or may not have been useful, but whose non-periodicity rendered them much more difficult to filter out. The process could either be done afterwards, by fitting a model of the 'average cycle' perfectly synchronously to the periodic noise in the soundtrack, or online, where the process was slightly more involved, and revolved around creating predictions for the periodic signal based on the 'average cycle' and removing them on the go. Only problem: if the period of the noise suddenly changed (e.g. the helicopter pilot changed the throttle setting), then the filter had to be reconfigured. Luckily, the engineers that designed it gave it limited capabilities to detect small changes in the 'average cycle' of the incoming signal and adapt to them.

As such, when the processing was done in real-time, the system would actively search for the periodic noise component within the incoming signal, lock on to it and make sure that it still matched the average cycle template. If it consistently matched the average cycle template, then all was fine, but if not, so long as the change was not too fast, the system could adapt to it and change the model template to suit the new, altered dominant frequency. The trade-off in this design was that the more quickly adaptable the system was, the more likely it was to confound some spurious signal with a change in the average cycle pattern. At any rate, experience had allowed the engineers to design something that works in most 'journalistic' circumstances rather well and the sound expert was perfectly happy with that.

Eventually, all preparations were completed and the connection went live. Ramsay gracefully announced his viewers that there were important news coming from Miles' team and managed to seamlessly blend Miles' news story to the one coming from Thompson, who was now reaching Vauxhall. The screen was split again between the moving images coming from the ground, from Thompson, and the mostly static images coming from the air, from Miles. That news cast was absolutely sensational. The sheer magnitude of the events the reporters were capturing sent shivers down the spines of all their viewers and everybody within the Thompson and Miles teams was silently thanking the communist army for allowing them the privilege of covering the news story in such a spectacular way. Not that the communists didn't benefit from the publicity all this news coverage bestowed upon them, of course, but still it was polite of them to invite journalists from the Kropotkin agency to cover the news like that instead of just letting the 'Workers' bulletin' alone to be privy to such preferential treatment.

A few more minutes passed with intense commentating from all 3 reporters, namely Ramsay, Thompson and Miles and then things got really interesting. Thompson's BMP reached the houses of parliament and stopped on Westminster bridge by the railings, offering a great postal card view of the houses of parliament, while the rest of the military column advanced. The tanks and battle droids then formed a wall surrounding the Westminster shopping mall whilst BMPs parked nearby and started unloading their troops. Meanwhile the helicopter with Miles' team slowly lost altitude until it was at just the perfect distance from the ground that allowed the journalists to cover the event from above. At that point they briefly noticed that very close to them, although slightly lower in altitude another helicopter was hovering. That one was carrying the journalists from the Workers' bulletin and had been airborne for much longer. Whilst Miles was covering the news of the gates of Zone 1 being breached from the tubular bridge above the communist gate, the journalists from the Workers' bulletin were already in their helicopter covering it from farther above, as it turned out later. Either way, how the Workers' bulletin covered the story is irrelevant at the moment. The important thing was that Thompson from the ground and Miles from the sky, both covered the capture of the Westminster shopping mall. From large loudspeakers the communist army politely beckoned shoppers to make their way out of the mall where they would be searched for weapons and subsequently allowed to go home with their shopping items whilst at the same time a number of platoons was making its way towards the entrances of the mall. The people inside, naturally panicked, but the army was doing its best to keep them calm, reassure them that they would be allowed to return home and that nobody was going to be hurt so long as nobody assaulted the communist troops. After all, a perfectly bloodless invasion was going to be something very important for the communist government to boast about later on if achieved.

In the end, the evacuation of the mall proceeded according to plan, particularly as people saw that nobody was firing and that the troops were all behaving gentlemanly, and as a result calmed down significantly. It turns out that politeness paid off in the end. Whilst people were being evacuated, more military columns converged at Westminster, reinforcing the already strong force that was stationed there. Every time such column arrived, Miles showed some footage of it and then returned the image to the mall itself to keep covering the evacuation procedure. However, when the 5th converging column arrived, something was different. A parade of BMPs came through the rest of the troops all the way to Parliament square instead of just sticking to the end of the queue like all other incoming columns had done before. In fact troops that had arrived earlier were creating a secure corridor for these BMPs to go through. Eventually they stopped right near the entrance to the parliament and stood there unmoved. Shortly afterwards they were joined by a single other BMP that came from a different direction. Miles knew not what to make of this strange behaviour so he decided to mention the fact casually and continue covering the evacuation.

A couple of hours after the commencement of the operation, the mall had been evacuated and another hour later the infantry troops within notified their commanders that the building was clear. These events were imparted with the news agencies by the army's press office via a live connection. Only after both the evacuation and the securing of the Westminster mall was complete did the mysterious BMPs reveal their secrets. Thompson's own host BMP had been now repositioned so that it stood a bit out of the way yet roughly in between the mysterious BMPs and the entrance to the houses of parliament whilst the helicopter carrying Miles lost even more altitude and 'parked' itself near the

Workers' bulletin helicopter a few tens of meters above the tip of the Big Ben clock tower. Then, finally, the moment they've all been waiting for arrived: the 'special' BMPs started moving, one by one parking with their rear towards the entrance to Westminster. The first one opened its door and 8 very well-dressed people came out of it under the armed escort of 2 communist soldiers in parade uniforms. Thompson and Miles did not recognise them immediately, but eventually they did remember: It was the Prime Minister and much of his cabinet. Turns out what had happened was that the communists planned their invasion during a plenary session of the UK national parliament so that they could race to the hotel where they were meeting and capture them all at once; and apparently it had worked. Nobody was told of this in advance, naturally, for reasons of secrecy. At any rate, the 2nd BMP followed suit, churning out another 8 MPs and 2 uniformed soldiers, then the 3rd, then the 4th and so on until all 646 MPs were inside the building of parliament. The soldiers escorted them through a secure corridor that consisted of regular troops and eventually they entered the old chamber of the house of commons, which many of the MPs had never seen with their own eyes due to the expensive admission ticket -the chamber had for a long time been a museum, charging £200 for a single visit-.

    Finally, the last, solitary BMP that arrived separately from the others also opened its doors to reveal just 6 people: 4 guards in very extravagant parade uniforms -clearly officers- and the royal couple of King Harry and his wife, who were at that moment deeply regretting the dismissal of the entire royal guard to cut costs following the removal of the royal grant by act of parliament years ago. They solemnly made their way to the entrance of the parliament and Thompson's team along with colleagues from the Workers' bulletin followed them inside as they slowly paced through the historical building, through impressive corridors and staircases and in the end all the way to the assembly chamber of the house of commons. The couple entered the chamber just as solemnly and all MPs stood up, as protocol demanded. This extraordinary assembly was going to be chaired by the king himself. Everybody seated themselves except the soldiers who stood in attention, lining the walls of the chamber, and the king, who stood up courteously so that his wife could seat comfortably in the old chair of the speaker for the house of commons.

    Outside, Miles had covered the short walk of all MPs and the royal couple and was now wondering what to do next when a large helicopter made its appearance. It was all bright red with a hammer, a sickle and a molecule in bright yellow on its tail. It was being escorted by 6 other helicopters; helicopters that had orders to take the hit themselves should a missile approach the red one. Miles figured whoever was in there was very important. That assessment turned out to be correct. The helicopter landed on the green of Westminster and 15 people came out of its large hull: The general secretary of the communist party of the communist zone, the minister of defence, the minister of foreign affairs and a couple of old generals, all surrounded by 10 guards in parade uniforms, but fully armed. They also made their way into Westminster and then to the assembly chamber of the house of commons where everybody was seated in perfect silence and the camera crews from the Kropotkin and the Workers' bulletin news agencies had occupied vintage points that allowed them to capture nearly the whole chamber in one shot. The doors opened and the cameramen immediately turned their lenses towards them to capture images of the powerful 5 entering the assembly chamber. The 5 made their way to the centre of the chamber, in between the place where the PM and the leader of the opposition used to usually stand and lock horns. The 5 bowed respectfully from the hips towards the royal couple, except the general secretary who simply bowed his head, equally respectfully -especially considering his station as a head of state-. The royal couple responded by bowing their heads too. Then, the minister for foreign affairs handed a luxurious brown leather envelope he was carrying to the general secretary who opened it and took out a couple of papers. He arranged them, handed the envelope back to the minister and broke the tense silence:

'Your majesties, and recognised royal couple of the United Kingdom of Great Britain and Northern Ireland, members of its elected parliament, we are the leaders of the communist party of this country and the party's armed forces. Following a disgraceful decline of our once great country, a total destruction of the power of the state in favour of capitalist business interests, the full dismantling of the social security network and the unacceptable growth in social inequality, all with the blessings of the democratic governments of the past 5 decades, we have decided to rebel and take over control, turning the United Kingdom into a communist state. Our air force dominates the sky, our ground troops dominate the land and the disbanded national military can no longer defend your interests to the detriment of everybody else in this country and abroad. Your capitalist masters have caused the crisis that brought your ultimate demise, they have caused the inequality that fuelled anger and tension against you, you all have sold us the rope with which we will now hang you and sold out even the means by which you could have potentially prevented it from happening.

In my hand...' he raised his left hand. '...I hold two papers. The first paper is that of your unconditional surrender. We hereby demand that it does not leave this chamber without 650 signatures: All MPs', both royal signatures, the minister's of foreign affairs...' he indicated towards his minister. '...and mine.' A very brief, but complete silence ensued before the secretary of the party continued: 'In my other hand I have the paper pertaining to the abdication of the royal couple. There is no place in modern society for hereditary power and honour. It must, instead, be earned rather than inherited. After the unconditional surrender treaty is signed, the royal couple shall abdicate the throne. That is all.' he concluded and placed the papers on top of the ancient table before him.

Silence ensued as the communist dignitaries ceremoniously stepped backwards, giving MPs enough room to walk past them and sign. The guards beckoned them in an orderly fashion to step forth and sign the treaty, forming an organised queue. Signature after signature Zone 1 was handed over to the communists while the world watched. Finally the royal couple stood up and stepped forward to sign the treaty and then the communist dignitaries stepped forward again and signed the treaty one by one. When the general secretary signed the treaty himself and put his elegant, black & gold pen down a short silence ensued and then, as if choreographed in such way -which it was, by the way-, the bells of Westminster abbey started ringing in a rhythmical, solemn, sombre tone. Outside in the helicopter Miles saw the union jack being lowered ceremoniously, folded by uniformed communist soldiers with mathematical precision and replaced by the red flag with the hammer, sickle and molecule.

Back inside, the general secretary took the surrender treaty and passed it to his minster of foreign affairs, who placed it into the brown leather folder. He left the other paper on the table and the powerful 5 took a couple of steps back. Then the secretary looked at the royal couple sombrely. They understood what was required of them, stepped forward and signed their own abdications. The king then offered his crown to the general secretary who refused it stating that he is not and never will be king, following which the king and queen placed both their crowns on the chair of the speaker for the house of commons. They then both stood up, one either side of the chair of the speaker. The powerful 5 bowed from the hip, with respect, this time all of them. The royal couple followed suit, remaining graceful even in defeat and the general secretary spoke again: 'I believe this concludes our session today. I wish you all good luck.' at which point the powerful 5 executed an about face and started making their way back to the red helicopter. Shortly afterwards the assembled MPs started dispersing. The camera crews stayed on for a while longer while their respective news anchors were commentating on the events that had just occurred and then they too left.

The events of that day precipitated an enormous amount of change in the country. Very shortly the army secured the entire Zone 1 of London and the other central zones of big British cities and disbanded the financial heart of the world. Debt worth trillions was suddenly written off and the economic crisis was at once resolved. The communist government immediately announced that the new banks it would set up would play according to the rules set out in international treaties. It also declared that whoever was owed money from British banks would never get them back, but those who owed money to them would never need to repay them either. This immediately placed all governments in the world to their side as British banks had lent about 50 times as much money as had been lent to them in return, so economically it made a lot of sense to keep the situation as is. In the following months the other zones of London were also forced to surrender, which they did. The royal zone surrendered at the request of the royal couple to avoid bloodshed, for example, while the dictatorial zone surrendered in exchange for assurances that in the case of an unconditional surrender the dictator, the high-ranking members of his cabinet and army and their families were allowed to flee the country. The communists agreed to exiling them forever, however when the time came to exile them, they confiscated everything they had except £3000 per person and then let them go and start a new life elsewhere from the beginning. As for the countryside, the large corporations that owned the land were given an ultimatum to turn their land over to the state within 6 hours. The move was made to ensure that they would not remove everything valuable on the way out. Sabotage of the land and farming equipment was punished by forced labour and so was the attempt to flee the country with valuable equipment or too much money. In the Confederation, voices in favour of merging into the communist sector grew stronger, probably with the discrete help of the communist security services, until less than a year later, the voices grew strong enough to precipitate change. Thus, the entire Britain turned red and started a new chapter under a communist government. The future of the country was uncertain and a lot was hanging from the ability of the communists to prevent themselves from being tempted to repeat the -often blood-chilling- mistakes of the past.

  For Miles personally, it was the definitive end of an era. Having lost his place in Zone 1 he got used to living first in the Confederation and then in communist Britain. Kropotkin's diaries news agency kept operating normally, but was under government control from that moment onwards. The communists proved to be fairly liberal as employers and kept the tradition of giving fair amount of time on the podium for all opinions and maintaining the main newscast as impartial as humanly possible, at least in the beginning. As for the future, who knew what would happen? Even more personally, amidst all the upheavals and political shifts not all was uncertain and worrying. The fact that the communist state eventually covered the entire of Britain meant that Miles could finally be reunited with Martha. Cliché as it may sound, they did marry and lived together ever since, giving birth to a son and a daughter. For a long time since those epic events they went to the royal botanical gardens at Kew -they retained their name in the name of tradition and history- and visited the rich collection of plants, as well as the giant oak that the communists planted on the day the surrender of Zone 1 was signed. They called it the 'Victory tree' and it was genetically engineered to grow to a height equivalent to 15 floors of a regular building; and within 20 years it did. The trunk was so thick that it took 80 people holding hands to fully encircle it. Far up amidst the branches of the giant oak, a restaurant was built, gracefully integrating the wooden structure of the restaurant itself with the natural network of sturdy branches that the giant oak possessed. At one side, of the tree, about 20m away from the trunk, an elevator surrounded by a spiral staircase reached up to the level of the tree-top restaurant and then led out to a tasteful wooden corridor with ornate balustrades which itself then led to the balcony of the restaurant. Below the wooden bridge and cleverly disguised as a series of logs, the plumbing and electrical veins of the restaurant escaped from the wooden structure. As for the daily provisions, they were brought in through either the elevator or a purpose-built crane at the rear of the restaurant early in the morning (food ingredients etc.) or late at night (empty beer cans for recycling etc.). Miles, like many people enjoyed going there for a lovely meal every now and then, and so did his wife and children.

On a final note, the daily diaries kept by the members of team Thompson ended up in their intended destinies. Thompson and Miles published theirs whilst O'Brien showed his to the new director of the Kropotkin news agency and was indeed promoted to 'in front of the camera'. In the end he ended up hosting a comical show -sic- with political connotations. Yusef's version was embellished with literature and elements of fiction and became a well-selling story, Johnson's version became his personal memory box and Mrs. Wilkins' became a story for her children first and grandchildren later.

PART IV: TRANSCENDENCE.

CHAPTER 16: A MORNING IN THE BAHAMAS AND THEN A SCOTTISH BURGH.

'So that's what happened.' he concluded. It was bright and sunny that day. That was predictable. He wanted it to be bright and sunny just like everybody else there, so it was. Miles was lunging on a comfortable chez-longue by the seaside, his wife Martha next to him on an equally comfortable chez-longue, listening with undamped fascination. Just next to him, on one more chez-longue, protected from the bright sun by a large sea-umbrella stood his two children and their spouses facing him and his wife, while the little grandchildren, about 15 years old both of them were sitting on a comfortable towel between their grandfather's chez-longue and that of their parents, also under the refreshing shadow of the sea-umbrella.

'That was a brilliant story grandpa!' said the little boy.

'Yes. Great story!' repeated his little sister.

'Oh father, no matter how many times I hear this story I never get bored.' said Miles' son.

'Indeed. It seems you have quite a story to tell papa. Not many people can say they've undertaken such journey, had such experiences and been transformed quite so utterly in the interval of a few short years. You have definitely got a very impressive story to tell.' said his daughter-in-law.

'Oh well...' said Miles and snapped his fingers. A large glass of cold and refreshing chocolate mousse materialised in his hand. He took a sip out of the brilliant, highly viscous drink. '...I guess you could say that. I have lived in Zone 1, the Confederation and then communist Britain. A rare combination. But above all else the journey I took around what was back then Zone 2 and the conversations I had with people there were quite something.' he concluded.

'It honours you that you undertook such journey without any obligation to do so. It did you good, father. It did you a lot of good to broaden your horizons so.' said Miles' daughter.

'Well, to be fair it was only reasonable to tour Zone 2 before deciding where to settle. So not all credit should go to me for that.' said Miles holding the empty glass in his hand closing his eyes and letting it de-materialise again. He then proceeded to place his muscular arms behind his head, raising his sunglasses and gazing at the blue-green sea and the little waves that were gently hitting the sandy beach.

He was in his mid 70's as it was the year 2100, but his body was that of a young, fit man. His wife similarly was of a great age, but had the body of a very attractive young woman. In fact, everybody who had grown beyond the age of 25 possessed a fit, young body with a 'physical age' of no more than the aforementioned 25. In essence, age had lost its meaning in the world of 2100 as peoples' bodies didn't age any more, nay they remained as fit as their users wanted them to be without any need for exercise or healthy dieting. In fact, the very act of eating and drinking had become obsolete and so had the entire curative branch of medical science. Human bodies became effectively zero maintenance and the aforementioned obsolete acts of eating & drinking became merely past-times, hobbies.

Back to reality, Miles' son in law entered the conversation:

'You are right, I suppose, but that does by no means diminish the magnitude of the achievement. I mean travelling so much and particularly learning so much. Whether you wish to thank luck or yourself for that the matter of fact is that you did it and you are now a better person for it! Either way, you could have just as easily simply toured Zone 2, found a nice place to stay and then shut your eyes and ears to what was happening all around you; yet you chose to look, listen and learn!' declared the man assertively.

'Heh. True enough, no?' said Miles and then continued: 'Shall we go for a short fly? What do you think dear?' he concluded by asking Martha. She lifted her large 1950's style sunglasses, smiled at him and replied:

'Certainly darling. Let's fly over to the coral reef and swim amongst the fish.' she said very happily.

The rest of the family nodded and the children jumped up and down with joy before everybody stood up and started hovering. Miles led the way as the family casually flew over the sandy beach first, then over the crystal-clear waters of the Carribean. Soon the beautiful coral reef came into view and the family descended, eventually sinking into the warm water. There was no need to breathe, so the family simply enjoyed the swim amidst the fish. While down there they could also speak normally. The surrounding water did make them feel lighter, but did not interfere with their vocal cords. As such they ended up enjoying their swim while at the same time uttering various exclamations of amazement and wonder at the cornucopia of colours that adorned the underwater wonderland. Brilliant fish were swimming swiftly through the intricate structures of the corals as algae rising from the shallow ocean floor were gently waving airily in response to the movement of the water around them. A myriad of small arthropods and other sea critters were crawling here and there on the living coral rock or the sandy bottom of the ocean. Every now and then sea birds would dive into the water like arrows, pick some unfortunate sea creature in their beaks and resurface again to enjoy their meals. The family enjoyed the brilliant sight and the kids darted through the water, getting close to the reef and playing with the fish, the anemones and generally the sea life around them. The parents were content enough to see the children have fun; they knew they were in no danger. Nothing was going to hurt them, that was technically impossible.

Eventually, the family decided to return to their comfortable chez-longues by the sea-side and so they did, hovering above the surface of the water along the way. Once seated comfortably, a set of drinks materialised in their hands, mostly coconuts filled with refreshing juice and a hole through which a bendy straw exited the hollow fruit. The members of the family commenced sipping the sweet, sweet juice with satisfaction whilst still enjoying the beneficial rays of the sun. The sun was their friend. It couldn't harm them in any possible way, it could only do them good. From a distance behind them, the beach-bar, a structure made out of straws and dried bamboo shoots mixed with good old-fashioned wood, emitted funky Latino music at a comfortable volume. The barman was dancing gently along the pleasant rhythm of the maracas as the guitar and the small chorus of voices chanted in Spanish. Yes, that was what life should be like. Being in a place like this whenever you like, working if and when you like, being close to the ones you love whenever you like.

All around the family, people from all over the world were having fun, playing with Frisbees on the beach, playing volleyball on the sandy courts nearby, running along with their pets -dogs and cats mostly-, enjoying the warm water of the Caribbean sea or simply walking along the breathtaking beach just at the thin strip of sand that was periodically covered by water on the 'up' phase of the small waves and left dry on the 'down' stage. The people spoke to each other in their own languages, but everybody understood each other. Just then a couple passed by where the woman spoke Spanish, and the man Portuguese and they understood each other perfectly well. Miles understood them as well and so did his entire family even though none of them was a Portuguese or Spanish speaker. Not that the couple was saying anything of particular importance or gravity; merely idle chatter.

It was the 14th day in a row that the family enjoyed in the Bahamas and the story Miles was telling the rest of his family had just ended. The kids were beginning to grow tired of the scenery and were beginning to ask their parents whether they could return to the English countryside, or maybe a castle in Scotland. The parents agreed that it was time for a change in scenery so they imparted the idea with their own parents and the rest of the family -the in-laws- and once all agreed they all closed their eyes. Elegant, European clothes materialised all around their bodies and they were transported straight into a large room with walls made out of heavy stone. The change in atmosphere was sudden. Miles was now wearing a full set of rich Scottish land-owner clothes. His attire included a kilt, thick white socks, shiny black shoes, a warm jacket with a tie and a traditional Scottish cap for his head. His children and their spouses chose something far less (stereo)typical of Scotland, opting for either an elegant suit of tweed with a green, velvet vest, complete with a tweed cap -for the men-, or elegant yet warm dresses of various shades of green -for the women-. The children were simply clad in warm, casual clothes.

As for the room, it was beautiful. A large fireplace dominated the scene with a large mammoth pelt laid over an open area before the fireplace. Comfortable sofas surrounded the pelt with a couple of rocking chairs sitting either side of the fireplace. A set of ornate, brass tools that were intended to manipulate the coal and wood in the fire was conveniently placed next to the rocking chair on the left. Behind the sofas, a thick strip of high-quality predominantly red carpets with little discrete yellow ornamental strip patterns by their sides and small emerald green diamonds with yellow edges along the centre of the lines of the said carpets crossed the room to the left of the fireplace from the door beside the fireplace to the one on the opposing wall. At the same time a branch of the luxurious carpet veered off towards the right so that it would cross behind the sofa that was facing the fireplace, make its way towards the right and then turn left until it was behind the sofa to the right of the fireplace. What area the mammoth pelt and the luxurious red carpet didn't cover was revealed to be made out of solid stone. As the carpet's main branch crossed from one of the aforementioned doors to the other, it split the room in two distinct parts: a large, square 5x5m area that included the fireplace, the mammoth pelt, the sofas and the secondary branch of the carpet, and a much smaller 2x5, area where the floor was covered by a small, shiny wooden parquet podium. Just by the stone walls of the small area stood from one end to the other: a medieval armour, a yucca plant, a small bench with ornate legs and a comfortable-looking red velvety padding on top that looked like a large hassock or a nice piano chair, another yucca plant, a bookcase with old tomes, neatly arranged in alphabetical order on the shelves, yet another yucca plant, another small bench similar to the first, yet another yucca and finally another suit of armour. Above each small bench hung an old fashioned portrait that looked like it came out straight from the 18th century, the suits of armour were standing each by one door facing each other, and everything else in the arrangement faced towards the sofas in the other side of the room. As for the other side, the walls were lined with sturdy, wooden book cases, separated by thin strips of solid wood, out of which small candle-holders protruded at about head height, each accommodating a triplet of candles that provided additional illumination to the room. Above the carefully crafted mantelpiece of the fireplace stood an 18th century clock with intricate hands and Latin numerals, and above it stood a portrait of a fictional 'Earl of Glynarlock'. The ceiling was very tall and arched like that of an ancient cathedral. Above the bookcases in the 2x5 area were a couple of very tall arched windows akin to those found in medieval churches, through which a murky sky could be seen. This was the permanent residence of Miles and his adorable wife

Martha.

Once in there, the kids darted off, going through one of the doors, presumably to make their way to other parts of the castle and play hide & seek, or get their Wellington boots, pick up the family's greyhound and go exploring in the grounds of the castle. If one could elevate himself to the height of the windows of the aforementioned room and gaze idly through the large, arched windows, one could see a large green area full of hillocks extending ahead until a forest, behind which the ground sloped downwards until a 'loch' could be seen, behind which there were some low, Scottish mountains with relatively little vegetation. All of this was under the murky, cloudy sky of Scotland. Meanwhile in the room, Miles sat in one of the rocking chairs whilst Martha did the same in the other one and both covered their legs with warm blankets in a careau pattern with white and black stripes against a brown background. Their children and their respective spouses sat themselves comfortably in the sofas next to the rocking chairs as their parents (or parents-in-law respectively) began rocking rhythmically back and forth in their elegant chairs. Miles took his beloved, luxurious, black metal & wooden pipe from a nearby shelf just at the side of the large fireplace and placed it in his mouth. He used a match and box of matches from the same shelf to light it up and then started puffing away serenely. The smoke was pleasant and smelled of natural herbs and forest fruits. It wasn't tobacco, but even if it was, it couldn't hurt him. His body was -just like everyone else's- indestructible and untouchable by disease. The children and their spouses, seated as couples embraced each other warmly or rather the men placed their arms around the necks of their wives and the wives held their husbands' torsos in their arms, very warmly and lovingly. It was a beautiful scene of family serenity.

This is as good a point as any to introduce the family properly. Miles' son was named Arthur and was an engineer. He worked as an electronics designer with his own work schedule. He didn't work for a company. There were no such notions any more. He worked for the 'hive', as they called it. More on that later. His wife, Sonja, was also an engineer and worked on the same project team. Miles' daughter was called Elvira and spent her time as a philosopher, whilst her husband, Marek, was an artist. The children were called Victoria and Atrus and were learning in school. School was not really necessary, as they could learn things at the press of a button if they so chose to do, yet it was found out that humans respond better to acquiring knowledge in a fairly slow -by the standards of a computer-, but structured environment where one piece of information comes only when the correct background for it has been set up and 'digested' properly. Still, in modern humans once a piece of information had been learned, it was not forgotten unless that occurred willingly.

At any rate, the family stood comfortably in the cosy room with the exception of the children who had eventually chosen to go outside with the greyhound and play in the woods, maybe trek on the mountains, or even fly for a while over the loch. If they wanted to they could always visit the local village and enjoy some pastries or other food, or simply teleport back to the castle. The pleasant crackling of the fire was the only audible thing in the room for a while until Arthur spoke:

'Father.' he said.

'Hmmm?' said Miles dreamily in response.

'How was it living under communism? Did it not crush your individuality?' Arthur asked.

'Good question. I'll answer, but out of curiosity, how come you're asking me this right now?' inquired Miles.

'Because you also lived in Zone 1 and the Confederate sector before. That's why I'm asking. Mother should also know I suppose. Anyway, I've been thinking about it since you told us that story again.' replied the son.

'Interesting question.' repeated Miles. 'Now let me try and answer it...' he continued pensively. 'The problem is that people tend to think of individualism and freedom of expression only as the ability to express one's self and act against a background of social rules and norms. However, I've realised later on that we are not simply defined by what we express, but also, and possibly even more so, by how people around us will be influenced. There is no question that being allowed to express ones' self is a step ahead of not being able to do so, however if people around will pay no attention and one's actions will have no effect on others, then I surmise that would lead the example person very quickly to apathy, or even insanity.' said Miles equally pensively. Arthur shook his head as he listened closely. Miles continued: 'In Zone 1 I was free of restrictions and even above the law for as long as I could afford it. One could even get away with murder if he could pay the price. However, because everybody lived in his own bubble world, everybody was so 'emancipated' that one had no reason to care for others and was thus designed by the very society to be selfish and ruthless. It was incredibly difficult to really reach out to others. We were all mindless islands, scattered in an ocean of plenty, with no connection to one another. What I'm trying to say is that in Zone 1 my personal actions were not hampered by pretty much anything so in theory I could be myself, but being so isolated from everyone else made me not much better off than a savage or a hermit living along in an otherwise deserted place and that was soul-crushing. When the ancient Greek philosophers were talking about humans being social beings they certainly implied much more than merely our propensity to talk to one another. We are defined by our interactions with one another, and intimate companionship -not in an erotic context- moulds us into who we are. If we are given too much free hand and compelled to isolate ourselves from one another we don't get too far.

In the commune it was very different though. There you were part of a community where your opinion was valued and respected or at least considered worthy of hearing by the others. Your actions were never disregarded and cooperation between members of society was encouraged. One didn't have to be particularly sociable to fit in as such differences were respected. However, the spirit of engagement in public affairs found very fertile ground in the fact that ones' views were heard by others and taken into consideration. An opinion in a commune was always appreciated. The very act of forming an opinion was seen as positive despite its implications, much like we often reward effort rather than just result. There I felt at peace both with myself and with my neighbours. There I felt that I could genuinely express myself freely, even though the rules binding my actions were more, numerically, than in Zone 1. What I'm trying to say is that in the Confederation I was supposed to be technically 'less free' than in Zone 1, but somehow I felt much, much more comfortable to be myself.' he concluded and a small pause ensued as Miles was gathering his thoughts. Sonja interjected:

'I think our individuality needs to be, let's say 'fed and watered' in order to blossom, just like a plant. Perhaps Zone 1 didn't water your soul with enough social interaction for it to blossom as it did in the Confederation. After all, is it not true that a plant's growth is not defined just by the container, the pot it grows in, but also by the quality of the soil it casts its roots through and the amount of sunlight and water available? Similarly judging societies and their capability to support individualism just by looking at their sets of rules is like trying to assess a plant's prospects of growth judging by the size of the pot alone. At best these rules impose an upper limit, no?' she argued brilliantly. Miles nodded approvingly. He hadn't thought of it that way before.

'I suppose you are right...' he answered. 'The sets of rules will be the upper limit, but will then also proceed to create and define a society around them and play a huge role in moulding the characters of those living within it. That will create an 'environment' around each member of that society, let's say. And that environment will provide more or less 'nutrients for the soul' if I'm to stick to the gardening simile.' he concluded carrying his daughter-in-law's argument to its logical conclusion.

'Doesn't that render the very notions of individualism and collectivism somewhat incomplete?' asked Marek with interest.

'I guess so.' answered Martha. 'Yet the notions are still useful. I still see them as a ledger that can go between the full subservience of the individual to a group to the complete disengagement of the individual from the group. Thus, the notions are still useful, yet still not enough to explain the complex social interactions in the real world. As we just demonstrated, if you are at the extreme individualist end of the ledger it doesn't mean that your individuality per se can reach the peak of its capabilities, in fact it will lack the means to reach it -loosely speaking- even though nothing will be forbidding it, as such, to do so. Similarly, I think we can all agree that if we end up on the very opposite end of the ledger, then it will simply not be allowed to reach that peak.' she argued.

'So does that mean that societies geared towards the middle of the 'ledger' will perform best?' asked Elvira.

'It looks so.' said Sonja. 'But it can't be that simple. The problem is not 1-dimensional. If someone is subservient to a group, you don't only need to know the measure by which he is subservient, it is probably impossible to measure anyway. The point is you also need to know how exactly he is subservient to the group. Arguably, if in society A the individual is subservient to the surrounding society in that he must have certain opinions about politics and in society B the individual is obliged to wear the same clothes as everybody else, then arguably the person in society A is just as subservient to society as the person from B quantitatively, yet the net effects are very different.' she stated.

'And how about the fact that looking the same as others induces you to think more like others and lose your sense of identity?' interjected Arthur.

'Ah... That's a secondary effect I had forgotten about. Either way you get my point.' replied Sonja. The others nodded in the affirmative.

'Oh well, that made an easy and straightforward comparison between society impossible.' said Marek jokingly.

'Well, you weren't expecting anything different, were you? It's the old administration fallacy: If it's important to know, it can't be measured reliably, if it can be measured reliably it's either incomplete or misleading.' said Elvira. Everybody chuckled at the utterance.

'Otherwise expressed as: The product between the usefulness of a parameter and the ability to measure it is always constant.' observed Arthur prompting another round of civilised chuckles.

'Either way, what was it like in the communist society then?' asked Sonja.

'Yes, I'd like to know that too.' added Arthur.

'Well, under communism there were many rules and regulations that one had to adhere to, however in the end the communists in government proved much wiser than their predecessors. For example, the communist party, instead of becoming a monolithic fossil, decided to welcome pluralism within its ranks, encourage debate and difference of opinion, but in the end act as one under the general secretary and his cabinet. Thus, the communist party became host to a far, far more colourful collection of opinions than the democratically elected UK parliament in the last few decades of its existence and certainly even more than what was seen in the crude and primitive predecessors of the communist party that made a mess of the Soviet Union and countless other countries. The communist party effectively became synonymous with the government itself and the lack of any mechanism to discipline the 'official party line' as such, meant that people were elected in the congress based on their beliefs and voted according to their beliefs.' replied Miles.

'And how did the government act in a concerted way then?' asked Marek.

'The government was the central committee and the general secretary who ran the country between sessions with, I dare say, dictatorial powers, but had to fight for their re-election afterwards. Either way, the way the system did not reward them with either excessive emolument or power whilst actually at the steering wheel, meant that the only reason they did wish to run the country while at the helm was because they thought they were doing the right thing. If they had to bow to policy changes in order to get re-elected, they felt they were not being themselves and would rather lose their posts and try to convince others that their opinions were the correct ones. For the record: transparency in government and the relatively small gap in living standards between politicians and the citizenry also meant that people tended to enter politics out of conviction rather than for the rewards associated with the job.' answered Martha.

'And what prevented the people in power from simply altering the rules to suit them?' asked Elvira.

'The fact that the basic rules of society could only be changed by referendum and the fact that any contravention of a very strict politician's code of conduct was seen as blasphemy and meant immediate loss of office. At any rate, as I said, the people who tended to enter politics were there out of conviction because of the effect of exactly such rules and regulations.' replied Martha again.

'Wouldn't that make their policies rather short-termist though?' asked Marek.

'Not necessarily. People in the assembly were unlikely to change their fundamental views very much over their tenures. As such the main consensus tended to remain mostly unaltered during a Peoples' Congress tenure. Moreover, there was always a president of the Congress that would try to keep things in order like a good diplomat and negotiator.' answered Martha.

'Hmmmm...' mumbled quite a few in the present company taking a break to consolidate what they'd just learned. Arthur broke the silence in the end:

'Ehh... Going back to what we started with, how was the communist system in the end for your individualism father?' he asked with polite hesitation.

'Oh yes, of course. That. Right.' Miles scrambled to answer. 'In the end it wasn't too bad. The decision of the communist party to encompass pluralism within itself ended up rendering the word 'party' rather obsolete. The mistakes of the past were thankfully not repeated. Art was not censored, people were not restrained for their beliefs, the police state did not emerge and eventually that huge apparatus that started off monitoring citizens from behind the shadows was slowly deactivated and used only under legal circumstances for security. In fact it ended better off than the paranoid 'big brother', Orwellian democratic society we got after 2000 all over the world. I was quite surprised to be honest. Like everybody else I expected the communists to fail and end up in a dreadful dictatorship like last time.' concluded Miles.

'So your personality blossomed under communism then?' asked Arthur once again.

'I could say so. I never had as much say in my community as I once enjoyed under the system with the communes, however small local councils and tower-block administration councils and other civic organisations as well as various clubs and societies at the local cultural palaces largely made up for that loss. That's how I could take up chess and trekking with your mother. In the end we were quite happy. We did not feel oppressed or under serious danger of being incarcerated without legal grounds or a chance to speak our own side of the story. In fact nothing of the sort ever happened. Also, admittedly, this balance also solved the inherent problem of the commune system, namely its scalability. The communist society worked as a unit from the very bottom to the highest echelon of power.' Miles concluded.

'I see...' said Arthur. 'But there is one more question.' he continued.

'Sure.' encouraged Miles.

'In our society there are no longer countries, governments or anything really. We are even freer from a technical point of view than you were in Zone 1, yet there is no such apathy as you experienced in Zone 1. How is that?' asked Arthur.

'Ah, son...' said Miles wearily. 'You can't imagine the intense pressure of competition that permeated the entire rotten society of Zone

1. Competition for limited resources, when combined with nearly full freedom of action makes beasts out of men. That's why society always needed so many rules, so many complicated rules to keep things together and move on. Here...' he continued opening his arms slightly and indicating his surroundings. '...we live in a society that is post-shortage. Everything we need or want can be ours with extremely few restrictions. That's why we even have dragons flying in our skies; dragons that are completely harmless yet give so much pleasure to our children.' he concluded.

And indeed he was right. Much like an unconstrained, random distribution was even, a.k.a. 'normal' (like a throw of the dice) and a constrained random distribution typically exponentially or otherwise skewed (like a Boltzmann or a Planck distribution where energy is limited), a society with limited resources tends to create friction amongst its members which must be at least contained, if not exploited, and a society with unlimited resources tends to create cooperation. After all, it is much easier for people to be polite when they can afford it and when they know others can't hurt them and even more so have no reason to do so. Arthur contemplated all that and uttered:

'And thank goodness for that...'.

'Now child, don't be overly modest. It is because of engineers such as yourself that all of this has become possible, no?' said Martha. Arthur nodded positively. He knew the history and how mankind had come to conquer the limitations of nature, in a sense even master the rules of the universe themselves. Thus, he didn't give as much thought to the observation as a complete stranger, an alien to the planet was expected to do. Instead he changed the subject gently.

'Oh well... I suppose we did our part, no? But that's all history. Now we can finally break free of our greed and need for expansion. I remember how in the 20th century great scientists such as the legendary idol of science, Stephen Hawking, declared that for mankind to survive, it would need to expand beyond the Earth. Or Tsiolkovsky. Wasn't it him who said that the Earth is the cradle of mankind, but one cannot remain in the cradle for ever?' said Arthur and the others nodded affirmatively. Arthur then continued: 'Well, Tsiolkovsky was proven right, as we are now conquering the depths of space, yet Hawking was proven wrong, at least for the time being. We no longer 'need' to break free of our cradle, but we certainly want to. We no longer need to expand our civilisation beyond the so-called final frontier like modern-day space conquistadors, but we want to see what it is like out there like tourists. We no longer want to take our civilisation to the outer reaches of space and turn more of space in a reflection of our image, but for the first time we are genuinely more interested in learning about it instead.' he concluded solemnly.

Indeed that seemed to be the case. Mankind had begun to send faster and faster space probes in all directions to explore space and in the 'new and improved' version of mankind meant anyone had access to the cameras and general surveillance equipment mounted on those probes and could literally see what the probe was seeing as if the space capsule carried one's own eyes in outer space. For planetary landers things worked similarly and people could experience what it would be like to walk -or rather roll more often- upon the surface of a planet and beneath an alien sky. Naturally when it came to controlling the probes not everybody had access, except the people who actually were responsible for running the modules. And how many times indeed hadn't Miles and his family enjoyed the wonderful views from the surface of Mars, above the tumultuous clouds of Jupiter or just over those layers of Uranus and Neptune that were constantly ravaged by storms of unimaginable ferocity?

The small company's contemplations, however, were soon interrupted by the sound of the arriving children. It had started raining outside and they chose to quickly make their way back to the castle. They entered the impressive burgh, wiped their feet perfectly dry on the large mat at the entrance, crossed various hallways and eventually made it to the living area where their parents, uncle & aunt and grandparents were sitting.

'How was it children?' asked Miles.

'It was great grandpa!' answered little Atrus with a wide smile on his face. Victoria nodded in sign of agreement to her brother's statement.

'We had great fun with the doggy too!' continued the little sister. Miles and Martha smiled whilst the children's parents asked them to prepare for lunch. Everybody stood up and exited the room, crossed various corridors and ended up in an impressive dining room with a long table, adorned with hovering candelabras and various decorative elements out of brilliant crystals, and covered in an impeccably white tablecloth. Perhaps it was no longer necessary to perform the tasks of eating and drinking, however for the family it was more of a social occasion and the opportunity to tickle their taste-buds with delicious treats from all over the world. Caviare, sushi, curries and many more dishes materialised on the table and were eaten with great gratification as the people seated around the table took turns to impart humorous stories and anecdotes with the others. Miles, for example, imparted with his family the story of the first time when he, as a journalist, visited one of the first functioning nodes of the 'hive' whilst Martha told one of her numerous stories of her encounters with travellers from the time when she was a border guard for what used to be a tiny communist sector of

London. Thus the afternoon passed with great conviviality and generally in good spirits. Afterwards, everybody set about their work, as they always did after a joyful meal.

From here onwards, there is little point in following what the family did very specifically since their days passed in the same note. Instantaneous travel, much enjoyment and socialisation not just amongst themselves, but also with many friends, work and the use of what seemed like supernatural abilities. It was a joyous life and all of it was owed to the 'hive'.

CHAPTER 17: THE HIVE.

The 'hive' was mankind's greatest achievement. It allowed everybody in the entire world to live a life with very few limitations; in fact most of those residual limitations not technically impossible to get rid of. It had rendered medicine obsolete, just like the very acts of eating and drinking and even sleeping, as we've seen. What possible technological achievement could generate such impressive results? As it is probably very easy to guess by now it was cybernetics. The hive was nothing more than a vast distributed computing network upon which the entire mankind lived. For that reason, people no longer needed real bodies. All they needed was enough hard-disk space to store their personalities and enough processing power to 'run' them and generate the world around them.

At the heart of the system stood a physics engine that modelled the world, just like those found in various computer games, and a vast network of sensors around the globe. Detailed and very painfully collected data from various sensors here and there generated a virtual universe and updated it with new information as time progressed. The sensors could be anything from thermometers in the Sahara to imagery received at a radio-telescope. As such, the computers of the hive's network generated a virtual universe from a set of measurements coming from the real world. They then used the engine to update the universe as time progressed and until the next set of measurements was ready, much like a Kalman filter does. Of course the story was not that simple. The measurements need not come in synchronised batches so questions of when to update what were immediately raised. Further issues arose when people decided to change things around them, such as materialising chocolate in their open palms or flying like birds. The system, therefore, also needed to know when to break its own rules of 'physics' that stemmed from the engine. That was what people called 'the World module' of the system which was tasked with creating a universe that people could live in.

Another part of the system was 'the Human module', tasked with 'running' the inhabitants of the world. Just like a brain would run a human body, the human module of the hive made sure that its inhabitants led normal lives. After all, the whole existence of a human being can be explained by complicated, yet perfectly logical physics. From the way our mitochondria generate usable energy by using nano-turbine molecules like the ATP-synthase, to the way electrical impulses in our brains generate an input/output pattern that we call human personality everything is explicable by the universal laws of physics, everything is susceptible to simulation and ultimately everything is engineerable. For this reason people no longer carried out their thoughts in intricate networks of fleshy neurones that communicated to each other with clumsy and slow neurotransmitters, but in electronic circuits that not merely simulated that very process, but also improved on it making it faster and more efficient. A human being of the year 2100 was no longer a heterogeneous mass of organic materials, riddled with bio-sensors -optical rods and cones, cochlear cells of the auditory system, thermo-receptors, baro-receptors and the rest of them- armed with actuators -various muscles- and coordinated by the nervous system. A 2100 human was a being of no constant physical presence other than whatever dedicated circuitry 'ran' him in the human module of the hive. The input was either simulated inputs from the world module of the hive, or real input from the real world when necessary or wished for -like the example of the space modules-; the output was an equally simulated set of changes to the world module that were visible by the other inhabitants of the world -although even that was not strictly necessary-. That had to do with the rules of the hive which we will examine later. Also, on certain occasions the output could be linked to robots and machines that existed in the real world. The people working for the maintenance of the hive, the space programme, etc. were good examples of people who used this capability as part of their work. As for the processor of the 'virtual human', it was the dedicated circuitry of each person within the distributed network of the hive; circuitry which could be easily replaced by a spare if necessary and could be manifesting its physical presence anywhere in the real world. Note: the human module was also tasked with safeguarding the memory if its inhabitants.

Yet another important module of the hive was its so-called 'Executive module', which was tasked with maintaining the hive running. It involved anything from essential tasks such as maintaining the power plants (including the successors to the ITER ultimately successful project), mining for resources and repairing damage or physically extending the circuitry of the hive, to less essential but also important tasks such as running the space program. The executive module had armies of robots at its hands and those were either operated by AI, or by humans who ran them directly much like a demon possessing a mortal body in medieval mythology. Moreover, the executive was equipped with factories that manufactured spare components or anything else physical that was needed for the operation of the hive, laboratories that conducted research in the real world, mines, power plants etc.

Finally, another very important module of the hive was the set of rules it included, the 'Law module', which had originally been decided upon and designed by the engineers who created the hive in the first place and was then given the ability to change under certain circumstances, i.e. by majority vote. One could speak volumes of it, its origins and its history, however it might be interesting to examine the issue in the context of how it was created to begin with.

Back in the 2050's, scientists managed to create a scalp that could read a lot of information from the brain's cortex and later in that decade also re-create memories from an external drive, or simulate feelings with appropriate neural stimulation. In the 60's, some of the neural processing was successfully diverted from the brain to electronic circuits, so for example initially mundane things like cerebellar associative memory and parts of homoeostatic auto-regulation were performed partially on computer hardware -with spectacular results, particularly in the memory department- and later on higher cognitive functions followed suit. In the 70's the degree of outsourcing had grown so much and covered all the fundamental tasks of the human brain so completely, that with large enough sensor arrays, actuators and circuitry carrying out memory and cognitive tasks, losing one's actual, physical brain was no worse than a person of the 20th century suffering a very minor and completely recoverable brain lesion as a result of, say, lobotomy following an equally minor cerebro-vascular incident (mild stroke). Much like the people who tested the electronic scalp in the 2050's, people who had suffered that fate during experiments could use their training in using computer screens as outputs to provide their fellow researchers with very important information. There was the monumental and legendary example of Yoshida, Matsumoto who was hooked to a computer under such circumstances for the purposes of research, but suddenly an accident involving a careless lab assistant severed the connection between his brain and his body. The unfortunate man was the first to suffer that fate and his colleagues were extremely concerned of what had become of him. In the end the story took an unexpected twist: The body remained comatose after the incident, however the terminal screen upon which Matsumoto was able to easily display text to communicate with his colleagues started 'talking' like him and asking his colleagues questions, such as why he could no longer feel touch, temperature, hunger, thirst etc. all of a sudden (the experiment was concentrating on audio/visual and cognitive tasks). That's when his colleagues realised that Matsumoto's personality had been preserved in the machine. Naturally, the first thing people then wondered about was what would happen if only about 50% of one's cognitive tasks were linked to the computer. Most expected that the person would essentially divide and create two similar personalities, each different from the original and incomplete, one remaining in the mortal body, and the other living within the machine. At any rate, nobody knew since none volunteered for such experiment, ever. The 2nd thing to cause many to scratch their heads was whether Matsumoto in the machine was the same as the original, or a copy or simulation with all his original memories and traits. The catch was that from the outside it would be absolutely impossible to tell the difference and even Matsumoto himself would be unable to tell whether he was a copy of some original self or actually himself as both original and copy would behave in exactly the same fashion. Eventually a philosopher provided the following explanation that swayed the vast majority of the world to his side. Let's quote:

'I believe that Matsumoto is the original one because the change was gradual. His mind expanded to control his original brain plus so much more. Eventually unplugging his brain at the end was not something that had terminated him and created a copy like in the case of teleportation atom-by-atom. Imagine that you have a pipe and you drop inside it a drop of water. The drop falls and falls and falls until the pipe ends and then there is a gap. Finally, after the gap it enters another pipe and upon exiting it you capture it. Now, if I was to drink the droplet while it was crossing the gap and then replace it with another droplet that I throw downwards at exactly the same position and with exactly the same speed, you wouldn't be able to tell that something peculiar had transpired. Let's assume I can perform the substitution without any delay in time for this particular example. Similarly if I hide away after my act, the droplet itself, having no memory of the past and not seeing me in the picture would deduce logically that it dropped through both pipes, just like you would deduce when capturing it. Naturally the analogy is not perfect, but please try to see the key points in it. Matsumoto is, in this example, a drop that fell through the 1st pipe, but the 2nd pipe was not perfectly aligned with the 1st one and a little part of the drop was spilt out of the 2nd pipe whilst most of the water simply crossed, migrated if you prefer, from the 1st pipe to the 2nd.' said the philosopher sending waves through the world.

And technology marched on: In the 2080's migrating one's mind into a machine and then abandoning the mortal body became standard practice and researchers found a way to make the process work even for infants. With the data gathered from all the infants that abandoned their bodies while they were still children, the 2090's heralded the arrival of the first entirely artificial humans. They were simulated as embryos by the engine of the world module and then their neural systems were built from scratch by the human module. For that reason the last people to ever be born were born in the 2090's. By 2100 mankind was technically extinct, yet still so alive in its own world. For the record, the last people to have lived fully fruitful lives and died of natural causes at near their life expectancy were born in the 1960's.

During this long process of migrating humanity from the rather drab and limited existence of the human body to the solid, replaceable and engineerable body of machines, researchers examined the notion of trying to tweak reality a little in so much as processing the inputs coming from the sensors to the 'brain'. In the beginning this simply confused the subject, but then experiments were done where the subject was given the option of choosing whether to 'read' the true input, or the tweaked one. A very interesting such experiment involved 'cyborgised' -as they called it- people who had the option of ingesting some foodstuff through their own taste-buds and assess its taste, or simply ingest the foodstuff and receive an altered version of its taste whilst cutting off input to the 'brain' from the real taste-buds. The experiment found that subjects tended to choose the altered taste if it was better than the real one. The next stage of the experiment let people choose how the taste was altered before reaching them and then let them also choose whether to use the real or the altered taste, and sure enough everybody chose the altered taste, which was mostly chocolate, steaks etc. Finally, the subjects were given the option of ingesting different sorts of food and then altering its taste in which case everybody started eating healthily and feeling as if they were devouring a chocolate cake at every meal. Naturally, matters such as the natural connection between the fullness of the stomach and the feeling of hunger also had to be regulated, but the experiment showed that letting people alter their own reality could mean they would be more inclined to act in 'the right way' yet feel more motivated and happy in doing so. The principle was extended to its natural conclusion: reversing thermodynamics. Creating a reality where doing the right thing feels good and is easy to do, unlike in the real world where doing the right thing may or may not feel good, but is almost always the hard path to take. That's why there was infinite energy inside the hive, why everybody lived in their dream house, could fly and teleport freely and be completely free of the need for nourishment or sleep.

However, as the system progressed and the tweaks evolved towards this reality, some rules had to be imposed. Many rules were there not for technical, but rather psychological reasons. For example it was found that imposing rules that made obtaining happiness the product of effort went a long way in the domain of character-building and creating active people rather than lazy, gluttonous, shamelessly self-indulgent degenerates. Such rules were also the most powerful cure for the crushing boredom that invariably and inevitably follows omnipotence. Other things such as imposing limits on how much the actions of a person within the hive could affect another were intended to prevent a situation where a human makes another human suffer. As such, anybody had the option of completely ignoring anybody else he chose to, as if that other person didn't even exist. Furthermore, other characteristics of the virtual world that were common with the real one, things such as gravity, electromagnetic waves (including in the optical range), typically trees, the sun etc. were there simply because people would otherwise find it too surreal; too difficult to cope with. Finally, a special rule meant that somebody's residence could not simply be manipulated by its owner and changed at will like cups of tea or writing tools could. The reason was to allow the home owner to feel a sense of stability and permanence about his home, with the full sense of security and comfort that comes along afterwards. For example one rule geared towards the resident's comfort was that only the owner an authorised people could teleport within the residence at will. In fact all of the rules were there to make sure people would feel comfortable rather than going insane or abusing their new world, drunken from the dizzying temptations of a world of endless possibility. Yet even this was changing as newer generations with fewer memories of a far more restrictive reality began to be more creative in their use of the new world. They found the real world, which they could visit via the executive module's robot and the world module's sensor networks, very restrictive since they could not manipulate reality with the ease that the hive allowed them to manipulate what was *their* reality. The older generations who had lived a good part of their lives in the real world had no such problem.

Nevertheless, the real world was still there and had to be dealt with. If for any conceivable reason the hive could no longer procure energy for example, the inhabitants of its virtual world would die like everything dies -real of virtual- when there is no energy to sustain it; it is an absolute rule of the universe. At the same time, however, the hive was far more efficient in creating the ideal world that everybody craved for themselves with the smallest possible 'energy footprint'. All it needed to fulfil any man's reasonable dreams was a relatively little amount of electricity. No longer the need to house, feed, water, shield from the cold, train and generally maintain the inefficient human body. That meant that cities all over the world ended up mostly abandoned; old relics of the past that were slowly being reclaimed by nature as mankind now only acted in those parts of the Earth where fuel, raw materials, factories and laboratories were to be found. London, just like other mega-cities of the world such as Tokyo, New York and Bombay were now simply massive agglomerations of forgotten and abandoned buildings. The old skyscrapers of London, the glass towers that once symbolised the financial might of the City still stood eerily against the typically cloudy sky of London, refusing to give to natural decay -still-. Animals now roamed the streets and parks of London freely again and completely released of their fear of eradication by a mankind that once completely dominated nature around it. Mankind, as we saw, had transcended its own existence and no longer needed to control nature and accommodate it to its will with the intensity of the past, and once again it had come to harmony with it. Grass was once again beginning to grow between the cracks in the streets of London but this time it was welcomed. It was time for nature to reclaim and recycle what mankind had used in its long, 10.000-year long journey from the invention of fire to transcendence.

Simultaneously the achievements of the human race during this path were preserved by special robots and by people who did it out of love for history. Important monuments such as the pyramids & sphinx, Angor Wat, the forbidden city, the Taj Mahal, the Acropolis, the blue mosque of Samarqand and the exquisite mosque of Isfahan, the Hagia Sophia, St. Peter's cathedral, the Vasily blazheny cathedral, the Hermitage, the Louvre, the Burj Khalifa Dubai -widely seen as the first 'real' skyscraper-, Kansai international airport and the incredible multi-layered city district in Tokyo (Odawara-ku ookaigai -The Odawara district multi-floor city-) were preserved with reverence as symbols of mankind's progress through the centuries. Naturally there were many, many, innumerable other such monuments of architecture and also a vast collection of monumental objects of a different nature such as paintings, sculptures, musical manuscripts, cars, robots etc. that could also be mentioned. Such objects were preserved in very real museums around the world that people could visit by embodying themselves into special robots even though few did that, as most just took the virtual tour instead.

At any rate, the new balance between man and environment greatly influenced the 'labour market' too. Labour as such had more or less lost its meaning ever since mankind achieved transcendence, however certain jobs -as mentioned before- still had to be done and were being carried out with discipline. The high degree of automation and the incredible quality of AI systems meant that for the most part the hive could run itself, maintain its power generators, mines and industry and generally survive just like a living organism would. In short, most tasks were handled by the hive itself. For that reason, only a small collection of other essential tasks, such as making changes in the rules of the hive, repairing damage that for whatever reason the hive could not fix itself etc. still had to be carried out by volunteers who thenceforth 'worked' for the hive. Engineers like Miles' son and his wife Sonja carried out such tasks. Other 'jobs' that were mentioned before, still available to volunteers, were those of scientists who had to carry out their experiments in the real world and progressed the scientific march of mankind, as well as a vast ocean of artists, philosophers and generally speaking men and women of culture -again gender had lost its practical meaning now being just maintained for psychological reasons- advanced the cultural level of the world. Finally, another class of jobs that was not mentioned before was the so-called 'military'. Again the concept of an army had been lost along with the physical existence of mankind and the competition that it created, however the 'military' of the hive was responsible for scouring the skies for potential threats such as meteors or comets and look into the Earth for earthquakes and volcanoes, so generally speaking, it searched for threats that could compromise the circuitry or power generation and management systems of the hive. Then it attempted to take the best preventive action against them. For that reason a sizeable arsenal of super-powerful bombs and other weapons was still maintained in functioning order. However, this time mankind was certain not to bring about its own destruction through these weapons, but merely protect themselves and for that matter the rest of nature around it from alien, as well as indigenous threats.

And it was thus that the new era of effectively limitless possibility dawned upon mankind. Miles was lucky: he had lived to be part of it. He had gained the immortality sought by people since the quest for the philosophers stone, and what's more, his wife and children and grandchildren had also lived to see it with him. Who, in the dark and dirty ambience of the middle ages, would have imagined that the magic device that turns any substance into gold and grants eternal life was not some bemusingly complicated rock, but an incredibly complex computing system?

And finally, a bit of trivia: the first computer that was designed and used specifically to 'transcende' a human being was funnily enough called 'the philosopher's stone'.

EPILOGUE.

The year was 1.000.001 A.D. Miles no longer existed and at the same time was never gone. As mankind eventually got accommodated to the incredible world of the hive, initially by making more and more liberal use of the super-senses that the hive allowed, then by incorporating into their virtual minds abilities that normally machines perform much better than humans -such as fast calculations- and eventually by accumulating incredible amounts of knowledge, merging personalities with other people and generally expanding the realms of their mind to well beyond what was normally accessible to an obsolete biological brain, even one as intricate as the human brain, humans changed. They became more than human. They became a form of intellect that would have been well beyond the wildest understanding of humans back at the dawn of civilisation. The world module had changed its simulated world so much that it no longer resembled anything in the real world. The very notion of a human had been rendered obsolete, let alone such simple and mundane notions such as home, sky, air, animals etc. As such, Miles was now part of a hive over-mind; an intelligence that connected everything and everyone. He was there, yet not there. It was very difficult to explain it, but the best way to put it was that we was at absolute harmony with his environment. It could not be called happiness, or joy, or even enlightenment. It was impossible to describe with such antiquated and mostly obsolete notions such as those. After all, seen from outside all it was, was a collection of signals propagating through infinitely complex circuits. Applying those notions to something so foreign and alien would most certainly confuse people who had not lived to see it happen. Even the very notion of a feeling was now obsolete and in no way applicable to what had become of mankind. The best way to describe the change in real, engineering terms would be to say that the input/output patterns of the system had changed beyond recognition.

  This begged the question of why all this process kept going on. Why continue 'living'? -If we can even apply such word to the hive.- What was the purpose of it all? Yet the answer was probably strikingly similar to the one applied for people: there was no inherent meaning. It was just a process that continued on and on and had acquired enough sentience to be self-aware, judge its predicament and even terminate itself if it chose to do so. The journey, not the destination is what makes life worth living. There is no destination for that matter. And the hive mind saw merit in this and set about understanding the universe and seeding life wherever it could so that it could give the gift of the journey to other, alien beings. Beings that were seeded from organic molecules catapulted into space by the rockets of the hive and nurtured to create life beneath alien skies. The hive was still functioning and seeding and growing life, just like a farmer seeded and grew wheat or corn; and then it watched. It watched civilisations rise and fall or even reach transcendence either just as it had done, or in a completely different way that even the mighty hive over-mind had never thought possible. It watched and didn't intervene as the aliens evolved into distinct species and enjoyed the journey of life. And once it had seeded the farthest reaches of the galaxy, and sent its robotic seeders far beyond even the remotest stars of the milky way, bound for a myriad of other galaxies and tasked with nurturing life even there, the hive shut itself down. It's huge metal structures that housed its circuits, its robotic executive arm, its mines and everything just fell suddenly silent, their mission accomplished, nothing else left to do, no pending tasks. The circuits of the hive stopped conducting and the flow of artificial life was ended, all that was left behind being the lifeless husks of the infrastructure that had once sustained it; husks that perhaps aliens in the future would discover and stare in amazement at. And thus, the hive ended. It had nothing more to 'live' for.

Commenced: 12/11/2010
Completed: 27/12/2010
1st correction completed: 1/1/2011

Made in the USA
Lexington, KY
19 April 2012